Klara's JOURNEY

Klara's JOURNEY

A Novel

Ben G. Frank

Marion Street Press
Portland, Oregon

Published by Marion Street Press
4207 SE Woodstock Blvd # 168
Portland, OR 97206-6267
USA

Printed in the United States of America
ISBN 978-1-936863-47-1

Cover design by Sy Waldman

Library of Congress Cataloging-in-Publication Data—pending

To my lovely wife, Riva,
who helped me pursue a dream and see it come true.

1

Odessa, November 1917

"The hell with the Czar."

"Who said that?"

"I did."

"Get your books and get out."

"The hell with you, too!" she yells back at the shocked teacher. The stunned class cringes as they watch the tall thin teenager dart from her desk and exit the Russian-history class in School No.1 on Nikolaevsky Boulevard overlooking the Black Sea port of Odessa.

"What a mouth on that Jew girl. Off to Siberia with her, like all the other Bolshevik kikes," sneers instructor Igor Devushkin.

"Now class, as we were discussing before we were so rudely interrupted, on page 38, as the Czar said: 'Where the Russian flag is planted, there it remains forever.'"

•

She is Klara Rasputnis, daughter of Rev. Gershon Rasputnis.

No one comes around the night of March 2, 1917, to arrest her. Instead, the news that day lands as a bombshell: Czar Nicholas II has abdicated and nearly all Russia hails the fall of the tyrant. It's the first Russian Revolution.

Eight months later, civilians, workers, and soldiers still continue to march in the streets under huge red banners. Each night brings shootings and shouts of "bread and peace." Street meetings are held. Workers gather in factories; soldiers in barracks.

One night, Klara wakes up sticky and sweaty. Her head throbs. Her arms ache. Her large and penetrating, tough-looking brown eyes bulge. She slides off the bed and grimaces as her feet touch down on the frozen wood floor. She foregoes looking for her slippers. Instead, she dons her white, thread-worn bathrobe and shuffles down the hall to the bathroom.

"My God," she gasps. "The moon, it's red. Blood red. How can that be?"

•

Muffled sounds waft in from the frigid, outside world. Peering through the arch-framed windows facing the courtyard, she spies a mob of soldiers warming themselves around fires burning in empty gasoline cans. Some kneel in the snow as they study a torn map of Odessa. Some whisper. Some lie quietly on makeshift stretchers. Others shout, groan, moan, gasp for breath, and call for water. The pleading yet odious sounds cause Klara to shiver slightly.

"Time to go," she says. Closing her eyes she counts the hours until she boards the train.

•

He is Mischa Rasputnis, only son of Rev. Gershon Rasputnis. He's in the next room; his strong upper torso emitting goose pimples from a winter frost. Shivering in his shorts, he runs into the bathroom, stands on the freezing floor, and lets out a long, relieving stream of urine into an old, broken, enamel toilet. He washes his hands and splashes the freezing water on his flushed face and hostile eyes, eyes which message anger at Klara's leaving instead of him. He pulls on his baggy pants, a heavy woolen shirt, and heads for the apartment's small eating area where he gazes at the most luxurious breakfast he's seen in three years. He can't restrain himself. He runs to the table and gobbles down two slices of white bread, a spot of nearly melted butter, and imported Turkish jam. Best of all, two fried eggs—all washed down with *chai*.

"Time to go," he says to his sister wondering how in hell his mother got hold of such scarce, luxurious food in war-torn, revolutionary Russia.

•

She is Zlota Rasputnis, wife, mother. She sits and stares at these oldest of her five children. It's like a dream, thinks the 38-year-old, well-shaped woman, medium height, thin face, long nose, tightly curled hair parted down the middle. "Your children grow up before you know it," she says to herself. Klara is seventeen and Mischa sixteen. "My God, where did the time go; infants one day; grown-up the next."

"I'm ready Momma," says Klara, breaking into her mother's thought.

The two look at each other in what is probably the longest second in their lives until Zlota says: "Go in peace; arrive in peace." She kisses her oldest daughter on the forehead. The two embrace; it will be their last.

Looking into her mother's misty eyes, she chokes. "Don't worry. I'll find Papa."

"Mischa," says Zlota, observing that the teenager is so hungry, he's devouring the last crumbs and seeds on the plate: "Meet the Lubavitz family in the main hall of the station. They'll be waiting for Klara. No side streets, mind you. Tram's ok. Army patrols are out and about. Heard them this morning. Make sure she gets on the train and don't leave until it departs. Then come straight home. Understand?"

He nods.

"And Klara. Listen to Mrs. Lubavitz. She's a smart woman. Knows her way around."

Before leaving the house, Klara follows the age-old Russian folk custom of sitting on her suitcase and reflecting, meditating, praying, or wondering what lies ahead before embarking on her journey. Mischa waits outside their apartment at 21 Proharovskaya Street. It's the end of November 1917, a few weeks after the "Glorious October Socialist Revolution."

·

"Our lives are changing, Mischa," Klara says in a soft tone as they head for the train station. She doesn't want to aggravate him; she knows he is seething with anger because he's not being sent to find father. Klara, flashing a subdued smile, wonders if Yevgeny will be at the station. Will he bring her flowers? A gift? Underneath her fur-lined woolen coat, she's wearing a short, brown dress, divided by a brown sash around her waist, with three buttons adorning the front. Her neckline is opened slightly exposing a long thin neck covered with a woolen green scarf. Her face is full, highlighted by a receding forehead, topped off by wavy light brown hair, a small straight Russian nose, a sensuous mouth. She is blessed with very long muscular legs.

Lanky Mischa avoids the side streets and leads his sister down Proharovskaya Street toward the station. Even with her brawny legs, Klara can barely keep up with him. As she follows, she notices his lips are tight; his eyes glued to the road. A frown appears on his unshaven, boyish face. At this moment, he's not the lovable Mischa as neighbors and friends have labeled him. She knows him better; she calls him a wolf in sheep's clothing, a description some later would attribute to Klara.

Last night, he, too, decided he would get away from Odessa. "If Klara goes, I leave. I'll be a general and ride on a white horse. No more with Momma and those giggling sisters of mine. Babbling all the time: 'Mischa, do this'; 'Mischa do that.' The only reason I stayed all this time was that before he left, Papa said, 'take care of your mother. You're the man of the house now.'"

Mischa notices the streets are deserted. A few lights blink on and off as the city awakens. An eerie glow pinpoints discarded banners, their revolutionary slogans giving way to the reality of hunger caused by the disruption of food trains.

He can't believe how quiet she is.

"She'll soon be out of my hair. No more putting me down. No more taunts."

A few blocks from the railroad station, loud noises cause the two to crane their necks this way and that toward the direction of the deafening blast of voices.

With daybreak, the streets are full of people weaving in and out of the shadows of dark buildings and running toward the station. Hastening to the terminal are motorcars and small trucks sounding loud horns as passengers cover their ears from the irritating and shrieking noise. With no room inside the vehicles, the riders cling for dear life onto the wooden truck rails as they balance themselves on the running boards. The crowd converges into the Razdelnaya Railroad Station. Most of the building's light bulbs are broken. A shadowy yellow glow illuminates the dank station with its peeling brick walls. At the entrance, empty garbage barrels smolder with fires that could level the station if not controlled.

Outside the rail depot, brother and sister observe a group of soldiers: their great coats soiled and smeared with dirt; their leg wrappings caked with mud; their shoes stuffed with newspapers for soles, their dirty caps crawling with lice.

Inside the drafty station, birds fly in and out of empty windows, ticket booths are shut, and large clusters of people move back and forth like the ebb and flow of the ocean splashing against the nearby sandy Black Sea beach. They have nowhere to go on this cold, blistery day.

The two young people enter the building and scan the hall for the Lubavitz family, their eyes swishing owllike seeking their target. This way. That way. Up. Down. Left. Right. Over the heads of soldiers—all the while inhaling foul air.

"Watch out, Klara," yells Mischa, as he pushes her aside to avoid stepping on a crumpled-up woman sleeping on the floor, an infant cradled in her arms.

Mischa knows the two of them will have to claw their way through the mob just to get near the train.

The terminal is packed with long lines backing up to the hall entrance blocked with crippled soldiers and sailors, many of them hobbling with makeshift crutches, their heads drooping down as they try to hide their frightened eyes and tight faces while they plead with passersby for a piece of bread, or at least a few *kopecks*. But the police are merciless in moving them out of the path of incoming travelers.

"Where are you, Lubavitzes?" Klara mutters, knowing full well she could spot the family miles away. "Come out. I want to see you. How dare you keep me waiting? Where are you, my next-door neighbors? You're supposed to be here."

"Maybe, Klara dear, they couldn't stand traveling all that distance with you and took the early train," Mischa quips with a smug smile.

"Quiet. How can you say such a thing," replies Klara. "Oh, God. What am I to do now?" she whines. "Where are they? We're not late. How could they desert us?"

Two policemen watch Klara and Mischa disagreeing with each other.

"Papers."

Klara relinquishes hers.

Mischa hands over his temporary pass.

The officers examine the documents.

"You're not traveling, right?" the policeman asks Mischa.

"No, Comrade officer. I'm going to the Army."

"Good," smiles the policeman, turning to his companion and uttering, "hard to believe there are cowards in the Army who are deserting and going home and here's a youngster ready to fight for the Revolution."

"Safe journey," he tells Klara, tipping his hat in mock salute and handing back the documents.

"I'm leaving, with or without the Lubavitzes," Klara whispers to Mischa. "I'm not waiting until those filthy Cossacks beat me to death. I swore I'd find Papa, and I'll do it."

"Klara. Come home. You can't go alone."

"Try me. Where I'm going, everyone goes."

"If you go, I'll go with you."

"You can't. You don't have travel papers and you don't have a passport. You don't even have a ticket. They'll think you're a deserter. They'll shoot you. Besides, you have to protect Momma and the girls."

He shrugs and turns away.

"Did you hear me?" snaps Klara. "Don't ignore me. You know that makes me furious."

Then, on the other side of the station, Mischa spots a long-limbed lad pushing his way through the crowd, his face distorted, his teeth clenched. He looks as if he's about to leap onto a rehearsal stage. Holding up a rose, Yevgeny Aleksandrovich waves; raises his right hand, signals with a finger, and shouts: "Be there in a minute!"

"Well, mind my soul," says Mischa. "I don't believe it. Look who's here, Klara. You're saved; Prince Charming to the rescue. You knew he was coming, didn't you?"

"I swear I didn't."

She looks straight into Mischa's distrustful eyes, which say: "My own family always turns to someone else, even a complete stranger. I'm not good enough for them."

"Yevgeny. Here we are," Klara shouts with joy, hoping he'll rescue her.

But Yevgeny never has a chance even to say hello, or to wish Klara fare-well. Right then and there, the gates leading to the Odessa-Kiev-Moscow-train platform open and the crowd bursts through the gate like a swollen river sweeping away everything in its path, as if the raging North Sea was pouring through a leaky Dutch dike.

The indecision is over.

Mischa takes Klara's suitcase from her, grabs her hand, and shoves Yevg-eny forward. The trio run for dear life. All around them, people are shouting, shoving, and scrambling.

"Follow me," commands Yevgeny now in the lead on the dimly lit platform. Unlike the other men, women, and children, they avoid the first and second already impassable train car doorway, and crawl under the third carriage.

"There's a door on the other side of the carriage. I know these cars. I worked in the yards last summer," Yevgeny hollers.

He's right. There's no one on this side, observes Klara, straightening herself up on the other side, and hoping her back hasn't been wrenched out of place. Up they go into the already packed car. Only a few seats are left. Klara grabs a seat next to a young woman. Mischa lifts her suitcase up onto the overhang shelf.

Three loud beeps of the engine reverberate above the din of the crowd.

"Get off! Get off!" yells Klara. "The train's leaving!"

"Here take this," says Yevgeny handing her his crushed rose. Stooping, he kisses her on both cheeks. "Good luck," he says, as he turns and pushes his way out through the compartment into the crowded corridor of frantic mothers and crying children.

"Got your way again," utters Mischa with just a slight touch of sarcasm, as he bends over to kiss his sister. She rises and throws her arms around his neck, almost choking him in a bear hug. "Take care of yourself, Mischa. Papa and I'll bring you over. We won't forget you. Don't do anything foolish. Look after Momma and the girls."

The train lurches forward, but doesn't move. Mischa turns and fights his way through the crowd. He looks back at Klara who already is busy talking to the young girl seated next to her.

"She's already gabbing," he says to himself as he notices Yevgeny stepping off the train.

"I'll never see her again. Never," he says, as he, too, descends to the plat-form. Momma'll be furious with me. I let her go without the Lubavitzes. Who cares? I'm leaving, too. Last day at home."

As the line of cars begin to roll away, Mischa stands and watches, a slight smile on his face, like a child gazing at the caboose of a toy train moving on the tracks.

Shaking his head, he begins to walk away. He recalls that a little over three years to the day, his father left for Canada. Now, the Rasputnis family has disintegrated. Papa's gone. Klara's gone. Soon, he'll be gone, despite what Klara said. Only Zlota will be left with the three younger girls, Ann, Lillian, and Sonya.

"Her journey's just beginning," says Yevgeny who's waited for Mischa. "All the plans in the world don't make a journey."

"I'm worried," replies Mischa remorsefully. "Not sure she'll make it. This is going to be a long trip, one might say, a journey to the grave."

"Hope she keeps a diary," utters Yevgeny. "She can title it 'Klara's Journey.'"

2

As Klara boards the train leaving Odessa, nearly eight months have elapsed since the first Russian Revolution of March, 1917 that overthrew the Czar. A Provisional Government headed by Alexander Kerensky has been formed and a touch of democracy has enveloped the country. But even that dim, democratic light is extinguished on November 7, 1917, when Red workers and sailors capture government buildings as well as the Winter Palace in Petrograd and install a Bolshevik government. That seizure puts an end to the Provisional Government and its freely-elected officials. The putsch, known as the "Great October Socialist Revolution," proclaims the world's first Communist state, a state that will crumble 74 years later.

Much of this story takes place during the Russian Civil War. Actually, the conflict begins when the Bolsheviks, or Communists as they later would be called, grab power in November 1917. From that point on, Vladimir Ilyich Lenin will turn the nation into a class war of the proletariat against the bourgeoisie. Opposing the revolutionaries are the Whites, a term used loosely to refer to all factions that battle the Bolsheviks. White strength derives from army officers, Cossacks, and the bourgeoisie—from the far right to the socialist revolutionaries. Shortly after the Red coup, three leading Czarist generals, Alexis Kaledin, Mikhail Alekseev, and Piotr Krasnov, flee to the Don area to regroup and form what will become the White Army.

By the end of 1917, power is in the city streets. Cruelty, fanaticism, and wonton killings become part of this erupting nation. The Russian novelist Maxim Gorky writes "that the dark instincts" of the Russian people will "flare up and fume, poisoning us with anger, hate, and revenge." He is indeed prescient.

Klara Rasputnis will witness the bloodletting.

•

Loneliness makes us look around for someone. Like a magnet, the traveler is drawn to meet others and Klara is no exception. Besides, nowhere in the world are journeys by train as time consuming as in vast Russia.

At first, passenger Rachel Gorodetsky gazes out of the stained window and scans the frozen fields of the Ukraine. Blankets of snow cover wheat, corn, and sunflower fields.

Quickly tiring of the all-too familiar scenery, this young, voluptuous girl with big sad brown eyes, light blond hair, and a small nose leading down to full lips, turns to Klara: "*Du bist a Yid?* (You are a Jew?)"

"*Ya. Shalom Aleichem.* (Peace be with you.)"

"Where're you going?"

"To Moscow, to see my aunt," lies Klara, who will not tell her the truth until she feels she can trust her.

"I'm happy to be out of Odessa. But you're going to see Moscow. The Kremlin's amazing," says Rachel, who then rambles on and on explaining how long it took to validate her papers for travel. When she turns toward Klara, the cantor's daughter notices she appears to be short with a firm, full bust.

"Me, too," answers Klara, still not disclosing that she's going farther than anyone in that train car: Across Siberia, Manchuria, Japan, and the Pacific Ocean to Canada.

Klara holds back. She's just starting out. Yet, without the Lubavitz family, she needs companionship.

I have to make her like me, she thinks. I mustn't show off. Can't force myself on her. Have to remember Papa's words, "familiarity breeds contempt."

Time and distance, loneliness, and separation loosens tongues. By day's end, Rachel tells Klara that she lives across town in the Greek section of Odessa. Since her father serves as an accountant in the mayor's office, the family has a good apartment in a mixed neighborhood.

Klara doesn't have anything to boast about. "We're not rich and we're not poor. Being in the middle isn't that good either," she jokes. She doesn't tell Rachel that her father, Gershon, at times, gets paid for his singing with a chicken instead of rubles.

"Call us '*bourgeois,*'" she whispers, looking around cautiously, hoping no one hears her proclaim that now-forbidden word. She has to watch her mouth and temper. In the new Russia, it's better to look and act poor.

As for their apartment on Proharovskaya Street, Klara tells Rachel it's large and comfortable. "It's in the Jewish section; near Hospital Street in the Moldavanka section. You know, the area where supposedly all those shady characters live," she says with a sneer.

Already, Klara misses the busy apartment, decorated in the latest Russian motif, bright blue and orange colored painted rooms. In the sitting room, a love seat against one wall, and an English wingback chair on the other. Usually, everyone crowds onto a large green sofa that holds all the children who pounce on it or plunge down deep into it as if on a trampoline.

"Before the War, we were never hungry. We had stylish clothes and went to Russian schools. One problem, though: We're the Reverend's children so we had special rules: Like fish in a bowl. Outside, we must behave. Can't be like other children. No pranks. No knocking on doors and then running away. No throwing snowballs at adults," she tells Rachel.

Klara stops for a moment. Wanting to make an impression on a person is especially important for her, a skill that'll help her get through very difficult situations. She exaggerates her father's stature in the community.

"My sisters and brother and I are proud of Papa. He walks tall as a soldier. Non-Jews don't harass him. He's a member of the Jewish clergy. Christians know he gives concerts for affluent Jews and they attend these gatherings, unheard of in other cities."

"Does your father make you go to synagogue on *shabbos*, too?" asks Rachel.

"Are you joking? His singing gets us out of bed before dawn, rain, sleet, or snow. Even on Saturdays, he whips himself into shape, more so than on a weekday. 'This is my warm-up practice,' he tells my mother, adding, 'we must eat quickly. Let's go.' Momma hurries to the synagogue for services and listens to him as if she were a parent watching her child perform in a school play."

"Actually our work begins on Fridays," she exaggerates again. "Dust the furniture. Clean house. Bake *chaleh*. Help with the cooking. Set the table."

Zlota has wrapped sandwiches for Klara that she now shares with her new friend and the two munch on black bread and dried meat. Zlota has included some fruit that she scrounged from neighbors and friends, all of whom love Klara. Zlota would never have been able to collect and borrow enough money for Klara if she hadn't pawned some jewelry. The cash amounted to about 100 rubles, a lot of money in those days. Still, Zlota was under no illusions it would be enough, considering the rampant inflation sweeping through Russia, the devaluation of currencies, and the empty coffers of the government. Along with the money, she handed Klara a pearl necklace with instructions to sell it when needed. She also gave the young girl a railway ticket, but it was only good to Moscow. She figured the Lubavitzes would help her daughter in lieu of Klara watching over their young children during the long trek. That's the way it was in those days.

The two keep the conversation going. Rachel wants to avoid having to look out at the dreary sky and bleak landscape. So they do what passengers do to pass time, they talk. Running out of words to describe wartime fashions, they fumble through their purses and makeup kits.

Klara flashes pictures of her family, again painting them in a favorable light, including Mischa. "Am I lucky to have such a brother," she lies.

Rachel does not offer up any photos. Struggling with her emotions, she turns to the window. Then, like floodwaters, she pours out her troubles.

Klara can't understand how a father could strike a daughter; how a husband could throw out a wife; how a brother could beat up a sister. Though

Mischa could get violent—he once pushed her—he never punched her.

"Why didn't you fight back?" Klara asks.

"In Russia, a father's like a Czar: Absolute ruler. Lord of the family. Oriental despot. Wives bear it. Children obey."

Klara explains that she learned that the weak are often willing to be the victim. What she doesn't say, but feels, is that Rachel resembles a prisoner who has given up. Her new friend, so it seems, doesn't mind being imposed on, especially after Klara sees a large, circular fading black-and-blue bruise on the girl's right arm. What's the origin of that, Klara wonders.

"A piece of advice," says Rachel. "Stay away from soldiers. Don't ask directions or questions. Don't fall for the lie that the police are your friends. They help little children and old ladies, but not big girls. Don't go near them," she advises Klara, turning her face toward the window and staring at the snow-covered fields as Klara stores information that will aid her and help save her life.

•

The train swings north through the dark and frigid countryside. When the car rounds a bend, the passengers hold on to the arm rests as the train rocks from side to side. Sometimes the car sways like a boat on the ocean. The bunks are three tiers deep, not more than twelve inches between the upper loft and the roof of the car. Who cares if the windows are dirty? Nothing to see anyway but white hills of snow. Both girls close their eyes again and again. Drowsiness comes over them. A bright moon follows them and lights the way for their steam locomotive as it chugs its way over flat snowy lands. When they're not dozing off, they read; with Klara devouring a book of short stories by Anton Chekhov, and Rachel, *Anna Karenina* by Lev Tolstoy.

An old peasant woman sits nearby and curses the unheated car; she wraps her feet with a blanket. What stories that *babushka* could tell, thinks Klara, surmising that everyone must have a deep secret.

Rachel appears not to have money problems. The teenager likes Klara and invites her to sleep with her in a compartment Rachel's father arranged. "There's an empty bunk above mine, and the *provodnik* just loves me."

When the cabin man walks by, she winks at him. He motions and shows the attractive young ladies to their first-class births, where he brings them food, and receives an exorbitant tip from Rachel.

"Remember, look down the corridor before heading to the bathroom. You never know who's there, especially early in the morning. Watch out for the *moujiks* (peasants); they're usually drunk and smell and have wandering hands. Yes, there are good and bad people in the world, but if you're alone on a journey, stay away no matter how kind they look."

As the train plods north through the Ukraine, sleep overcomes the two and they slip into a deep stupor. In the middle of the night, however, Rachel whispers up to Klara that she can't sleep and has to get down. Slipping on a grey woolen robe she stands in the corridor and tries to overcome her fear of tight quarters. She has previously overcome these bouts of claustrophobia by commanding herself to go back to bed and acting as if her mind is blank. It usually works.

"Are you alright?" asks Klara, thrusting her head out the curtain. "You look like you've seen a ghost."

"Actually, I've got one on my shoulder. He's a monkey. He's always there. Can't you see him? Been with me all the time. I'm sure he'll haunt me the rest of my life," she says climbing up back into bed.

As Klara falls to sleep, she believes she hears Rachel sobbing. Or is it the howl of the wind blowing in from the vast steppes of Russia? Soon, the black night melts away and is replaced by a grey dawn as the train rattles through the dull, fog-shrouded countryside.

3

Mogilev, November 1917

Klara and Rachel's train is detoured to Mogilev, White Russia, a city with a bustling life and a population of about 50,000. Located southwest of Moscow, the city serves as the headquarters of the Russian Imperial Army, an army that has suffered more casualties than any other army that ever participated in a national war: two-and-a-half million killed, or forty percent of all the losses of the Allied Armies. "No other country paid near the price for the folly of 1914," wrote Douglas Smith in *Former People*. The girls are unaware that the Russian troops who are stationed in Mogilev denounce Bolshevism and affirm their loyalty to the fatherland and the Allies. General Nikolay Dukhonin, who commands a huge force of 100,000, leads them. The Bolsheviks order him to open up negotiations with the Germans. He refuses. In the ensuing showdown, his troops become demoralized and go over to the Red side. Local mutinous soldiers join a Red Army detachment that arrives in the city. They lynch General Dukhonin on December 3, 1917. Mogilev is now a Red stronghold.

•

Klara and Rachel learn that in wartime, timetables are discarded. What is touted as a three-day trip can take weeks. At times their train jogs along for hours, then stands dead on the tracks. Sometimes their home-on-wheels is shunted into a siding and they sit waiting for their train to clank out of imprisonment. Sometimes, they can feel the switching movement from track to track. The teenagers are beginning to lose a sense of time and their route. Combine the constant checks by police or self-styled Red militias with the mounds of snow blocking the tracks, and it is obvious why their long winding path to Moscow is traversed at a snail's pace.

At certain stops, however, passengers are allowed to get off and stretch their legs. Reboarding, they return to their coach.

Taking turns sleeping during daylight, Rachel teaches Klara how to doze off. She takes a deep breath, followed by a few more deep breaths. She then forces herself to yawn quietly. Her head slowly starts to droop downwards. Soon, Klara is dreaming of her father welcoming her into his warm, bear-like arms on a strange distant shore. No one could hug better than he.

Fresh snow lay on the ground one morning as Klara presses her face against the train's dirty window and searches the wintry landscape as if she's looking for someone. To fight boredom, she counts the number of gloomy, low-roofed sheds, the huge barns, and the landowner's cottages.

But her mind strays, her concentration ebbs as the long journey ahead clogs her thoughts. To think about the future frightens her; the past three years have been so terrible.

"Was I born the wrong time, wrong place, wrong circumstances?" she asks herself. Having read a great deal, especially on the Sabbath when there was basically nothing to do, she knows history and she makes a good historical connection to her date of birth, 1900. War with the Japanese when she's four; the Russian Revolution of 1905, World War I when she's 14; and now at 17, two revolutions—the latter one vomiting up the Bolsheviks. And to top it off, there's talk of civil war and this *devushka* from Odessa is heading right into it.

One night, the two girls, along with the other thousand passengers in the over-packed coaches, suddenly discover that they're in Mogilev and are forced off the train. Carrying their luggage, they crowd a station platform, their angry faces displaying shock that they are nearly 400 miles southwest of their destination.

"Fighting on the tracks," warns the conductor. "This train's going back south. Two trains should be coming in, one to Moscow, the other down to Kharkov. Don't ask me when. Better you go inside."

No lights guide them into the Mogilev station house, only voices. Meaningless chatter and sharp, musty odors fill the doorway to the station.

"God, the station smells like a toilet," says Rachel as Klara follows the girl's marker, a white furry hat. Stepping over sleeping bodies, she can only hear snoring, moaning, sneezing, crying, and whispering that fills the dark station's waiting rooms as the occupants cram into every nook and cranny of the damp shelter. Officials, black-marketers, and soldiers all bundle up and sleep on the cold floor. "Hope that train comes soon or we're dead," says Klara. "I pray we get to Moscow."

"No! Let's go to Kharkov," counters Rachel. "The Bolsheviks can't get to us there. The Cossacks have occupied it and they're too damn busy feeding their faces to bother us."

"Does it really matter? Right now, we can't go anywhere. We don't have a train," declares Klara, fixing the scarf around her exposed neck. She feels a slight chill. The temperature is dropping. A freeze has settled over the city. The two stare at a few of the soldiers brandishing fixed bayonets. Standing motionless on the platform, they look as if they wouldn't stir even if a train does come along. One sentry is posted outside the telegraph office.

Nobody enters this communications hub whose messaging systems are down anyway. They all move to the platform.

"I'll tell you what," volunteers Klara. "Just so we don't argue later, let's take whichever train comes first. That way, we'll be able to stick together. I really want to go to Moscow. But no matter, I'll go with you to Kharkov if that train's first. It's out of my way. But it won't be so bad. Maybe I can get a better connection east."

"I know. You're going all the way to Vladivostok. Aren't you?"

"How do you know?"

"Simple. In your sleep you keep saying, 'Vladivostok to Canada.' Sometimes it's 'Vladivostok to America.'"

Klara smiles and, while looking into Rachel's sympathetic eyes, reveals what's bothered her since they left Odessa: "I was supposed to go with a family, but they stood me up. Maybe I should have gone home. My brother wanted me to do that. My mother's probably angry as hell that I went alone. But I couldn't quit before I started, now could I?"

"No. You're right, once you begin, you've got to keep going."

"She'll understand. I'll write or get a message through to her once we get to some kind of normal place. Right now we've got to get out of here."

"Alright. I'll go with you. Whichever train comes first," agrees Rachel.

The two sit on their suitcases. Cringing from the freezing wind from the *steppes,* people curl up under blankets. Babies cry. Mothers yell. Peasants snarl. Drunks snore. At night, some pace the platform; others eat as if it was a Sunday feast.

But not Klara and Rachel. They utilize portion control of the food the *provodnik* on the train packed for them, but eventually they have to dig into their own pockets for nourishment. They sit and wait. Minutes seem like hours; hours like days. Finally, they, too, lie down on the cold station floor. They barely sleep.

The frigid, sunless morning brings on the same routine. Constantly listening and looking out for a train going northeast or southeast, they keep a smile on their faces, a smile that is infectious and these Russians, who know how to throw a party, begin to stir and come alive, especially when Klara and Rachel burst forth with traditional Russian ballads, their girlish soprano voices pleasantly serenading weary travelers whose eyes constantly scan various platforms in the station.

Impatient, a few men get up, walk around, and begin to push everyone back. The audience forms a circle around the two men. The dance is about to begin. Klara notices the two shed their great coats and shiver slightly. No matter, they will warm up as soon as they begin to move their arms, at first ever so slightly and then wildly in the air. Lowering themselves down on their haunches, they slap their thighs and at the same time kick their feet out in front of them.

"These guys are good," Klara says to herself, as she watches them balancing themselves so they don't fall on their backsides. Up and down they jump, like a rising top; it's the *hopac*, the national dance. The dance and song help the refugees forget their troubles. While Klara holds onto every kopeck, she realizes she has spent a dozen rubles already just on food.

•

A week later, a train, hissing and clanging, puffs into the station.

"Get ready. Let's go," says Klara, grabbing Rachel by her arm.

"Where's it going?"

"Can't tell yet. But wherever it is going, we're getting on. Wait. It's the Moscow train," declares Klara, happy to get out of the confining station and head toward her choice destination.

"Nah," says Rachel, as she pulls Klara's arm. "Know what? Let's wait. Won't be long now. Let's go to Kharkov. I've got relatives there. We'll be treated well."

Klara is speechless. Everything has gone so well between the two of them and now this.

We've just started and already she's changing plans. And it's not good to wait for a second train, she thinks.

"Wait a minute. You agreed. First train in, we take. How do you know the Kharkov train'll ever get here?"

"I talked to the conductor. He told me the Kharkov train is a good train and well protected. Besides, I've changed my mind."

"But we agreed."

"We agreed? We agreed. What are you some sort of lawyer or something?" challenges Rachel who is angry that this girl whom she treated so nicely, dares to argue with her. "We agreed is all you can say," she adds in a mimicking tone. "Makes more sense to go to Kharkov."

"No it doesn't. Moscow. Remember, we said whichever train comes first. And that's that. Besides, I heard the Germans have hired gunmen to rip up the tracks. There's still a war going on. I don't know what that conductor told you, but he told me that the Germans are racing through the Ukraine. 'Trains going to Kharkov often don't get through,' he pointed out. If the train had been to Kharkov, I'd have taken it with you. Your word is your word. You promised."

"Well, I'm not going to Moscow. I'm waiting for the Kharkov train."

"Good-bye then," says Klara holding out her hand.

"You're really serious. You're going to break us up because I said I'd go with you on the first train. If you're that stubborn, go to Moscow! Go to hell.

You're no friend of mine," Rachel shouts as she turns and moves to the back of the platform, leaving Klara's hand hanging in midair.

"Okay. If that's the way you want it," says Klara, her face flushed with anger. Without hesitating, she grabs her suitcase and boards the Moscow-bound train.

"I'm not stopping for anyone," she mutters as the train leaves Mogilev far behind. Deep in thought, she tells herself, "I've got to stick to my plan. I'm not giving in to anybody."

•

But an hour out of the station, the train grinds to a sudden halt. "Shit! Maybe I should've gone to Kharkov with her. I could've reached the Volga from there and connected with the Trans-Siberian via Samara to Ekaterinburg. Maybe I made a mistake. Would have had company. A promise is a promise. 'A person is as good as his bond,' Papa always said. Better it happened now. Only be trouble later."

But she wasn't comforted by the logic. For at that very moment, bandits, belts of large bullets strapped over their shoulders, burst into her carriage as the train stops at a provincial station. "Any Jew Communist in here," yell the intruders. Nobody moves. The conductor tries to intervene, but they push him aside.

"Over there. Get that *zhid* (dirty Jew). Grab him."

Two Cossacks get hold of a tall teenager, a young worker with a peaked cap who's sitting five rows in front of Klara. Flinging him to the floor, they pound him with their fists and kick him with their tall booted feet. Klara, who has slunk down in her seat, can still see that his face is bloodied. They drag him along the floor, kick him, hurl him outside, and depart.

The train moves out. A few hours later it stops at yet another station.

"We'll be here for at least three hours," instructs the conductor. "You can get off the train and walk to the nearby market if you want."

A family next to Klara promises to watch her suitcase.

"But don't miss the train and be careful of black-marketers," they warn.

When she buys apples and bread, she notices that the proprietors of the stalls keep looking over their shoulders, eyeing their sacks of food. Security guards, with menacing eyes, and clenched fists, stand watch.

Nearby, a young boy, hatless, mounts a soapbox and sings: "Boldly, we'll go into battle for the power of the Soviets."

And less than a block away, another lad sings: "Boldly, we'll go into battle for Holy Russia and wipe out all the Jews."

"Hope to God I'm out of here before they come after us," Klara says to herself. "Wonder if they sing songs like that in America? If they do, where would I turn?"

Back on the train, the family who has watched her suitcase, loans her a week-old Moscow newspaper. Klara spies a headline declaring: "Riots Against the Bourgeois."

Getting ugly, she realizes as she reads that gangs are looting shops and middle-class houses, grabbing the owner's jewelry and vodka. Women and girls are raped. Security forces have fled. No police to protect civilians. What should have taken Klara at most a day to reach Moscow has already taken nearly a week. *And I'm going to this place? What am I, crazy?*

"It's taking this train forever," says Klara turning to her new neighbor. Next week, it's December."

"Just let's get there safe," answers the woman.

"You're right," replies Klara realizing again she wasn't going to get any sympathy from this lady, a heavy-set woman in her forties with two kids in tow. She seems to treat young people as infants. She barely mumbles 'good evening,' observes Klara who suddenly feels very tired and begins to doze, her head nodding off like an old woman. Her body rocks in time to the rhythms of the swaying rail car until the train comes to a stop, starts up again, halts and jolts again. Two hours' delay for every hour moving forward is the train's new timetable.

Klara knows how long a wait it'll be by the way the engine enters a station and screeches to a halt. She gets so tired of handing her papers to inspectors that she keeps them out on her lap. Her baggage is searched repeatedly, even though she has a passport marked "ballet instructor." Without the title, she might not have been able to stay on the train. She knows that anyone involved with ballet in Russia is treated like royalty.

God bless Yevgeny. He knew what he was doing when he helped me fill out the travel forms. Me! A teacher? Thank God nobody ever checked.

The train creeks along the track. The click-clack, click-clack of the wheels lull Klara into a half sleep. Without Rachel, she can only doze. She watches her cardboard suitcase even though fellow passengers say they'll look after it. She's learning not to trust anyone.

As her eyes close, she remembers the children's voices resounding through her home in the Black Sea port of Odessa, the outings with her father, his soothing songs warming her soul. Deep in the slumber of sleep, she awakens to a new day at 21 Proharovskaya Street.

4

Odessa, July 1914

Before World War I, Russia had the distinction of being "the most anti-Semitic and politically divided nation on the European continent." In the fall of 1905 alone, there were 690 anti-Jewish pogroms and 3,000 Jewish murders. That year, in the Odessa suburbs of Moldavanka and Slobodka, 800 Jews were killed, about 5,000 injured and 100,000 made homeless. The Czar's police supplied the illiterate Russian Orthodox rioters with arms and vodka for the pogroms, which lasted for four days.

Over the next decade, the Jews of the Russian Empire will have four choices: emigrate to the West; join the Zionists rebuilding the Jewish state in Palestine; stay in Russia and maintain Jewish social, religious, and cultural institutions; or "throw their lot in with the Bolsheviks."

History records that only a minority of Jews joined the Bolshevik cause and those who did found themselves in the leadership of the Party. Although Lenin and the early Communist comrades are not "overtly anti-Semitic," Jewish merchants and businessmen will be targeted later as scapegoats of the new regime, just as they had been in the old one.

During the Civil War, Jews will be caught in the middle. The Whites inflict and tolerate pogroms and exclude Jews from their administration, though Jews serve in the White Army. In the Ukraine, however, Whites and the Ukrainian bandit Symon Petliura unleash the worst pogroms. "If we include all those killed, wounded, raped, and orphaned by the violence," throughout the country, the victims number a million, according to Ruth Gay in *Safe Among the Germans*. After White atrocities, many Jews, "for their own self-preservation," gradually side with the Communist regime. The Red Army will contain Jewish officers and commissars, though individual Red units also will kill Jewish civilians. A decade later, Stalin and the Party will begin to close down the "fading world of Russian Jewry."

•

His name is Gershon Rasputnis. His family doesn't need the loud chimes of a grandfather clock to rouse them at first light. Nor do they house an infant who shatters their slumber just before dawn. Nor do they own a rooster to coax them out of their warm, quilted blankets to begin the day. His melodic voice gets his dreamy tots up every morning. Bellowing, cooing, whispering,

19

chanting, he spouts fast notes and slow notes. His sweet sounds move up the scales, down the scales, over the scales.

Gershon Rasputnis never misses an early morning rehearsal at home. Even when he has laryngitis and has to silence his voice, he recites prayer texts and music sheets by mouthing the words and hearing the tunes in his head.

God help those around him if he has even a touch of the sniffles or a hoarse throat; the apartment becomes an apothecary. At first, his remedies include hot tea with lemon, steaming chicken soup, fruit juice, honey spread on bread, honey mixed in tea, as well as spoonfuls of honey to soothe the raw throat. He also resorts to sprays and herbal concoctions, and at bedtime, he downs a shot-glass full of *schnaps* to sweat out germs. That's what he did until another cantor told him to drink ice-cold water, which he said shrinks the vocal cords; where-as, heat expands them and makes them even more irritated. Whatever worked he did it; God forbid he should face the high holy days without a voice.

Actually, Gershon is what they called *a baal koreh*, a reader, though every-one calls him cantor. He chants prayers. Whether he isn't good enough, or the congregation can't afford a cantor, Klara never figures out.

Late in the day, before evening prayers, Gershon can be found in his small book-lined room, silently working over tunes swimming in his head. He never stops improvising. He knows almost every word of every prayer by heart and can interpret them for his listeners, often adding a few flourishes of his own. Since he pleads to God, he feels he has to be Orthodox, although he wishes, at times, he can waver a little. Music is his life; everything else is secondary.

"I'm on trial when I sing in the synagogue. I have to be as good as my last performance," he explains, trying to account for the slight nervousness he has before he has to perform. "All eyes and ears are on me. God wants to hear a pleasant voice. So does the congregation."

Klara, the oldest, has heard family stories: How they moved from Zhitomir to Odessa where she was born. How Papa set up a draft-tight separate room for himself, a quiet place to rehearse and study. In that room facing the court-yard, he installed a form of cork-insulation onto the walls to mute the sound.

Even before Klara and the toddlers could talk, they were instructed never to enter the forbidden room when the door was shut. It's as if their father lives on another planet. Whenever they crawled on the floor, they were turned away before they could bang on the door. By the time they can walk, no Rasputnis child would dare invade this inner sanctum, except in an emergency. "If the door is closed, don't come in," Gershon repeats over and over again. They obey. Even when Zlota enters by mistake, he shouts: "Don't disturb me when I work!"

Once, Klara got so excited about the praise she received from an unusu-ally strict teacher, she forgot the rule. She burst into the room, only to see her father's face immediately change from deep concentration to a distorted look of rage. The message was clear: "Don't do that again."

When practice is over and the doors opened, Gershon emerges, takes a deep breath, and flashes a smile. Hastening to the kitchen, he brews some tea, smears butter and jam over a piece of white bread, and kisses and hugs anyone in sight, no matter what they're doing.

"Papa, Papa. A kiss for me."

Klara gets there first, pushing the others aside.

"Me, too," says Lillian, the third daughter, who, even as a child, senses that a burden has been lifted from Papa when he leaves his study room.

As for the youngest daughter, Sonya, she'll have to fight her way to grab father. But when she succeeds, he lifts her up into the air and plants kiss after kiss on her soft face.

Gershon remains a father in love with his children and they sense his warmth, his tickling beard, and his warm lips lighting up their faces and caressing their soft, wavy hair.

Childhood days pass quickly. Every morning before she goes off to school, Klara scurries down the passageway to the bathroom just off the kitchen where Papa is shaving. His woolen undershirt hangs loosely over his suspenders, which are draped over his black pants. His full face is covered with white soapy suds. As his eyes are fixed straight ahead at the mirror before him, he steers the sharp shaving blade over a salt-and-pepper-fuzz and neatly carves the goatee with surgical precision.

"That's my Papa!" she exclaims to herself as she takes in the full measure of the man whom she feels favors her over the other children. Of average height, he's a good-looking 36-year-old. His hair is always neatly pasted down. A long, full nose enhances his somewhat oval face; bushy eyebrows frame dark brown eyes. Even though his suits are out of fashion and shiny with wear, he carries himself well.

He loves Odessa. "This town has a soul. How good it is to live like God in Odessa," he says, repeating the often-quoted description regarding the metropolis. At the same time, he curses "those anti-Semitic bastards, the Czars. They're hypocrites. They needed to populate the city so badly that they made an exception. 'Let the Jews settle in Odessa.' Fine. But what about the millions languishing in the Pale of Settlement, that huge ghetto?"

But one thing in his life is wrong. Officially, he does not hold the rank of cantor in this city of cantors. He had come from Zhitomir to study with the masters, get experience, and then obtain a cantorial position. "How long do I have to wait?" he often asks friend Shaul. The latter shrugs his shoulders.

Even before their marriage, wife Zlota knew he had dreams for the future. He recognizes that in Odessa, he's going nowhere. He's sure he can succeed in America. "My America," he calls it. "So many Jews there; they certainly need cantors."

Thoughts of emigrating to Canada, where he has relatives, enter his mind. "There's gold in the streets," his relatives write him and assure him that he can obtain a position as a full-fledged cantor. He's convinced it'll take years until he overcomes the competition in Odessa.

Gershon rides the trains to get to his "culture events," as he calls them. Frequently he takes the train to Kharkov, Vinnitsa, Kiev, Bialystok, and even Zhitomir. And, when he does, he goes in the morning, less chance that a drunk will board the train and scream at him, "*Zhid (dirty Jew)*." He boards a car in the front so he can observe the fleeting farmlands, as well as hear the purr of the engine. The song of the wheels circulates above his fellow passengers, who snore, cough, and munch on sunflower seeds.

The routine is the same. As soon as the coach doors are unlocked, most rush to secure a seat on the always-crowded train, aptly named "the Kiev-local." As the train pulls out and heads through the suburbs, passengers begin to relax—some even smoke; others read. A few ride for a while and get off. At times, fellow passengers converse with him. He doesn't like to talk; he's afraid he, and any Jewish companion he meets, will lapse into Yiddish and the *goyim* will hear him. He always keeps his hat on; he does not want everyone to see his skullcap. Actually, it doesn't matter, he realizes, non-Jews can sense he's a Jew. "Where are you going?" they ask. He mentions some inconspicuous town because unless a Jew has a special *prokhodnoyo*, a residence permit, or transit pass, he can't enter the big city of Kiev. Off-limits.

He avoids staring at the homeless, starving children begging on station platforms.

"Is this 20th century Russia, 1914?" he asks himself. "We're living in medieval times. Children go hungry. Look how veterans from the Japanese War hobble along on crutches, stopping only for alms."

Gershon gives a few coins.

In late spring, 1914, Gershon is invited to attend a concert in Kiev given by the great cantor of the day, Moshe Stashefsky who is going to conduct a workshop on voice modulation, a skill in which Gershon admits he needs improvement. But how can he get there?

He hasn't been able to buy train tickets and a pass in advance. His blood boils every time he has to stand in line at the city hall for what he calls "a piece of paper" that gives him the right, *the right*, mind you, to travel to another city. Besides, there's no guarantee that the bureaucrats will give him permission to enter Kiev. They'll be suspicious and will question him. They'll check and see how many times he's visited the city and wonder if he's transporting revolutionary literature.

"We need more time to check. Come back tomorrow."

So, instead of bothering to report to the police station, he decides that he'll be defiant, though he should know that defiance never works in the land of the Czar. He should have recognized trouble. He should have realized that if a Jew opens the door just a little, thinking it's safe, new difficulties slap his face: Workers' demonstrations, arrests by the Czarist police, pogroms, and corrupt officials.

As luck has it, the day he leaves for Kiev, workers' strikes against proposed pay cuts for civil servants break out in Odessa and Kiev. When laborers walk off the job, the police move in to crush the work stoppage.

On this warm day, every Cossack in Odessa and Kiev is out on the lookout to catch and nip in the bud any planned demonstration. They are aware that Jews often travel without a permit. They watch out for these violators. But Gershon wants to beat the system, though he realizes that if the police don't pick him up on the train, they can collar him in Kiev. And that's exactly what happens. A few days after he departs to attend Cantor Stashefsky's workshop, Zlota receives the following letter:

Dearest Zlota,

I know you will forgive me. I only hope God will.

How could I have been so stupid to put you and the children in danger?

It's all because I'm so damn impatient. I hate those long lines at the municipal building just to get a permit from the police to travel to Kiev, even if it is only for a day. How many times have I said to you, 'what kind of country is this when only a Jew needs a permit to travel to another city?' I thought I could get away with it. But as my friend Shaul told you, I got caught. They picked us up right outside the Kiev synagogue. Shaul had a permit and I didn't. I tried to explain. I am a rabbi—they don't know the difference between a rabbi and a "baal koreh." I thought I could fool them as Rev. Yakovsky did a month ago. But the police were out in full force.

"No excuses, Jew," said the one who grabbed me. He dragged me by my neck and pushed me into the carriage. They put cuffs on my hands. I must say, so you and the children, God bless them, don't worry, they didn't beat or punch me. But they were disgusting and I could smell the vodka and garlic on their breath.

When we got to the police station, they threw me into in a padded cell and I could hear their laughing. 'We caught a big fish today,' they joked. 'A rabbi, no less.'

Zlota, my friend Shaul knows what to do. Listen to him. I know you will do this. Please make sure you bring me enough to eat. They offer me hazer (pig).

Again, don't worry. I'm not in any danger. They are not putting me into Kievskaya Prison, thank God. I am in Podol Prison, near the park. Each prisoner has his own cell. The cell next to mine is empty. It'll be full later, I'm sure.

You know, I don't like to give sermons. But after this, enough. We're getting out of here. We're going to Canada. I'll go first and bring all of you over after I get a position.

Love and kisses to you, Klara, Mischa, Ann, Lillian, and Sonya.

Not losing any time, Zlota applies for and receives "permission-to-travel" papers. In two days she's on her way to Kiev and pays the fine to get him out. "I'll take him in any shape: no legs, no arms, even blind," she tells the officer in charge.

"My God. They didn't touch you!" she exclaims when they open the gate and let him out into the sun-drenched street.

"A shave and bath is all I need," he says as they walk down the street under the stares of suspicious passer-bys. "The prisoners didn't give me a hard time. My singing came in handy. I entertained them with Russian folk songs."

"I'm sure you didn't sing Kol Nidre," says Zlota, smiling as she observes his stained vest.

"I didn't have to," he answers, laughing for the first time.

"Let's get going. I've got a lot of work to do. Applications. Forms. Tickets. I'll get affidavits from relatives in Ottawa. I must do this now. If I don't, I never will," he says, taking Zlota's arm and guiding her toward the train station and back to Odessa.

5

When Jews emigrated from Europe at the turn of the 20th Century, the plan was the father, or breadwinner as he was often called, went alone, made money, and then sent the family train and boat tickets to join him.

·

"He wouldn't dare leave us," says Ann as the girls prepare for bed.

"Oh, you think so, do you? Well, you're wrong;" interrupts Lillian. "His boat tickets arrived by messenger this morning. Saw them with my own eyes."

"Who's going to tell us stories at night?"

"It'll never happen," Klara assures the girls as she tries to usher them into bed.

"Nobody'll take us for walks. No picnics on Sundays," chimes in Sonya. "No circus."

Klara puts on a happy face before the young ones though she also questions: *Would they all have to move and leave school? What about their friends and their cat, Petrushka?*

On the other side of the partition, Mischa lies in bed on his back, staring at the dull, grey ceiling with its single, dangling light and listening to the chatter next door.

"Girls! Don't believe everything you hear," he shouts. "Papa's not going. Klara, stop teasing those kids. Go to sleep."

A few nights later, Klara wakes up screaming. Gershon and Zlota run into the room to calm her. "Gershon. Cold compresses, quick. She's burning up."

"Papa. Don't go."

That morning, Ann, who wouldn't miss singing lessons with Mrs. Nemsov for anything, refuses to go to her teacher's studio. "I have a sore throat," she suddenly declares.

The next day, Lillian gets up at the breakfast table and runs out screaming, "I'm not going to school. I don't feel good. My stomach hurts."

As for Mischa, he's sadder than the rest. The 13-year-old is sure he's "Papa's boy," and the thought that he'll be gone is incomprehensible. "The house'll be unbearable," he says to himself. "Bad enough now. Females always fussing over their hair, looking at themselves in the mirror, trying on earrings, giggling over the boys in the class, and yes, even breaking out in tears for no reason at all. Besides with Papa not around, they'll all gang up on me. Papa, don't go."

And Klara? Her father was indeed the only man in the house. Mischa, however, was not a man, he was a sibling and Klara treated him as if he was a sister. But if there was anyone Klara was afraid of, it was Papa. She admired and loved him, but became frightened if he as much as raised an eyebrow in her direction. Yet she sensed that if he left, the connection between the two of them would grow stronger.

"Papa, Papa. Please. Take me with you," she pleads.

He stares at her.

She knows the answer.

One night, Klara dreams that Papa gets lost while trying to find his way home. She is sent on a long journey to find him. Klara believes dreams come true. That dream, like many before, is prescient. She's too young to realize that sometimes what you wish for reaches fruition.

Meanwhile, they wait. The days pass. Klara senses that Papa'll depart soon.

Gershon does not have the money for passage to the New World. Relatives raise and send the funds for his one-way ticket to the U.S. and then onto Canada. He's fixated on one idea; becomes obsessed with it. He's heard you can live wherever you want in America, travel, and move anywhere without a permit. For now, that's enough for him.

At day's start, Klara usually wakes up first. She rubs her eyes with the back of her hands and mumbles to herself. "Get up and face the world." But on that hot late July morning in 1914, however, she sits up in bed in a state of shock. She can't focus. Something's wrong. Stretching her neck, she peers out through the open door and spies suitcases and a trunk lined up in the hallway. Outside, rain is beating down on the roof. The biting wind crashes off the shutters. Except for the heavy breathing of her three sisters lying in the large quilt-covered bed next to her, the house is deadly silent.

No sound. No voice. No chants. No prayers. No scales. Papa's not singing. Impossible! She can't remember a day in her life when she hasn't heard Papa reciting scales in the morning, every morning, even on the *Sabbath* and holidays.

"No. No," she screams as she jumps out of bed. "He's closing his suit-cases."

Gershon says his good-byes. He nervously moves from child to child. "Six or seven months. That's all it'll take. In the spring, I'll send you boat tickets and we'll meet in 'my America,'" says the admired father, flashing a reassuring smile.

He has promised himself to leave his family as best he can, without tears. A friend tells him not to do that, just go quietly at night and spare the family a wrenching departure. Gershon'll have no part of sneaking off like that.

"Now Klara, stop crying," he says, putting his arm around the shoulder of the slim teenager, and kissing her on her large forehead, his eyes downward and locking into her eyes messaging, "I'll miss you."

Mischa's next. He stands at attention like an officer in the Cadets. Gershon's hand is on his son's arm. "Be strong, Mischa. Remember always, you're the man of the house now."

When he slides over toward the younger daughters, they can't restrain themselves and rush up to him, hunting for a little space in which to hug the husky man. Youngest Sonya grabs onto his leg and wails, "Don't go. Don't go."

"Only six or seven months," he again promises, as he disentangles the children's arms.

And with that, he puts his hands over their young heads; closes his eyes; and recites the priestly blessing over his children. He then sits on his suitcase for a minute or so and gives a final look at his family, picks up his luggage, places another peck on Zlota's cheek and bounds out the door to the waiting for-hire horse tram, which serves as his taxi to the train station.

The family stands together at the doorway. Klara dabs at her moist eyes with a wet handkerchief. Mischa stands erect, aping his fellow high school students on the parade ground—imagining his unit's being reviewed by a general. The young wide-eyed daughters nervously shuffle about, craning their necks for a view of the departing carriage, now just a moving, black speck far down on Proharovskaya Street.

Instinctively, Zlota gathers her flock to her, the two young ones on one side, Klara and Ann on the other. Mischa stands away a bit and aloof.

I'm glad we rehearsed this departure, Zlota thinks. *I didn't know he was such a liar.*

Gershon told a white lie when he said six or seven months. He sensed it would be more than half a year. The made-up number, six or seven, was correct, though. Not six or seven months, but six or seven years.

Gershon Rasputnis is last seen sitting next to the driver and reciting the Talmudic "prayer for a safe journey," known as the "*Tefillat ha-Derekh.*"

"May it be thy will, O Lord my God to lead me forth in peace, and direct my steps in peace … and deliver me from the hand of every enemy and ambush by the way…."

He's on his way to "his America." Little does he know that a month after he abandons his family, World War I will descend on Russia. The conflagration will change the lives of the Rasputnis family and millions like them.

6

Klara Arrives in Moscow, December 1917

Unlike Petrograd (St. Petersburg), the Reds had to fight tooth and nail for Moscow during the Bolshevik Revolution. Street battles lasted six days. Workers suffered heavy losses but overcome the well-organized defenders of the Provisional Government and their White supporters. Four months later, on March 12, 1918, the Soviets moved the capital from Petrograd to Moscow and began to face off against the regrouped Czarist generals in the south.

The Reds will kill thousands of innocent people in the name of the masses. The Whites will murder thousands in the name of the Czar, though many Whites—while pro-monarchist—want to reconvene a Constituent Assembly. Many see the Bolsheviks as fanatics who will not preserve what is left of the defeated Russian Army nor honor the pledges Russia made to the Allies before the Czarist regime collapsed. Neither side takes prisoners. Dead men tell no tales.

Moscow was not only suffering under the coldest winter on record, but also "facing hunger on a scale more massive than any they had known in modern times," according to W. Bruce Lincoln in his book, *Red Victory, A History of the Russian Civil War.*

While Klara is in Moscow, Cossack units in the Don and Kuban regions resist the new Red government. Having supported the Czar, they set up autonomous units located in lands far from what they call "Bolshevik anarchy."

Meanwhile, making good on their prerevolutionary promises, the Reds sign an armistice agreement with Germany and Austria ending the fighting on December 17, 1917. Russia is out of a foreign war but will soon enter another bloody conflict, a civil war that will cause, as author Brian Crozier put it, "a catalog of horrors, which will bring hunger and depravation." More will die in the war through famine, disease, and atrocities than from military action. To this day, no accurate statistics exist, but it is estimated that from 1918 to 1922, seven to ten million men, women, and children died in this bitter struggle that tore Russia apart and left "a lasting scar." "Russia descended into savage anarchy beyond imagination," writes Douglas Smith.

•

"God, I'm shivering in this damn, unheated train," Klara says to herself as the landscape outside Moscow begins to change with fewer empty fields and more towns popping into view.

Klara dares not look outside. She doesn't want to stare at the crowds lining the tracks.

Reluctantly, she prepares to leave the train. So she summons her courage and winds herself up like she always does when anxiety flares up. *Big city, here I come.*

"*Mosk-va, Mosk-va* (Little Mother Moscow) in ten minutes," booms the conductor. "*Moskva Matushka,*" he repeats. Quiet in the car. Not a word. No one moves.

Crawling into the Aleksandrovsky Station on Tverskaya Zastava, Klara Rasputnis' train is welcomed into the 12th century city, once the Byzantine heart of the Russian Empire.

Waiting to get off and looking out her window, Klara spies a single female figure. The woman is waiting for somebody. *Is that Rachel? Looks like Rachel. Damn it. Look closer.*

Her mind is playing tricks on her. It's not Rachel!

As Klara descends from the train, she shivers. "Gotta be 10 degrees below zero. God! Never felt so cold in my life," she says to herself, pounding her arms with her fists to improve her blood circulation in the frigid night air.

The station has turned into an armed camp. Bolshevik posters appear on the walls. Red Guards loll around—their woolen hats emblazoned with a Red star. They move in groups of twos and threes and stalk the dark station hall as they eye weary travelers sitting on their luggage and guarding their bundles, their bags, their packing cases, their rolled-up mattresses, household utensils, and gramophone horns.

Bagmen sell flour, potatoes, and vegetables at black market prices. Men, women, and children huddle in dark doorways and as they sleep they are covered with newspapers across their shoulders, giving them a sense of warmth. Youngsters, their feet wrapped in rags, beg for food, their haunted faces gaunt. Dressed in sacking, they appear half starved and diseased as they huckster their wares.

"Alms for the poor. Alms for the poor," pleads an old man.

A mother instructs her 10-year-old daughter how to beg and how to stay away from other hawkers, as well as making sure she gets the correct change.

Klara realizes this station is not a railway depot. It's a hotel, with no clerk on hand to vent one's anger for the haughty attitude of the staff.

Although track announcements are rarely made, hundreds of hungry, anxious people know when a train is ready to depart. The word gets around like a raging fire. Mobs rush the gate to get on board. Away from Moscow. Away from the war. Away from the Red Revolution. Away from the Civil War. Away from here to anywhere, as if a safe haven exists in this vast land.

She tightens her grip on her suitcase. She's frightened. "It's ok to be scared," she says to herself to calm her anxiety. "But don't show it, whatever you do. Mask it, Klara. Mask it."

Just when she's ready to walk away from the mass of humanity in the station to go to the Kazansky Station on Kalanchevskaya Square for passage to Siberia, the streetlights in the terminal go out and the gates are locked. The authorities don't want people moving around outside late at night; too dangerous. Now she has to wait until dawn and sit for a few hours in near darkness.

Dawn. Snowing again. She leaves the station and enters the biting cold. Moscow remains dark. Women, carrying their babies, shiver and knock one foot against the other for warmth. Tykes approach her, offering to carry her suitcase. They assure Klara they'll drag her bag anywhere in Moscow, for a small price, of course.

As she walks, hard snow blasts frost into her shoes. Klara moves past old wooden cabins squeezed in between ramshackle apartment houses. She notices pavements are torn up and abandoned cats crawl through rubbish bins. Old women in headscarves come out to shoo them away. Workers pull down their fur-lined hats to ward off the freezing snow. Moscow trembles. What has become of Mother Russia?

Klara's muscles tense as she moves briskly down a noiseless wide boulevard. Afraid of being followed, she enters a crowded marketplace, past fish stalls selling mackerel. She's hungry, but so are the emaciated beggars around her.

"Give me a bit of bread, little mother, for Christ's sake," says one little urchin.

"Don't have any, little one. Here's a ruble," says Klara dropping the coin into the child's nearly frostbitten hand.

She proceeds, street by street, alley by alley, only pausing to scan some book stalls which have proliferated as the upper class, cut off from their funds by the new Communist government, try to raise some money by selling precious collections.

"Can I get something to eat?" she asks a woman who has taken out some bread at her makeshift stand selling trinkets. "I'll pay you."

"Don't have much. Stale bread, a piece of herring, onion, and garlic. But I'll share it with you," says the woman. "Don't want your money. My good deed for the day."

Exhausted from the cold and her long walk—already an hour—the girl from Odessa decides to jump on a trolley pulled by horses, known as an *izvoschick*. As the wagon heads toward Aleksandrovsky Station, Klara enjoys the emptiness of the city covered with a thick blanket of snow. It calms her.

Klara's decided to go to Chelyabinsk where the Lubavitzes were to hole up for a few weeks, according to what Zlota told her. Maybe, just maybe, they are there; even though, by this time, the hatred of those so-called friends of the family has begun to torment her. Still, she knows she must try once more to find them. She's convinced her trip across Russia will be safe in a small group.

As Klara alights at the station, large groups of travelers mill around the main entrance. Others are drinking hot tea from homemade containers. Standing in place, guards shuffle from side to side, trying to keep their circulation moving through their tired bones. New arrivals carrying boxes, suitcases, and crates get as close as they can to the main entrance.

She has mastered which line to choose for ticket validation; which train carriage to climb aboard; when to sleep; how to guard her baggage. She knows how to find the platform of her train and since no one usually is in line at the gate hours before scheduled departure, she often can board at will and grab a window seat. She knows that Russians respect an unwritten law that declares, once you get there and put a bag or a coat on an unoccupied seat, it's yours. After that, she smiles; possession is nine-tenths of the law. Isn't it? Or is it brute force?

Klara realizes that Moscow is not Odessa; the police control the crowds better, though hooligans who jump the line often knock women and children to the ground.

By now, Klara feels she can look at railway personnel and know whether a friendly soul hides behind a stern face and dark narrow eyes; how to find someone who'll be nice to you; and maybe even tell you the truth.

She spies a young conductor by the door studying a timetable.

"How do I get to Chelyabinsk?"

"Well, there's an old Russian saying about trains," he says as he fixes his eyes on Klara's inquiring facial expression. "You can go by the fast train which they say is slow, or by the slow train which is even slower."

She smiles.

"Just kidding, *devushka*. Go to the east gate. Better chance to get on there," he says winking at her.

Klara blushes and turns away.

"Oh, you'll have to change at Ekaterinburg."

She hastens to the ticket office, but first has to get past the guard at the gate. She succeeds by smiling at the soldier who lets her pass. The line is long. An unshaven old man, twitching his hands slightly, hunches over the counter at the caged window. He's been there a long time.

Murmurs erupt from the crowd.

"Next," someone shouts out from the middle of the line. "You're asking too many questions, Comrade Grandfather."

"Enough already, old one," echoes another tall youth shouldering a rifle and standing further back in line.

"Move on," says another trooper immediately behind Klara.

The old man turns and sneers. "I'm sick. Don't be so rude. I'll summon the police and tell them you're abusing me."

Laughter erupts in the line.

"Well if you're sick, move away," replies a soldier. "Have some consideration for others."

"No," fires back the old man, proud, haughty, not realizing it's a new country, a Bolshevik country where force heads the list instead of civility.

"That's why they call a line a line. You'll have to wait your turn," the elder lectures the soldier. "Besides, I was in the war before you," he says, puffing up his chest. "The 1904 War."

At first, not realizing he's talking to a deserter who is so angry and bitter that he'd have killed his own father at that moment, the grandfatherly-looking man now begins to shake; his eyes open wide and his pupils begin to bulge when he senses that another youngster walking up to him is going to grab him and haul him away.

No words are exchanged, but everyone in the line watches as this angel of death leads his victim outside. Klara does nothing.

A few minutes later, the trooper returns and takes his place in the row.

"The comrade's right," he tells the person behind him in a voice that reaches the end of the queue. "A line is a line. But where we're sending him, he won't be bothered with impatient people like us," he adds with a smirk on his face.

Arriving at the ticket booth, Klara buys a one-way ticket to Chelyabinsk via Ekaterinburg for 10 rubles. She dares not look at the soldier behind her. He's waiting his turn. She's learned not to make a fuss.

Soon she approaches the gate whose posted sign reads "Chelyabinsk." She knows that that Russian city is on the Asian side of the Urals, a gateway to Siberia. She envisions the longest train journey in the world, 6,000 miles through an icy wilderness. She remembers reading how the exiles were linked foot-to-foot with iron chains and sent to convict prisons in the north where either they work or die. *Is that my fate?* she asks herself.

At that moment, the station doors open. People rush in.

Quickly finding a seat, Klara will have to wait for the all-clear sign, two short bell blasts—followed by a jolt of the cars—and then the long train will begin to glide out of the terminal.

She fidgets, eager to get moving. The time for departure has long gone. She plants her nose up against the stained window to better focus on the far end of the platform so she could avoid the screaming newsboys bombarding her ears. "Famine Hits Ukraine," they shout, words that knife deep into her brain and stomach.

The headlines unsettle her. *Why this now?* she asks. Had she not entered the train that morning in a state of euphoria? As she thinks about the family back home, her face is punctured with gleeful smiles and she whispers to herself, "In a way, except for my ballet classes, I'm glad I'm out of there. A new life for me," she repeats over and over again, even as she utters: "Papa. I miss you. I'll find you. Believe me, I will!"

She watches the train fill up with battle-fatigued soldiers and anxious families pushing and fighting with each other to board. One hour extends into two, two into three, three into four. Listening to the newsboys repeating the headline, "Famine Hits the Ukraine," Klara imagines long bread lines are forming in her home town of Odessa; beggars are invading its streets; children—perhaps even Ann, Lillian, and Sonya—are putting out their hands as they plead for a mere morsel of food; old men and women are rummaging through garbage cans; roaming gangs of youths are accosting carriages along Pushkin Street; and hooligans are grabbing bags of groceries from helpless women. Is Mischa performing his duty and watching over the family? It's agony not knowing.

Her despair, however, is broken as a woman with her teenage son and three young girls, apparently ages seven through 16, push their way into the compartment. The woman is tall but plump, a long, pleasing but narrow face, short brown hair.

"Oh my goodness; my eyes deceive me," says Klara to herself. "Am I seeing my mother? Can't be."

She remembers Zlota's face as gaunt, her eyes sunken, cheeks emaciated, lips parched.

"Is that Mischa who's moving into the next compartment with a peasant woman? Across the aisle are the girls, her sisters, Ann, Lillian, and Sonya, cuddling up to their mother.

"Please," says the woman with four children. "Join us. Eat something."

"No thanks. Just ate," fibs Klara who hasn't eaten all morning and whose stomach is calling her names, as Zlota used to say. But wait, better to be hungry than accept gifts from strangers, Klara was taught.

The woman takes out porcelain dinner plates from a large bag and loads them with strawberry-filled *blini* and sour cream; bulging, heavy-layered chicken drum sticks; brown and white bow-tie kasha; several boiled onions, thick slices of black bread smeared with cherry preserves, and little balls of red caviar. To wash it all down, a large jar of cold, green borsht passes around from thirsty mouth to thirsty mouth.

This well-fed family savors each bite. The woman picks up a newspaper with the same headline that Klara spied earlier: *Famine Hits Ukraine*. She reads the words, with absolutely no physical or emotional effect, except that the muscles around her mouth tighten as she chews pieces of dark meat.

Never one to be silent, Klara points to the newspaper and shouts above the din:

"See that headline? 'Famine Hits the Ukraine.'"

"Ukraine? Don't know anyone there. Thank God we're here," declares the woman. Looking up at Klara, she forces a smile and returns to her paper.

Turning away, Klara looks outside—just in time to see a tyke standing on a baggage cart, his eyes taking in their compartment. Hands outstretched, his sad eyes seem to search for a morsel of food.

Inside the train, the oldest boy, wiping his mouth to clear away sticky food, sees the child outside looking in on them and reaches over Klara to lower the window blind.

Klara wants to get up and slap the teenager and lift the shade. She doesn't dare. She's learning to use her brain and restrain her anger.

The situation on the train platforms is constantly getting worse. Panic-stricken men, women, and children—fearing they won't get on in time—hurl their trunks, their bundles, their boxed-live chickens into the carriages. Women wink and smile at the conductors. The mere thought that her mother, Zlota, might have to surrender her flesh to a storekeeper or the landlord to feed and house her children, gags Klara. She can't stop coughing.

Impulsively, she rises; grabs her suitcase and darts for the door.

"Where you going?" the woman with four children asks, her voice and face expressing bewilderment.

"Leaving. Going back to my family in Odessa. They need me."

"You crazy? Back there? Might as well jump in front of the locomotive!" exclaims the woman, as Klara pushes through the doorway and into the crowd in the passageway.

"Momma! Why is that girl doing something so stupid as getting off the train?" shouts the teenage boy.

As Klara lands on the platform, a blast of cold wind bites her face. The sting energizes her as she spots an empty train across the track with a wooden sign on its side, marked "Ryazan," south of Moscow. Even if it's out of the way, she can change there for Kiev and then onto Odessa.

She has no time to run to the ticket office to exchange tickets, so she has to purchase a new ticket from the conductor for seven rubles. When the conductor hands it to her, she notices the empty car behind him and pleads: "Comrade conductor, please get this train moving. I've got to get back to my family."

7

Gershon Rasputnis Arrives in Vladivostok, September, 1914

Cantor Gershon Rasputnis is comfortably ensconced in Vladivostok, in the Russian Far East, six thousand miles from war-threatened Western Russia. He's quite capable of taking care of himself, of adapting to a new environment. When he left Odessa, he was forced to travel eastward because of the German advance into Russian-held territory.

Now, for the first time in his life, he's free. Taking advantage of his new situation, he becomes a "wild buck." He does, however, write Zlota that he arrived safely in this port city on the Pacific Ocean.

It will be the first and only letter he'd ever write to his family:

> Hills. Hills everywhere you go. Up a hill. Down a hill. Hills and more hills peopled by Chinese, Koreans, Japanese. I am told they have fueled a brisk wartime economy. You can see a harbor full of foreign ships bringing in equipment and arms for the Russian war-effort.
>
> You should have seen what I looked like when I arrived here. Unruly beard. Crumpled suit. Old-fashioned English tie. Ukrainian leather boots.
>
> I've been detained on some passport matter. I'm filling in at the synagogue for the regular cantor who is ailing.

Ending with a prayer for her and the children, Gershon notes it's risky to put cash in the mail. Nevertheless, he encloses several hundred rubles so they won't have to dip into savings.

> I'll write more and send more money soon.
>
> Love you all, Gershon

"Gershon. Listen. I've good news for you," says Boris, the Cantor's cousin. "The break you've been waiting for all your life; it's here, though God forbid we take advantage of a death. But fact is fact. Cantor Elie Cohen just passed away."

Only a second, that's all it takes for Gershon's brain to decipher the news that Cantor Elie Cohen is dead. Oh, how quickly he conjures up the pleasing image of his standing on the *bimah*, draped in his white gown, crowned with a tall, box-like ceremonial white skull cap and reciting holy prayers before the Vladivostok congregation of 300 and growing.

"I'll do it. I'll take it. Did you ever know me to turn down an opportunity or a ruble? Imagine," he goes on unashamedly, "when I walk down the street they'll call me, 'Cantor.' Some will even say 'Rabbi.'"

He's shouting so loudly that the driver turns abruptly, his expression demanding a lower voice from the occupants.

"Easy, Gershon. You don't have the position yet. For goodness sake, mask your feelings," cautions the cousin who knows Gershon already has the job. The holidays are only a few weeks away and this congregation on the Pacific, 10 time zones away from Moscow, certainly can't get a replacement so fast.

"Get a good night's sleep," says Boris. "Tomorrow, I'll take you to the synagogue. They know you're coming."

The taxi continues to speed along the city's cobblestone streets. "Vladivostok. Vladivostok," murmurs Gershon to himself, as one would utter a lover's name. To show his excitement, as if he was in a paramour's embrace, he voices the city's nickname, "Vladik, Vladik." He savors the sound as he looks out of the car window and gazes at the sea, and imagines the congregants wishing him: "A good Sabbath to you, Cantor Rasputnis. A good Sabbath to you."

At that very moment, as the sky darkens, he lets his mind wander over this Far East land and can feel a prayer shawl ceremoniously being lowered on his shoulders that places the mantle of respectability for the clergyman from Odessa. Now, he's truly Cantor Rasputnis.

He can taste the honor.

Two days later, Gershon receives the following letter from synagogue leaders:

> Dear Reb Gershon Rasputnis,
>   This is to inform you that the Board of Directors of Congregation Ahavas Shalom has appointed you to the position of Cantor for a term of one year. Please come to our office on Sunday, to sign a contract.
>   Daniel Chernick,
>   Board of Trustees.

Legal contracts have a way of being extended. Gershon Rasputnis finds himself in a predicament. Death lies behind him in war-torn Russia and death lies ahead of him in a perilous journey across the ocean. Far from the battlefield, he chooses a safer, merrier, indulgent life. He keeps his wife and children hidden in a far-off compartment of his mind.

"Have you noticed, our new Cantor smiles so nicely," congregants say to each other after meeting the former citizen of Odessa. Gershon has learned to keep a smile on his face at all times. "The Odessa-smile," he calls it; an ingratiating grin sewn onto your countenance, like a handstitched patch covering the elbows of his jacket. He has practiced being gregarious. He commands himself: "Wind yourself up like a clock when entering the synagogue. No one wants a dour rabbi or cantor."

While he agrees the clergy should be aloof somewhat, he also feels they must flaunt a smile. When a congregant has a problem and seeks out the rabbi, he or she wants his spiritual leader to be comforting, even if the matter is serious or difficult to solve.

In his room, he practices smiling as well as standing straight with good posture—head high, shoulders back, eyes forward. He rehearses entering and exiting a room, a bow, the kissing of the female-host's hand.

The new cantor becomes friendly with Harry the haberdasher who's a member of the congregation. Gershon has resolved to dress well, for though a frontier town, Vladivostok follows the Siberian commandment that its professional men look distinguished.

One day after services, Harry the haberdasher, calls Gershon aside.

"Cantor, forgive me. I've been observing you. Allow me a professional prerogative: I think you have to change the way you dress. I can help you. Come to the store tomorrow."

The haberdasher teaches him color combinations. "When you are giving a concert at Mrs. Rosenblatt's house on Sunday, wear your blue blazer, a white shirt, grey pants, and this plain tie."

New mannerisms are essential: How to dangle his gold pocket watch to attract attention and indicate affluence. Pressed clothes, shined shoes, haircut every two weeks; a manicure for his beard. He trims his moustache and goatee with preciseness; it hides his ambitions.

Even though congregants know he's married, they try to fill his time with women, not just any kind of woman, but a woman willing to entertain him at dinner.

"Guess who's lunching with us on Sunday," Mrs. Rosenblatt tells friends.

The wealthy congregational ladies fall over each other in planning who will have the most prestigious gathering of the season. Whose soiree would bring city officials or famous actors and actresses? Gershon loves to perform in these houses. It gives him a chance to show off the arias he has heard and studied at the Odessa Opera House, such as "Kuda, Kuda," from Pushkin's *Eugene Onegin*, in which Lensky (friend of Onegin) asks, "*Where have you gone, O golden days of my spring?*"

Flattered, and feeling young at heart, he notices which women approach him at the end of each party exclaiming how much they enjoyed his singing. Clearly stating her address, one asks whether he would accept a future invitation. Some women even come up to him unaccompanied. He amuses himself with the thought that one widow would have thrown herself right at him—right

there in front of everyone. Other women shake his hand and even stroke it as
if to say: "How nice you are. How gentle." Some ladies do not dare introduce
themselves without their husbands. Yet he perceives they manage to maneuver
their seductive eyes to convey they would visit the Cantor alone.

"Come back to my place. You can stay over," whispers the cantor one night
to a congregation lady whose husband, a merchant, has traveled to Harbin in
Manchuria.

Late at night, she brings over a few things in a small bag.

The large soft-cushioned red sofa stands in the middle of the den. He serves
up thick, black Turkish coffee. He puts his arm around her waist and kisses her.
He draws her closer. A few words like, "you're the reason for my smile," and
"you're always in my heart," and he begins to undress her. She's young, with
a thin, muscular body like Klara's.

Once at night.

Again later that night.

She takes a bath.

He takes a bath.

They bathe together.

She leaves at dawn.

A few years later, he won't recall her name.

8

Train Back to Odessa? December 1917

Armed groups of various political persuasions move to the battlefield to engage the Bolshevik revolutionaries. This civil war, however, is not just soldier against soldier; it mushrooms into class struggle—workers against managers, peasants against landowners, poor against rich.

Because of Russia's huge landmass, this civil war is fought in phases, not as classical warfare. The conflict will consist of few fixed fronts and massive battles, more like partisan skirmishes and mopping-up exercises. The engagements will be spread over different geographical areas. In constant flux, troops will move along major railroad lines. Large unoccupied areas will exist between warring armies.

•

Klara, who is now beside herself waiting for the train to take her back to Odessa, will never know until much later about Gershon's philandering. She only knows that at this moment, her conscience plagues her for leaving her mother and sisters. As we have seen, she has decided to leave Moscow and return to help the family. To her outside world, parents, friends, teachers, and instructors—she appears to look and act decisively.

But like a Talmudic scholar, Klara almost at once begins to question her new plan. "Why am I giving up and going back to Odessa? For a brother who's always fighting with me. For my sisters, they'll fend for themselves. For Momma, she'll manage. On the other hand, I gave my word. I promised I'll find father. I'll make it. I can't falter. I've got to survive," she concludes.

"But they're so vulnerable in Odessa. Who knows what Mischa is doing? He hates being at home, especially since I left and he wanted to be out of there. Chances are he went and joined the army. No. I've got to help them."

Still, she's consumed with doubt, doubt that now envelops her mind even as she boards the Odessa-bound train.

The locomotive neither warms up nor moves. Klara waits.

Once again, Klara inhales the aroma of freshly baked *pechenya* wafting up from the platforms into her welcoming nostrils.

The anticipation and warmth from the overheated cars bring on sleep. Visions of her mother appear before her. Even though Klara wants to touch her, she can't reach her. Someone is pulling her the other way; it's Gershon, her father. She visualizes him as sick and emaciated. Her mind verbalizes his pleading: *Come Klara. Help me.*

But she sits there in a stupor. No one talks. No one interrupts her drowsiness. Her head rests on her chest. She has entered dreamland and though she wishes she can destroy the deep-seated wish to be with her father, she fails because she truly misses his hugs and kisses, his support, even his favoritism of her over the others, an extra kiss, an extra wink, a look that signals she's something special.

Pulling at her is Momma, the girls, and the city she loves. Her dream places her on that grand 240-step Odessa street staircase, the "Odessa Steps," on which she climbs up and down, counting each step. She feels the quick pulse of the city as she romps over its cobble-paved courtyards, the byways and arteries that feed the heart of the port city, including frantic Deribasov Street, full of pedestrians; majestic and sleepy Pushkin Street whose stately homes were occupied by grain traders; pretentious Catherine Street with its old fashioned houses, and yes the gold-trimmed Odessa Opera and Ballet Theater where she saw her first ballet performance. All this flashes before her and commands her to go forward or retreat.

Just as the warmth of her hometown begins to thrill her, a single, shrill locomotive whistle shatters her dream. Startled and shaken as she comes out of her sleep, she moves her head side to side. Where is she? It's Moscow, not Odessa.

The catnap has wiped away the mental cobwebs. Reflecting on the struggle to get this far on her journey, she realizes what she must do.

The train lurches. Again she is startled. Last chance. In a minute or two, she'll be heading home, her quest for her father, a failure.

She remains frozen. No energy to get up.

"But I just left the other train," she says out loud and the debate begins all over again, with both sides of the argument battling for her mind. One idea, however, begins to overwhelm the other. Maybe she should go back to her old railway car and continue onward in her journey to find Papa. "I love him," she says to herself.

She wishes she had an omen; something or someone to spur her on whichever way she goes. At that very moment she sees a sign—a Communist banner hanging on the brick wall outsider her window:

"Change course if necessary, but press on."

Maybe I'll make that Red slogan my own, she thinks, as she notices that her old Siberian-bound train across the tracks has not left the station.

"Go already," she shouts angrily to that train facing east.

Meanwhile, a few soldiers board her train.

"Damn it," she says to herself, remembering Rachel's advice: Stay away from soldiers.

The troops begin to unload their gear. Rucksacks come off the shoulders of these tough Red Guards. She sinks down in the chair. But the troopers spot her.

"Off the train," commands one.

"What do you mean? Off? Why?" she answers back, surprised at her talking back to a soldier.

"This train's going to Ryazan, correct?"

"Not any more, Comrade Citizen. We're commandeering this train. Orders of the Central Committee. Get off. Be quick now."

The decision has been made. She grabs her suitcase, moves down the aisle and steps down onto the empty platform. Only the conductor stands guard across the way, at an open door of the train to Chelyabinsk.

"All aboard," he yells in a deep, throaty voice, taking her ticket to Chelyabinsk. "Thank God I saved it," she says to herself. "God wants me to go on my journey, otherwise, he wouldn't have sent those soldiers," she adds, smiling and holding her bag up to a young man standing on the car steps.

Pushing through the car, shoving people, uttering over and over again, "excuse me, please," she threads her way back to her compartment. Her seat's still empty.

"You've returned," says the mother with the four children. "Got some sense knocked into your head," she snickers. "I told everyone this is your seat. 'She's coming back,' I said."

"Thanks," says Klara, heaving her suitcase up onto the luggage rack. She's exhausted.

"Here, eat something. I saved some *pirozhki* for you, and some fresh *borscht*. My name is Marya Ivanovna Kovchenko and these are my four children, Leonid, Vera, Ludmila, and Yevgenia."

"Pleased to meet you," answers Klara who begins to eat the meat-filled pastries and drinks the cold beet soup. She forgets the famine. She forgets the hunger of the populace. She doesn't forget that the food is not kosher, but she must eat and she hopes God will forgive her. Nothing must stand in the way of her journey.

"Anyway, how far are you going? You never did tell me," questions Mrs. Kovchenko.

"Chelyabinsk, by way of Ekaterinburg," answers Klara.

"Oh, we've got a way to go yet," says the woman.

"Yes we do," replies Klara, already pondering a problem that constantly nags at her, but will never be completely answered until much later. What daughter or son can tell the truth even to herself or himself about a father who is wonderful on the outside, but can change in a moment, in a day, in a week. How could he leave his family, his flesh and blood, and then forget them? How could he abandon them to their own devices? On the other hand, maybe he couldn't help it, she thinks, so for the moment she pushes it all aside. She has to concentrate on getting to Vladivostok. *If by chance, Papa's there, I'll find him. If not, it doesn't matter; I'll find someone to help me, to give me food and shelter, until I can get to America.*

Her thoughts are interrupted by the whistle, the jolt of the train pulling out of the station. Even if she's not going back, she is reminded again of her life back in Odessa, the years she recalls so well, especially after Gershon left for Canada in 1914.

9

Odessa, Spring 1916

When Gershon left Odessa, Zlota made a promise to herself: She never would allow the children to think Gershon is dead or has deserted them. Now nearly two years later, she's jealous of him. Why doesn't he come back and rescue them? To them, he has disappeared into that wide continent that is Russia. The war prevents mail from getting through. The money he sent is long gone. She becomes bitter. Why her? Hate creeps into her body. Is she a woman spurned?

Zlota writes to Gershon's relatives in Canada, supposedly inquiring about his health, stating that she has not heard from him for a long time but of course that could be because the war hindered his journey and mail often didn't get through. Has he arrived? Do they know where he is? She heard he reached Vladivostok. But has he landed in America or Canada? She tries to frame the wording in such a way that they won't suspect that she's inferring that he deserted her.

No reply. Perhaps they never got the letter. If they did, she suspects, they wouldn't tell her the truth anyway. Why would they? Why would they want to get mixed up in a family squabble?

Everything around the Rasputnis family is decaying. Odessa, their great city, the most important shipping center of the country, an important rail junction and port, is shrouded in darkness. The electric supply station has been destroyed by fire. Zlota used to reach under the mattress for the hidden packet of rubles. Now that money pouch is empty. Prices have doubled, no new clothes, no meat.

At first, the family acts mature and responsible. Quarrels are limited to squabbles over sugar or food portions that everyone watches, fearing the next person is getting more.

"Leave me alone," Klara shouts at Mischa.

"Me? Leave you alone? You kicked me."

"Stop it, you two," demands Zlota. "Don't we have enough problems? We don't know where Papa is. Have you nothing better to do than fight at the dinner table?"

It doesn't help. Klara fights with Mischa, and Mischa with Klara. Zlota has her hands full keeping them apart. Yet, as sometimes happens between siblings close in age, when they put aside their need to be aggressive and tease one another, they begin to confide in each other, especially when talking about their real loves; in this case, she, the ballet; he, the military.

Change for the better occurs for Mischa. He loves to watch the soldiers drilling in a nearby football stadium.

"Commands ring out," he tells Klara one day. "Officers parade between the ranks. Their eyes stare into the trooper's face. They scan the soldier's uniform. Boy, do I ever want to be with them. My bayonet ready to stab the cursed German beasts."

At night, he imagines that he leaps from the trench and hurls himself against the vicious uns. He has found his identity.

Klara, too, doesn't stay home that spring of 1916. She has thrown herself into dance. She jumps out of bed before dawn. Even as the morning chill causes her to shiver as she stands on the frosty floor, she covers herself with her blanket to preserve body warmth. She moves fast these mornings, stepping into a large tub of hot water for a quick sponge bath; drying off with the coarse towel; donning her underclothing, tights, a gym blouse; dabbing her powdery makeup on her smooth face with a few drops of perfume behind her ears— perfume she took from her mother who feigned ignorance of the theft. A slice of black bread, a cup of tea and she's out the door. She never misses a dance class. She's never late.

"I am good at this," she whispers to herself one day after a rehearsal in which she pushes herself. All of her physical and mental energy now goes into ballet. She has little time to argue with either Mischa or Momma or her three younger sisters. Ballet stands for discipline, exactness, and punctuality. Don't waste a second. The dancer must arrive at a certain spot on the floor at a certain orchestra note or trumpet beat. Despite her regular school classes and delays, she manages to move about war-suffering Odessa.

Thank goodness Momma urged her to join a division of the Imperial School of Ballet. Starting out on the lowest rung of the school's ladder, she could move up to the Mariinsky Theater class. But first, she has to obtain a position in the *corps de ballet*.

Zlota fantasizes Klara will attain fame and fortune as a ballerina. Her daughter is especially good with *fouettés*—a step with which a female dancer whips herself into spinning like a top, rising and falling on the toes of one foot that remains on the same spot throughout. Through her camber feet, the limber arch of her back and her beautiful long arms, she uses every step as an expression of character. Everyone is struck by the formation of her thigh muscles: shapely and extended by black tights. Her leap is phenomenal.

Mornings, she hurries to the large room of the ballet school with its tall windows running down both sides of the papered walls. A gallery circles the top of the hall adorned with portraits of celebrated teachers, ballerinas, and the Czar.

Zlota supports Klara in her efforts. She skimps on clothes and saves coins so Klara can have some spending money, which is all she needs since ballet schools are heavily subsidized.

Zlota knows that her daughter hates household chores. Instead of pushing her to clean, Zlota encourages her to dance. "Dance, Klara! Dance!" Just the mention of a step can cause uninhibited Klara to twirl round and round, like the tops children spin in the street, only the dance setting takes place in the middle of the living room where Klara feels unleashed and proceeds down the apartment's hallway, a *jeté* here, a grand *jeté* there. When she's angry or furious with Mischa, she *pirouettes* to calm down. Often she jumps off the family couch and dances and dances, her face lit up like an actress on the Moscow stage. And she can act.

Klara's fine, executed movements graduate her from dance class to class, from troupe to troupe. She manages the fear. "Just get past the first few steps," she instructs herself. She's good and she knows it.

Many of her dreams are scenes of her performing on stage. She realizes that she has to move up to the next stage in the life of every classical artist or athlete, the audition that makes or breaks a professional career.

So in the spring of 1916, when the snow has just about melted, Klara walks into the school she has called home for seven years.

"I've got to do this," she says. Like the acrobat climbing up to the high wire, like the swimmer poised to dive in during a swim meet; like the violinist walking onto the huge stage for a debut, this is Klara's moment. Past the unguarded door, past the quiet halls and the empty seats, through the dark wing curtain, she steals onto the silent stage floor.

"God, it's scary," she whispers to herself. Droplets of perspiration drip on her forehead. Her cheeks warm red. All of a sudden, coming right at her from behind the red velvet curtain, looms a muscular male, his long arms extended in executing an *entrechat-quatre*, a jump into the air and then rapidly crossing his legs before and behind each other, each crossing being two movements.

"What style. What grace," she says to herself, and good looking, too, she observes in the few seconds that his boyish blue eyes, blond hair, and clean-shaven face pass before her. She's about to pivot around and flee the dim-lit stage but can't; he's got his eyes on her and she notices his exceptionally long and strong legs. His magnetic face draws her closer.

"Are you here for a tryout?" he asks politely.

"Not exactly," she stammers. "I live in Proharovskaya Street. I just came in to ..."

"Why is it that nobody admits they come here to see if they can get into our company?" he finally says, making sure she's attractive before extending an invitation.

He notices her inviting, small brown eyes, her friendly, smooth face. She's cute and tall, just a tad shorter than he. Probably Jewish, he thinks, though he's not sure; she has a small and straight nose. Anyway, who cares? As artists, we're above all that, he pontificates.

"Come in, please. "I'm Yevgeny Aleksandrovich. Do you dance?"

"Yes," she answers meekly.

"Good. Mikhail Dvorovenskev's not here. We're rehearsing alone. Follow me."

She's dazed. She's in the hall of the Mariinsky, the famous Mariinsky Ballet Company. The mere sound *Mariinsky* sends a quiver through her body. The company is rehearsing and performing, despite the war. Newspapers carry stories about these dancers. Even in war-time-Russia, performers, dancers, clowns, musicians, actors, remain the elite.

In the warm, sunlit rehearsal room, Yevgeny tells her to take off her coat. Young members of the troupe, going through their exercises, stare at her threadbare black tights and tight blouse and motion her forward.

"Join us at the *barre*," says Yevgeny. "You know the routine," he winks.

"When you're ready, go ahead. Out on the floor."

Klara Rasputnis does not need much encouragement: Taking a deep breath, she fires up that stored-up energy and pushes aside the fear that would stop others to leap onto the floor—she will make it look as simple as one leg after another.

"*Jete, Jete*," commands Yevgeny! "Perfect," he cries as she lifts her legs. Then come the words she knows will be next, "*entrechat-quatre.*" Perfectly executed.

Watching her one would have thought that this young, resilient 16-year-old could stretch her legs all the way from Odessa to the capital in Petrograd and fly there in seconds.

For two long hours the next day, she dances and runs through her exercises. Director Mikhail Dvorovenskev is back and he accepts her; she's good.

Despite relentless, tense muscles, aching back, and sore, bloody feet always in need of bandaging, there are rewards. Just to be with the dancers gives Klara a lift, like a stevedore raising a crate of fruit with one hand. She is hungry to learn and longs to be with them and like all the members of the *corps de ballet,* dreams of being a star. "When I'm there, it's as if I am in the luxury of the Winter Palace," she tells Mischa one day.

She walks with them, laughs with them, jokes with them and forgets her hard life. Most of the time, the group frequents the Greek café on Krasnyi Lane. She loves the noisy sounds: tinkling glasses, clinking cups, hissing steam, and the flirting waiters whispering sweet and touching words into the ears of eager young girls with glowing eyes and inviting smiles.

Klara has little money, so she always hopes some comrade will add a few coins to her contribution to pay for her coffee or tea. God forbid she should order *baklava* and spend twenty-five kopecks, her budget for the day. Like her, most of the ballet members are teenagers, slightly older than she and some would say more mature. They carry themselves well. Possessing strong slender bodies, they watch what they eat, a challenge because fruits and vegetables are hard to come by in wartime. They're obsessed with their bodies, their muscles, and their feet. How to take care of them? For hours on end, in the privacy of their rooms, they stand in front of the mirror and stare hard at the shape of their naked bodies as if their eyes were locked onto the body of Michelangelo's David.

Like Gershon preparing for Sabbath services, Klara will practice and practice. "I must," she will say, and like her father even if not physically walking through the exercise, she will formulate the steps in her mind and visualize a leap forward. It relieves the stress.

Performances thrill her. Later after the rehearsal, as she walks home to Proharovskaya Street, a smile comes to her lips: "If only Papa could see me now."

But Gershon Rasputnis cannot watch his daughter. He has already made it to Canada and with his family far away in Odessa, his thoughts of them have been checked at the door.

10

Odessa, Winter 1916

By 1916, the public realizes that Russia is losing the war. Shouts and arguments break out in cafes, bars, grocery stores, bathhouses, courtyards, markets, and houses of worship. A "stagnant and oppressive" atmosphere hangs over the country. The shattering defeat at Tannenberg and the Masurian Lakes in 1914; the epic retreat in 1915 from Poland through the heart of the Pale of Settlement with its dense Jewish population; the repeated offensives and counteroffensives in Galicia; and the fighting in other sectors of the Eastern Front continue to cause Russia enormous casualties.

And the Jews? When Russia's military situation became desperate in Poland and Western Russia in 1914–1915, Czarist Supreme Headquarters orders the expulsion of masses of Jews from areas near the front. Hundreds of thousands of Jews are ordered to leave their homes. The Czarist regime does not trust its Jewish citizens.

Meanwhile, Russian armies are running out of supplies and ammunition. "Up to 25 percent of Russian soldiers sent to the front are unarmed, with instructions to pick up what they can from the dead," writes Nicholas V. Riasanovsky in *A History of Russia*.

•

At first, Zlota, naïve and impractical, is unsuited to the tough, scheming world of deprivation that plagues Russia as it enters its third year of World War I. Often at a loss about what to do next or what is best for her and her family, her daily task centers around getting enough food to feed them. Deprived of sleep, run down from poor nutrition, living on bread, garlic, and a piece of onion, the family manages to survive. Often, she resorts to begging soldiers for a little chocolate for the girls.

With Gershon gone, she and Mischa have come up with an idea to help make ends meet. Since they're a musical family, Zlota can sing and Mischa can play the violin. Now they will turn their talents into money. The plan takes shape one day when they hear gypsy music coming from the courtyard where the husband of the family plays an accordion and the mother and children are working the crowd for money. Zlota and Mischa decide they'll go to local workers' clubs and entertain them at their meetings in factories or warehouses. Papa made money entertaining at concerts; why can't they do it? They know the routine.

The plan works. The laborers and the soldiers at the military installations love Mischa. He's so serious. But when it comes to entertainment, he can be jovial and rouse the audience with his violin. As he plays, they're up on their feet dancing as only Russian soldiers can do when they're in a good mood and fortified by vodka.

Singing and playing his violin with gusto, he accompanies Zlota, who puts the laborers in an even happier mood, with the Ukrainian peasant songs she learned in Odessa.

Who knows what the men do after Zlota and Mischa go through their routine. What happens in those little private rooms the laborers secretly set up? She makes sure the two never see the next item on the agenda. She knows that these men could be the most imaginative impresarios of burlesque in any land.

But one night Zlota can't find Mischa. Thinking he already headed to their apartment, she leaves with a soldier who lives in her building. She's sure she'll find Mischa at home. But he isn't there. About to leave the club, he's pulled back into the room by Nikolai, the chairman of the evening program and a hearty man who always cusses and visually undresses any pretty *krasavitza* that prances by.

"Stay with us. We'll make a man out of you, yet. Ach! I can see you're worried about Momma. Tell her I made you sweep the floor," spats Nikolai.

"And now, gentlemen, please welcome Helena, the Greek."

The stripper is 30 years old. She has been on her own since she was his age, 15. "If nobody gives you anything in life, you'll take to stripping like a fish to water," she tells friends. She's good looking and she knows how to entertain with her body. Pleasant. Friendly. Plump with white breasts and a soft and bulgy stomach that sports a few shallow folds. She's at that plump bodily stage because she can't resist *kasha* and potatoes.

On this night, when she rises and began to shake her two beacons, the men roar with approval. She herself becomes aroused, and her inviting, light-pink nipples rise. She's their dream girl and they instinctively want to suck her breasts and put their long, hard instrument into her.

"Bravo," yell those present, including many troops back from the front. When the soldiers are really drunk—and that's often—and when they offer her a generous fee—Helena pulls down her under-leggings and dabs some heavy whipped cream on her white thighs, all the way to her black, hairy bush. She lies on her back on the bench. Acting like children in a candy store who grab a sweet offered up by a teasing proprietor, these grown men rush up and push and shove each other out of the way to be the one to lick the cream. Soon, one finally gets down on her, and begins sucking in the cream. He keeps licking, slowly exacting every morsel, ever forward up her thigh until his tongue enters her soft, milky area and he sucks at the muff between her legs.

Mischa sees it all. At first he just stares, his eyes wide open. Certainly better than the dirty French books the boys pass around in class or the sneak look he once managed at one of his sisters in the bathroom. When he focuses again on the licking sex act before him, a brief tremor overtakes his body and he can't for the life of him control the surge that's rushing through his penis that rose between his legs; the wave that warms his mind and body. He shivers and feels the silky liquid wet his pants. "Damn it," he says to himself. "Thank goodness it's dark in the room; nobody can see my stained trousers. They'd roast me with laughter." Embarrassed, he walks the long way home until his undershorts dry. He swears never to look again at what those workers call entertainment.

One night, however, temptation pulls him again and the thought of the forbidden area between the woman's legs entices him. That night, Momma left early and told him to come right home after he rendered his part of the show. But instead he hurried into the curtained room and was welcomed like a comrade. Like the other workers, he, too, one of a dozen, mounts Helena who drapes herself on the cot. Helped and guided by her movements, he clumsily thrusts his sex into her, and pumps his body up and down and that's all he needs and out it comes. He shudders with a deep sigh. Now he's a man. When he exits the cubicle, they slap him on the back and roar with toasts. "Here's to our newcomer."

Most of the time that war year of 1916, however, Mischa is just a roving Jew wearing a hat, a woolen coat, and carrying a violin case in a city that's starving. School classes are held, but all eyes are on the war and soon, even schoolteachers are called up to the army.

Meat, which most of the time comes from horses, is cut rotten. Communal dining rooms sprout up everywhere. Endless lines of thin, sad people form outside bakeries whose shelves quickly become empty after opening at dawn.

Yet food, drinking, and dancing always can be found in the cafes on Niko-laevsky Boulevard. If they don't have an engagement at a workers meeting, he and Zlota sing in a café of artists, poets, journalists, soldiers, and sailors laden with weapons and grenades. The troops sit on stools arranged around crude tables. At the end of the night, the café owners throw Zlota some black bread to take home.

Begging and playing the violin is not Mischa's first love. Like a thief in the night, he sneaks out of the house to participate in Army drills. Sometimes the Army band marches in a dress rehearsal. What Mischa does not know is that one of the officers, Sergei, standing on the training field, has seen the boy's eyes light up as he watches the parade. From his position near the fence, Sergei can spot a potential recruit when he sees one. Certain boys come every day and stare. That's how he snares his best enlistees. He'll go up to them after the parade and ask, "Young soldier. Want to join us?"

One day, Sergei approaches Mischa. "I've been watching you. You look strong. I've got a job for you."

"What's that?" Mischa asks meekly.

"We want you for something special: A bag carrier, a *meshetchnik*, a sort of messenger.

Sergei explains that with the black market growing, they're starting a group of *meshetchniki* who will collect used clothing or household articles and transport the goods to sell to peasants outside the city. In return, the peasants barter them flour, cereals, meat, eggs. The bagmen then haul the black-market food to customer's houses in the city.

Mischa loves the sound of the word "*meshetchnik*." It means he'll be able to travel. Anything to get out of the city, away from bothersome Klara as well as join a group that makes life exciting for him.

Sergei cautions Mischa that a Jewish bagman cannot let on he's Jewish, even if Jews on the train he rides are assaulted. Jews are often robbed along the way, especially when the train stops at a small-station hut when passengers jump out, stretch their limbs and pump water from samovars.

Bagmen are feared, he is told. Travelers in the aisles have to move aside when they come into a car. Because of his training in the Cadets, Mischa has developed bulging arm, leg muscles and broad shoulders. He will use his shoulder and belly to butt his way through a crowded compartment. The sack will become his battering ram as he puts it in front of him to clear a path toward an empty seat. Later, when he arrives at his station, he'll have to fight other bagmen to hire a carriage or sleigh.

"At first, you'll be just like the other bagmen so you won't arouse suspicion," explains Sergei. "Later, when we really organize the bagmen movement and if you do well, we'll have bigger things for you."

"Okay," says Mischa. "I'll let you know." He already knows the answer.

At ballet, Klara has become good friends with Yevgeny Aleksandrovich. From the very moment he brought her into the group, he guided her. He teaches her how to placate Mikhail with a polite 'thank you.'

"Don't react to his criticism. Just answer, 'Yes, of course.'"

He practices with her. He encourages her. He persuades Corps members to be nice to her. She's attractive to him but he never shows it. He reflects that if she ever leaves the city, he might flee Odessa with her. But in the end, he won't go. He won't throw away a dance career for a young woman. Sleep with her, yes. Marry her, no.

As for Klara, she keeps Yevgeny at a distance. But she can't keep Momma away:

"Maybe you should leave Odessa."

"Don't even think that, Momma!"

The subject's dropped.

"They've instituted further rationing," Yevgeny tells Klara one cold morning.

"My God! What's happening? It's getting worse."

"The war. We keep losing the battles with the Austrians and the Hungarians. By the way, Klara, are you leaving? A lot of Jewish families are packing up and traveling east.

"I'll never go. What would happen to ballet? But you're right about one thing; something's bound to happen."

Neither had long to wait.

11

1917 is a year historians will be parsing for generations. A whole empire will turn itself upside down, as the Russian people overthrew Czar Nicholas II. More than anyone, the Czar "who was imbued with a hatred of the Jews represents the symbol of tyranny." By March 1917, discipline among the troops collapses. Soldiers massacre their officers. The front simply disbands into chaos. Most men go home by whatever means they can find.

The Czar's rule had caused soaring inflation, severe rationing, harsh food and fuel shortages, and long bread queues. Joy and celebrations greet word of the abdication everywhere, notes Douglas Smith.

•

Thousands pour into the streets from their cold, dreary apartments, from their dismal shops, and dirty factories. They carry huge red banners flowing in the wind as they march from Cathedral Square to the corner of Richelieu Street.

"He's quit. He's gone. The Czar has abdicated," they proclaim, shaking their fists into the air and hugging, kissing, and slapping the backs of friends, relatives, and even strangers.

"Come on. March with us!"

"Can't. Gotta get home," Klara excitedly replies, tearing herself away from a reveler who runs off before Klara can finish making her case.

The crowd's joyous shouts—wafting up to the rooftops—grow louder. Red, the color of revolutionary socialism, appears everywhere. A burst of energy fills her young lungs, her body, her legs. The air becomes electrified.

Klara watches people waving red banners and placing homemade red paper flowers into their lapels. Many slide red armbands up their sleeves. They hoist soldiers on their shoulders. Others cheer weary lads who drive by in overloaded trucks and fire their rifles into the air. Some dance and lift vodka jugs to toast the Czar's collapse. Strangers talk to each other and ask about the latest news. Policemen are nowhere to be seen. Trams have ceased running.

"Down with War! The Czar and his rotten wife are our misfortune," an old man standing next to Klara declares. "Army supplies never arrived; food rotted in railroad yards. Thank God they're gone."

The next day, ex-soldiers parade in the streets. No one calls them mutineers anymore. At night, their rifles and bayonets bristle in the moonlight.

Climbing into trucks and carrying red flags, they throw out paper proclamations grabbed by outstretched hands.

"We'll pillage! We'll kill! We'll cut throats! To the gallows with the Czar. The bourgeoisie are vampires."

For a week, Klara watches troops march down Odessa's broad avenues. Civilians break into their ranks. One big party. Soldiers, officers, marines, and workingmen—stepping along as they transform the cities arteries into veins of red.

"Down with the capitalist ministers." "Down with the land owners." "Down with the bourgeoisie." "Down with the capitalists." "Down with War," they shout and shout and shout deep into the night.

Klara cannot believe the ease and suddenness with which the Czar collapsed. "His house went down like a stack of cards," observes ballet member, Svetlana, the next day at rehearsal. "By the way, Klara, you were great in class. Every one of us wanted to yell out a loud 'hurrah' to you for cursing the Czar like that. You've got what boys have and the women joke about," says Svetlana, giggling. The two continue laughing as they embrace each other, neither of them knowing that within seven months their newly found liberty will be hijacked by Bolshevik revolutionaries.

Meanwhile, Odessa begins to change. Tram conductors are pleasant: "Citizens. Please have your fares ready," is the new greeting of these managers, instead of the old, "Fares, fares, fares." Overnight, everyone becomes polite. Men don't grab seats. Swear words give way to "Please excuse me; pardon me."

The situation for Jews is better. A week or so after the fall of the Czar, Klara bursts into the room. "There's a proclamation issued removing all restrictions on Jews in Russia."

"Can't be true," exclaims Zlota.

"It's so. It's so."

Overnight, although nervous, Jews walk with their heads just a little higher; they remember the old adage "New king, new troubles."

As time goes by early that year of 1917, after the Czar was toppled, the privileged and the underprivileged began to clash. The Provisional Government and the local soviet councils are at loggerheads.

By October 1917, chaos engulfs the towns and cities of Russia.

The underground group of Bolsheviks and the authorities constantly collide as the Reds encourage peasants to seize land.

One night, the first week in November, Mischa sits down at the dinner table and as he begins to eat his bowl of kasha, he tells Zlota: "Deserters are everywhere, terrorizing everyone and clogging railways. Do you know what I heard?" continues Mischa. "These deserters find a space on the trains heading toward Siberia. They climb onto the steps on the bumpers, the roofs, and engines. But soon their hands freeze so badly that they plead for someone to kill them. I've also heard that their own friends shove them off the cars to make room and save their own skins."

At least now we have the right to travel, thinks Zlota, realizing that perhaps the proper time to make a move has arrived. Soldiers are loose and undisciplined; they shoot innocent civilians. Bandits and rapists operate out in the open. Odessa is no place for a teenage girl. Her reasoning tells her that if Gershon is not coming to get them, Klara can go find him.

Meanwhile, Communist radicals placard the city with their program: "All Power to the Soviets." "Peace." "Partition Large Estates." "Workers' Control of Factories."

One day, a news item reports a bizarre coup on November 7, 1917, in Petrograd: "*Bolsheviks storm Winter Palace. Overthrow Provisional Government.*"

True to their word, the Reds seize power by force of arms. Nobody stops them.

"Tovarischi (comrades)," the Bolsheviks declare in their widely distributed pamphlets: "The revolution has triumphed in Petrograd and Moscow. All power is in the hands of the soviets of soldiers, peasants, and workers. Peace, bread, and land."

Zlota now calculates that if Klara stays in Odessa, her life will be meaningless and end in shambles. She fears the worst. She imagines former officers fondling her at their drinking parties in the cafes. She begins to hear rifles firing in the early hours of the morning. People are disappearing, either murdered at night or fleeing by day. Had she herself not seen soldiers dragging a group of suspects to a nearby park? She didn't stay to see what happened. She and her daughters dare not go out into the street.

One day returning from the market, she passes an apple stand. As she continues down the avenue, she hears shouts from behind her. Turning, she sees several soldiers arguing with an old, woman apple-seller over the price.

A single shot rings out.

"Oh my God," Zlota gasps. "They shot the woman."

But nobody hears Zlota. Nobody helps the woman who falls to the pavement. Instead, Zlota watches as the crowd rushes the stand and takes as many apples as they can carry, all the while avoiding the body of the dead woman whose red blood stains the dirty snow.

Zlota's only thought now: How to get Klara out of Odessa? How to do it? Why not just send her to find Gershon. But where is he? In Vladivostok? Unlikely. Three years have passed since they heard from him? If anyone can find him, it's Klara. She'll need papers to get to Vladivostok. Zlota can get a travel permit from neighbor Miriam's husband, a big shot in the local government.

But will she be safe? All these thoughts plague Zlota. Her daughter will be safer, she surmises, if she can find a family to take her along. And that's how Zlota comes up with neighbors, the Lubavitzes. They had planned to go a long time ago. Maybe now they really are leaving, though unfortunately, Zlota will learn they are going the long way, east through Siberia because the Germans and Russians are still fighting in the west and refugees often can't get through to sail from Germany, a popular exit point for the U.S. and Canada. Perhaps they'll take Klara with her. But what about Mischa? He'll want to go. He'll be furious if Klara's chosen over him. But I need Mischa to protect the girls and me. Thus is her reasoning.

So Zlota does what she has to do. She lies. She tells Klara that she heard from a neighbor that Gershon is in Vladivostok; he's sick and hasn't left for Canada. Klara should go there and if he's still there, take care of him. Then the two of them eventually could proceed to Canada. If he's not there, Klara can sail alone. Relatives in Canada will help her reach Papa if he is already residing there.

I'll feel guilty if I don't do this, Zlota thinks. I want her to live and I will succeed, even if it means causing trouble between her and Mischa.

"I'm not going to give up ballet. Never."

"Papa's sick. Someone has to go to him."
"Not me. Forget it. Drop ballet here? No, not even for Papa."
Mother and daughter stare at each other.

Life in Odessa becomes unbearable. News of beatings, rapes, shootings, and killings permeate the city.

One day, Klara leaves class late. Her fellow ballet class students have been asked to stay back; director Mikhail Dvorovenskev wants to discuss upcoming performances. Not unusual because utter chaos rules during the day. Bands of soldiers often barge in and disrupt classes. So at night, the group often meets to hear Dvorovenskev's plans for forthcoming programs.

"Anyone going my way?" Klara asks as they finish the meeting.
"I can walk you as far as Proharovskaya Street," says Nicholas.
"That helps. Don't have far to go after that."

On the way home, Klara and Nicholas discuss the company, the opinions of some of the group's stars, their next performance, and Dvorovenskev's presentation.

The two are now engrossed in deep discussion, but still manage to watch their step as they move through a damp fog enveloping the street. The moon gives off a weak light. Street lamps are out. Few candles light the blacked-out pane-glass apartment windows. A few pedestrians hurry along, their shadows moving alongside the grey, dull buildings. Soon, they reach Proharovskaya Street and part.

Now, Klara hurries along. Lost in thought, she never sees the ugly, strong hand that grabs her and tries to pull her into the doorway.

She summons all her strength to free herself and shouts, "stop, stop, police, police." Attempting to push away from the tightening grip and the octopus-like hands of her assailant who keeps yanking her toward an apartment building entrance, Klara claws at him. She tries desperately to scratch his face. But he pulls her into a bear hug against his body.

"Give me your lips, you bitch," he growls, trying to kiss her. His heavy, unkempt, sharp whiskers cut into her face. Caught, but still managing to move her head backwards and sideways, she calls up every ounce of muscle power she can and she does what every rape victim can do and should do if she can; she lets go with an hysterical scream, that sounds like "ai, ai, ai" and lifts her knee straight up, right up into the attacker's testicles.

"Awl!" he growls; his scratched voice bounding up against nearby windows and ricocheting down snow-covered, icy streets.

Finally, someone opens a door and yells, "What's going on out there?"

So hard had been her kick that Klara's assailant is choking, gasping for breath, and wreathing on the pavement.

She, too, is breathless.

Hearing nothing, nor seeing anyone in this dark, foggy night, the neighbor slams the door. Klara thinks she's free but standing on the side and watching the struggle is another assailant who now lunges for her. Shocked that she's being attacked again and caught off guard because she successfully felled the first soldier, Klara stands paralyzed. The new attacker tries to pull her into the doorway, but the sound of a bullet rings out and this predator quickly grabs his knee and falls onto the pavement. As he sits on his backside and attempts to move, someone approaches and kicks the intruder in the stomach and the groin, causing him to cry out in pain.

Klara doesn't stay to see her benefactor. She flees down the street.

"Klara, run like the wind," intones a very familiar voice behind her. "Keep going," commands Mischa Rasputnis who at that frightening moment is proud he's protecting his sister.

The two sprint for several blocks, never exchanging a word, not even when they reach the safety of their apartment.

For several days, they never discuss this incident on Proharovskaya Street. She knows when to leave well enough alone. She never asks: "How? Where did you get that gun? Why were you following me?" She realizes he has a secret life of his own.

His often sullen expression, his angry eyes seem to be messaging to her, "No questions."

Mischa, however, tells Zlota what happened. Somehow, the three keep the story of the attempted rape out of earshot of the other children.

One night when only Klara and Zlota are up and sipping tea from tall glasses, Zlota blurts out, " Go to Papa. You can't stay here. They'll get you."

"I know."

"Leave with the Lubavitzes. They're going in a group, like a caravan. With numbers, you'll avoid attackers. Here, they'll kill you."

"But my ballet group? My classes? No. I won't. Absolutely not. Can't go. Can't live without them."

"It's best you go."

"No."

"I guess you haven't heard they have ballet all over the world," Zlota says with a slight, sarcastic touch. "Once we're all together, you'll continue."

"Not the same. Russian ballet is the best. Besides, I'm doing well here."

"But you must go nevertheless," Zlota says with such determination that her eyes fix onto Klara's, and she leans forward and points her finger directly at the girl in such an unmistakable commanding gesture that Klara rises and storms out of the room.

Next morning, Klara asks Zlota, "What about Mischa?"

"Don't worry. I'll handle him."

"Alright already. I'll think about it."

But Zlota can't calm Mischa.

"You'll never make it," Mischa tells Klara after he heard from Zlota that Klara was leaving, "You of all people know what they do to young girls. Just like the other night, a Cossack'll grab you. That'll be the end of little Klara. I'm the one that should go. I have military training."

"It's better if I go," responds Klara. "You shouldn't leave Momma. Remember the night you warded off that intruder trying to break into our apartment? When you shout, it's a man's voice. What do I sound like?"

Mischa gets up in a huff, doesn't say a word, walks out, and slams the door.

That night, Mischa tosses and turns in bed. He remembers he can still sign up with the Red Guards. "You'll get a new pair of boots," Comrade Sergei said. "And at least one hot meal a day, I promise you."

Yes, the day after Klara departs, he'll call on Comrade Sergei, and snapping to attention, he'll declare: "Comrade Mischa Rasputnis reporting for duty."

He, too, is beginning to believe that Russia can only be changed by violent revolution. He will fight for the Revolution and aid their cause.

12

Immediately after overthrowing the government, the Bolsheviks solidify their rule throughout the Russian Empire. Relying on local soviets to take over the governments of towns and provinces, they begin to make bold moves.

In January 1918, the Reds apply the *coup de grace* against the one institution that could conceivably halt dictatorial rule. They disband the democratically elected Constituent Assembly. Any semblance of Russian democracy is dead from that moment. More than any other event, this closure is the watershed that sets the chain of events in motion leading to the Russian Civil War. The Party does not tolerate dissent; its message is, "Citizens, either you keep quiet until you are silenced; or you move over to the opposition Whites; or you flee into exile longing for a homeland you will never see again."

During that winter of 1917–1918, the Reds launch offensives against the Whites in the Ukraine and the Don. The opening salvos are fired in the conflict, according to author W. Bruce Lincoln, a battle that will "cast its terrible shadow across the Russian land." Russia will continue to expand its sea of poverty and cruelty as it has done for centuries.

•

As the snow clouds release their white flakes on the black, iron locomotive fighting its way eastward toward Siberia, boring expressions cover the faces of weary passengers. Beneath the picture-book scenery of frail wooden houses burdened with mountains of snow and frost lie the despondent Russian people, bitterly cold and famished: their livestock has been left untended, no grain to feed them.

Delay after delay. Day after day.

"Empty fields and impassable roads are all we see," Klara tells the woman with the four children who welcomed her back to her seat. "Boring."

"So are the passengers," replies Marya Ivanovna who is occupied by her knitting and has observed that Klara has not yet learned to adjust to the "white nothingness" that covers this land in which the trains don't work, the government doesn't work, and the people don't work.

Klara is fidgety. She jumps up a lot. She walks around, talks to fellow passengers. After she has tired herself out walking up and down the aisles, she sleeps.

"Wish we were in Ekaterinburg already so I could get on to Chelyabinsk," she tells anyone who will listen. They shrug their shoulders.

"No way to know how long it'll take," the conductor answers curtly to all who ask. He, too, stares out at the desolate Siberian snow falling steadily on onion-domed buildings.

Luggage clogs the aisles. Families have taken everything with them: household goods, blankets, sheets, pillows, and even scissors for cutting up sugar to put in tea tumblers.

A break in the monotony, but not in the danger facing the refugees, always occurs when the train stops. Passengers descend to inhale the bitterly cold, fresh air, to exercise and bend and walk on hard icy earth. They mill around on the platform and nod here and there to familiar faces. Everyone buys something and Klara realizes she can spare a ruble or two from her dwindling supply to buy some *chai*, cabbage, or black bread, if any is to be had at the station. And if there is, she buys a little extra to squirrel away.

At rest stops, travelers fill every nook and cranny of the station platform. Klara notices that cars often are shunted off to a siding, while express trains pass freely, disclosing *wagons* packed with prisoners along with sounds of war and fighting in the distance. When the battles get closer, passengers automatically duck as bullets ricochet off a train car.

In this deep-freeze land of central Russia, gunshots become as common as birds chirping in the trees. So are the prolonged stops.

Klara and Marya Ivanovna are friends. The matronly woman clothed in a proper, long, swollen skirt and long-sleeved dark top, hails from the ancient town of Suzdal, north of Moscow. Her husband is a government inspector who was transferred to Chelyabinsk. The family is joining him. The children are overjoyed; no school and a train ride to boot.

Though tempted, Klara does not tell the woman she is Jewish. Long ago, Gershon and Zlota hinted that it wasn't necessary to announce your religion. "We're different and no matter how detached you become from Judaism, you'll always feel like a fish out of water. Once you indicate you're Jewish, the situation changes, sometimes a little, sometimes a lot, but the relationship is modified. You'll sense they'll begin to look at you differently."

Before Klara's new family digs into never-ending food supplies, which they now conveniently share with Klara at every meal, they bow their heads in prayer. Klara lowers her head and silently recites her own blessing. Then, after eating, Klara looks out the window and utters the long passage of the grace after meals. Her mind has absorbed the melodious sounds of her family sitting around the dinner table and reciting the prayer. Often her lips move, but Marya Ivanovna probably notices nothing and if she does, she probably thinks Klara's reciting her own private prayer.

Klara always wears a colorful *babushka* over her head. Wanting to look like an average peasant girl, she doesn't wear makeup or a short dress. She doesn't want to be a mark. She makes a point of sticking around the family—becoming friends with the children, telling them stories, walking them through details of placement and fundamentals that make up the foundation of ballet. When she tells them she's in a ballet company, their admiration soars.

Marya Ivanovna takes to Klara because the girl from Odessa gives her a hand in moving the family's baggage in the compartment's luggage rack. She helps her prepare snacks. She watches the children during rest stops. The woman likes the teenager's outspokenness and courage. In a day when children disown families to fight for revolutionary causes, Klara's story to find her father resonates. Though somewhat sarcastic, Marya Ivonvna is kind, and though aggressive; she's polite—yet suspicious of people. She'll help Klara because she trusts her and even gives the girl from Odessa some bread and meat that the teenager wolfs down quickly.

One day, she offers Klara much needed advice regarding travel: "Whenever you want a favor from an official; tell them you need their help. Never get angry. Never argue. Once you argue, you've lost. Don't demand to see a supervisor unless necessary and when you do, make the request in a kind manner, not hostile. Above all," she stresses, "follow your instincts. Never hold back. Move fast. Remember, don't be dragged down by misfits. Besides, rich people don't like to socialize with poor people. Even if you're not rich, follow that principle. Believe me, it's better to be rich than poor despite what the Communists say. Do what's best for Klara, and above all, avoid political discussions. By the way, Klara, you don't have to pull the wool over my eyes. I know you're Jewish."

"But how...."

"Not necessary to explain," says the woman, a sympathetic grin on her face.

A half hour later, passengers hear the guttural voices of Cossacks shouting outside that they were boarding the train and demanded everyone stand up.

"Klara! Quick! Hide under my skirts. Do as I tell you," yells Marya Ivanovna, lifting her bulging and free-flowing dress.

For some reason that she'll never remember nor be able to explain without smirking, Klara listened and didn't hesitate to crawl under Mrs. Kovchenko's bulging skirts. Remembering a ballet exercise, she moves into a fetal position between the lady's slightly spread legs. She puts her thumb and finger over her nostrils, so no-one would hear her heavy breathing and at the same time smother the disgusting smell emanating from Marya Ivanovna's soiled under-pants that Klara thanked God the woman at least wore rather than go without any.

Klara could hear the Cossacks' boots pound the floor as they quickly passed her in the aisle. She prayed she wouldn't laugh and at one point bit her lip at the incongruity of it all. Finally, she heard the bang of the door and the bustle in the car and climbed out by lifting up the woman's large skirts.

"My god you're shaking," declared Marya Ivanovna.

"It's nothing, I'll be fine. Thank you so much, you saved my life," says Klara.

"I didn't think they would go after my daughters; they're too young for them."

"I've got to get some air. Be back soon."

"Didn't want to take a chance on those brutes grabbing you!" Marya Ivanovna hollers after Klara who's already scampering down the aisle.

The next morning, the train comes to a crawl after a long night moving through dangerous territory as bandits roam the area and are known to attack trains that slow down on steep grades.

"Where are we?" asks Klara.

"Just after Perm" says Marya Ivanovna, as the train now shrieks to a sudden stop.

"Twenty minute break, comrades," announces the conductor; his welcoming words send a bolt of joy through Klara's body, especially since they are from this cranky and depressed-looking official who has ruled their lives completely. He's the Czar of the train, and he acts like the former despicable ruler. He has the key to the bathrooms, decides who gets on and off and when, and can move people ensconced comfortably in their warm seats out into the cold corridor.

Winter has smothered this harsh land and Klara and company have been cooped up in aged cars whose wood covering is peeling away like a caterpillar shedding its skin. Ahead is the heart of Siberia and its frozen, white birch trees. The young girl from Odessa needs some air.

Outside, a rare, sun-filled winter day infuses Klara, who loves to roam in parks. She jumps down and inhales the crisp air cooling her face and lifting her drowsiness and spirits.

Despite the weariness, she's pleased she's on her way. Good to be alive, she thinks, pushing aside fears of war and battle that accompany and face her and her companions, whoever they might be.

As if a scene is then created specifically for this moment of joy, she spies a soldier smoking a cigarette. He is blowing smoke rings into the air.

She can't see his face for his back is to her. All she notices is that he's tall, broad shouldered, with black hair combed backward in the popular student style. His uniform, though wrinkled and worn, fits snuggly. His rucksack, which has a Red Cross logo printed on its worn cover, is full. An insignia on his jacket's epaulettes make him out to be some sort of officer. He has removed his woolen hat, strapping it onto his belt. He flexes his muscles a certain way; stretches a certain way; bends a certain way. Turning and seeing Klara he smiles and says, "Thank God for Mother Nature, eh?"

Their eyes connect. She's not sure it's his words or his good looks that send a slight tremor through her body. His features are pleasing. Even though covered with a great coat, his muscular build seeps through and his deep blue eyes envelope her. His thin nose fills out a kind face. His smile is infectious. She's attracted.

With a slight grin, she blurts out her name: "I'm Klara Rasputnis," and with the words, her forehead becomes sweaty, her palms moist. She wants the meeting to continue.

"Pleased to meet you. I'm Vladimir," he answers as he again flashes a warm smile. Standing and staring at each other, frozen in time, young handsome Vladimir Sergeyevich Milovich and attractive Klara Rasputnis like what they see in each other.

A strange feeling of excitement again comes over her.

Only his words, "we'd better get back," breaks the spell. "Where're you sitting?"

"Car number 11, compartment 5," she replies without hesitation.

Five minutes after the rest stop, the youthful Red Cross worker shows up at car number 11, compartment 5. Klara introduces the soldier. The children are excited. Army men are Gods.

Like a mother meeting her daughter's boyfriend for the first time, Marya Ivanovna sizes up the suitor. She discovers that Vladimir is not only a Muscovite, but from a once well-off family. His father, who became a Bolshevik overseas, has just arrived from exile in Canada to join the Communists. Before the War, the youth attended a military academy near the Kremlin.

"With such a very impressive father, you're a very important person. But how is it you're in the Red Cross? Not fighting like all the young men," posits Marya Ivanovna bluntly.

Klara's face flushes with embarrassment, thinking this woman obviously can't tell the difference between a soldier and a soldier of mercy.

"Well," he says hesitatingly, "I don't believe in killing. I want to save lives."

Before he can continue, however, Marya Ivanovna lets his remarks sink deep into her mind. She gets the point; he possesses authority as he's with the

Red Cross. The woman has learned that she must make and keep the acquaintance of anyone who can help her. She will pass this on to Klara who will polish her skills of manipulating newly found companions along the way, male or female, and in Klara's case, mostly male.

"You two young people, please move outside," pleads Marya. "I've got to get these children to sleep."

"Klara. I have to get back. I'm not alone," says Vladimir as the two stare out of the window into the newly arrived fog that creates a near total blackness.

Trying as hard as she can, Klara can't hide the disappointment, at least to the extent of frowning slightly and averting his eyes.

He notices and soothes her with a "No, nothing like that. But I do have a friend with me: Dmitri, a former schoolmate and Moscovite. He's a security agent for the railway."

"Where is he? I'd like to meet him," says Klara smiling, reassured Vladimir does not have a wife or girlfriend with him. "Your wish is my command," smiles Vladimir, who at that moment sees Dmitri pushing his way through the crowded corridor. "Where you headed?"

"Right now, Chelyabinsk. And you?"

"That's great. So are we."

"Ladies and gentlemen of the court," jests Vladimir when Dmitri catches up to them. "May I present agent, Dmitri Abramovich Dudin. Klara, meet Dmitri. Dmitri, meet Klara. Sometimes, he helps me get people out of jail. He does all the work and I get all the glory."

"Nonsense," replies Dmitri, perturbed at the introduction. "He's too kind and only trying to make me look good," says the young man who is short and stocky, with long hair, also combed back. His face possesses small tiger eyes, eyes that blink as they search the area. His red stubble of a beard makes him look much older than Vladimir.

"Dmitri prefers to travel incognito. If the enemy takes over the train, he can disappear among the passengers and strike back," explains Vladimir. "We worry about bandits. They hide among us, shoot up trains, and rob the passengers."

A bulge, obviously a pistol, is easily recognizable on the side of Dmitri's pants. Later, Klara will learn he stole it from a drunken soldier in Vladivostok, the last stop on the Trans-Siberian railway. She's heading there, so maybe, just maybe, he'll help her.

"Dmitri has a little problem, however," Vladimir tells Klara in a loud whisper that is meant to be heard. "He's a sweetheart, but does he have a temper."

"Don't listen to him," grunts Dmitri. "Anyway, got to go. Nice meeting you. We'll be in Ekaterinburg in a few hours, I hope, and then we've got to get another train to Chelyabinsk. I'll be in Car Number Two," he informs Vladimir.

"I don't like the looks of several fellow passengers. Our conductors wouldn't recognize trouble even if someone whispered to them that he was Ataman Grigorii Semenov, the Cossack bandit."

"He doesn't tolerate fools very easy," says Vladimir. "He mouths off. He insults strangers. Bad policy to possess with a war ravaging the country. People are touchy, ready to kill if provoked. Not that he looks for trouble; it just comes to him. Tells people what he thinks. At the last station, he lashed out at a kiosk attendant, berating her because the soup was cold.

"Some people are meant for trouble. Add on the Russian curse of alcoholism, and you have human beings who are bombs with short fuses," continues Vladimir. "Not only does he drink; he guzzles it. Brings out the worst in him: sadness, boredom, disgust with life. He thinks vodka relieves tension and makes him feel good. But it ruins his work."

Vladimir stops talking. His mind wanders. He's transported out on the battlefield to shootouts, no-man's land; he's running with a stretcher or he's back of the lines visiting a prison camp and burying the dead.

In the front car, Dmitri sits with a unit of Red Army troops as the now darkened train heads for Ekaterinburg, held by the Revolutionists.

"Comrade Boris, pass the vodka and some bread," demands Dmitri, even as his voice remains plaintive. The warm, biting liquid calms him down. His thoughts turn away from his present task. He closes his eyes and recalls that afternoon on a blanket. He's a teenager lying atop a hill in a small forest clearing just outside of Moscow. This was a nice moment in his life. He recalls the voluptuous body of the peasant girl Dunia and how they explored each other's bodies. He longs for her now. He wants to recapture, better yet, relive those moments, moments he would remember the rest of his life: How he took her mouth into his; how he fondled her breasts; how she kissed him and hugged his body. He would try to feel the total madness that came from later losing himself in her. He wants more.

But more's not to be. After four long years—first in the Czar's Army and then in the railway police—he should have been discharged. The war continued, however; and she disappeared. He had been with other girls, but they were never like Dunia.

Now his assignment states he is to stay on trains, though his bosses seem to have forgotten him in the mass movement of people across the Russian continent.

The rattle of the train lessens. The soft whispering rhythmic sound of the wheels causes Dmitri's head to droop down as he prays he can sleep and dream about Dunia. He's almost there in fantasyland when pain bolts through his stomach, causing him to feel he's going to wretch up his whole inside.

About to throw up, he wobbles forward, aware that the white liquid he drank could have been diluted and spoiled. Breaking out in a sweat and stumbling along the aisle, he begins to fall, but grabs hold of a railing and manages to reach the landing where the steel train door is open for some reason and he can puke out his guts. Shaking from the freezing air, he realizes he's not alone though he wonders again why the train door is open.

"You there! Get back into the car," growls the conductor who has been walking through the train. A few recent shots of vodka have warmed his body and brain.

"Can't stand here while the train's moving. Can't you see the door's open?"

Whether it was his churning stomach or his roaring head, or his deep anger, or his lack of self-control, we'll never know.

"Who the hell are you to tell me what to do," roars Dmitri not yet realizing that the formidable and hard-faced man facing him doesn't know he's a railway agent.

"I'm boss in this train," shouts the conductor out over the noise of the locomotive.

"Who says?

"I do," replies the conductor seizing Dmitri's left hand.

At that, Dmitri lifts his right arm and lands it square on the mouth of the conductor. The quick blow cuts the man's lip and causes him to release Dmitri and cover his mouth as he leans back to the wall of the carriage. Dmitri thinks he's scored a knockout punch, so he doesn't reach for his revolver. But the conductor—blinded by his rage at being struck by a civilian, humbled by his humiliation at the hands of a passenger and suffering from a pregnant lip—rebounds from the wall and like an angry bull, charges ahead. Both his arms are forward like a double-battering ram, yelling for all he is worth, "you bastard."

But drunk as he is, Dmitri tries to sidestep his attacker. However, at that very instant, the train sharply turns as it negotiates a long curve. Dmitri, caught off guard, leans forward to grab the side railing but misses it and helplessly flies backwards out the door. The only noise heard that moment thirty miles from Chelyabinsk is a shriek that quickly fades away.

Dmitri Abramovich Dudin is gone, over the embankment, down the slope.

The wild turn throws the charging conductor sideways and he again bounces off the wall onto the floor and though bruised, he lands inside. Taking out a handkerchief and dabbing his busted lip, the conductor peers out into the darkness. Dmitri's gone.

No one could live through a fall like that. That idiot has met his maker, thinks the train official. The bastard. He tried to kill me, me, chief conductor Alexander Kirpichnikov.

Vladimir hears the piercing scream. He pulls the emergency cord. The train comes to a screeching halt. The armed guards rush him. He shows them his pass.

"We can't stop the train for long," says the officer in charge of the unit. "This is January, remember, and the weather's going to get worse. We'll be a sitting duck and risk the lives of all the passengers," he tells Vladimir. "We'll send out search teams from Ekaterinburg. We can guard the train there much better. I know you're going to Chelyabinsk. You can work on the case from there; it's only 130 miles away.

The officer is correct. Around them stand only a great ocean of cedars and snow accompanied by a solitude that causes horror in each passenger.

Vladimir again questions the conductor who maintains that Dmitri was drunk and fell out.

"Tried to stop him and pull him away. Swore at me and punched me. Gave me a bloody lip. My God! It was terrible. Sudden turn unbalanced him. He must have been drinking."

Unwittingly, the trainman touches on Dmitri's weakness. Everyone knows that Dmitri drank a great deal; they have no reason to doubt it was an accident.

The shocked civilians are shooed away and return to their carriage. The train starts up and soon picks up speed as Vladimir makes his way to Dmitri's seat where he notices his friend left his rucksack. He finds a large paper envelope filled with stacks of thousand-ruble notes.

A group picture of 20 farmers comprises one of the two photos he retrieves from his friend's wallet. They are Russians; they don't smile. In the first row, one short, stocky lad of about eighteen stands with a pitchfork at his side, the farm tools taller than he. In the second row, far right, an older man with a sun baked, wrinkled-face positions himself in the middle and holds a large steel hammer in his hand, while next to him, at the end of the line, is a stout woman with a stern face, blond hair, dressed in a white jumper. Atop her head is a colorful babushka. In her hand is a sickle whose blade reflects the beams of the sun to the tall grass. The woman has that look of a murderer about to wield this slicing weapon, the sickle, the *serpi*.

Yes, the hammer, the *molot;* and the sickle, the *serpi*. Both instruments will become the national flag of the Bolsheviks and the flag of the Union of Soviet Socialist Republics. In years to come, these farm pictures will become posters, emblems, and statues that appear all over the Soviet Union. "Workers of the World Unite," will be imprinted on the banners.

But that is yet to be. Vladimir's mind wanders to Klara as he picks up the picture of Dmitri's buxom blond. The picture is signed, "Love you, Dunia."

"Yes, that's her," says Vladimir to himself, as he recalls Dmitri showed him the picture a million times. How many times, thought Vladimir, did Dmitri lift the picture to his lips, smile, and move it back so he could stare at Dunia's beautiful figure. How many times did Dmitri mutter to himself, "come to me, my beautiful one," as he gazed at her unobtrusive nose, eyes that glistened even on cloudy days, her long blond hair through which Dmitri used to run his fingers.

Vladimir returns the pictures to the knapsack. He'll turn over Dmitri's money to headquarters in Chelyabinsk. He could keep it, but he'll give it back. Though he doesn't know it, his Red Cross report says "Leader Vladimir Sergeyavitch Milovich is a dependable, trustworthy Russian, a credit to his country, the kind that gives you hope in Russia's future."

"We knew each other's every move," Vladimir tells Klara as the passengers scamper from the train in the Ekaterinburg station. "We'll find him."

"Hope so," she says, recognizing the anguish on his face. "I thought he was nice."

"As a Red Cross officer, I can make sure you'll get on the train to Chely-abinsk. If you're with us, nobody will give you a problem. We'll take good care of you," he adds with a reassuring grin.

She smiles back.

"Thanks. Of course. Appreciate the ride," she continues, adding firmly, "I guess we're going to see a lot of each other."

"I guess we will."

13

Chelyabinsk, February to May 1918

In March 1918, one of the most significant milestones in early Bolshevik rule will take place in the Polish town of Brest-Litovsk. Russia will end her war with the Central Powers. Not every Communist leader is in favor of the pact. Bolshevik leader Vladimir Ilyich Lenin prevails, however. He is compelled to reach "his understanding" with the Germans: to get Russia out of the war. That's why the Germans, who financed him, sent him from Switzerland to Russia in the first place; to foster revolution, create chaos, seize power, and end the war so Berlin could transfer troops to the Western front. Lenin now needs peace desperately and he will pay any price to solidify his dictatorship over whatever land remains for him.

After the Reds end the war with Germany and desert the Allies, the new Red rulers face a supreme test. Can they survive? "That Treaty," notes historian Brian Crozier, "is a disaster for Lenin and his Bolsheviks." The Germans acquire an enormous swath of territory from the Soviets: the Baltic states, part of Belorussia, Ukraine, and southern Russia as far as Rostov on the Don; thus including 40 percent of its industrial proletariat, 45 percent of fuel production, 90 percent of sugar production, 64 to 70 percent of metal industry, 55 percent of wheat. The Russian Empire has collapsed.

Allied capitals denounce the treaty as "capitulation, surrender." Russia must be kept in the war. A few vow to force Moscow to continue fighting even if they have to send troops onto Russian soil to engage Berlin and prevent Germany from transferring soldiers from the east back to the west, which is exactly what Germany does after the pact is signed. Thirty-three German divisions, some 400,000 men, will show up on the Western Front.

•

When the military transfer train finally arrives at Chelyabinsk, Vladimir seeks out the military commander who is waiting for him at the station and tells him of Dmitri's probable death.

"Trouble ahead. You must remain in town," the commander says. "Civilians will be housed in barracks. Women on the left side of the square; men on the right side. Families go into that huge barn down the road."

On this dark, gloomy January day, Klara observes scores of makeshift sledges lined up in long rows with baggage men standing at the edge of the station. They await the crowd of surging, shouting, cursing, shoving refugees. Klezmer players from the Ukraine entertain these arrivals whose only wish is to head east.

But they will go nowhere. Snow has covered the tracks and the station has burned down. Only the walls and holes for windows remain.

When the clouds break, the light from the moon brightens the few remaining plastered white walls stained with black and brown smudges of greasy hands. The station stinks. People grab the first waiting *droshky* to flee the stench.

A month and a half after she left Odessa, Klara takes a quick look at Chelyabinsk and frowns.

Barely a dot on the map of the vast Russian Empire and located on the eastern slope of the southern Ural foothills, Chelyabinsk seems to be weighed down by old wooden cabins, rickety buildings on unpaved streets, onion-domed churches—all trapped by the scourge of war and mounting revolutionary fervor.

Vladimir tells her that Tartars founded Chelyabinsk in 1736, now a vital link to the Trans-Siberian railway, a refueling station, a railroad hub; population about 45,000. Somewhat off the beaten track, it thrives as a passenger stopover for weary travelers, a home to beggars, gamblers, whores, explorers, trappers, adventurers, and exiles who, despite impending disaster, feel no desire to push east, deep into frightening, snow-covered, Siberia.

Since the city nestles on the eastern flank of the Ural Mountains and is situated about 1,400 miles from Moscow, its populace lives off the trains that stop to take on civilians or soldiers on their way to Far East bases as well as to load up with coal, household and military supplies, and mail connecting to trains going on to Moscow or Vladivostok.

In the days ahead, Klara will watch Chelyabinskis run up to the cars and sell their wares of food, drink, souvenirs, provisions, health- and personal-care items. Many are walking-pharmacies, pushing pills, herbs, and oils for every known illness; a tablet for a headache, a tablet for indigestion, a tablet for morning sickness.

For now at least, Klara has an advantage to staying in Chelyabinsk. Vladimir's Red Cross group has access to food supplies so she can eat to her heart's content. Unlike Petrograd and Moscow, food is available here, at least for now. Vladimir gives her money to buy food for the two of them and for his small staff. She finds peasant women who sell fruits, vegetables, and kasha, especially those *pirozhki,* hashed meat or cabbage wrapped in flour dough and boiled in grease like a donut. If you have money, a hearty Russian breakfast can be procured: thick cream, porridge, three-egg omelet flanked by crisp blintzes topped with heavy cream and berries and washed down with black *chai*. During the deep freeze of winter, there's always a shot of vodka to warm one's inner soul, though Klara is wary of taking more than one swish.

But she knows the bounty won't last; bread will become scarce. She notices that hungry thousands are fleeing from the cities. Conventional wisdom has it that it's better to be in the countryside than a very large metropolis.

Even though she realizes she has miles and miles to go, Klara Rasputnis delays her departure. Anyone who looks at her these wintry days sees she is radiant, with eyes that shine, with color in her cheeks. She has a boyfriend. Has she fallen in love? "You'll know when it happens," a cousin once told her.

She is housed in a huge dormitory with single women like herself as well as young orphans traveling in groups. Pork fat, pumpkins, and potatoes are her daily fare. One of her worries remains—the overcrowded conditions; refugees may be carriers of typhus and threaten her.

News from the outside world is often filtered and colored to one's political views and false hopes. Though war news saddens her, Klara has learned to try and brush off those depressing thoughts; they just don't enter her mind anymore. She just waves them away, like a dog shoos away a flea. A woman on the train, she recalls, told her "your mind is your best friend or worst enemy," and later instructed Klara to pull her earlobe when she has obsessive thoughts.

Her soft, brown eyes light up as she saunters down the main street each day. Inside the few open stores, she listens to conversations, unobtrusively of course, trying to pick up morsels of information that later she will pass onto Vladimir who separates the items into "possible," "impossible," "needs to be checked," or just plain "rumor."

Vladimir has taught her the skill of asking questions. "There are no dumb questions, only dumb answers," he jokes. "You'd be amazed what you can pick up. Sometimes, I walk around a room and pick up tips and items that make sense out of this whole mess. Yesterday, I heard German prisoners are offered 200 rubles per month for food, room, and clothing if they join the Reds. Most don't. That's why they wander around here, with nothing to do, except rob and kill. Be careful, Klara," Vladimir warns her. "Especially now."

"I hear you," she replies impatiently.

Klara constantly studies Vladimir's face, his deep penetrating eyes, his muscular, straight body. She's afraid that one day when she wakes up, he won't be there. When he's at the police station working on Dmitri's case, she discreetly peeks through the window. She wants him to know that she's there and true enough, she's never far away, especially since Vladimir put her to work in a Red Cross dispensary. She keeps accounts and passes out supplies. He trusts her and she receives a few rubles a month for her work. She manages to save. When his face reddens when she's near him at work, as though embarrassed before his comrades, inwardly he is all smiles. He thinks about her all day and eagerly awaits dinner, when single men and women can mingle in the dormitory and their hands touch and they whisper endearments to each other.

The days pass: February slips into March. The snow begins to melt ever so slightly, and the birds begin to hover over the several thousand lakes in the region.

One evening as she stands alone on a street above the station and next to the Metropole Café, Klara waits for Vladimir. Looking below to the railroad tracks, she watches the huge flow of humanity moving eastward through the western edge of Siberia. Though still run by a Soviet of People's Commissars, Chelyabinsk remains a city of flight.

Sometimes Klara asks herself: "Why am I still here? I should be on my way to find Papa. I'm putting it off." She blushes at the thought of procrastinating. For now, her boyfriend is her rock. Father's a long way off. She's constantly pushing aside a voice in her conscience that tells her to get moving toward Vladivostok.

At night, the guilt feeling torments her. "I feel like I'm removed from the rest of the world. I should really get going. I gave my word and here I'm sitting like a bump on a log."

"Got to stay alive," Klara tells herself upon awakening the next morning. "Getting harder to find food. Concentrate on getting enough to eat and keeping warm."

She's getting restless. She dreams Momma and Papa come home at night and find her and the children sleeping. Father bends down and kisses her. Mother tucks her under the blanket.

She remains indecisive. To go forward, however, to get back on a train can be a death warrant, she rationalizes, though it's true; with sabotage, the situation has become so bad that passenger trains are canceled or pushed aside.

Despite the threat of the Reds stretching their long arm of terror east from Moscow into Siberia, a mood of complacency settles over the area. Some put off their journey; lulled into believing the Red storm will never come. Moscow, still the center of the universe, is a long way off and local soviets have not yet accepted "Red Terror."

As a worker for the Red Cross, Vladimir moves freely about town, frequently with his newfound love. One day in early April, on a walk through the outskirts of town, he and Klara find an empty, three-room log cabin, the kind that dot this part of Siberia. Scavengers somehow missed the structure. Though deserted, it's in good condition; the former tenants must have abandoned the hut in a hurry because they left food, furniture, everything in place, even family photos. And they even left the key to the door on the single wooden table. Klara and Vladimir move in; they're a couple.

The house boasts an old-fashioned Russian oven, a combination heating furnace, baking oven and cook stove. The oven—nine by five feet, and four feet in height—stands in one corner of the kitchen that just happens to be the largest room of the house. Since the stove is located in a corner, it's actually heating two adjoining rooms. Sometimes, when they shiver in the night air of a Siberian frost, Klara and Vladimir take a chair and climb up to the top of the oven where they sleep, hugging each other in the deep warmth.

One particular morning Klara awakens and notes that Vladimir has left for work. She hastens to their favorite haunt, the Metropole Café that is more like a soup kitchen than a restaurant. People are standing in a circle discussing the latest situation. Gossiping about local officials, they joke about attempts to form a new Republic of Siberia that will fly its own flag and hold its own parliament.

"Maybe they'll even have the courage to resist the Bolsheviks," says one customer. "The Reds are beginning to concentrate their position in Siberia."

Her mind is fixed on one object only and it's not the emerging Civil War. Even when she sits in the café, she stares at him. Love changes everything, she realizes as she daydreams they're living in America, though that fantasy is interrupted when she remembers she still has to reach those far-away shores. Father is waiting. Yet she remains.

Spring indeed has come to Siberia—always welcome after the long, freezing winter when the sun is hidden for so long, especially in the snow-covered, sub-arctic, evergreen forest, known as the *taiga*.

But April ushers in the hungry spring of 1918 and with it, famine. Already, food stands have disappeared from the Chelyabinsk railway depot. The peasants have stopped shipping food supplies and hoard them for themselves. During the day, former Russian prisoners of war creep into town, push people around and gobble up every piece of chocolate and biscuit they get their hands on. "It's better than eating black bread, soup and kasha," they declare.

With famine, comes typhus, festering in the filthy bathrooms and striking at the bodies of demobilized soldiers who crowd the train stations even though the rail system itself has just about collapsed. Historians will record that typhus rivaled hunger as Russia's greatest killer that first year of the Civil War.

One morning, at the hour when the sun is already high in the sky over Chelyabinsk, Vladimir, who has been working for quite a while, arrives at the café. He kisses Klara on both cheeks. They sit down and hold hands. They stare at each other. They order coffee and bread from the owner who, because he likes the two lovebirds, slips a little butter and jelly on their plate to help them swallow the stale, black bread.

As the sun embraces the city, Vladimir tells Klara: "Look how beautiful it is now. Welcome to Siberia, my love. Not the Siberia of ice and snow. Not the Siberia of exiles and prisons; but the Siberia of pines and fir trees."

"Stay this summer," he pleads." You'll love it here. Besides, we'll be together. The situation's getting better," he tells her putting his arm around her, holding her and repeating in a hopeful voice: "We'll take trips; go swimming; they even have dances outdoors in Chelyabinsk."

"Vladimir, need I remind you there's a war on," she replies.

"There's a lot of talk that the Whites are going to win," he says.

"Nonsense! Even I know that all those groups will never unite. Leaders are suspicious of each other. Don't trust each other. Those White groups work at cross purposes. No, we've got to get out of here soon," she declares, somewhat overwhelmed by the revived guilt that rises to plague her. Even though she realizes her lover is sitting before her and will protect her and comfort her and even though she will have a strong shoulder to lean on, she keeps hearing a voice that haunts her. "Get on with it, Klara."

On one bright May morning, Russia's political future does not concern the two lovers. The sun is shining; it warms the soul. Only Siberians seem to know when spring-summer sun gives off enough heat to make their bodies feel good again. And this year, warmth has arrived early. The couple is told that officially, it is 86 degrees F. "And this is Siberia?" they ask.

Vladimir throws caution to the wind and comes up with the idea that the two of them take an afternoon off and head out to a small lake, just outside the city. They'll pack a picnic lunch of cheese, a few hardboiled eggs, an onion, radishes, black bread, all of which Klara can snare from the dormitory kitchen. He'll add a few cans of sardines that he can obtain from the commissariat.

The lake is not far, a mile down the main road. Nobody is fishing today and few farmers stop at this watering hole, off the beaten track. Bathing suits don't exist in this part of the world.

Vladimir's active imagination conjures up a scene of them swimming nude and touching each other, but he quickly discounts the idea. Even if isolated, people do wander by the lake area and if spotted, he could be reported. Visions of someone stealing their clothes on the beach while they're naked in the water confront his sensible and cunning mind.

Now if that happened, how would they walk home without clothes? That'd be funny, he thinks, as a big grin covers his face. He's quite aware of the consequences of a Red Cross officer being caught without clothes and accompanied by a young girl.

So they bring old clothes; he a pair of colored shorts and she, dark, summer leggings and a jersey top. They change in the woods behind bushes, he to one side; she to the other. As Klara removes her blouse and slips out of her bra, a strange sensation overcomes her. She shivers slightly until the hot air warms her white breasts. She opens the buttons on her skirt and lets it fall to the ground. She wishes she had a wall mirror to look over her dance-formed body. She's sure it pleases Vladimir.

Her borrowed swimming outfit, however, won't win her a medal in the fashion gazette. Her mind wanders. She can only hope that someday she and Vladimir will walk along the *Boulevard des Anglais* in Nice where all the wealthy Russians wintered before this horrible war.

Now dressed in this makeshift swimsuit, she steps out and decides not to wait so Vladimir can stare at her. She gracefully runs forward over the pebbles that dig into the soles of her feet. She doesn't feel it. She's a gazelle, a ballerina always.

Vladimir catches up and entering the cold water, they hold onto each other; each feeling the sensuous skin of the other—sending goose pimples over their bodies.

Frolicking in the water, they float on their backs, hug each other, kiss and hug; kiss and hug—their faces wet with cool water. Spreading out their thin blanket, they lie on the pebble beach and look up at the sun and cloudless blue sky.

He loves to look at her smooth, filled-out body, her sensuous thighs, her perfectly formed breasts that lead his eyes below to that imaginable black area atop her thin long legs. He would shed his makeshift bathing suit in a second. But he knows better and observes convention in the lake.

Again, they wade out in shallow water to a small raft and lie on their stomach. No talking; total silence underneath a cloudless blue sky as they stare into each others' eyes.

"This is wonderful," says Klara finally. "How can this be? Nobody'd ever believe us. Forget the war. This is the life. Maybe someday we'll have it. Yes?"

"Hope so," he says reservedly, smothering her wet face with kisses. He is breathless.

Sun and water have moved them; though they wait until they return to their secret room where they quickly rip off their clothes and thrill each other and afterwards lie panting and saying to themselves, "Yes, this is the life."

Klara and Vladimir draw closer.

Aware of fighting up ahead, Vladimir continues to try and persuade her to stay in town.

"Trains on their way to Vladivostok are all lined up in the railroad yard. They're waiting for engines," he tells her. "Don't worry. I'll never let you go alone. I'll go with you. We can always hop on together when the time comes."

Vladimir has no trouble slipping away from the barracks. No one keeps tabs on him. As for Klara, she has come up with an excuse for the other ladies in the dorm so they won't ask where she's going every time she walks out. Besides her Red Cross work, she tells them, she has a job with a family.

"No. I'm not a governess or nanny, just taking care of a few children."

Yet if one of those fine ladies followed Klara from the dormitory, they would see her walking briskly toward the station, her arms swinging slightly forward; her shoulders pushed back. A smile breaks out on her face; her eyes glisten. She is attracted to the smells of a few delicacies left in the market, especially the cabbage, peppers, and onions. She wants to get closer, the aroma reminds her of home.

The actual bedroom Klara and Vladimir sleep in once served as a young girl's room. One can see pictures from girly magazines; pictures of actresses on a huge wall mirror; bottles of *eau de toilette* spread about. An iron-wrought double bed and a wooden three-drawer bureau make the bedroom a very livable place.

Everyone knows they're living together. Still, they never enter the residence at the same time. That's the way they did things in the era before the Communists preached their free-love philosophy and no one was discreet anymore. They bring utensils, clothes, and knick-knacks to the apartment: Sheets and blankets, a small mosaic table, another wooden table for their meals. From this new home, they can look out the window and see the birch trees, a canal, and the church.

And with a night of lovemaking behind them, their energy spent, their bones rejuvenated and their muscles relaxed, sleep overcomes them.

When they awake, they return to their dorms. Not together. He, first; she stays behind tidying up. Then she leaves. No frowns on her part, no guilt. Klara Rasputnis remains content.

•

One day as Vladimir is about to depart, she urges him to stay.

"No. Have to go. I'm on duty."

An early morning fog covers the town and he shivers standing on the cold floor.

"Vladimir, come back," she says, smiling and turning on her side, her elbow supporting her in a position that enhances her ripe breasts.

He sits down at the edge of the bed. They linger longer than expected. He's kissing her. Those few moments of tender touching so electrifying in early morning hours seem like a lifetime to both of them.

On this day, however, their joy quickly ceases when they hear shouts and knocks on doors of nearby houses. Soldiers are searching each residence.

"Open up in the name of the Revolution. We're looking for traitors and deserters. Open up! Be quick," yell the soldiers at the house next door.

The two lovers stare at each other.

"Shit," he whispers. "Get dressed. Quick! If they find you here, they'll jail us. I'll stall them. No. No wait. Don't. No time," he adds as poundings can be heard on the neighbor's entrance.

"They'll be here in a few seconds."

"Open in the name of the Revolution."

Vladimir hastily picks up his pants and tightens his belt.

"Grab your clothes. Get under the bed. Right away," he utters quietly. "I'll tell them I sleep here during the day while I'm investigating Dmitri's case. Underneath you go. Don't breathe," he says trying as best he can to avoid looking at her warm, naked body.

Making sure she gathers all her clothes, Klara slithers under the bed. Large balls of dust surround her. She hopes she has taken everything down into the darkness.

"Just a minute, comrades," shouts Vladimir. "Hold on. I'm coming. I'm an officer in the Red Cross," he yells deliberately to prepare them.

He has his shorts on; his hair's disheveled. He decides he'll tell them he's been sleeping. They'll believe it. Yes, that's it. He's with the Red Cross and works late at night.

Vladimir opens the door slightly and flashes his international Red Cross identification.

Opposite is the sullen and grim face of a lieutenant dressed in a khaki shirt and dark brown pants with a thick black belt holding them up. Next to him stands a young lad in civilian clothes, wearing a black tunic, black leather jacket and pants covered partially by knee-high boots. A commissar, he brandishes a revolver.

The officer sports a tired, worn face, a wild mustache, an unkempt, dirty-blond beard. His dark, frightened and cruel eyes that have observed a seamy life scan the room.

The younger civilian is obviously a Jew, thinks Vladimir. He has a Jewish nose, long, wide at the bottom. Yes, that's how you tell a Jew, by the features of his nose. The three look at each other. Each pair of weary eyes welcomes the other, at least for the moment.

The lieutenant is aware that the man at whom he is starring is his equal because the Moscow government has recognized Vladimir's international organization.

"What is it?" says Vladimir in an official, commanding, military voice.

"Sorry to bother you," says the lieutenant trying to avert his eyes. "We're looking for White counter revolutionaries, traitors, and enemies of the people and spies.

"Of course. But none here, Lieutenant," answers Vladimir rubbing his eyes and yawning loudly, casting a worried eye to the so-called civilian commissar. "Sorry. I work nights and I've been on the case of a friend of mine who fell or was pushed out of a train. Happened a while ago. Perhaps you've heard of the incident? Dmitri's his name, a railway agent."

"Yes, something about it," answers the lieutenant.

"By the way, have you seen this man?" the teenager asks holding up a cracked photo to Vladimir's eyes.

"No. Can't say that I have. What's he done?"

"He's a spy for Czechs. Causing trouble. We'll catch him. And when we do..."

He doesn't finish his sentence, but Vladimir, who yawns slightly, gets the message. The word "catch" sends a tremor down his spine. He doesn't have to be reminded that Klara is naked underneath the bed covered with worn blankets. He dare not look around the room for any incriminating items.

But let us suppose that if Lieutenant Slutsky had not left, but taken a flashlight and got down on all fours and lifted the blanket and moved the flashlight underneath the bed, the light would have illuminated a very shocked young lady. She's frightened as hell, biting her tongue for fear of being caught, and yet, on the other hand, she's happy. She has recognized the voice of the teenager. She wants to shout out his name:

"Mischa. Mischa. It's Klara. Your sister. Here I am."

She doesn't utter a word.

The lieutenant, raising his arm and giving a proper salute, mutters:

"Dosvidanya."

"Good-bye," answers Vladmir.

The door slams tight. Safe. The soldiers won't bother them anymore. Klara peeks out from under the bed.

"Damn it; it's stifling down here. Yet, it's better than under Mrs. Kovchenko's dress," she recalls.

Vladimir doesn't say a word. He's deep in thought as he dresses. Picking up his rucksack, he kisses Klara and as he leaves, he shakes his head and says, "That was close." They both laugh.

"He's free. He's alive. My dumb brother is alive," she says to herself, holding back tears.

But what if I'm crazy? What if it wasn't Mischa. No, it definitely was Mischa. His deep voice; I'd recognize it anywhere."

Mischa's alive and she's happy for the moment. She can't fathom it completely, but whenever he's near, her dislike of him fades, like a cloak of hate lifted from her shoulders.

As she picks up her clothes and moves over to the washbasin to clean herself and the dress, flashes of those years in Odessa before she departed appear before her. But she isn't in the city on the Black Sea; she's in Chelyabinsk, and she and her brother have changed.

14

Brother and Sister Meet in Chelyabinsk, May 1918

Historians have called the time between the October 1917 Revolution and the spring of 1918 as a "kind of interregnum" in the war in Siberia between the Reds and the Whites. By May 1918, extreme food shortages exist throughout the country. Famine is acute. Fortunately, a new organization, the Joint Distribution Committee, affectionately called "the Joint," founded in 1914, brings food and supplies to needy Jews in Ukraine and Russia. With the demobilization of the army, guerrilla warfare breaks out and sabotage is rife throughout Siberia. Prices are rising because peasants withhold food and refuse to deliver it to cities and towns to be sold in exchange for Soviet money.

"Russians began to bury their dead as the spring thaw came," notes author W. Bruce Lincoln. The country is starving and its citizens are clad in rags, barefoot and hungry. Moreover, as Red Russia pulls out from the World War, the Allies begin to carry out their threat to intervene. On April 4, 1918, Japanese and British forces land in Vladivostok. All told, about 160,000 foreign soldiers will join the battle to stop the Reds.

Back in Odessa, the "hungry spring" of 1918 bombards the remnants of the Rasputnis clan, a mother and three daughters. They have watched thousands flee the Bolsheviks and arrive in their port city on the Black Sea. These mobs of homeless, hungry people hope to sail away. Nothing functions, unemployment is widespread. Inflation is rampant. Odessa is starving!

•

Standing there in the cabin they call their "lovers nest," Klara Rasputnis has taken a quick bath and prettied herself up a bit. She hurries; she doesn't want to miss her brother.

Now what? Should she tell her brother that his sister was under the bed, naked? Never! she thinks, smiling as she recalls the scene. He would surely beat Vladimir to a pulp for sleeping with his sister, and a *goy* no less. But who cares?

Still, other unsettling thoughts plague her. What if Mischa doesn't like him? What if Mischa tells her to drop him? Mischa's a hunter now; Vladimir could become his prey. A stalker doesn't let a victim escape. She has to find Mischa first, however. He can't be far.

Minutes later, she's on the busy streets of Chelyabinsk—looking for her brother. She's sure she'll find him. What if he tells her to leave town immediately and move again on her journey? What if he won't help her? What if he deserts her? Thoughts she quickly dismisses. She knows how to soften him up, she thinks.

Across the street from the train station, she spies a group of young soldiers and a civilian. That's him. They're talking. They shake hands. They say goodbye and split up.

"Don't make a scene," she tells the teenager who can't believe what he's hearing. He wants to smile and even hug her. "Look straight ahead. Talk to me as if we know each other. Just like we're brother and sister,"

"I don't believe this," he says as laughter overcomes him.

"Neither do I. Keep walking. Cross the street. See the café over there. I'm your sister. Remember: Don't attract attention."

They disappear into the crowd.

"Two *chai*," orders Mischa.

They sit quietly waiting for the hot tea. They purposely act like an old married couple on a Sunday afternoon, sitting in a restaurant or café and already talked out. The tables are tight, pushed together. Waiters have a hard time maneuvering around them; it's a balancing act. They dare not tilt their trays too much in the smoke-filled, crowded room.

On the train to Chelyabinsk, she learned that one never talks about the person sitting across the aisle from her. Too many spies around. One refers to that person in front of her as if that individual were someone else and somewhere else, when it's really the man or woman facing her that you're discussing. Talk like that doesn't arouse suspicion.

"So, tell me. What happened to Yaakov?" she asks with a sly wink.

"Yaakov accepted a special job with the Army the day after you left. Before he left town on his first assignment, he made sure a fellow agent looks after his mother and younger sisters and gives them a few rubles a month so they can survive. He owes him. And Yaakov's traveled all over since you last saw him. They even gave him a new pair of boots when he joined up. Still have 'em on," he says pointing down to his polished footwear.

"And you're alive, thank god, and a big shot, no less," she says, somewhat proud of her younger brother and relieved to hear that Momma and the girls are safe. "You must be doing well with your job."

"I was lucky. They like me. They had their eye on me. They saw I was good as a *meshetchnik*. That was good training for learning how to travel and getting around all kinds of officials. Anyone with a brain can rise in the ranks in the Red Guards. Already, I have commanded soldiers, mostly peasants who could be my father. Those poor guys. Most of them don't even know what they're fighting for. They've been sucked in because everyone in their village went over to one side or the other. The Bolsheviks realize this, that's why they've started to send an information officer to every unit. His job? Feed them the party line. He's called a commissar, a Red invention.

"Right now, that's me. Lately, I travel incognito. I dress in civilian clothes. With forged documents, I can move in and out of the lines. Anyone bothers me on the Red side, I give them a password that guarantees their leaving me alone and I tell them 'I'm in the new secret police, the *Cheka*.' They back off immediately. Who wants to argue with thugs?"

"If the Whites stop me, I've got hidden papers that I can pull out and show 'em I was in the *Okhrana* (Czarist secret police). It's dangerous, but I love the excitement. Better than a frontline soldier. What happens to people who live after they face death? Answer me that, Klara."

"War does that to you," she replies and then tightens her mouth.

The two stop talking. This is not my brother, she thinks. He's changed. He's harder. He's tougher. But then again, so am I.

Finally, Mischa speaks again, with a lower voice, as he continues to scan the café area. "I've seen soldiers returning home from the front. Embittered, they feel cheated by the fact that the peasants divided the land before they arrived. Many settle old scores. And they're convinced that all Jews are Bolsheviks. 'Aren't Trotsky and leading commissars Jews?' they say. But I know those Red leaders are Jews only by name. They might as well have converted to Russian Orthodoxy. They don't practice Judaism. They deny their Jewishness. Why call them Jews? Call them what they are: Communists, Leninists, atheists."

Though he supports the Bolsheviks, he thinks the Jews shouldn't be so eager to rush into the arms of the Reds. "One day it'll come back to haunt us, even though we'll contribute much to Soviet culture and thought. Eventually, they'll persecute and purge us. Communism will turn out badly for us," he says to himself, recognizing that these are thoughts you don't tell anyone, even Klara. For the present, he's a Communist, but he wavers.

"I'll probably have to leave. An intelligence officer's got to know what's happening. And don't think I don't know what you've been doing while you're moving through all this mess. You've got a boyfriend!" he states emphatically. Catching her off guard, he notices she's blushing.

"Nah," says Klara, embarrassed to talk to him about Vladimir. Quickly changing the subject, she replies, "I actually like it here." He doesn't press her about a beau.

The music blares from a group of musicians and drowns out their conversation. Customers enter the café. Several couples stroll out to the center of the floor with a new dance called the "foxtrot."

"I might stay here a while," she declares.

"Stay in this God forsaken town?" he replies, cutting her off. "Full of flophouses, all-night cafes, drunkards. People will soon be dying of hunger; getting killed by stray bullets. Dangerous to be on the streets. Keep your eyes and ears open. Everything's changing. The whole country's changing. You're changing. I'm changing."

"My mission's the same. I'm going to find Papa. I'm not going back, either. I'm determined. As Momma used to say: 'Either do it, or give it up.'"

"Who said anything about going back? You shouldn't. What I'm trying to say is, I'm not sure you should be journeying on, just to find Papa anymore. Go forward, but not for that reason. Listen, Klara," whispers Mischa, "there's something I've got to tell you. I've heard Papa's now a big-time cantor in Vladivostok. As a clergyman, he's invited to galas at town hall. He acts the court Jew, just like the privileged Jews in Europe. You may not want to believe it; but he runs around with women."

"You're crazy. Not Papa. Don't you believe it."

He could tell from her eyes, the way she looked down, that she didn't want to accept it. He'll have to convince her. "Klara, I read about him in a newspaper article."

"You don't believe everything you read in newspapers these days, do you? Let's not argue. You'll see I'm right." Mischa scowl is interrupted as a waiter approaches, pours some more tea, and puts down some black bread. He also places before them a variety of jams, gooseberry, Russian strawberry, cornelian cherry, paradise apple, and black currant. The sight of the toppings relaxes them as they smear the confection onto their bread.

"I don't believe this. Real jam!" exclaims Klara. "How much did you give him?"

"As Momma used to say, 'money talks, shit walks.'"

"But where did you get the...."

She doesn't finish the sentence, for Mischa's waving hand cuts off the word.

Neither talk. Now actually would be a good time to tell him all about Vladimir, thinks Klara. Otherwise, the two men could meet again by accident. What if Mischa comes to the dorm? What if one of the ladies informs on me: "Klara's not sleeping here."

Go ahead, she urges herself: *Tell him. He's your brother. He just wants to take care of you. Yet, brothers can be very jealous. But you'll have to tell Mischa that Vladimir's a non-Jew. God. There'll be hell to pay. I just can't do it.*

"See you later. Got to go." says Mischa interrupting her thoughts. "Where you staying?"

"Dormitory three. On Pushkin Street."

"I'll find you."

"How about you? Where you bunked?"

"The People's Barracks, 40 Khodofsky Street, near the factory."

"Mischa. I'm so glad you're here. Don't go. Don't leave Chelyabinsk."

"Have to."

They embrace.

He's gone.

Klara races to the corner of Kartsov and Lernovsky streets. She's excited. She has found her brother. She knows he has money. Even among Red forces, commissars have funds for their work. She'll get it when she needs it. At the same time, Klara hopes Mischa is sending the family something to tide them over. "I'm glad he's helping them. He should be. He deserted them." She walks faster. Loud conversations don't distract her. Yet she hears people yelling at each other: "White bandits snuck into town. Tried to assassinate government officials."

She thinks she sees Vladimir in the intersection. It's not him, although she notices the workers haven't yet exited Government House where Vladimir often has a morning appointment. She observes coachmen dozing off as they wait for customers.

"Damn it. He's not here. Where is he? Not like him to be late," she says to herself. She waits and waits. He doesn't show up.

"Never happened before. I was sure he'd be here. No talk in the streets of the Red Cross being moving out," she says to herself. "I'm glad I found Mischa. Need him more than ever. Maybe he's now my family rock to lean on. Besides, he's matured."

Klara can't tell if he remains piqued with her for being asked to find father. "I've got to be nice to him; he can help me and Vladimir."

When she awakens the next morning, she decides not to tell Vladimir about Mischa, at least not now. She's afraid; for even though Vladimir is a Red Cross worker, she's not sure of his politics, especially since she realizes in a civil war brother can turn against brother, father against son.

15

The Czechs Take Over Chelyabinsk, May 1918

Life in Siberia will change. The issue concerns the small Central European nation, Czechoslovakia, about to achieve independence. In 1914, when World War I breaks out, Czechoslovakia remained under the heel of the Austro-Hungarian Empire that forces Czech and Slovak men to fight in its army. Hating their servitude under the Austrians and Hungarians, thousands of Czechs are captured on the eastern front by their enemy, the Russians. But the Czechs willingly join their captors and form an independent unit that is now allied with the Russians against the Central Powers of Germany and Austria. This new group, 35,000 to 50,000 strong, is known as the "Czechoslovak Legion in Russia."

Since Russia left the war in early spring of 1918, agreement has been reached between the Czechs and Soviets for the Czech Legion to withdraw from Russia and ship out to France, via the port of Vladivostok—so they can fight on the side of the Allies. The Czechs hope that by joining the Allies, they will help advance independence for their country at war's end.

But because the German Army bars passage westward through the Eastern Front, the Czech transfer to Western Europe will have to take the long way around—a 6,000-mile-trip east along the Trans-Siberian railway to Vladivostok, then across the Pacific, followed by an overland journey through the U.S., and a transfer by ship across the Atlantic to France.

The Reds try to dissuade the Czechs from leaving; Moscow wants their manpower. Failing that, they insist the Czechs disarm before departure, a demand that the Czechs, strung out along the Trans-Siberian, refuse; they say they need the arms to defend themselves.

The situation comes to a head on May 14, 1918 during an incident in Chelyabinsk, in what is to be the first clash between the Czechs and the local Soviets.

•

Dawn! Morning light. Almost summer in Siberia and the sun shines on the pair. The two lovers hug and kiss. They found each other in a small square near the railway station. Vladimir explains he couldn't send a message.

"One of those surprise visits from Red Cross country director. It happens. I'm sorry."

"Understood," says Klara.

The two just stare at each other. They are young and oblivious to danger. Unknown to them is the saying "into each life a little rain must fall." Until now, with only a few mishaps, a golden warmth has lighted up their lives.

The next morning, chatter erupts as usual. Not far from where Klara and Vladimir sleep at night in their hideaway, a group of soldiers wearing uniforms similar to the Russian Army carry rifles with fixed bayonets. Speaking a different, though similar-sounding Slavic language, they pass the room of our two young people whose bodies are entwined into one as they lie there, a slight smile on their faces and listen to the voices outside. Soon, the two get up, stare into the sun; wash their weary bodies and amble down to the café.

Sipping hot chicory coffee and each eating a slice of black bread, Klara and Vladimir spot two soldiers in familiar uniforms, though with different insignias than Russia's.

"Who are they?" asks Klara. "What language are they speaking? Sounds Slavic, but ..."

"It's Czech. See the red and white markings on their Russian-style caps?"

"What're they doing here?"

"They come into the city from their army camps. They wander from town to town. This group, the Legion fought with our troops against Germany in the East. Now that we're out of the war, they want to leave Russia for France and fight the Germans on the Western Front so they can have their own country, a new, free Czechoslovakia."

"Come to think of it, I've seen them before. But not so many."

"They should be on the train or in their camp. Something's happened. Better go see. Could be trouble. They promised to relinquish most of their arms when they leave for the trains. Maybe they're refusing. Or maybe an advance party. I'll check. See you."

"Vladimir. Wait. I'll go with you."

"No. Liable to be trouble."

"I'll be fine."

Klara and Vladimir, two citizens of Russia, one an 18-year-old-Jewish girl, the other, a 19-year-old from a Russian Orthodox family just can't imagine that those wandering-about Czechs soon will clash with the Bolsheviks. Nobody does.

Klara walks part of the way with Vladimir.

She remembers that the Czech soldiers on the trains passing through town would often shout: "Going home. Long live the new Republic of Czechoslovakia."

"The Czechs and Russians'll soon be at each others' throats," Vladimir tells Klara. "The Czechs want to go and the Reds want them to stay and fight on their side."

"So that's what's happening."

"Partly. But it's confusing. Anyway, war's like that. Once it starts, it's uncontrollable. This happens; that happens. Nobody can figure out why. Wait here."

The two end their talk. Vladimir leaves Klara and heads to the sentry boxes just outside the station where the chief Russian officer stands.

She sees two trains crawl like a snail into the Chelyabinsk station.

One is a long, meandering boxcar train containing Czech troops. It's heading east in the opposite direction of their homeland and the long way back to Central Europe.

The other train, containing boxcars full of German, Austrian, and Hungarian prisoners of war—faces west. This second train, the one with prisoners, slides alongside the now-stopped Czech train. Cooped up in the steamy and smelly cars, the Hungarian prisoners are so despondent that they are ready to kill. So are the Czechs—especially if anyone stands in their way, and especially if it happens to be their old rulers, the Austrians and Hungarians.

Klara tries not to stare. She knows they'll harass her if their eyes capture hers. They'll call her names. They'll whistle. They'll try to seduce her with sign language. They'll think she's a prostitute.

She looks away. But out of the corner of her eye she takes in the tired, worn-out soldiers. Their hair is messed up; their clothes are disheveled. Many don't have caps. Even though standing, they seem to be asleep.

The trains stop. Both sides glare at each other.

She has seen those stares before; looks that kill, the half-frozen, homeless, starving bands of refugees wandering hopelessly across the land. Noticing the Hungarians on the other train, the Czechs sing *Hej Slovane,* their national anthem amidst Hungarian and German catcalls.

Suddenly, an eerie silence blankets the air.

The Red Guards, responsible for maintaining order, stiffen like cats backed into a corner. They feel the Czech hate rising; their eyes fixing their sights on the enemy. Muscles tighten.

"We're free of you at last," a Czech trooper yells out to the Hungarians.

At that, one of the Hungarian prisoners takes a lump of cast iron from a broken stove and hurls it at a Czech standing alone. The aim is good and it comes crashing into the trooper's head. The soldier moans as he falls to the ground. He's dead.

What then unfolds before Klara's eyes is a nightmare.

Czech soldiers climb over their cars. Their own Czech officers and guards can't stop them. Vastly outnumbering the Hungarians who are held in close and tight by Russian sentries, the Czechs charge the boxcar of the rock thrower. The Red Guards don't interfere. The Czechs push aside the Hungarian defenders. The attackers grab the stone hurler; and despite useless yells and shouts of protest drag him back to their own boxcar.

A Czech soldier comes up with a rope, fastens it over the Hungarian's head and around his neck. Joined by a few comrades, he pulls the prisoner forward to the landing between the cars.

Amid shouts of "hang him, hang him," the Czechs throw the free end of the rope up to their fellow soldiers on the train's car roof and these self-styled executioners lift up the luckless Hungarian by his neck. They raise him high into the open space between the cars as the victim begins to struggle. He claws the still air as his body slowly swings to and fro; his eyes look as if they're popping, his feet dangle, his arms, at first, wave up and down and then fall limp to his sides. He's dead.

Klara sees it all.

They let the body fall alongside the tracks below. Just another dead soldier. Silence. Both sides glare at each other. The Hungarians, still held in check by their Russian captors, make the sign of the cross as their train leaves the station.

Czech guards finally restore order to their own troops. The body lies prone and silent. The Czechs look away.

"Now get out," shout the Red soldiers who even though hardened themselves by war, are amazed at the action of the two groups. Before the Czech train leaves, the Russians round up the lynching party and several Czech guards and haul them off to jail.

"Good riddance to bad rubbish" say the Russians watching the Czech train leave.

"Did they have to kill the soldier throwing the brick?" Klara later asks Vladimir.

"No rational behavior in wartime," he answers. "Only hatred! The Russians feel the Czechs have gone back on their word by keeping and hiding arms. The Czechs say they need them as they move eastward across Russia. Who knows what will happen now?"

Not a long wait.

Three days later, Vladimir, finishing work at the clinic, heads home to Klara. He always longs for the afternoon to arrive, the end of the day. That's when tension and worry lift from his body. He anticipates her warmth and pleasure. "She'll be mine again," he says to himself.

Even if the air in Chelyabinsk is stifling him, even if he's sure trouble will soon break out, even if he hears people talking about the train incident, it doesn't matter—he begins humming and smiling and longing for Klara. He sings to himself.

"Gde eta ulitza? Gde etot dom? Gde eta devushka? Chto ya vlublyon?"

"Where is the street? Where is the house? Where is the beautiful girl I love?" goes the ditty his father taught him.

"Vot eta ulitza. Vot eta dom. Vot eta devushka sto ya vlublyon?"

"Here's the street. Here's the house. Here's the lovely girl I love." He mumbles the words so no one can hear him. He walks very fast.

Just before he reaches the street where he and Klara live, Vladimir is stopped by a member of the local Soviet and told the Reds are still holding the Czechs they picked up at the railway station.

"What! Are they crazy?" says Vladimir. "The Czechs'll be furious. They're not going to leave their own men behind bars."

"Everybody inside," command Czech soldiers who now appear on the street. "No harm will be done to you."

Later, people pour out of their houses. They welcome the Czech troops. Klara's neighbors are ecstatic. They are glad to be rid of the Soviets who have ruled the city. "Great," say the refugees, especially grateful as many now have a better chance to leave town and move east.

"Long live the Czech Army. Our liberators," they shout with joy, as Chelyabinsk will soon be in the hands of the White Army.

The locals join in the singing of Czech folk songs. Everyone's happy. "Let's have a party. Let's celebrate. Bring on the vodka," somebody shouts.

They may not realize it, but right before their very eyes, war has erupted in Siberia. Vladimir knows the Czechs. Once they start, they won't stop. The Czechs will begin to capture station after station along the eastern Trans-Siberian railway.

16

Klara, Vladimir, and Mischa Leave Chelyabinsk, June 1918

"Siberia's turning into an insane asylum," Vladimir tells Klara one afternoon. "I've changed my mind. There're no more Reds here. They've been chased out and everyone has a chance to flee this mad house. Now, Klara. Now's the time to get out. Going to be a bloody mess when the Bolsheviks return."

"I'm ready," she answers.

A few weeks later, returning to their hut late in the afternoon, Klara hurries up the steps. As she puts her hand under the mat for the key, a smile lightens her face.

"It's not here."

Opening the door, she shouts into the dark room, "Vladimir, Vladimir, I'm so ..."

Her smile vanishes. Her shiny eyes dim. It's not Vladimir; it's a stranger in a soldier's uniform with a Red Cross armband.

She doesn't step back, nor does she turn and run. Looking beyond the newcomer, she sees papers strewn about; clothes scattered on the bed; blankets piled high on the chair.

"Where's Vladimir?" she demands. "Who are you? "

"Vasilyev. Vladimir's friend. We're in the same unit. He told me where the key would be."

"Who did this?"

"Don't know. Asked myself the very same question: Why would anyone do this? Here's a note from Vladimir."

Klara eagerly takes the note.

Dear Klara.

I know all about it. You've got a brother, Mischa. He's here in Chelyabinsk. The talk is he's a Red. Be careful. Now that the town is White, they're looking for Red activists. That's probably why they came here. Fortunately, neither you nor I were here; a friend warned me to stay away, and I knew you wouldn't be back till later. Don't want to scare you. But because of your brother, you may be in grave danger.

I've got to leave for a short while. They're watching me, too. I don't know why, unless they think I can lead them to you and your brother.

That's why I sent Vasilyev with this letter. I also gave him 20 rubles for you; you'll need it. Please stay away from our hut. I'll find you when I get back, or I'll catch up to you if you move on. Don't worry. I'll know exactly where you are. Why don't you stay in the girls' apartment? No one would dare think of you being there. Don't take up their occupation. Just kidding.

 Love you, Vladimir.

"We better go," says Vasilyev, handing her a 20-ruble note. "Don't touch anything. Leave it the way it is."

"Sure. Can you give Vladimir a letter for me?"

"Yes, of course. Here's a pencil and a pad."

Standing in the hallway, she writes a short note.

Dear Vladimir, love.

 Taking your advice. Going over to the girls' place. Just like in the ballet or opera, you better come and rescue me, my knight in shining armor. Otherwise, I'll become like those girls. Just kidding, too.

 If I have to move on, love, I know you'll find me.

 With all my heart. Love you, too.

 Klara.

"Vasilyev, where is Vladimir?"

"Huh," he grunts. "Even if I knew, I couldn't tell you. If the Whites caught you and thought you knew where he was hiding out, do you know what they'd do to you? Don't worry. I'll see he gets the note. *Dosvidanya.*"

As he turns to go, Vasilyev looks at her, a comforting smile on his face. He softly touches her shoulder. "He'll be okay."

"The girls are home," says Klara to herself having walked to a house on Pulkova Street. "It's pouring rain; they can't stand on a street corner today." Since she has been in Chelyabinsk, she has seen their comings and goings. Everyone calls them the "girls." Klara knows they don't work in the house; they satisfy their clients in a building near the rail station. Some sleep during the day; others at night. Men are not allowed here. Even in this profession, the ladies are entitled to some privacy, they say.

Klara tells the girls her hideaway is being watched. They give her a bed in a small room. She's worried and frightened until sleep relaxes her mind and body, only to be broken by gunfire during the night.

In the morning, she dresses, leaves the house, walks fast, runs down the steps to the café. No sign of him anywhere. She decides she should go to the

Red Cross office and ask for Vladimir. And if that doesn't work, go to the new White Army headquarters. But that's too dangerous; her brother's a Red.

Obviously, the letter she gave to Vasilyev hasn't reached him yet, or if it had, Vladimir can't get to her. "What's my next move?" she ponders, a question that increasingly occupies her in this journey. Despite the dangers, Klara decides to leave. "Better to go, than to sit and mope. Try something, anything. Take a risk."

When she gets to Red Cross offices, however, reality closes in once again; the building is boarded up.

"What should I do now? I can't stay here, that's for sure. No time to lose. I've got to find Mischa and tell him all about Vladimir."

Back at the dorm, Klara asks a boarder: "Did you see a young man in a Red Cross uniform?"

"No. But come to think of it, someone did ask about you. He was in civilian clothes."

"What did he look like?"

"Good looking. Tall. Strong. Said he was going to Irkutsk. If you came around, I should tell you to meet him at the station."

"Thanks," Klara adds, "I better go."

It's risky but she decides to run back to the cabin, shoves some clothes into a new, smaller satchel she picked up the week before in the market for two rubles. The rest she leaves for the next couple or whoever occupies this cabin that became a home away from home, for she'll remember the time she spent here. Sitting for a moment on her suitcase, she prays for a good trip, rises, walks out of the hut, and does not look back.

And what does she find at the rail terminal? Jostling, shoving, elbowing. Porters solicit passengers. Mothers scold children. Fathers look worried.

"Where you going?" an official asks Klara who has been standing in the middle of the large waiting room looking for Mischa. "Let's see your papers."

"Here," answers Klara, as she hands him her documents. "I'm going to Irkutsk."

"I see," says the man who waves to two soldiers at the entrance.

Hurrying over, the armed guards glance at her papers.

"Come with us," says one gripping her arm.

"What's wrong?" demands Klara.

"We don't like your last name, that's what's wrong," he sneers.

"Just a minute officer. Leave her alone," orders a young man stepping in front of the girl and flashing his pass showing he's an officer in White Intelligence Services. "I'll take over," he says, grabbing Klara's papers back from the policeman.

The uniformed men back off.

"Now, you're with the Whites. Won't the Bolsheviks be looking for you?" asks Klara in a mocking voice. "Can't keep up with you, Mr. Chameleon; always changing your skin. You must know a good forger."

"I do. But you're gonna need one. Those papers expired. I'll get you a new rail transit pass when we get to Irkutsk. As long as you're with me, you're covered. As for my Mr. Chameleon activities as you call them, so far, so good. Until someone catches on." Mischa's eyes fixate. "Great. There's the train to Ekaterinburg. Just came in and they shunted it into the yards. We've got to get on it. Let's go."

Carrying a small sack of food for the trip, Mischa guides Klara past long lines of carriages until they reach the last car that turns out to be an empty *tieploushki*—a goods wagon with a stove in the middle, beds on the floor, and benches fixed to the sides in three tiers. Since it's a disbanded wagon for the wounded, movable steps have been placed at the entrance so the two climb up into the wagon.

But the train doesn't move.

Looking up and down the tracks, Mischa spots a railway worker, crouching down and looking from side to side as he approaches their car.

"Partisans are shooting in the next yard," the man yells up to them. "Get out of the car. Not safe."

The two are eager to get away from trouble, so they jump down and walk back toward the station to see if they can catch another train.

"Mischa, there's something I've got to tell you. It's, well ..."

"Not now, Klara," Mischa warns. " Damn it. He's there again. That short, bald headed man, with a beer belly and a pocked face. See him, over there; next to that kiosk."

"I see him."

"He's been following me. He's back. We'd better get out of here."

"Where to now? He'll see you getting on another car or another train. He'll warn his comrades. We'll get caught."

"Have to take that chance."

"You're crazy. They'll kill us on the spot."

"Let's go," shouts Mischa as he grabs Klara's hand and heads back to the freight yards. Now a few engines are warming up; steam jetting out of their fired-up engines; their shrill whistles warning anyone trying to board their cars.

"We'll follow the tracks. But be careful. They curve up ahead. Stay close. What did you want to tell me?"

Just as she's about to answer, shotgun blasts puncture the humid morning air in the freight yard and they crouch alongside a cattle-truck at the end of the train whose engine is spouting steam and is about to back up out of the yard.

"Klara. Hurry! The train's going to leave. Quick. Put your hands up onto the ledge. I'll boost you up into the car," says Mischa as he meshes his fingers of each hand into the other, thus forming a makeshift step-up. Throwing the small suitcase up into the car, Klara follows instructions as her muscular brother begins to lift her.

But just then, a loud shotgun blast penetrates the silence.

"Oh God! I've been hit. My leg," shrieks Klara as she flops onto the dusty, straw-laden floor of the car, which has jolted forward.

"Hold on. I'm coming up. Move to the other side of the car, away from the door."

Darting forward, he raises his two hands sideways up onto the raised floor and vaults into the car. Rolling over a few feet, he spots Klara writhing on the floor, both her hands tightly grasping the upper thigh of her left leg. His eyes rivet on the blood.

"Pain's killing me," she groans, her face distorted. "My leg. No more ballet. Damn it..."

He raises her bloodstained dress to the top of her leg so he can get to the impacted area. Her pleading eyes stare at him as the train picks up speed.

"Mischa. I must tell you...."

"Shh, shh," he whispers as he observes the raw skin is open, displaying a wound with ragged edges from which blood is welling up into the opening. "Don't talk. You need all your strength." Ripping off his shirt, he tears a piece of it and presses it against the wound and at the same time, he puts pressure on it to slow down the bleeding. "You're lucky," he says, still trying to comfort the wet-eyed Klara. "Only several pellets from a shotgun that hit your leg."

"Only several," she says sarcastically

Just then, he notices that Klara is also rubbing the spot where a pellet hit her in the abdomen. "I think my stomach, too," she stammers and wiggles a little as she lifts her dress higher, enough so he can see a slight stomach wound."

"Not only are you going to live, but I think it's only a deep cut in the leg from the pellet and a small pellet wound in your stomach."

"Only," she repeats.

Wiping away the blood off her leg wound, he tries to recall what the textbook says about venous bleeding. To stem the bleeding in her leg, he uses his shirt to push further into the gap in her thigh. He continues to apply pressure to slow down the bleeding. Working feverishly, he hasn't had time to ponder the impact of Klara's being shot. Though he's more concerned with her leg, he realizes he has to take care of the wound in her stomach. But in wiping away the pellet that hit her stomach, he cannot see a tiny fragment of dirty clothing that enters the sore.

"It's bad, isn't it?" she says, biting her lip.

"Calm down. Lie still. You'll be fine," he answers, looking around for something to raise her leg. He finds her suitcase and gently places it under her foot.

The shirt bandage is soaked with blood, though the bleeding itself has stopped.

"She'll be fine," he keeps telling himself. "You're going to live, Klara," repeats Mischa as he mimics their mother when one of the children got hurt. He gently removes the blood-soaked piece and throws it into the corner of the boxcar. He then applies a fresh bandage to her leg from what was left of his shirt.

"Drink this. Help you sleep," he says, handing her a small flask of vodka.

Grimacing, she swallows the jolting drink and, raising her hands, pulls Mischa toward her, kissing him on his forehead.

"Will we make it?" she asks, tears rolling down her pale, puffed-up face.

"We'll make it. We'll make it," he answers convincingly.

She's not so sure, however. Silently, she thanks God; it could have been much worse. "With the right therapy, maybe I'll dance again," she prays.

She's trying desperately not to despair. "Listen to your heart," she says to herself, over and over again as the train rumbles and creaks forward toward Irkutsk, about 2,000 miles distant.

For the next few days, her stomach irritates her.

For three days, the train, passing villages replete with birch, aspen, alder, and blank poplars, remains in a stop-and-go mode as it pulls itself alongside golden wheat fields. Wherever the train stops, and that is often, Mischa jumps down, gets water for his canteen, black bread, some potatoes, eggs, vegetables and a few slices of cold meat. The birds of Siberia, hawks, falcons, cranes, eagles, and geese follow Klara and Mischa as they flee to the unknown.

Finally, on the fourth day out of Chelyabinsk, the train halts. A moment later, their cattle-truck door is slid open and two Czech soldiers checking the cars command Mischa and Klara to get off. Although they don't speak or understand Russian, the soldiers comprehend a gift of several hundred rubles to allow Mischa and Klara to remain on the car until Irkutsk. The intruders seal the door and post a sign that reads, "Danger! Explosives on board!"

But the next day, Mischa looks out at a railway yard where he spies a passenger train. Mischa climbs off first; collars two porters to help him; instructs them how to lift Klara out of the boxcar and how to hold her up under her armpits, and leads them all to the train for Irkutsk. Fortunately, few local policemen stand guard in the station yard, which is in a state of chaos. As luck would have it and a few more bribes, Klara and Mischa are once again on the Trans-Siberian railway bound for Irkutsk.

This time, Mischa has secured two seats in a second-class coach that by some miracle was part of the make up of this very long train. So, a day into their continued journey, Mischa can leave Klara in a comfortable seat, get off and buy some more bread, kasha, and vegetables. He pays exorbitant prices with money given to him by his intelligence unit.

"Beat the Reds," says a farmer with sunken, staring eyes to a worker in the street.

"Kill the Jews and save Russia," yells one of the soldiers guarding the entrance to a boarded-up ticket agency.

A shiver runs through Mischa's body. "Always the Jews," he whispers to himself. The cutting wind seeps through the cracks of the wooden car and nips the two sleepy souls cuddling in the corner to keep warm. Her head's resting on his shoulder. For now, brother and sister are one.

Yet, beneath their calm, the two are very anxious. He doesn't know the Siberian city of Irkutsk, where they are headed. How good are the contacts provided him? he wonders. She's worried, too. She's not sure she can walk. Is she going to hobble around the city like a cripple and look conspicuous? And her stomach is starting to hurt. Even though it's spring, cold air moves in at night and that's when her leg hurts most. Reality has set in; she doubts she'll ever dance again.

Maybe I'll become a dance instructor, she thinks.

After a bowl of hot soup at a way station, their diet now includes biscuits, sweet chocolate, candy, and bread. At one stop, Mischa found enough boiled water to brush their teeth, wash, and for him, to shave. He's good at scrounging up food, especially since he has cash that can pay off the extortionate prices of black marketers.

They try to pass away the time, and when the silence gets too overbearing, they talk. But Klara notices Mischa is deep in thought; and she's sure he's thinking of a woman.

She catches him off-guard:

"What's she like Mischa?"

"Don't know. Never really got to know her," he says, realizing he can't hold back from telling Klara of the woman he knew briefly.

"It was in Moscow. Even though I was still in the Red Guards at the time, the Cheka under Comrade Dzerzhinsky invited me to a dinner where Comrade Trotsky was speaking. I was seated at a table with foreign correspondents and Jewish Communists. Waiters brought wine and lamb and rice. After we ate and drank, most of the guests left, I sat there alone for a few minutes.

"Then she came over. She was an officer and she was short. The minute she looked at me I knew her dark eyes were flirting with me. Her face was thin and long, a long short nose below a high brow. Because she didn't smile and I surmised that since she was in the Cheka, she had seen mass summary executions.

"'Do you remember me?' she asked, kissing me on both cheeks.

"'No,' I said, trying to regain my composure, as I was almost standing at attention, stiff as a board for I could tell her rank was high."

"'I don't think we ever met,' I said. 'But never mind. Have a seat, Comrade. Please.'"

"'I didn't know you were a commissar,'"

"I'm not. Just in the Red Guards. Comrade Dzerzhinsky's office asked me to attend. Apparently they're considering me for that post."

And who are you, may I ask?'

"'I'm Olga. And you're Mischa.'

"'I don't remember you, I'm sorry, Comrade officer.'

"'Back in Odessa when you were younger, you once asked me how children were born.'

"I laughed. Her face and body excited me. I wanted to grab her, hug her."

"'Come with me,' she said. We went outside the restaurant. She put her arm through mine. We walked a little and then I took her hand; it was gentle and the sensation thrilled me. We didn't say anything, nothing the whole time. A bright full moon lit our way.

In the morning when I woke up she was gone. I couldn't believe it."

"Continue," said Klara, amazed Mischa was pouring out the whole story.

"I went to Comrade Dzerzhinskys's office. I asked for Comrade Olga."

"'She's gone to the front,' they said."

"I must contact her."

"'Forget her,' whispered the soldier behind the desk.

"'But I can't,' I replied.

"You will,' he said. The strange thing, Klara, is that everywhere I go, I feel like I'm being followed. Not the usual White idiots, but that the entire Red Army itself is behind me. Somebody's watching over me. I've been in too many scrapes. I should be dead now. It could be God; it could be luck; and then again, maybe, just maybe...."

"She'll come back, Mischa. Believe me. If she loves you, she'll come back," says Klara, thinking of Vladimir whom she knows is out there somewhere in central Siberia and whom she's convinced will return to her. When he does, that will be the time to tell Mischa of her lover. For the time being, Vladimir is not around. Why even broach the subject? she thinks. Besides, if Vladimir knows about Mischa, then Mischa probably knows about Vladimir.

As they approach Irkutsk after a little more than a week of travel, they notice larger crowds waiting to board trains. These diseased and starved refugees want to get to Irkutsk, but they don't dare rush the train. Having seized the stations and rolling stock along the railway, the Czechs are in control and they crack heads to protect the line and cars for their own escape eastward.

Even though the Bolsheviks are gone, Klara cowers a bit. "Is this leg ever going to heal?" she asks herself. My god, what did I get into? Got to get out of Russia. Can't stay here. How can I make sure Vladimir comes with me?" she repeats over and over to herself. "Never, never did I dream this journey would be this long."

17

Arrival in Irkutsk. June-July 1918

The Russian Civil War in Siberia is about to begin in earnest. Humanity pours across the many miles of railway track to reach the area beyond the battle lines that keep changing; one day the conflict is further east, the next day west, one day further north, the next day, south. These refugees choose not to live under the Bolsheviks. The country has gone mad, they say. Under Lenin, the Bolsheviks believe the ends justify the means and they are convinced that only with the destruction of the "old order" could anything positive emerge. Red and White reprisals will leap beyond civilized standards. After the incident at the railway station in Chelyabinsk, which ignites the fighting in Siberia, the Czech "presence in Siberia," notes Ian Frazier in *Travels in Siberia*, will become a "wild card" destabilizing the region.

In early June, the Czechs disarm the Bolsheviks and seize power in Samara as well as Ufa. In the next two weeks, the Czechs roll over Red Army units that oppose them all along the railroad. They occupy Chelyabinsk, Penza, Syzran, and Novo-Nikolayevsk. They gain control over a huge zone of the Trans-Siberian railway, including much of the Volga region, the Urals, and Siberia. The Czech action will act as a catalyst for other anti-Bolshevik forces in the area and provoke a general uprising against the Reds all along the rail line.

Meanwhile, in Samara, mid-Volga, KOMUCH, the Committee of the Constituent Assembly, is proclaimed. Its goal: to act in an armed struggle against the Reds by reconvening the Constituent Assembly, restoring legitimate government in Russia, and canceling the Brest-Litovsk Treaty. On June 13, a Provisional Siberian Government is formed in Omsk.

Fighting back, Lev Davidovich Trotsky, (real name, Bronstein) has become war commissar, and commands the Red Army. A spellbinding speaker, he begins to galvanize dispirited troops who also begin to kill for no reason.

The Whites murder Communists and their sympathizers. Exile, death, suppression will be the price they will pay for their killings. The end will come soon for White Generals—General Anton Denikin, Admiral Alexander Kolchak, General Nikolai Yudenich, and General Baron Peter Wrangel who will not break with the policies of the Czar. "They are too firmly rooted in the Old Russia," notes author Orlando Figes.

•

Klara and Mischa are asleep as the bouncing car crawls toward its final stop. They miss the welcome sign just outside the city of Irkutsk. The date is July 15, 1918. The Reds are gone; the Whites hold the city.

Here lie the Asiatic goldfields that begin at the bend of the Angara River, about 3,300 miles from Moscow; the spot where the Irkut and Angara rivers meet. Lake Baikal, the world's deepest fresh water lake, is forty miles away.

Rousing himself from a deep slumber on this humid, blue-sky July morning, Mischa whispers to Klara. "Get up. We're almost there. Look. The Angara River. Look how deep, clear and beautiful it is," exclaims Mischa. "And those houses with gingerbread shutters."

The two stare at the scenery. At early morning's light, Irkutsk's smoking chimneys scatter smog over the dull bungalows made of tarpaper roofs. Blocks of these wooden houses are crowded together. Even with fences and iron gates, they are only a notch above wooden hovels.

Mischa's busy observing the bridge over the Angara River. He notes the railroad runs along the south side of the river, while the city is on the north. He can see the station is connected to the main part of the town by a pontoon bridge.

The two stand and look out at the great banks of fog rising from the water that runs free in the Angara River. They watch the swift-moving current as they travel past green pines, white birch trees, and dilapidated wrecks of boats pulled up onto shore.

The city seems to be talking to them:

"Welcome to Irkutsk, the capital of Siberia, the headquarters of the Trans-Siberian Railway, the largest and most substantial city of Siberia, the 'Paris of Siberia,' the capital of Eastern Siberia and Northern Asia. Here the steppes, the desert, the mountains, rivers, tilled lands, and tundra meet. That's the way teacher Golobochov put it," says Klara.

Mischa knows the city remains a magnet for fur traders, exiles, ex-convicts, prostitutes, and foreign travelers. The stores on the main thoroughfare, Bolshaya, are whitewashed and covered with stucco, green, and white roofs. Flickering oil lamps illuminate the back streets through which pedestrians must grope their way after dark. Bullet holes mark building walls.

He learned from his comrades that the governor has fled and abandoned about 100,000 residents to the fate of the Whites. Even so, life moves on. Amazingly, skating rinks, movie theaters, as well as performances of two professional theater companies are crowded. Gambling houses, saloons, restaurants, and hotels are packed.

"Look over there," shouts Mischa. He points to rings of acrid smoke clouding the blue sky. His eyes scan the horizon. "Must be the mansions of rich merchants. They're the first casualties in this Revolution."

On this morning, however, the city smells of summer with the wind blowing dirt and dust from street to street.

"So we're finally in 'the city of sable and gold,'" whispers Klara. "That's the phrase I used to see in the travel brochures in the Opera House," she says as she rubs sleep from her blood-shot eyes. Her mind hasn't fully absorbed the shooting incident. So she tries to get as excited as a tourist about to enter a new city.

"There's a woman here who knew Papa back in the old days in Zhitomir," Mischa says. "He once told me about her. Family name Ostrofsky. I have her address. I think I know the way. We've got to stay along the back streets. We'll stay there until you can get better."

"Get up. Can you stand? Station's coming up."

When Klara doesn't answer, Mischa, noticing her eyes are moist, lifts her up. She holds onto him like a drowning woman saved by a lifeguard. As the train enters the station, the two see that the streets are beginning to fill up with hundreds of refugees who have slept overnight at the station, or in parks, on benches. Despite the damage and decay, Irkutsk remains lively, full of hustle and bustle in the market. Horses pull rough wooden wagons of peasants; the few who still labor for the landed gentry who have not fled yet.

"Well, you're now halfway between the Urals and the Sea of Japan," Mischa says. "How about that, several thousand miles to Japan and then your long trip across the ocean. How's your leg? Got to get off now. Made a cane for you from a floor plank. Try standing," commands Mischa as the train comes to a screeching halt. As Klara attempts to get up, a blistering hot wind almost fells her. Mischa grabs her before she tumbles. He holds her by the arm. She groans, bites her lips, and stops tearing.

"I'll help you get down. I'll carry you. Hold on." He jumps down onto the gravel below and turns around, his back facing the boxcar. Klara lifts herself down onto his sturdy shoulders and like a camel whose crooked legs move swiftly over desert sands, Mischa begins to lumber step by step toward the station hall.

"Let me down. I'm too heavy for you. I can walk," says Klara after Mischa carries her a few yards. With the aid of the cane and holding on to him, she wobbles slowly through the yard and into the bleak, crowded station.

"You're doing fine," says Mischa, himself still shaky from the rattle and swaying of the train that has made him slightly motion sick.

"Well, what do you know? See. Look over there. A *kiosk*. Probably more food here than back in Moscow that has to import it all from farms. Those farmers aren't dumb either; they hoard crops and hold out for better prices," he explains.

Approaching the kiosk, the two can't believe what they see: Hot pies and bottles of beer. "Hot *pirozhki*," hawks the woman vendor who has hoarded the food and wants to get rid of it fast.

"Two pirozhki," orders Mischa.

"Five rubles.

"Five rubles? A month ago; it was two."

"Last month was last month."

"Speculator. Wait till the Bolsheviks get you."

"Leave it, Mischa. She's got to live, too."

"Don't worry, sister, Lenin, Trotsky, and company'll fix her. If I was in the *Cheka*, I'd ..."

"From what I hear, they kill a lot more people, for a lot less," interrupts Klara who watches Mischa put the rubles into the lady's sweaty hands.

"Let's go," he frowns, cutting off discussion. He doesn't like to get into political discussions with Klara. No one should criticize the Reds in his presence and he shouldn't associate with anyone who does. But for now, an invisible political truce has been established. Neither have the luxury of shopping around for an alternative ideology. Besides, Mischa has decided to play it safe, he believes the Bolsheviks will win and he's got a good job.

They're bleary eyed, their heads drooping. Will tonight be another sleepless night? They must be on the lookout for army deserters who might rob them.

Instantly, an explosion rips the town.

"Get down! Keep low! Let's get to the river docks!" shouts Mischa.

A second boom rocks the area.

"Ammunition dump."

"Let's get out of here."

"Stop. Stop," orders a policeman. "Don't go that way. Go back."

A mother, carrying her infant, runs up to the policeman and grabs him by the arm.

"Save my child. Save her."

Unconscious, the baby is bleeding, the back of her ripped dress already smeared with blood. The policeman at first ignores her. Too much to do. The explosion has unnerved him. He's frightened. What's one more dead child when thousands are dying? He waves her toward a nearby hospital carriage.

"They'll help you. Go!"

Fleeing the depot, Mischa and Klara soon find themselves in a residential area. With the help of a map, Mischa guides them to the Ostrofsky house. A middle-aged woman and her husband welcome them.

"Stay here as long as you want. But you'll have to share a room. So many Jews fleeing the war and the Bolsheviks. Don't worry, the Reds left earlier this month. They still have a lot of guerrillas hiding out here; they cause trouble, like that big explosion at the ammunition dump. But they'll be back. The masses are with them. They promise them everything: 'Bread, peace, land'. They're all lies. They'll turn out to be just as oppressive as the Czar."

"Now people can get out," interrupts Nathan, her husband. "We're a way station; just like it was in the old exile days when princes and princesses came here to serve time. Like them, we're still making false identity papers."

"Nathan, I hate to interrupt," says Mischa, "but Klara needs new railway documents. Could you...."

"No problem, she'll have them in a day or so. And they'll be perfect, I assure you."

She feigns a smile, but behind that serious countenance is the only question on her mind: Where is Vladimir? His letter said he would catch up with her.

18

The Czechs and the Whites still hold Irkutsk and many stations along the Trans-Siberian. They have freed thousands from the grasp of the Reds. But in one place they will be too late. On July 25, Czechs capture Ekaterinburg where Nicholas II, the last Czar and his wife and children were murdered on July 17. History will record that it's the Reds' "last, boastful, glorious act" in Siberia that summer.

•

Klara needs time. She is troubled. The wound has taken its toll. Not for one minute does Vladimir's face exit her mind. She even sees his picture in Mischa's countenance.

"Damn it, my life's a mess. I'll never dance again. I was so good. I could have been a ballerina. At least I could have made the *corps de ballet.* God, I haven't even arrived in Vladivostok and I'm shot. Will I ever get out of Siberia? Will I ever find Papa? What's happening with Momma and the girls? What'll happen to Mischa? To Vladimir? Will this love of mine leave with me? He says he's ready. But is he?" The questions now plague her day and night, especially about the family in Odessa. "Momma pushed me to go. It's not my fault Mischa left. I have to try and makes sure he continues to help them. Didn't Papa say Mischa was the man of the house?"

Klara is still in the room she shares with Mischa in the Ostrofsky house. As long as there's a chance that Vladimir will show up, she'll stay. She sleeps—the deep sleep that comes from not only the weariness of a long day, but from the emotional and physical strain that her wounds have caused her. Always tired and huddled in a quilt blanket, she is depressed and constantly dreams about the shooting incident and that Vladimir is with her—helping her up a long flight of steps. And at the top, awaits Papa.

Once she dreams the family is sitting on cardboard boxes and she escorts Vladimir into the room. Everyone's there to welcome her at the end of a long journey. She introduces him around. As they circulate through the crowd, everyone whispers: "But he's a *goy*. How can that be?" "Wait!" exclaims Klara. "They're sitting *shiva* (mourning period) for me as if I'm dead. I married a *sheigitz* (non-Jew), they say."

107

One night she dreams she's rearranging suitcases in a baggage room. She moves one bag over to the side. Another one on the other side. This one on top. No. Over there. Move the little one. Hour after hour she moves each suitcase until every piece of luggage is perfectly in place. The only trouble: No more baggage rooms. No more baggage cars. No more baggage trains.

One morning, Klara opens the window to let in the fresh morning air. Irkutsk is waking up. The birds of Siberia are chirping. Bright rays of summer-sun warm the house. Falling white flakes float downward. Not snow as in winter; but puffs of fuzz from poplar trees line the town's avenues. Horses trot on cobblestone streets. Life goes on.

About ten days after they arrived in Irkutsk, Klara suffers severe pain, nausea, and a high fever. She notices an abscess has formed on her belly and is draining. Mischa and Mrs. Ostrofsky are besides themselves and the pair decide to take her to the local hospital, which, though full up with war wounded, does treat some civilian cases depending on how important the personage. Mrs. Ostrofsky has connections. Mischa waits outside.

After a few hours, the doctor examines Klara and observes the healing scars on her leg and abdomen. "What happened here?" he asks.

She explains that she suffered a gunshot wound boarding a train in Chelyabinsk for Irkutsk. "I had an abscess on my stomach," she says, pointing to her lower stomach, "from that wound inflicted on me about two weeks ago. And early this morning, just before I saw the abscess was beginning to drain, I had severe pain in my stomach. I was nauseous and threw up. They tell me I was running a high fever," she informs the doctor.

The doctors realize that in this case, the deep abscess that formed on her stomach peculiarly drained into her abdominal cavity. After a further evaluation, he explains to her that this likely produced adhesions in her abdomen that not only will be a source of discomfort for the rest of her life, but could lead to an inability to conceive.

"Doctor! Do you mean that I can't get pregnant?" she asks.

"I didn't say that exactly. But it's very possible that the infection in the abdominal cavity damaged your tubes and will prevent pregnancy. If that is so, I'm so sorry," he says, not looking directly at Klara and quickly turning away.

From that moment on, the young girl from Odessa, now trapped in Irkutsk, realizes she can never be a mother.

The doctor has no time to further console her: What's a female's inability to have children got to do with the murder that is occurring in the civil war throughout Russia and soon will engulf Irkutsk?

The nurses treat her with medicine. But for the rest of the day, Klara will turn her head toward the wall. No tears come as she says to herself, "How will I tell Vladimir?"

A day later she is discharged. They need her bed.

As they bide their time, Klara begins to walk better, albeit with a slight limp. Mischa gives Mrs. Ostrofsky extra money to feed them, though the diet often consists of just above a quarter-pound bread ration and *shchi* (cabbage soup) and *kasha* (porridge).

Sometimes when she's alone, she picks up a prayer book and recites prayers. Her lips move and her body sways. She's praying with purpose, so far away from home. "God, please bring Vladimir back to me. I love him so. Let him be well. Let us get to America together. Help me find father. Help Momma and my sisters back in Odessa. And yes, stand by Mischa."

On nice days, Klara roams the streets, careful, suspicious. One day she walks into a general store looking for clean gauze bandages. But when the clerk says, "excuse me for a minute," and walks to the rear of the shop and begins talking to another clerk and both of them stare at Klara as they engage in hush-hush conversation, Klara leaves. She takes no chances.

Summer moves on. Every day more refugees knock on the door of the Ostrofsky House. "They all look like death warmed over," Klara says to herself, noticing that their clothes are dirty, their faces almost blackened, their eyes half-closed. Usually, their first words are: "Help us. Give us some food. Please get us out of Russia."

"What a night," says Mischa returning home early one morning from reconnoitering the railway station. "I was in a bar trying to pick up some information when I overheard three soldiers talking about a house of ill-repute, as they put it. I couldn't get over the description of the madame. He said she was beautiful, young, attractive, a Jewess, no less. But no fooling around with her. She's a tough lady. Yet customers want her above all others, though she doesn't oblige. Rachel was her name. Didn't get her last name. Wait. Golobetsky, an Odessean. Klara. My goodness, you look white. Are you're going to faint?"

"Where's that house? How'd you get there? Take me there."

"No. Definitely not."

"Mischa. Have you forgotten? You're my brother. Can't let me go alone on dangerous streets. You must take me," she says, in a commanding voice. "I have to see this *devushka*! Let's go. Now!"

"Are you kidding? Take you. Respectful women don't go there. Even to visit. Absolutely not!"

As soon as the sun set, brother and sister set out for "Relaxation House," at 19 Centralskaya Street. The night is black and they have to tread slowly. Mischa constantly looks around, eyes right, eyes left, up to the roofs of the darkened buildings. He holds Klara's hand as they walk, careful not to fall into the deep potholes. Dogs howl. Cats scamper. Only their footsteps are heard on the desolate street.

As they walk, Klara keeps repeating to herself: "I can't believe this. A Jewish girl, a prostitute? Preposterous. You know what the Bible says about a prostitute: 'Her punishment is death.'"

•

The two girls fall into each other's arms, hugging and kissing and crying as Mischa goes back out to the lobby and the two move into Rachel's private welcoming room.

"Am I glad I found you."

"Should've stayed with me," says Klara with a cross look on an otherwise happy face.

"You're right. Should've," replies Rachel, wiping fresh tears from her eyes. "Guess like you, I'm stubborn. You weren't so nice either. After all, I did help you; even gave you a comfortable place to sleep on the train and you desert me."

"I guess you want to know how I got here. I came to Irkutsk to find my sister. But she had left for America, via Shanghai. I could have accompanied you all the way to Moscow, but I wanted to head to Kharkov. What I didn't tell you then was that I was interested in someone. But he cleared out, too. The army later picked him up. In Kharkov, I had a lot of problems. Another fellow I knew from high school befriended me. We traveled together. He was so sweet. I fell for him. He convinced me it'd be safer if he kept my money.

"One morning, he said we had to get out of our room. He had to look for another hotel. Found one. We stayed a few nights there. Then he said he was going downstairs to find out if the trains were running to Irkutsk. Never saw him again. Took all my money."

"That wasn't the worst of it. I tried to sneak out of the place. You see the room hadn't been paid for. But the owner caught me. He was going to kill me because my boyfriend ran up a large drinking bill. He called a policeman. Would have taken me to jail. You know what happens to young girls in jail."

"'You can satisfy the claim, without a judge,'" the policeman told me, a sneer on his face. "I'll never forget that face, that grin. The bastard."

"Rachel come with me," says Klara, reaching out and drawing Rachel closer. "If you want to live, get out now."

"And leave all this behind? Never."

"If you don't ... when the Bolsheviks arrive; they'll kill you. You're the hated *bourgeoisie;* you're decadent and a private trader, no less. My brother Mischa's watching over me. He's brave. He'll guard you, too. He's got influence. He's waiting downstairs."

"There's something else I've got to tell you," continues Klara, finding herself pouring out the thoughts that occupy her mind every minute of the day. "I found someone. He's everything to me. Haven't told Mischa yet. Something happened; his unit got called up in Chelyabinsk. He's out there somewhere. I know he is. He'll help us, too."

"Klara, I'm so happy for you."

"Rachel!" interrupts Klara. "Please. Listen. Someone's bound to get you. They'll kill you if you don't give them what they want."

"Not me," she answers. "When it comes to what we do, there's no ideology. I don't know what it is, but when you show them what you've got on your chest and between your legs, they go nuts. Red or White," she snickers. "I rule them all. I'm the Czarina, their commissar. After I got here, I realized I had no place to go. No money. The owner fled when the Whites moved in. The girls liked me. They loaned me money. They knew I could manage. They think every Jew's an entrepreneur. I'm now a whore-business lady manager. But I don't get into bed with customers."

"But just to be around this place is demoralizing," counters Klara. "It'll only lead to trouble. Wrong element. And the police? What a joke. You warned me of cops and soldiers. Look what happened to you because of those bastards?"

"You're forgetting one thing that I didn't have back in that hotel. Money. Money corrupts. We give out bribes. We do it every day. I can buy my way out any time. Anyway, please come back tomorrow. Got to work now. They'll begin to come in later and I've got to get things in order. They'll want to pick up a girl for their little ecstasy."

The two began walking hand-in-hand down the hallway of the top floor; a long, dark corridor leading back to small rooms, each one with heavily beaded curtains serving as a temporary door.

Out of the corner of her eye, Klara spies a woman slipping out of her dress. Wearing black silk underpants and a black silk bra to match, she's starring in the mirror and gazing at her figure; moving her head back, constantly turning her body, her eyes focused on her thin frame.

"How sad," Klara thinks to herself. "It's almost as if she's checking herself out for an imaginary husband, instead of a drunk that's coming later. Could happen to anyone. God forbid."

"I'll come back tomorrow evening," she tells Rachel. "But who knows in this crazy world what will be by then."

A final embrace and then Klara pulls away, and without looking back, heads down the steps to meet Mischa.

Meanwhile, Mischa has been waiting for Klara in the large lobby reception room. The pale green walls with their frightening crucifixes and mysterious candles to protect the ladies as they sleep; ladies who dream of a different life: that of a housewife, a nanny, a society lady, anything but lying on their backs with their legs wide open.

Mischa watches out for "beauties" shuffling along the carpeted floors and staircase in this two-story brick mansion. But he only sees what he calls "ugly ones," when a tall, pock-faced Buriat walks over to him.

"Excuse me. Got a match?" asks the newcomer, obviously a native of the area. He towers above Mischa, who quickly summons up the match, lights the cigarette, and stares at the face of the Buriat native with high cheekbones, slightly slanted eyes, a rough pockmarked face, and a somewhat groomed moustache. The man smiles as he inhales the first puff of the cigarette. Playing with a small, wooden talisman, he draws in the smoke again and the drag seems to give him energy as it does to the addicted after reaching for a cigarette even before they completely open their eyes at dawn.

"By the way, what did they do here, import the ladies from an ugly convent?" says Mischa, stressing the word *ugly*. "I haven't seen a decent one yet."

The Buriat laughs, as he leans close to Mischa. "When you're on top of them in darkness, they all look same. You don't even have to see their faces. So, it doesn't matter if they're beautiful or ugly."

"You're right," laughs Mischa.

"I'm Hamid, medical inspector. No need to explain what I do."

"I'm Mischa. Glad to meet you. I'm waiting for my sister," he adds, pausing. "Oh no. Nothing like that. Banish the thought. She doesn't work here. She's visiting a friend, the Madame, I'm embarrassed to say."

The two talk about the war, about the future of the country, about their lives. "If you ever need anything, contact me. Come to our village; it's called 'Little Lena.' Ask for Hamid. No questions asked," he says. " I'd like you to know that we also hide people and get them across the border. For a fee of course, I'm telling you this in confidence. I trust you."

"Understood," says Mischa.

"Please excuse me, I'll be back in a few moments. Have to take care of a few business matters upstairs," Hamid says jokingly. "No, not what you're thinking. Just a short exam."

Mischa stares at the man. He believes he's sincere.

"Oh, if I could only just sit here," he reflects. "I'd be on another planet. No war, no hunger. No worries. Away from everything." He's afraid thugs are hijacking the Revolution and he's bothered by Comrade Trotsky's words. "Better to kill ten innocents, than to let one guilty go free. Create terror. Let them disappear. No one will know what happened to them."

But for now he does nothing, though he realizes that soon even his stash of cash will be depleted. Klara has to move on; there's no future for her here.

Hamid returns. After Mischa introduces the Buriat to Klara, brother and sister leave the building and head back to their room. He can tell from Klara's down look that Rachel won't budge.

The silence is broken by bloodcurdling screams.

"Mischa. What's that? Look up. There. On the roof. In front of that building. A priest. He's scanning the rooftop. I guess he's trying to bless that group on the edge. Yelling up to them. The guards are shouting up at them, too."

"We're dying of hunger," a man screams from the roof.

"The belfry in this Hermitage holds an isolation cell in the monastery," explains Mischa. "Prisoners are tied up. Abandoned for hours in the freezing cold. Some manage to cut their ropes and get out on the ledge. The priest obviously wants to stop them. That's why he climbs up to the roof, reaches the edge, and attempts to prevent them from leaping."

"Look at that one. He's crossing himself. Oh God. He's jumping," cries Klara burying her head in Mischa's shoulders.

Mischa stares. The man descends; his arms and legs flailing in mid-air.

"Let's get out of here." But Klara does not move. She is quiet. She has buried her head on Mischa's chest. Silent. No tears. He stands still for a minute to let her catch her breath. "Klara! Let's go. Please."

"Fine," she answers, wiping a tear or two from her eyes. Neither utters a word as they walk slowly back toward Ostrofskys' house.

Soldiers run past them toward the monastery.

"I can't take this anymore," Klara whispers to Mischa.

"You must. This is our life. Shootings, suicides, hunger, death, and disappearance. It's in the air we breathe. Don't get depressed over it."

"I'm beyond depression, Mischa. I'm numb."

"Let's go," he pleads again.

They start walking. Only now, Klara, usually talkative, is speechless.

Mischa waits. He senses she has something on her mind.

"What I don't understand," says Klara "is that over and over again, people ask for trouble. How could a person ruin herself? Even more stupid, Rachel thinks she can use her body as a weapon. One day some drunken peasant'll kill her."

"People do strange things. They punish themselves," answers Mischa.

"Me, too," she replies, realizing she must divulge what she has been trying to tell him for such a long time. She can't hold it back anymore. When he mentions "punishment," especially to one's self, it unleashes the secret.

"I have to find someone, Mischa," she blurts out. "I've lost a month."

He keeps a straight face and is silent.

"Mischa. I've a boyfriend. He's wonderful. You'd like him. A patriot. Works for the Red Cross. Educated and from a good family, too."

She dare not disclose that Mischa and Vladimir actually met in Chelyabinsk, the day she was hiding under the bed.

"Should have told you about him before."

"All this time you didn't say anything," says Mischa, trying to act the big brother and show he's a little hurt, though truthfully, he's touched she's finally telling him. "Nice you're confiding in me. One question: He's not Jewish, is he?"

"How did you know?"

"I'm not stupid. I listened. You told me all his qualities. I know if Papa and Momma were here, that would have been their first question. So I began playing the Momma and Papa card."

"What's the difference? Shouldn't matter to you," responds Klara angrily, raising her voice. "Besides, since you're in the Red Guards, you really believe like them. No religious garbage for you. 'Religion'll disappear in the new Russia. We'll all be one.' You've said it a million times: 'Religion's the opiate of the people.' Didn't Comrade Marx say that?"

Mischa doesn't answer.

Hesitating for a moment or two, trying to gather her thoughts, Klara finally blurts out: "Papa'd be ashamed of me. I know it. Marrying a *goy* is like betraying family, like murdering them. Cursed forever. Talked about for generations."

"Don't overdo it, Klara. Don't be so melodramatic. From what I've heard, if you take your boyfriend to America, they'll love him. They're not that religious there. All they care about is surviving in a new country where at least it's safe and probably easy to assimilate."

"Guess you're right. If Americans don't care about idealism, why do you?"

"No. On the contrary, it's the wrong kind of idealism. I now think communism is better; we want to change the lives of the masses who live in poverty and ignorance. Sure, some don't like what they're doing in Moscow, reign of terror and all that. But what choice do we have. At least the Reds are better than those Jew-hating Czarists. Somebody has to save Russia from them. At least I can do my part."

"Who are you? God?"

"Shh. Not so loud. You want to get both of us shot?"

"Mischa! How can I make you understand. None of this interests me. I've got to leave so I can find Vladimir. I can't do it alone," she says, hating herself because she's pleading with him.

Ah, that's it, he realizes. *She wants my help to find the boyfriend.*

"Come with me," she starts again. "Once we find Vladimir, we'll all go. He's certainly not committed, even to the Red Cross, though he wants to help people, too. We can make it to Vladivostok and avoid the civil war."

Mischa's silent. He's listening. *A new Klara?* he wonders. *Now she wants me to be with her and with her boyfriend. What else does she have hidden in that brain of hers? Why couldn't she have offered this 'togetherness' sooner, way back in Odessa?*

Mischa never completes his thoughts. Out of nowhere, the shrill sound of a train leaving Irkutsk, rings out. The blast signifies freedom; a chance to move forward, a little further from this gruesome war. "Far off is the train. So's the journey. So's the destination," he reflects.

The two keep walking. Each is lost in deep thought. "I've come this far. I'm not stopping." Klara says to herself. "Who comes first, Papa or Vladimir? No matter. Who says I have to decide at this time. Right now I need both, can't do without either."

Mischa says nothing more, but he's troubled. Despite his new ideology that religion will disappear in the new Soviet state and we're all one, he doesn't like Klara running around with a non-Jew. *Papa would never sanction it, and since I'm the man of the house, I've got to stop this relationship and I will. Yet I've got to help her, too*, he decides. *Don't want to, but I must. She's my sister; too much blood. Without me, she's lost. If I can get her to safety, everyone in the family will see how great I am. And that I would have been a better choice to find Papa.*

"Here's the tram back to the center of the city. Let's go," he says as he lifts Klara up onto the first step. "When we get off, let's walk along the river to the café. From there, I can see the train station. Been watching it for days."

"Still the intelligence agent, eh?"

"Don't be so sarcastic, even though you are a Rasputnis. You know what I'm doing."

Mischa helps Klara off the tram. They reach the café; grab two seats and order two *chai*.

Without warning, a shattering explosion rocks their area.

"The train station's been hit. Damn it!" shouts Mischa.

More loud booms.

"Out of here. Quickly," screams the café manager. "Can't you see? Bolsheviks. They're back. They're returning. A revolt."

"Run to the factory," he instructs a young boy. "Tell your father, the Reds are here. He'll know what to do."

"What's going on?" Klara asks the café owner again.

"Bolshevik guerrilla unit. They're on the outskirts of the city. Quick. Move. Look over there. Here comes trouble."

Klara and Mischa turn and see workers stream out of a nearby factory.

"To arms. To arms," yells a tall laborer brandishing a revolver. "Workers of all countries, unite!" he shouts, his eyes wild with rage.

A policeman, running up besides Klara and Mischa, is saying something they can't hear because of loud shrieks. Just then, the policeman falls. Withering on the pavement, his hand covers his chest as blood streams into the cobblestone cracks.

Shouts of "Hurrah!" come from the crowd as they charge forward. Mischa knows they'll trample Klara if they're not stopped. Out of the corner of his eye, he sees that the policeman is dead; the officer lies there, his arms over his head; his legs bent in half.

Mischa spots the man who shot him. The tall one with a fake smile on his face. "That one," he says to himself as he pulls Klara behind him.

"What am I to do now? Can't kill a comrade," is the thought racing through his mind at that instant. But he knows he must in order to save himself and Klara from the stampeding mob. Other police officers are shooting at other workers. "Get back!" they shout.

Leading the riot and coming closer to Mischa and Klara, the leader of the mob raises his arm to fire.

But a second later, he grits his teeth, his facial muscles tighten, his mouth opens. Stopped in his tracks, he falls over on his back, his eyes staring up at the sky.

Seeing their leader dead, the workers stop, draw back and flee in all directions.

Revolver in hand, Mischa runs over to check the body. Looking at his pock-marked face, his dirty, bloody shirt, he mumbles to himself. "What could I do? I had to save Klara."

The police rush to congratulate the civilian sharpshooter. Mischa quickly digs out his White identity pass: "I'm one of you, agent of the former *Okhrana*," he assures them.

"Thanks friend," says an officer, glancing at the documents.

"Did you see what happened? When you got their number one, they ran for it. Besides, it's only rumor the Reds are coming. Nothing so far."

Mischa drags the body to the side of the road where it will be picked up. He's not worried about the police questioning him where he got his revolver. He's concerned that one of the workers who just may have seen him in the past and recognized him will tell the Party. They'll ask questions. "Did you have to kill a comrade?"

"Klara. Let's go. Got to get out of here. If other White soldiers come, they might have my description. Even if they don't, the Red underground eventually will take over the city and they'll remember that I killed their leader. No matter if I tell them I had to protect my cover, they'll kill me, too. Go. Leave without me. The situation will only get worse. The trains are chaotic."

"I'm not going without Vladimir," she repeats. "Like I said, you two can team up. We'll get to America. To Papa. We'll bring Momma and the girls over."

"I can't leave Russia," replies Mischa impatiently.

And with that, she believes he'll never go. She's losing faith in him.

19

Klara Discovers Family Secrets, Irkutsk, August 1918

During August 1918, the Siberian war expands. Cossacks have set up independent fiefdoms. These forces will soon welcome the Allied "interventionists," which include Greeks, Italians, Americans, British, and Japanese. Entering Russia, these nations say they only want to protect Allied supplies in Siberia against German seizure. Most of the Allies, however, want to intercede in the civil war on behalf of the Whites.

•

The Czechs and the Whites control Irkutsk. The Reds have not attacked. All the more reason for Mischa to plead again with Klara to go now. He knows they're coming. But like his sister, he's too blunt. Timing is not one of his virtues.

One morning as they finish a light breakfast, coffee and a piece of black bread, Mischa says, "Klara, you must move from here. Get ready. I know a Buriat soldier. Met him when we visited Rachel. You can go with him. They're Mongolian nomads and they're intelligent. Their leader is a *shaman,* a type of witch doctor. They'll take care of you. They won't bother you. Hide with them for a while. And then he'll take you across the border.

"Alright already. I'll go!" snaps Klara, her anger rising toward this brother of hers, who clearly won't help her find Vladimir. "You're a nag. Always interfering in my life. I can't take it anymore. Leave me alone. You're a pest; you just want me out of the way."

Her eyes bear down on him. Out come all the hurts.

"You did that in Odessa, too. You're just jealous because Momma chose me. She had no faith in you. And did you ever prove it," she sneers. "You ran out on her. You've offered up all the excuses, but you even told me you left the day after I got on the train in Odessa."

"You ungrateful bitch. How many times have I saved your ass? More than that *sheigitz* boyfriend of yours."

She slaps him. The sting hurts and loosens his tongue.

"Go already," Mischa says, raising his voice. "I don't give a damn about you anymore. You're not my sister, anyway. You're ..."

Silence.

"I'm not what?"

"Nothing."

"Don't give me that. Out with it."

"It's nothing."

"You're not going anywhere unless you tell me," says Klara getting up, moving to the edge of the room. Turning around, she places her back up against the door. She folds her hands across her slightly heaving bosom. Her eyes burst with anger.

"What are you? A guard at a prisoner of war stockade?" laughs Mischa in a mocking yet agitated tone.

"Better tell me the truth. Out with it, you bastard," and she raises her hand, ever so slightly, but enough to warn Mischa, who though stronger physically, flinches. He knows this has gone too far already.

"Don't get crazy. I just lost my temper."

"Okay. Let's start over. 'I'm not your sister,'" she says, shaken by the very words coming out of her mouth. Standing resolute in front of the door, she, too, is not sure what this'll lead to; nor that she ought to know.

"Well, I guess you might as well know," he says, resigned now to tell the whole story.

"I'm waiting."

"Before I ran away to join the army; actually the day after you left, I needed some official papers. So I began rummaging through Papa's desk and found documents, wedding and birth certificates that ..."

"Go on."

"Can't."

"You already have. Just continue," she demands, realizing that once again she has power over this so-called strongman who's not weak, nor easily frightened by a bully. But he's afraid of her and she knows it. Yet, he wants to inflict damage, some kind of damage on this sister of his who has rejected and often trounced him.

"Go ahead. Come to the point," she says in that commanding tone.

"Well," he starts up again, hesitating, and then, after a deep breath, blurts it all out: "What I surmised from the documents was that we've got the same father. But our mother, Zlota; well, she's not your mother; at least not your real mother. Your mother is a woman named Gitel. A letter from Papa to a relative in Canada that was returned says she didn't want to be a mother or wife, so she ran out of him one night and fled to America and left him alone with an infant just a few weeks old. You're that baby. You were born in Zhitomir. Papa couldn't stay there. Disgraced, he moved to Odessa with you. Then he married Zlota, our mother or should I say, your stepmother. All the documents show me and the girls were born in Odessa. That's it."

Klara moves away from the door and sits down on a chair.

"Keep going," she says.

"No more. That's it."

"What's the woman's last name? My so-called real mother?"

"Gitel Kaganovich was the name in the documents."

"I don't believe this," responds Klara flatly, who has learned not only to challenge, but to put the opposite party on the defensive. You're making all this up. Like the Freiden brothers. One of them spread the rumor that the other was adopted. That's what you're doing."

"I wish it were so."

"What else did you find out?"

"Listen Klara. I didn't mean to tell you. Honest. But you get under my skin. Believe me. You're my sister; well, half-sister, anyway. At least, we've got the same father and the same temper," he adds, trying to make a joke of it. "I promise I'll never tell a soul. Nobody. Believe me."

"Sure! Till the next time we'll argue again and you'll shout it from the rooftops. That's when the secret'll come out, during a fight. "Wait. This can't be true. Momma never treated me differently. Not once. She even favored me over you. Nobody ever said anything. No whispers. I even overheard Momma and Papa violently arguing, but this ridiculous yarn of yours never surfaced."

The two sit quietly. And then Klara bursts into tears. "She's not my real mother. Where is this woman, Gitel? Got to find her," she utters between sobs.

"But how could she leave me? Why didn't she fight for me? A mother's supposed to keep her child. Men run away and leave their families, women don't! Why did she give me up? My real mother's not my mother. I have a stepmother who has been better to me than a real mother. Doesn't make sense," she decides finally. "I'll find her. Papa'll know where she is," Klara's voice cracks. Outwardly, she has succeeded in putting on a determined face toward Mischa, but inwardly, her stomach is churning at his disclosure that her real mother's in America. "Yes," she repeats, now softening her tone somewhat, "I've got to reach Papa.

Klara looks out the large window in the small room and gazes out at children playing in the street as the sun dims. Black clouds have set in. The sight of the boys and girls triggers a remembrance of long ago when she was so young, naïve and innocent; when she believed every classmate who came up to her and whispered in her ear, "I'll tell you a secret, but you'd better keep it quiet. Promise you won't tell."

She didn't repeat it, but the youngsters in her class did. Mischa will talk. Of that she's sure.

"I'm leaving," Klara tells Mischa. "Not with your Buriat either. I'm going to find Vladimir. The two of us will go to America. Not you. I've got to find Papa. He'll straighten this out. Now get out of my sight. I never want to see you again, especially after you insulted my love and you deserted Momma and the girls. You're just a jealous little baby because I went."

He waves her off. He's used to her outbursts. She has hardened him, too.

"I'm leaving also. You're on your own," he says. "And look who's talking about Momma. You didn't have to go. You could have stayed and helped her."

"You're right. I had ballet. I should have stayed. She forced me to go. And don't forget, because I went with you from Chelyabinsk on the train, I got shot. No more ballet. No children. You're bad luck to me. Go, already."

Mischa changes clothes. He has three black Russian shirts that button at the neck. He puts one of them on and then pulls on his black pants, steps into his boots, and fixes his workers cap tightly on his head. He packs underwear, a pair of dark pants, socks, and a sweater. By this time, he's furious. As he leaves the room, he slams the door behind him. The loud bang startles Klara.

"Take that, you bitch," he shouts from outside the door, making sure she hears his angry words.

A minute later, a heavy barrage of artillery booms out in the distance. Stunned for the second time that day, tired and alone, her mind full of anger, she wants to cry, to get it all out. But she can't. So she does what other depressed people often do in times of stress, she crawls back into bed, pulls up the covers over most of her head, and wonders if Mischa himself has given the command for those army guns to commence firing.

"He's capable of it," she thinks. She hates him so, especially when he is out of sight.

That night, after forcing herself to sleep, she wakes up in a cold sweat, shouting, "Papa, Papa!" She hugs the wet pillow as the shells land closer and closer.

20

Train to Chita, August 1918

As Klara proceeds east toward Chita, the Czechs continue to disarm the Bolsheviks. The anti-Communist KOMUCH, more radical than the Siberian Government in Omsk, is based in Samara and holds on along the Volga. Both the Siberian Government and KOMUCH form armies to fight the Reds.

Despite ideological differences, the Siberian Government and KOMUCH set up a five-man Directory composed of radical socialists and sympathizers. But dissension and party differences quickly make the Directory ineffectual. It's only a matter of time until it falls.

•

A whole nation is on the move. By horse-drawn sleigh or train, they are heading east toward Chita, capital of the Transbaikal territory and about 700 miles from Irkutsk. Klara believes if she can get to Chita, she'll make it. She and fellow refugees want to land into the hands of the "interventionists."

After she buys a ticket to Chita for five rubles, she waits for the whistle of the train. Finally, she boards an incoming train and closes her eyes, inhales a deep breath, and holds back tears as she hears shots fired from a car behind her. "Just a few seconds more and we'll be out of range. Chita here we come," she says anxiously.

However, danger from bandits looking for Jews will not leave her. A leader of one of the Jewish youth groups moves up and down the aisles of Klara's car and hands out small Orthodox crosses on a chain to all the Jewish women. "If soldiers board, quickly put this on and let it show," he tells Klara.

Later that night, replacement train guards come on board and move Klara to an empty compartment in an old coach car that inexplicably she now has to herself. The soft rocking of the train brings sleep for the night.

Early in the morning, she is woken by a white-haired, drunken Russian Orthodox priest with thick lips who staggers into her compartment. He's so bent over, he doesn't notice her. Klara is silent. He occupies the seat across from her and stretches out on his back. As he puts his hand on the front of his pants and unbuttons his fly he pulls out his red penis; she realizes it's the image of the red moon she sometimes sees in her sleep. She turns in disgust as this man of the cloth starts to masturbate right in front of her.

Literally leaping out into the corridor, she shouts: "Do something, please. Arrest him. Get him out of here!" she screams at several soldiers who try to calm her. She tells them the priest exposed himself. But Klara hasn't learned yet that a drunk—no matter a priest or general—is treated patiently and tenderly in Russia.

The troops talk to the priest who now has buttoned up his pants. He insists he hasn't done anything and says he's entitled to stay. He doesn't want to trade in his ticket for another compartment.

"The priest shouldn't be harmed," says an officer, now alone with Klara.

"Even in war time, a priest doesn't act like that," Klara snaps back, furious at the trooper's response and shocked at her standing up to a soldier in such an angry tone.

"Who the hell are you to talk about priests, you lousy *zhid*," screams the officer and raises his hand to slap her.

"Easy, sir. I meant no harm," replies Klara flashing an ingratiating smile and at the same time reaching down into her blouse and pulling out her cross.

He lowers his hand.

"As you can see, I'm no zhid, either," she says, opening her small purse and retrieving a twenty ruble note and quickly crumbling it into the soldier's hands.

"Alright," says the trooper, putting the ruble note into his pocket. Taking the priest by the arm, he leads him out back down the passageway.

A half-hour later, however, the man of the cloth returns.

"Go away. Please," pleads Klara, this time in a softer voice.

He doesn't leave. He won't move. The soldiers come back again. Another 20-ruble note to the officer who declares: "Take him to the baggage car and this time, lock him up."

"Hope I don't have to give out any more *bakshish*. Only 40 rubles left," whispers Klara.

As the train crawls through valleys of cedar and pine trees and crosses numerous small streams, Klara notices that the engine, huffing and puffing, climbs steeply and then snakes downward to give her the first glimpse of Lake Baikal, which every Russian knows is the oldest, deepest freshwater lake in the world, holding one-fifth of all the freshwater on the planet, more than any other single lake in the world.

The sparkling water calms the passengers and their hunger as the train curves sharply around the valley and descends nearly up to the water's edge and as it does so, Klara, whose stomach is beginning to rumble from lack of nourishment the past couple of days, nods off until a short while later, a sharp jolt jars her peaceful rest.

"Everyone off the train. Out. Quick."

"Here we go again," says Klara, noticing that her companion in the compartment is once again the drunken priest.

She rises to summon the guards. Before she can react, however, the man is on the floor, trying to kiss her feet.

"In the name of Christ, forgive me," he pleads, beating his chest.

Embarrassed, she doesn't know what to do. She's about to say 'stop mentioning Christ,' when she remembers the silver cross around her neck outside her blouse.

"Please get up."

"I have sinned. I have sinned."

"Come now. We have to get off the train."

"I'm Father Andrei. Please forgive me."

"Don't worry, Father. I won't turn you in," she says, noticing he continues to make the sign of the cross. Proudly holding her amulet, she rubs it gently as she follows the priest down the corridor and off the train. She calculates he can now be her protector, especially from the soldier she bribed.

As they exit the train, the priest is all smiles now. He is pleased to be accompanied by a young girl. He now has a cover, too: A grandfather-priest traveling with his granddaughter.

"Quick. Quick. Into the station hall," shout the guards, dividing the crowd into small groups. A station sign informs them they are in Slyudyanka, right at the edge of Lake Baikal, but the passengers know they won't be allowed to run down and dip their hand into the water for good luck. That's for tourists.

"What's going on Father?" asks Klara as they all sit down on the cold floor of the hall.

"Don't know. Too quiet."

Someone at the entrance shouts. "The Reds are coming."

"How can that be?" asks Klara. "We're too far away from the front."

"Maybe they're not Reds," replies Father Andrei. "Partisans, bandits, Cossacks. Take your pick. They're all the same," he says pointing to a piece of black bread in his rucksack. She picks it up and quickly devours it.

"Whoever they are; here they come," says the priest.

Klara notices their caps have no insignia. That's odd, she thinks, because in this part of Siberia, every group stakes out a claim to a land area and marks it with their emblem.

"They're young," she observes. "Black moustaches and no gray hair."

One of the soldiers, a teenager, approaches the priest and asks: "How old are you, Grandpa?"

"Sixty-eight," answers the clergyman.

At that moment, there's a buzz in the room as an officer enters.

"Sorry. We've got to leave. Sentry, tell those people we'll be back."

The teenager is instructed to stay behind for a few moments to guard the group. He moves his rifle this way and that. His hand is shaking as he lights a cigarette. He's waiting. But as he lingers, he continues to stare at the old man. He does not look at Klara who averts his eyes.

"We're moving on," he says, though he remains still, somewhat mesmerized. Someone outside yells: "Soldier. Come. We're going."

"How old are you Grandpa?" asks the youngster again.

"Sixty-eight and I'm not afraid to die."

"Who says I'm going to kill you?" he replies, again turning toward Father Andrei. He crosses himself, unaware that his comrades have departed. He's alone. He has willed it that way.

A shot rings out. People later say the young lad's face looked surprised, shocked, as if he couldn't believe that someone would do this to him.

He slumps to the floor.

"Let's go," says Father Andrei who with one hand puts the small, gold-plated pistol back in his pocket and with the other hand, offers to lift Klara up from the floor.

"*Nyet, Spasibo* (no, thanks). I can get up myself," she says, her face noticeably angry.

With one hand, she pushes against the wall and rises, not willing to tell the bearded one that she refuses his hand; maybe, just maybe, that's the one he used when masturbating.

Shocked into reality, Klara wants to attack the priest, a murderer, clad in ministerial garb, with the huge cross woven into his peasant blouse.

As he walks past the dead soldier, Father Andrei crosses himself.

For several hours, after they board the train headed toward Chita, not a word is exchanged between the two.

Klara is beside herself. She can't get over the fact that the man now sitting across from her actually whipped out a pistol and shot the trooper. The scene is so horrific to her that she begins to shake. "Maybe he'll kill me, too. What was I thinking when I got off the train with him back there? Maybe he'll just turn out to be an 'elder one,' a *startsy*. Most are good, honest men who wear rags and chains and renounce the world for meditation and prayer. This one's a murderer. He must have hypnotized the lad. I witnessed it. That's why the youth kept asking, 'How old are you, Father?'"

The scene back at the station continues to haunt her.

"Damn it," she says to herself as she looks at the priest, now dozing. "He's another Rasputin, the hated monk, the debaucher who had mystic powers over the late Czarina, and could hypnotize people. I should leave the train now," she repeats to herself, though she does not move. "Why am I hesitating? Damn it, Klara. Get up."

"How can I," she rationalizes. "Where would I go? We're in the middle of nowhere, far from Chita and the train's moving fast. 'What do I do? Jump?'"

She's afraid that if she gets up, she'll wake Father Andrei. "Leave sleeping dogs lie," she concludes.

But he awakens.

"Oh, precious one, thank goodness you're here," says the priest excitedly as he rouses himself and wipes his bulging eyes with his dirty sleeve. "You look tired my child," he tells Klara, running his hand over her upper arm as he tries to sooth her. "I'll get some tea from someone I know in the next car. Back in a minute. We'll eat something. You must be famished."

"Tea'll be good, and some food, too. I'm starved," responds Klara, realizing that she hasn't eaten since the previous day.

Moments later, the priest returns to the compartment. "Here, drink this. Hot tea. Some more black bread, too; it'll do you good."

He hands Klara a small loaf and when she takes it, his electric hands touching her arm sends a sharp, warm wave through her body.

She drinks the hot liquid and munches on a piece of the dry bread. The tea soothes her. But no sooner has she finished, beads of perspiration break out on her forehead. She becomes dizzy. She wants to blink, but she can't. Her eyes are focused on the priest's face with its long unkempt beard, the pure white hairs of which reach down to his back, and his belt is drawn tight around his soiled peasant gown. But she can't turn away from the steady gaze of his light-colored eyes in which not merely the pupil, but the whole eye stares at her. She is seduced.

"Sleep, my child, sleep," says his deep, monotonous voice, repeating over and over again, "Sleep, my child, sleep."

"I feel sleepy," she mutters, looking into his hypnotic eyes.

Klara Rasputnis succumbs completely to the power of this Siberian holy man.

A few hours later she awakes atop a wooden stove in a hut. She's a prisoner.

Klara would later learn that Father Andrei had been a monk. His real name is Boris Denisov. As a young man he was caught up in the wave of religious fervor that swept through parts of Siberia. He joined a religious sect that believed in a doctrine of salvation, though the group at times mixed religious fervor with sexual indulgence.

Klara does not remember what happened after she blanked out when he brought her tea and bread. How did she get to this small cabin with two rooms, one window, a stove, and a chair?

Father Andrei and his bandit henchmen will never touch Klara. Nor, as they move from location to location, will they ever tell her the name of the town where they hole up.

As dawn lights the sleepy town one morning, a warm mist hangs over the area. This time of year, the earth is fresh and covered with the blue and white Siberian iris plants.

"I had to get off the train," Father Andrei tells Klara when she awakens in her new home. A nearly unfurnished bedroom holds several cots. The room she is in serves as a kitchen and sitting room with a long wooden table and three chairs on each side.

"Soldiers boarded the back of the train. We were in the front. I was told later they began to ask passengers if they had seen a priest with a young girl. Apparently he killed one of their comrades, they reported. I couldn't leave you. They'd have tortured you and obtained a full description of me. One of my comrades helped me carry you off."

"Where are we?" asks Klara.

"Can't tell you. You see, I'm adopting you. You're my granddaughter. You'll be part of my cover when my group moves from town to town. That's all you need to know."

"By the way, let me introduce Gura Maslovsky," says Father Andrei pointing to a short, heavy but muscular man sitting in the corner. "He'll guard you. He'll not harm you, even though we call him 'Gura the killer.' He's a Jew, son of a baker. He enjoys killing people. They say he weighed about ten pounds when he was born. Working in the family factory as a child, he would lift heavy boxes with ease. He could have been a weight lifter. He murdered his wife. They were about to hang him, but we sprung him.

"Can't believe it, can you? I'd save a Jew from the gallows. I despise them. But I need a strong man. Besides, I have converted Gura to our religion, though he's too dumb to know it. He may smell of garlic and vodka, but he won't harm you, even though he looks like a gorilla.

"Tomorrow you'll come to our hideout in town. This time, I may need you to accompany us on a short journey. We know you're a Jewess; it's in your papers. Your father carries the family name of Rasputnis, very close to that fakir in the Winter Palace, Rasputin. Your father's first name, however, is 'Gershon,' a Jew name."

Except for the single light bulb that dangles from the ceiling on a long wire, the large basement room in the abandoned factory looks like an overused storeroom. In the dark corners of this damp and dreary space, four men stand checking revolvers: opening and closing the chambers, cleaning and re-cleaning gun-hammers, inspecting and clicking fire pins.

"Where is she?"
"Why you bringing her? No job for a girl."
"She'll be fine."

Klara stays at the gang's hideaway, which, she notices from the sounds of passing trains, must be near a rail station, as the locomotives slow down as they pass their hut. She's their cook, maid, all-round cleanup girl, though she's always accompanied by Gura who helps her in the preparation of meals, such as *pelmenye* (dumpling soup), *potchmak* (tartar buns with spinach), *garshochki* (mushroom stew). The gang proceeds from town to town, village to village; robbing, pillaging, hauling in money, working behind the lines; calling for rallies and demonstrations, and stirring up the crowd against the existing order, whichever one is in power for the moment. One day they battle the Reds, next day the Whites. At the first sign of danger, however, these bandits who often rob trains, pull out.

Klara does not care about the ideology of the group. She's not part of their killing and robbing. She's decided, however, to play along with the group, not fight them or they'd lock her up. "And let's be realistic," she says, "they're feeding me." She'll wait for the opportunity to run away. "Please hurry, God. Help me get away. I'll get my revenge," she says to herself. "They'll be punished. All those who forcibly keep me back from my journey and who prevent me from finding Vladimir and Father will suffer."

"How many Red sympathizers did you kill today?" she often asks her returning heroes. She has learned to put up a good front even as she listens at night to the trains that appear to stop nearby.

One day, two weeks after she was kidnapped, the gang doesn't return to the hut. Hours pass. Klara stares at Gura and Gura at Klara. Two neighbors stop by and say the priest and his men have been hanged in Posolskaya village square. Apparently, they didn't inform the police where Klara and Gura were hiding.

"Let's go, Gura. We can catch the next train," Klara says, noticing that Gura has left the key in the latch in the inside door and didn't lock it after the peasant women left.

Gura paces the floor.

"Gura, let's go," she pleads.

"No. Stay here. I don't believe. Can't be. Father Andrei, dead? *Nyet.*"

When he turns and goes to retrieve something from the stove, Klara jumps up, grabs the key, opens the door and locks it from the outside and bolts the cabin. She hears Gura pounding on the door; it's only a matter of minutes before he'll break it down.

"Oh my God, if he catches me," she utters as she notices the railway tracks just down the street. If the tracks are here, the local rail station must be nearby, she surmises. With Gura now pursuing her, she runs down the tracks, praying that her sprint will get her to the crowded station where he won't dare touch her.

"This time, I'll fling myself on the mercy of the police," she says. And then it happened. A loud bang. She'll never know if it originated left or right, in front, behind. Only a single rifle shot. No more footsteps. No grunts. Only a thud as the heavy body behind her hits the ground. Gura Maslovsky is deceased.

Klara stops; looks at the stiff, fallen body and removes Gura's money belt, from which she grabs fifty rubles. No one is in sight, and she doesn't care who fired the bullet, as long as she reaches the station, which she learns is in the town of Posolskaya where she waits for the next train.

With Gura's money, she buys, some clothes, a new rucksack, and even writes her name on a baggage tag, a gesture to prove to herself she's alive.

She also picks up a fish soup known as *ukha*, as well as provisions for the train ride ahead for about 10 rubles. She notices the market place is full of forgers, "writing-liars," as they are called. The only difference between the various craftsmen doing their job is the cost. She pays 10 rubles, slightly more for a good one; he does his work well and even tells her of a free hostel where she can stop until she can move on.

Father Andrei and his gang are gone. Who's watching over her? Who's following her? Mischa? Vladimir? God? A few days later, with a three–ruble ticket she boards a train for Chita.

21

As the train heads to Chita, Klara will learn about a new combatant against the Reds whose very name strikes fear into the heart of those traveling through Siberia. He is the hated Ataman of the Siberian Cossacks, Grigorii Semenov. He stands medium height, with square broad shoulders, an enormous head that boasts a flat Mongol face from which gleam two clear brilliant eyes that belong rather to an animal than a man.

During the winter of 1917, he gathered a large force in Harbin, Manchuria, and six months later, marched into Siberia. With Japanese aid, he establishes himself in Chita. His army of Russians, Buriats, and Mongols stops trains, murders hundreds of passengers, and burns whole villages. A terrorist, he kills at will, especially Jews. He is known to grab Jewish women, rape them and then toss them out of a moving train. Rumor has it he supports a Jewish mistress upon whom he lavishes jewelry. He allows a Yiddish theater and a synagogue in Chita, which is the junction of the Trans-Siberian and the line that runs to Manchuria.

•

"*Devushka* (young girl). Please move your suitcase. Bags go on top. How about some room to breathe," challenges the deep, but firm voice booming at Klara. At first, she doesn't hear the pleadings of the new passenger. The noise from the engine, the creaking wheels, the loud conversation of the passengers, challenge her hearing. Besides, she's daydreaming of Vladimir, tall, strong, handsome Vladimir.

"Come on. I'll help you lift them onto the rack. Too many suitcases. No wonder it's so crowded in here," says the newcomer whose heavy-accented voice annoys her.

Klara looks up at the intruder. He's short, very heavy, with broad shoulders, hair sheared in a crew-cut style. His shiny, brown eyes highlight an oval face that features a long, straight nose. She can see scabs on his crown, a fact of life in Civil War Russia. He's about 17, but acts older, as do all young men who age in wartime. Klara can smell his sweaty body. He's unkempt; his shirttail is hanging out, his pants almost falling off his narrow hips. She smiles.

"That one over there. Is that knapsack yours? Don't worry. I'll lift it. I'm Hercules," says the lad whom Klara already has dubbed "little fat boy." And if she finds out he's Jewish, she'll call him "little fat Jew boy."

A show-off quality pervades his every move, a swagger, something Klara can't tolerate.

"Ah oh," laughs Klara to herself as she gazes at the newcomer's dangling gold *mezuzah* (amulet) as he bends down.

"Come on move, a little," he pleads. "Don't make me shout for the guard."

"Shhh. Be quiet, Jew boy. The Cossacks will get you."

"No. Not Jew. Saw the amulet, did you? Took it off a dead Red," he explains, preparing to heave her rucksack onto the shelf.

"What are you doing? Stop," Klara gasps. She never lets her bag out of sight, let alone let anyone touch it. "Don't you dare move my bag."

"I wouldn't raise your voice if I were you. I know who you are, Klara Rasputnis, Mischa Rasputnis' sister; or should I say, Commissar Mischa Rasputnis."

"What? Where did you get that idea?"

"Well, I noticed the new baggage tag on your rucksack. Your name's on it. Bad idea young lady. You could get into a lot of trouble. Besides, I know Mischa Rasputnis. He's a brave Red soldier. I assumed he's your brother. See how smart I am."

Klara stares at him. The last name in the world she wants to hear is Mischa Rasputnis, so she changes the subject: "I suppose your name is 'Ivan Ivanovich, of royal blood.'"

He bursts out laughing. "Actually, no. I have a Jew-name of all things, Osip Bernstein. It's a long story. Anyway, you should know that I'll help you during the journey."

"How can you help me? I'm not used to such *muzhik* behavior. And I don't have a brother named Mischa," lies Klara. "My brother's back in Odessa. Must be another Rasputnis," she declares, hoping he falls for it.

For a moment, both stop talking.

He could be an informer, she thinks. *How is it he's on a train in civilian clothes?*

"Have it your way. But I'm here if you need me," he says, not telling her that he did not sit down opposite her by accident; he had her description and was tipped off she would be on this train.

A sudden jolt, a shake, a rattle and Klara's train halts.

Boarding are White Army soldiers shouting a one-word command: "Papers."

Other troopers with bayoneted rifles come from the far end of her car.

One is dressed in a soiled White uniform, carries a big pistol in his belt, no holster.

Klara is slow getting her papers out of her bag. No matter how many times this has happened before, she's terrified, but tries to mask her feelings by faking a calm smile.

"Hurry up. I don't have all day. Want to end up in a prison camp?"

"Just trying to get the pass out of my bag, officer."

"Don't you dare answer back. Keep your mouth shut, damn it," he yells and raising his hand, he whacks her on the head. The blow almost fells her but she straightens up only to hear the soldier shout, "If you weren't a woman, I'd beat you to a pulp! Nah. I'll leave it to Ataman Semenov, our friendly bandit."

Another soldier who has boarded in the front of the car, yells back, "Need any help?"

"No. I'm fine. This one's mine. I'll handle her."

"I'm sure you will," snickers the other soldier up front.

Klara, shaking her head, averts looking at the soldier and hands him the documents as she cements her lips and looks down at her shoes.

"Where are you going? A beautiful girl traveling alone? Are you really alone? Or is he with you," demands the soldier pointing to Osip whose face is buried in a newspaper.

"No," she answers. "Alone. I'm going to my auntie in Vladivostok."

He hands back the document.

Turning from Klara toward the teenager, the soldier asks, "You a Jew?"

"*Nyet*," says Osip convincingly. "Armenian. My passport. See; it says, 'Armenian.' Born in the town of Homat."

"Well, you look and smell like a Jew. Besides, you have a Jew name, Osip Bernstein," says the soldier glancing at the youth's papers.

"Every time I apply for a new name, the authorities laugh. 'Good for you,' they say. 'You deserve a Jew name. Suffer. Just like Christ suffered at the hands of the perfidious Jews.'"

"I'd change that name anyway if I were you." As the soldier moves forward, he doesn't look back at Klara or Osip who now feel relieved, so much so that Osip takes out a sharp pencil and quickly writes a note to her:

"Klara. Please go to Amursky Park. The entrance is on Yaraslav Street, across from the Odessa Café. There's a statue of Muravyov-Amursky. Can't miss it. Wait there for the Red Cross worker."

Klara stares at the young man sitting across from her. A smile comes over her face, although her hands are shaking. Her headache from the trooper's hitting her is gone. Even the ache in her stomach from hunger is gone; the pain that was caused by her finishing too fast all the food she brought on board from Posolskaya. She's so excited she wants to run over and kiss this messenger of good tidings, but as she gazes at him, she notices he's looking around and at the same time, he covers his lips with a single finger that messages, "Don't breathe a word."

"Welcome to the rail yards of Chita," says Osip who's getting up from his seat. "We're arriving at the station in the town center."

Klara is hungry and impatient. From the window, she can see the food displayed on a food stand counter. Alighting at Chita station, she runs over to the stand and for a few kopecks picks up slices of black bread and some weak tea. Klara notices that people seem to be running in different directions and bumping into each other; arms flaying, mothers calling children, men arguing.

"Welcome to Chita," says Osip. "Here Slav meets Mongol. Lots of Chinese goods coming through here. That's why the Jews came here. Lots of trade, but utter chaos. Anyway, see you on the road. Good-bye for now."

Klara doesn't pay attention. Chita could have been Hell frozen over, as far as she's concerned. She'll soon be in the arms of her soldier boy.

Nothing bothers her on the streets of Chita that August of 1918. The shoving, the pushing, the long lines for food, nor Ataman Semenov's crude soldiers patrolling the streets.

As she walks quickly, shots ring out. Klara blocks them out, though sometimes she flinches. Men whistle at her. Klara doesn't hear them.

Maybe that's Vladimir down the street in that doorway, or he's on that passing truck, or on top of the roof, or over there with soldiers.

"Have a look," she says to herself. "I better find the statue in the park."

She passes boarded-up shops. Porters stare at her. She's reminded of the little fat boy from the train. "Let's see. What's his name? Osip? That's it. How can I forget him? Will he cause trouble?"

It is then that she hears a familiar voice. Osip Bernstein has caught up with her.

"Go away," she says, waving him away. She doesn't want him around when she meets her lover. She forgets, however, that she needs him. She has been asking herself: "How did he know I was on the train. How did he recognize me? I never saw him. Probably had a photo. And how does he know both Mischa and Vladimir? Has he been following me? Did he shoot Gura? Turning the corner, she stops an old woman.

"Excuse me, *babushka*. Is this the right way to the park on Yaraslav Street?"

"Yes," says the woman," looking over her shoulder. The *babushka* is about to continue when she notices a young man approaching them. The woman walks away, but still manages to yell back: "Go straight. Straight ahead. Can't miss it. Across from the Odessa café."

"A schoolboy. That's what you are," Klara shouts at the figure again coming up behind her. "Why you following me? Clear out, Osip; or whatever your name is. Can't you see I'm going to want to be alone with Vladimir?"

"I understand. But let me walk with you. You don't want to be alone in this town. Too many bandits. Too many Cossacks. You're a target."

"Okay. But as soon as I get to the park on Yaroslav Street, you go."

"For sure."

The two walk on. The park is farther than she thought.

"Osip, when was the last time you saw my brother?"

"Mischa? Actually, last week, I helped him get back through to the Red lines. They pay me as do the Whites when I work for them. None of them know who I am. I've got false papers for every contingency. They think I'm loyal. I keep quiet. I took him to headquarters. Now there's a good human being. A great soldier. One thing for sure, he'll do anything he can to keep you out of harm's way."

She's about to ask him how he came in contact with Vladimir.

"This must be the park," says Osip. "Yes. I'm sure of it. There's the bench. By the way, my real name truly is Osip Bernstein. I made up the story for the police. Actually, that part of the name, Bernstein, belonged to a wealthy Jewish banker who gave my father a loan. Therefore, my father named me after him. See that statue."

"Osip, do me a favor. Go now. I'll be alright."

"Sure. Here's a piece of fruit and some chocolate for you. See you."

Klara's not listening. She's waiting.

22

Chita, August 1918

The Bolsheviks now move to take over Siberia. However on August 2, 1918, a joint British-French force captures the port of Archangel and backs a puppet government for northern Russia. Soon afterward, an American force lands and fighting erupts between the three-nation Allied force and the Reds.

Meanwhile, Czechs and KOMUCH forces capture Kazan in early August and seize the entire gold reserve of the Russian Empire. For the Whites, the way to Nizhny Novgorod is wide open. But the Whites hesitate and that gives Trotsky a chance to transform "a vacillating, unreliable and crumbling mass" into a formal Red Army that in a year will see White Armies crumble before his Bolshevik onslaught. He implants discipline and strength to his forces who retake Kazan on September 10, 1918, and press on against Simbirsk and Samara, the capital of the KOMUCH government, which he captures on October 7. The pendulum begins to move toward the Communists.

•

Klara and Vladimir don't talk.

They don't say: "Where were you? What took you so long?"

She doesn't say, "I'm freezing out here. I've been waiting for you."

He doesn't ask, "How do you feel?"

Their lips meet. They kiss and hug.

"I thought I'd never see you again," she finally says.

"I'll never leave you. I love you. I knew I'd find you. Actually, I knew where you were.

"How's that?"

"It's a long story," he sighs as he pulls her toward him, kissing her again. He's aroused. He pulls her into him. She doesn't move; her lips are moist.

"I'll tell you later. Come on. Let's go to the café. It's noisy there, but safe. I'll tell you everything when we get there."

Taking her arm with one hand, and picking up her small bag up with the other, he finally asks: "So, how are you?"

"I'm in heaven."

They stare at each other.

"Vladimir, when you were gone, I said to myself, 'I'll take you in any condition. Even if your arms and feet were cut off. Just come back to me alive. I love you."

"I love you, too. I've waited a long time for this," he says, squeezing her hand as they arrive at the café where Klara notices old men, their heads down, singing. They sound like an off-key orchestra, noisy, loud, shrill. Laughter, shouts, declarations, and toasts fill the room. As they enter, a soldier smashes a plate against the wall. Klara stiffens. She spots a lonely soldier; his head nestled on a table of empty bottles and dirty dishes. He's snoring.

An argument erupts nearby. One combatant shouts the familiar Russian curse: "You should return to your mother's womb."

In a crowded corner of the café, another fight breaks out. Nobody pays attention. They keep drinking. They keep hearing the word, *Nazdarovia* (to your health) over and over again as soldiers stand up and throw the clear vodka down their raspy throats and also hurl the empty glasses against the wall. The room reeks of alcohol-stained tablecloths, cigarette butts, and spoiled food.

A tipsy lady dances and prances on top of a table. She teases the soldiers by holding her dress up just enough for the men to peek up her legs. She wears no undergarments. Their heads roll and circle to get a better view, their eyes bursting out of their sockets at forbidden fruit.

In another corner, embracing couples stand against the wall, holding tight, body to body, and smothering each other with kisses.

Klara and Vladimir sit down at a large table by the door. A friend of Vladimir's waves to him to come over. But Vladimir signals to him with a slight nod of his head to his right. The man sees Klara and understands.

"Nothing has changed; has it?" remarks Vladimir. "These people are drunken slobs. And they're supposed to be the future of Russia?"

"A war's on. Remember."

"A war? This civil war is not a war where one army fights against another. This is terror! The French Revolution all over again. Soldiers go wild. No restraint. They kill as if they're swatting a fly."

"A vodka for me," he says to the bored-looking waiter who silently stands at their table and admires Klara.

"*Chai,*" she orders.

"Bring her some food; whatever you have," orders Vladimir. "We'll pay."

The two stare at each other.

"So what happened? Why did you disappear like that?" she asks.

Lighting a cigarette, taking a deep puff, exhaling as if it was his last, he proceeds to talk as if a flood is gushing from his mouth.

"Without warning us, they pulled out our Red Cross group. I couldn't even write a note. Banned all communication, they did. Anyway, we're staying put, for now."

"You'll move again. There's a war on, remember."

He ignores her comment.

"Thank God I knew when you left Irkutsk, though I must say we lost track of you until you surfaced in Posolskaya."

"But how could you know that?"

"The dispatcher at the train station who knew I already was in Chita sent a message to me through a conductor friend of his. You were spotted in Posolskaya. We have contacts up and down the line. I hired someone to follow you. He has a network at every railway station.

"You're kidding?" responds Klara, smiling. "Ah. I know. That Armenian. The little fat guy. Osip something...."

"He's not Armenian. He's Jewish."

"Don't make me laugh. He's Armenian. He told me so."

"A disguise. He looks Jewish. So he says he's Armenian. Even though he's heavy, he's everywhere. He's a spy for the Bolsheviks and he's a spy for the Whites. He works both sides. I saved his life in Irkutsk. I could have turned him in. I didn't. He's been helping me ever since."

"You're kidding."

"No."

"You think he left you alone in the park. He was across the street all the time. Turn around. By the doorway. Someone's waving at you."

"Fat boy," she utters in astonishment after she glances across the street. From the doorway, comes a flippant wave of the hand and a wide smile. Osip then lifts his hat off and bows like a Cossack.

"Had me fooled."

The waiter interrupts them by setting down some *borscht,* a vegetable stew known as *swekolnik,* and some black bread.

"Klara, you know I love you."

Then, taking a deep breath, he hurries the words, "Klara, I've come to marry you."

Fumbling in his pocket, he comes up with a ring, an antique, white gold with diamonds, baguettes. "It's yours. Marry me. You're the one."

"Oh, my God!" she exclaims. Her eyes shine. "Who? Where did you? Oh Vladimir, it's gorgeous."

Both stare at the ring.

She's silent. Wrinkles appear on her forehead. He awaits her answer.

"Klara, what happened? You look so sad. Just to marry me?"

"No. No," she interrupts, "it's just that ..."

"I'm not Jewish. Is that it?"

She doesn't answer. She doesn't want to answer. She refuses to answer.

"Vladimir, I'm so happy. Let's not talk about those things."

The two are quiet. Only the loud noise in the café can be heard.

Klara thinks. Life's getting more complicated. That's what Rachel said. I laughed then. But look at me now. Can't get any more involved than this, especially when Vladimir's a different religion.

Her mind is racing. Should I tell him I can't have children. No! Not now. Don't want to blackmail him into feeling sorry for me and marrying me.

Besides, what kind of wedding are we going to have: Jewish or Christian? A *mishmash?* she continues reflecting. Who would marry us? One of those monks? We never even talked about this. We love each other. Who needs marriage? So we'll live in sin, as they say. But what if Momma and Papa find out? One look at Vladmir and they'll know he's no Jew. They'll disown me. They'd never talk to me. A darkness would descend on my father as though I left the world. I'm sure I could find a rabbi who would marry us. I'm going to live my life. Not someone else's. I'm not going to do something just to please someone else. I'll always be Jewish. And yet, when he's angry, Vladimir'll call me 'dirty Jew.' I'll be the scapegoat. But the war has postponed everything, even marriage. There's no guarantee he or I will survive this. I'm too young to be a widow.

"A ruble for your thoughts," he blurts out.

"So much money for a ring. I guess I'm worth more than a kopeck."

Now he's quiet, pensive, frowning, thinking:

What about my parents? They'll want to disown me. Even my Communist father, despite his protestations about the church, won't like the idea of me marrying a Jewess. When the grandchildren come, they'll change their mind. I know what's coming in this war; it'll get worse. How are we going to exist? Right now I'm in Chita. No one knows what's going to happen next. Why am I doing this? Why get married? Doesn't make sense. We'll continue to be lovers. Nobody need know. After what I've seen, I don't need religion, at least not to interfere in my life. They have a lot of nice things, those Jews. They believe in one God, the Ten Commandments, and all that. They're smart and they don't drink.

Her voice reaches his ears. "Oh Vladimir. Yes. Of course I'll marry you."

He feels her arms around him. She plants kisses on his neck, ears, eyes. Her eyes are wet. She's been crying and he didn't even notice.

He hugs her. Almost in shock, he repeats: "You said, 'yes.' You said, 'yes.' 'Yes.' We're going to be husband and wife."

They kiss and hug. A park is one thing, but in a public place. Again, young lovers usually don't care who watches them. They are oblivious to prowling eyes. This is Russia, 1918. Love, hate, death. They're all the same. Nobody stares at the dead or the living.

"Come. Let's go," says Vladimir breaking off their embrace. "It's late. I share a room in Settlement House. We'll celebrate our engagement. My fellow officer is out on patrol tonight. Nobody else lives there anymore. Family fled. We requisitioned the house and got it. Put up a sign. 'Red Cross Office Depot.' Osip comes there. He runs it, though there's nothing to do."

"Vladimir. Wait. One thing. We can't get married here. In Vladivostok. It's safer," says Klara, as they get up from the table. Vladimir nods. He's listening. But his mind is far, far away.

"We can live here for now. I've got a couple hundred rubles hidden away."

"I don't have near that much," says Klara. "Maybe 20 rubles left. My brother," and she stops talking for a second. "Vladimir, no secrets between us. My brother, he's always near me. He probably hates me, but I've come to depend on him. I believe he'd protect us if the Reds break through. I never told you this. But you do know him. You met."

"We met? When? Where?"

"You met each other in Chelyabinsk. That young civilian who came with the lieutenant to the door in our apartment. I was under the bed," she says, blushing.

"You're joking. You were?" and he snickers. "That was your brother? Oh God! What if he'd have found you?"

Vladimir bursts out laughing and she joins him.

"Not funny," says Klara, smiling herself, but then quickly trying to fake seriousness. But it doesn't work. The two are now laughter and kisses. She pushes aside any anger. He does the same. People who love each other can do that, at least they try to do it.

They leave the café and hasten out into the night. The cold wind, hurling itself off the Mongolian desert, forces their heads downwards. They walk fast.

"He doesn't know it was you," she shouts above the chilly blasts. "I didn't tell him," she yells even louder, blushing again and still laughing as she thinks of the incident. "I only told him I had a boyfriend."

"So much has happened," Vladimir reflects. "I'm sure we'll feel this way tomorrow and the next day and every day of our lives."

"Klara, let's go. Too much talking is not good. Only love and kisses," he says as he smiles sheepishly and takes her hand.

As they pass another noisy tavern, someone throws a glass out into the street; it crashes into bits and pieces right in front of them.

Others would shudder. Others would cringe. Not this Russian couple.

"That's good luck. God's with us," Vladimir says as he puts his arm around Klara's waist. Her body is tight, muscular for a woman; she's a dancer after all. Her flab has been burned off. She still possesses stamina, plenty to get her through the next leg of her journey, that is, if she moves on. For now, not a chance. Father will have to wait. She and Vladimir are almost one.

23

Tragedy in Chita. August 1918

Chita, a 16th century stockade, once became a destination for banished "politicals." Those pioneers were Decembrists, exiles who erected huts, drained marshes, filled in swamps, started businesses and at the same time brought culture to Siberia, including literary societies. No wonder the name "City of Exiles" stuck.

The town never forgot these intellectuals. They named the main street, "Damskaya," after the brave wives who accompanied their husbands into exile in 1825. Later, criminals and political exiles who lost themselves in the vast Siberian lands changed their identity and practiced the scams they had learned in the teeming cities of European Russia. They gave Siberia a bad name.

About twelve thousand residents occupy Chita, this small municipality on the Trans-Siberian railway that is surrounded by a district of plateaus and mountain ranges separated by wide, deep river valleys and guarded by hills. One valley at Chita opens into Mongolia; it's an escape route.

•

Like many of towns she entered, Chita, with its wooden sidewalks and wooden homes is far from paradise. She doesn't have time to look around, however.

The couple is as happy as they were in Chelyabinsk. At night, their bodies are knotted together in the Settlement House; Vladimir's roommate has moved out. They eat well. Vladimir brings food from the army camp. He manages to get off on Sunday afternoons.

"Klara, you can't stay here," says Vladimir early next morning even before the cold sun bursts through grey skies. I've just found out I've got to leave soon. We're going east in a few days."

"Where can I go?" she asks.

"Stay in the room till tomorrow morning. Then go to the station and get on the train to Harbin in Manchuria. A lot of Jews there. Osip'll go with you, at least as far as Zabaikalsk, this side of the border. I'll join you there. Here's the money for the ticket, plus some."

"No. I want to go with you."

He pulls her toward him. She rests her head on his chest. She wants to cry, but dares not. She has to show him she's tough, too. Embracing, their young bodies clinch. They go to bed. Sleep and love. Love and sleep.

Dawn breaks. The Siberian sun rises and shines over three thousand miles between the Ural Mountains and the Pacific Ocean, a total of five million square miles.

Klara prepares to leave the apartment. Vladimir is gone. She never heard him leave. Her sleep was deep. She thinks she remembers how he bent down and kissed her on her brow. "Yes, he did that," she mutters to herself.

When she gets to the station, it's boarded up. Soldiers bar crowds from entering the building. There's activity on the tracks: A train has derailed; it rests on its side, wheels hanging in mid-air. Bodies are strewn about under carriages. Workers are hammering away at the twisted tracks. "Sabotage," a soldier tells Klara.

"Sabotage?"

"Yes! No trains today."

Obeying Vladimir's instructions, Klara goes back to the house. As she walks the crowded streets, she debates whether they had been right to wait. Maybe they should have gotten married. She would have followed him anywhere.

Arriving at the house and climbing the broken steps, she enters and scans the large sitting room. She can hear Vladimir moving about in the back room.

"I tried. But no train," she says.

"Yes, I know. I heard the news, a derailment. You must be hungry. Have a bowl of *kasha*. Got it from the commissary. I'll heat it up for you."

"What do we do now?" asks Klara.

"They'll fix the tracks today. Then we'll try again tomorrow. You know our motto," he says with a determined smile on his face. "Never give up."

"You're telling me. But when will this all end?"

He doesn't answer.

At dawn the next day, Klara wakes to a banging on the door.

"Klara, open up. Klara. Quick. Vladmir's been arrested." If it had been anyone other than Osip, she wouldn't believe it. But Osip knows everything. "Yes, arrested. Do you hear me? He's at the police station."

"What for?" she asks, letting him into the apartment.

"He's supposed to have said that Whites were treating Red prisoners badly."

"I'll get him out. Whatever it takes," she says as she knots her kerchief and pushes Osip aside and hurries to the police station.

But there's nothing to do. Vladimir's superior came in from the field and freed him. From now on, however, the police will watch him.

Once again, he gives her funds for the journey. "Put this in a safe place; you know where." Vladimir blushes as he hands her a pouch when they meet outside the jail. "There's a 20-ruble note and some rubies I bought from a Cossack for an identity pass before the police picked me up. You're going to need a lot of money."

As she leans forward to kiss him, he says, "Don't. They're watching me. A kiss on both cheeks, like we're cousins. They don't like Jewish girls kissing us, and believe me Klara, you look Jewish. Love you. Now you should go to the station. I can't be seen with you there."

Her eyes embrace him. She kisses him on both checks and turns to leave. But impulsively he takes her arm. He won't let go. "No matter. I can walk with you for a block or so," he says.

They smile at each other.

"I love you Klara."

"I love you, too."

They walk side by side as she hides the pouch in a deep skirt pocket. No talking. No embracing. Just two young people moving down a street on a summer Siberian morning. Two young people looking into each other's eyes. Two young people so aroused by urges in their bodies that for a few seconds, they don't hear shooting that erupts at the end of the road—small arms fire announcing trouble, bringing on fear, hatred.

"Guerrillas. Guerrillas," someone shouts.

"Down, down, everyone down," Vladimir yells as he draws out a hidden revolver and turns toward the sound of the shots. He fires several times.

"Klara, get out of here. Run. Go. Into that café over there. Hurry."

She doesn't move.

Crouching, Vladimir grabs Klara's arm and pushes her hard toward the café. His forward motion propels her forward and though she almost slips, she finds herself hunched over, moving in toward the intended direction.

Vladimir rises and fires again.

She stumbles; falls to the ground; but gets up and moves toward the café. She doesn't look back. She can only hear his words: "Go to the café. Don't move, whatever you do."

Klara reaches the café. She's moved fast, faster than she can imagine in spite of her limp. She can't remember how quickly she ran, maybe like back in ballet class years ago. Oh those runs and leaps!

"Down. Get down," a harsh voice in the cafe commands her.

Rat-tat-tat sounds a nearby machine gun. Bullets crash through the windows of the café. Glass shatters. More shots are fired.

"Where're they coming from?" she wonders.

Glass smashes to the floor. She shivers. Fire breaks out in a far corner of the café. She shivers again.

A waiter, his long apron spotted with blood, crawls on his belly and reaches a spigot. Raising his body slightly and crouching, he picks up a nearby bucket, fills it, then gets up, and pours water on the blaze.

Smoke envelopes the room. Klara, still on the floor, drags her body under a table and buries her head in her arms. Black. Everything's black. She can hardly breathe.

"Got to get out of here," she tells herself. Up she goes and dashes out through the back door into a yard full of garbage and discarded furniture. She closes the door behind her, almost automatically, for she recalls she read somewhere, closing doors helps prevent air from spreading a fire. Stumbling, she moves around the café, along a broken fence. The fetid air chokes her. Step by step, she hugs the fence along the bullet-ridden building and moves around the side to the front of the café where the shooting began.

The street's empty. No noise. No shooting. No trucks or carriages. No one, except a civilian with a revolver stands a few feet from her. He wears a red armband.

At the exact moment he turns toward her, she shouts at him, forgetting her usual fear of the police and soldiers. No longer is she prudent, the man she loves is gone. She forgets she is talking to a Red guerrilla. "Where is he? Where's the Red Cross worker who was here?" shouts Klara.

"Well, if you mean the bastard who was firing at us; he took off," says the guerrilla, his penetrating eyes still searching the now-silent neighborhood.

"A whole bunch of them were shooting at us. We came under fire. But they ran. He's probably gone; ran like a chicken. If we'd have caught him.... Anyway, get out of here, now!"

"You probably killed him. We were going to get married. You're the bastard," she screams as she starts pounding the soldier with both her fists, harder and harder. "You killed Vladimir and he's a Red Cross officer no less," she says, and flings herself at him, her arms beating his chest.

The soldier breaks out in nervous laughter as men often do when faced with the opposite sex waving their hands and fists at them.

"Killed him? Where's the body. Don't be stupid," he says, continuing to laugh.

"You fired first. I was here. I heard the shots," she responds.

"Go," says the guerrilla who is obviously the leader of the group and who now exhibits a loss of patience. Sudden anger appears in his voice. "Be quick about it. There's nobody's here," he declares as he again gestures to the empty street, "No bodies on the ground. Go before someone takes a potshot at you. Besides, we're underground and if they catch you with us, you're dead."

But Klara is blind with rage and fear and guilt. She let Vladimir walk with her. She raises her hand again to strike the soldier again, but he is too quick and ducks out of the way, as one of his comrades approaches and bangs her head with his rifle butt.

"Damn it. You shouldn't have done that," the Red officer tells the soldier who butted Klara. "Apparently that shooter was a Red Cross official. Not good. We don't need an international incident over one of those guys. Get a wagon," he commands a fellow soldier. "Take her to the hospital. Act like you're a civilian. You just picked her up off the street following a wild shooting. Leave your rifle with us.

"You there," he hollers to another comrade. "Go with him and stay with her, too. If she comes to, keep your eyes on her. Don't leave her. Don't touch her. No harm to her, understand. That's an order.

"Tell the hospital authorities she's a friend of a Red Cross worker. She said his name was 'Vladimir.' They'll probably know of him. Apparently, he's a big shot in the area." The two place her on her back in the wagon. She's in and out of consciousness as they pull the wagon away.

"Well," says one of the Reds, "we followed orders. We really shook up this neighborhood just as Comrade Mischa Rasputnis ordered us to do."

That was all Klara heard that morning: "Comrade Mischa Rasputnis ordered us to do." The rest of their conversation faded away.

She won't recall the terrible pain inflicted on her; nor the two men transporting her in a wagon to the hospital and then the blinding bright lights above her head; the nurse at her bedside. She'll only recall that her brother ordered a Red mission that killed her lover.

But where's the body? She'll never ask that question. Others will.

24

Awakening, patient Klara Rasputnis lying in bed three, ward seven, sees only white: White sheets, white blankets, white uniforms, white nurses' caps, white doctor coats, white walls—all reflecting purity, cleanliness. The sights in her mind, however, are people and pills. She sleeps; they give her pills. She sighs; they give her another pill. She wakes up; they give her a pill. She talks; they give her another pill. She shouts; they give her a pill. Sometimes they give her food and then they give her another pill. They just don't know what to do with her.

The days fly by and she is treated as a very important person; a big shot's relative. Osip has fixed it.

"How did I get here?" she asks a guard.

He doesn't answer.

A young man, dressed in peasant clothes, walks into the ward.

"Nurse. Nurse." Klara shouts. "Don't believe him. He's not a civilian. He's a Red agent. A spy. Arrest the Red bastard. Shoot him."

Patients stare. The nurse stutters. The doctor says nothing. They all know he works for the Whites; they've seen his credentials.

"She's delirious," say the nurses shaking their heads.

"Shh. Shhh. Calm yourself," says a nurse tidying up the blankets that Klara has kicked off the bed.

The patient rambles on: "He's a Red officer. He's a Red, I tell you. How many times do I have to repeat it? Get him out of here. Out!"

She throws a brush at him. He ducks.

"Oh God. God help me. Go away."

But Mischa Rasputnis visits her every day.

"Nobody's been found," he tells her every day.

"Don't lie. You killed him. You did it. Till I die, I won't believe anything else."

"No use arguing with you. Don't you understand?" he whispers in her ear. "I ordered my men to shoot wildly in various parts of the city to stir panic. How did I know you and your boyfriend would be in that neighborhood at that time? No matter, I think he's still alive."

"Get out!"

He sits there and stares at her. Try as he must, he just can't convince her. So why does he keep coming back to her? he wonders. Why does he bear the insults, the curse words and the hateful expressions, even going so far as to reveal his true identity that fortunately no one believes. No matter how much he wants to distance himself from her, he can't. One day he'll get over this family guilt trip, he tells himself.

Mischa's thoughts turn to the past. "Why should I care? Truth be told, I wanted to go find Papa. I would have gotten there much sooner. She stole my dream," he repeats and repeats over and over again. "But that's the past. Now I have a new dream. I'm not a quitter either. Russia's my homeland. Maybe the Reds are right, capitalism is finished. Maybe life'll be better for Jews under them; all religion will disappear. Maybe.

"As for Klara, let her think what she wants. Let her go crazy. I didn't do it. I didn't kill her boyfriend. We don't know where he is. Why worry? On the other hand, she's my sister. Well, alright, half-sister. Yes, pretty much the same flesh and blood. So if anyone wrongs my sister, I'll revenge her. That's the way it is. I'm the man in the house, Papa told me so."

Klara lies there, day after day. "Why me?" she asks.

She sulks. She wishes she died on that street. And yet the next minute, she wants to live. She knows Mischa can save her. He always does. He even risks his life as he is dressed in civilian clothes and carries a fake identity.

Mischa realizes his underground job gives him the power to watch over Klara's journey. But it can't go on this way. If he's going to keep his sanity, he has to get her out of the country quickly and far, far away from him, so far away that even if he wanted to, he couldn't associate with her.

That's it. Get her out. Get her out of Russia. Problem solved.

"He did it. He did it," she cries out at night. Klara is being treated for shock and nerves.

One day, however, she lets him talk. After all, he has brought her a book of short stories by Anton Chekhov. She should be a little nicer to him. A new thought has entered her mind. Maybe, just maybe Vladimir's alive. Maybe he wasn't killed. But she dismisses it quickly and firmly; if he wasn't shot, he would have come back by now.

Late one afternoon, the nurse ushers in a visitor.

"Well what have we here," says Klara. "Little fat boy. Little fat Jew boy. Can't fool me anymore, Osip Bernstein. You're an Armenian? Hogwash. You're a Jew!"

"So you found out, eh? I admit it," he confesses. "Anything wrong with being Jewish?"

"Nothing. Nothing. I'm teasing you. Being sarcastic. Runs in the family," as she takes his arm and moves him closer to the bed and whispers:

"Osip. Listen. Have you heard anything about Vladimir? You're in contact with both sides. You've got friends with the Whites. Tell me the truth. Is Vladimir dead?"

"It's strange. Nobody really knows. Then again, they don't care. People are disappearing every day. Casualties of this bloody civil war."

"Osip. Damn it. Let's get out of here. I've some money, jewels. I'll pay you. Find me a home and then we'll go." She turns away and hides her head in the pillow that absorbs her tears of anger.

"I can't do that without…"

"I know; you have to ask Mischa. You work for him. What can I do? I hate him. But go and talk to him. Tell him I'll go. He's the only one that can arrange it. He's got power, even with the Whites. He'll help me. He'll save me. He watches over me. I know that. I've got to get to my father. Tell him. He'll arrange it."

"Okay, Okay. Don't cry. I'll do it. I'll contact him. But you can't travel now in your condition."

Nurses continue to watch her. They observe her shuffling down the hallway. Never would they believe she's a ballerina. Now, she looks emaciated, weak, slouching, limping, breathless. Her dancing days are over.

Osip takes her back to the apartment she and Vladimir shared. She sleeps. She sleeps long hours. She sleeps full days. He brings her food.

"I want Vladimir. I want my father," she utters deliriously.

One night, a week later, she wakes up feverish and sweaty. Her head throbs. She manages to lift herself off the bed and grabs her thread-worn bathrobe lying on the floor. As she shuffles across the room and down the hall to the bathroom, she looks up through windows in the skyline and gasps: "The moon. The moon's red. Bloody red. How can that be?"

A nightmare. Just like in Odessa. The frightening whistles of the trains, accompanied by loud gunfire, fill the night with fear. One night she dreams she's thrown into the fiery, wooden boiler of a puffing train engine. As the hot, orange-red flames begin to sear her body, she escapes through the engine's chimney and lands in the arms of her father in America.

Later, she dreams she runs and runs and leaps onto a departing boat, just as the vessel slips away from the shore. Or was it a departing train? No. It had to be a boat. How could a train float on water?

Everywhere she walks in the unheated, boarded-up house, she imagines Vladimir's near her. She stays here in Chita to hide; but knows she has to leave. The Communists will come for her. They're probably looking for her now. Maybe they found out Mischa's a double agent. They know she's his sister.

Dreams return to Klara. One worse than the other.

In one, a man comes into her room.

"Who's there?" she shouts.

A voice replies: "You're not in a room. You're in a parked automobile, in the passenger's seat. There's no driver."

She looks again. A man approaches the car. "Take this. I don't want to be seen with it." He places a revolver on the empty seat on the driver's side. It's Vladimir's pistol. She screams.

Next night, she dreams she's back on a train. There's a fight in her compartment. A man is stabbed. He falls to the ground. He's bleeding. Klara stares into the bright night sky and screams: "Something's happening. The moon. It's red. Bloody red. How can that be?"

Osip has no choice. He has to take her back to the hospital that now resembles a vast morgue. Stacks of bodies fill the hallways. The stench's unbearable.

"Papa. Where are you?" she shouts one morning until the nurse comes. The doctor takes pity on her. He gives her a shot with a long needle. "Take her to my house," the doctor instructs. "She can't stay here anymore and she can't return to her present place. Too many memories."

Even though they didn't know the doctor, they accept his offer.

She has no photo of Vladimir. She only visualizes Mischa's hateful face.

"He killed my lover."

With near total willpower, she reinforces her unconscious desire to be loved again. But it is a marred wish. In one nocturnal fantasy, she walks into the private room of a military officer. She's naked and he's only wearing his army shirt. She sees his phoenix rising. He stares at her pubic hairs and as he does, his eyes open wide. He trembles a bit and grabs her and they both run out. They hail a carriage and cling to each other. As he climbs on top of her, a herd of reindeer bear down on them. Klara screams; her partner flees. She can't flee. He has tied her hands to the rails of the carriage. She sees the swollen face of the first reindeer, it's about to leap up onto the carriage and crush her. Or is it going to rape her? She'll never know. She awakens.

The doctor's house is a typical *izba* located on the outskirts of town. She sleeps late every morning. Her room is replete with table, chair, a portmanteau, even a window facing the garden.

She's stronger now. Long, pleasant dreams now replace the nightmares. One night, she dreams she's at an outdoor party of the Buriats. They sing; she's energized. She's ready now.

Next morning, Klara eagerly awaits Osip, who holds her prisoner in the doctor's house guarded by a security agent. "Hurry. Damn you. Get here already," she says to herself as she paces the floor and runs over to the window looking out onto the open green fields beyond.

"He visits me every day. Maybe he's got a crush on me. Today, like every day, we'll end up walking the streets of Chita so I better take a jacket. Drizzling slightly."

•

On their walk this chilly fall morning, Osip and Klara stop in front of a silver store. She stares at the window display: pendants, table settings, candelabras. She dislikes jewelry stores, especially since she took off Vladimir's ring. No sense wearing it now; she'd be a mark among the thousands of fleeing refugees, many of whom already have become urban bandits. She had since placed the ring alongside the rubies and the necklace in the pouch, which she hides in her bra.

No sooner was she mesmerized by the magical windows when three hooligans push past them, knocking her against the wall. They brandish revolvers and wave their arm and yell as they push the two into the vestibule.

"Lie on the floor, you two."

From the ground, Klara spies one of the bandits smashing the plate glass window. As they seize valuables, they fire their pistols into the air. People cower in nearby doorways. A young man tries to stop them. They shoot him in the head. Klara turns away. Now's my chance. I'm out of here.

Backing down toward the end of the block, the bandits continue firing. Osip gets up and pulls out a revolver. He jumps into a doorway next door and fires. His back is to Klara who thinks, Osip'll never let me leave Chita. He works for Mischa, and I can't leave until my brother gives the okay. I'm trapped.

And so she takes that first step, that first step needed to start action. She runs from Osip, who doesn't hear or see her break away. Down the empty street she flees, even as bullets career off buildings and people duck all around her. She's not stopping. Giddy for a moment; she's a kid playing the game, a kid running away from someone who's trying catch her, as in hide-and-seek. "Catch me if you can," she says laughingly. "Get farther away. Go," she instructs her body and mind. "No time for warm ups. No time for running in place or stretching. Put tracks between us. A *droshky*. Find a *droshky*."

She scans the street, looking here and there, just as she did that long-ago wintry day in the Odessa railway station when the Lubavitzes didn't show up. As the name Lubavitz goes through her mind, she utters two words, "dirty bastards." She hates them and for the moment turns all her anger toward them, just as she mentally kills or blames anyone who halts her progress. If the

Lubavitzes would have shown up that morning, none of this would have happened, she rationalizes. To Klara, a person's only as good as his or her correct advice. Otherwise, they're no good.

"Ah, there's a carriage," she says out loud and runs over to the *droshky*. Calmly and quietly she beseeches the driver: "Railway station. Please."

Even before the man in the carriage seat can say, "Get in," she realizes she may have made a mistake in grabbing the first cart she sees.

"He's dirty!" she exclaims silently, as if one's dirty clothing matters to a young maiden fleeing for her life. His unkempt beard and disheveled hair blowing out from under his weather-beaten cap frighten her. A short scar runs down the side of his left cheek; his nose is broken, and his stooped body emits a sweaty odor. He smells. To Klara a person who gives off a bad smell is not only unclean, but irresponsible. Moreover, the driver's face worries Klara; his cat-like eyes seem to her as if he is about to pounce.

"Shit! What am I getting into," she whispers to herself.

As he yawns, she sees his cracked teeth.

"No turning back; got to go with him."

Summoning all her energy, she climbs aboard the carriage.

"How much?"

"Two rubles."

"Fine. Go!"

The *droshky* takes off; its movement calms Klara who realizes how lucky she is. By chance, she just happened to take her money belt from the room; it contains nearly 50 rubles. But as the carriage gains speed, Klara holds tightly onto the sidebars. The driver begins to whip the horse over and over again. He seems enraged about something, cursing, yelling at the horse, standing up in his seat. Holding the whip in his right hand, he slashes the nearly deranged animal, over and over again.

She closes her eyes. She can't bear his beating the horse and for a few blocks the animal responds with increased speed until it shifts into a slow trot. The cool fall air rips Klara's face, and her eyes become watery and begin to burn. She's shivering. Exhausted, she begins to doze off as the vehicle rolls down the street. She wants to yawn but catches herself. It's useless. She lowers her head and for a few minutes enters a dream zone where she finds herself at a round, wooden table, her elbows resting on coarse wood. She gazes at the crisp, new playing cards she holds in her long fingers. And who's opposite her? None other than brother Mischa whose sneer she barely makes out in this shadowy room.

"I win. Beat you," Mischa shouts, throwing his cards up into the air, his shrill words shattering to pieces his sister's visit to slumberland.

Seconds later, the carriage executes a sweeping right turn, forcing Klara to open her eyes. Another few blinks and the conveyance stops and anchors itself at the side of the road.

"*Chto eto* (What is this)?" she roars at the driver.

No answer from the man whose head is resting firmly on his chest.

"Why have we stopped?" she asks as she jumps down and looks around the busy street. Everything is moving; only her *droshky* is at a standstill. She stares at the driver. He seems frozen in a sleep position. Gently, she pulls him backward. His bulging eyes roll skyward. He's dead. She knows the look.

But nobody is observing her or the driver. Death is a common occurrence. Face down in mud or snow, bodies litter Siberian streets.

Only by chance does Klara look down at the driver's warm, fur-lined boots. Take them. He won't need them anymore. Good price in the market, she thinks.

But as she debates whether to remove the boots, she spots something that causes her quickly to forget those enticing, well-soled shoes: About 30 rubles are visible in the driver's thick money bag resting comfortably by his feet on the floor.

No one's looking. No one sees the dead driver. He could be taking an afternoon nap.

"The purse. The money purse. Grab it," she instructs herself. Conscience no longer exists in Russia, private property is not stolen, it just changes owners.

If I don't take it, someone else will, she philosophizes. Everything's up for grabs, especially with the Communists. 'What's mine is mine, and what's yours' is mine,' she snickers, remembering she has no clothes other than what she's wearing, no jacket, no suitcase, nothing. She needs the money. She picks up the bag; puts it under her coat and leaves the carriage.

As she waves good-bye to the driver, she laughs to herself and walks towards the station, Turning the corner, she pauses, looks around again, catches her breath, and walks very fast.

Arriving at the Chita station, she quickly finds a black-marketeer, buys a blouse, undergarments, skirt, stockings, some chicken and black bread, and yet another cardboard suitcase. The transaction leaves her with 35 rubles.

After obtaining a ticket from Chita to Manzhouli for five rubles, she heads out to the railway tracks at the far end of the terminal. Like every rail station in Russia, this one, too, is besieged by crowds clamoring to get in the cars, only to be met by rifle butts and the words, "*Nyet mesta* (no room)."

Trying to reach the rail car, therefore, is no easy task. Already, train roofs are crowded. Woman and children are lying flat on top of the attached boxcars; men kneeling or standing up. "Get this train going or Osip'll catch up with me," Klara repeats to herself as she climbs aboard.

A whistle. A jolt. A look out the window. A forward motion. And the train jerks forward and moves briskly. She has yet to notice that the carriages are filthy. Dust and dirt cause her to sneeze. No bedding, only straw on the cold floor. No provisions. She has enough money to buy food at the next station. All she has to do now is journey on.

The train heads due east out of Chita and follows the left bank of the Ingoda River and hurls itself right through the open steppe. As it passes the town of Darsun, someone exclaims there's a sanatorium nearby.

"In our condition, maybe we should all go there," pipes up a young man.

"Not for mental cases, comrade," someone contradicts. "This one's for cardiovascular and intestinal ailments."

"That's for me. I have a terrible stomach ache."

"After this trip, I'll probably have that, too," replies a youngster.

Soon they reach Karymskaya, a small industrial town first settled by Buriats. Then onto Kaidalovo, the junction for the railway to China.

Passengers settle back to the music of the wheels murmuring "East, east, south, south."

Once the train leaves Kaidalovo, Klara feels exhilarated as their temporary home on wheels steams along on the branch line in the direction of Manchuria. Crossing the Ingoda River, the train again heads through the steppe.

One would think people would be less fearful; after all, they are out of Russia proper. Not so. Not on this train. They remember the name, Semenov, the ataman, the bandit. He's been known to wander down here. When the train is forced to stop, talking ceases. Eyes scan the land. "Please God. Don't let's see that bastard."

As if that wasn't enough, these people have another new name to fear; none other than Semenov's buddy, Roman Nickolai Maximilian von Ungern-Sternberg, known as the "Bloody Baron."

Everyone knows they'll have to run the Baron's gauntlet, especially when they get to the next town, Dauria, 200 miles from Chita, on the railway line to Manchuria and close to the border. This small hamlet, surrounded by a marsh of red reeds, is the Baron's execution camp.

Dauria stands quietly on the main line of the railway, replete with a station house, a barracks, and a small hotel. A small church with its tall spire can be seen from miles around as can a fort constructed of red bricks that is positioned in the nearby valley.

A day later, the train stops in a railway yard in Dauria. A passenger opens the car door. Klara can see right across into the stationmaster's hut. A group of soldiers enter the shack. She absorbs their gestures; their officer is trying to get the station master to let their train situated across the tracks go ahead of the east-bounder in which Klara's riding. He agrees and the intruders leave.

Shortly afterwards she sees the stationmaster give another train also head-ing east, the go-ahead. "Is he out of his mind?" she thinks. "Letting another train go first; they'll kill him."

Klara judges correctly. Cruelty and sadism win. A moment later come the heated words. "You bastard. How dare you," yells an officer. "Get him," he commands his soldiers who proceed to drag the station clerk out of his hut onto the westbound tracks. They hurl him onto the ground and tie his arms and legs behind him. They stuff oil rags into his mouth and push his head onto the icy train rail and hold his legs. They tie him so tightly that only his head hangs over the rail; it's the guillotine. In two minutes a west-bounder roars through the station.

Just another headless corpse on the tracks.

Klara looks away. She's alone again.

25

Klara and her fellow passengers realize that they are the lucky ones. They have heard that back home the Bolsheviks are killing off the bourgeoisie in order to bring about the Communist utopia. Because they are desperate, the Bolsheviks inaugurate mass arrests and executions, accompanied by the suppression of freedom.

Known as the "Red Terror," and inaugurated in the fall of 1918 with the assassination of Bolshevik Moisei Uritsky as well as the attempt on the life of Lenin, "this ruthless campaign" aims at eliminating political opponents within the civilian population. But it rages out of control. Killings soar as the "Red Terror" which will destroy the entire noble class, spreads into Russia's provinces. All those involved with the Whites are to be shot. "The threat of death hangs in the air" and "the thought of death became commonplace ... The very word 'death' ceases to be fearsome," according to W. Bruce Lincoln writing in his book, *Red Victory*.

In the countryside, Red Army units are beginning to engage in the forced requisitioning of grain from the peasants. Because of this act, in 1921 more than a million will die from starvation in Voronezh and the Volga provinces alone when drought destroys the harvest. In 1921–22, famine and disease sweep through the Volga region killing five million.

•

Long after the killing on the tracks, the passengers remain silent. Even though death has been with them, they can't slough it off, not yet at least. Others are immune to the killings, like stepping on an ant. If a man or woman gets shot, well, they're just in the wrong place at the wrong time.

But that's the past. Now the passengers quickly cheer up as the dilapidated engine burning wood and shooting sparks from its cone-shaped funnel finally begins its journey toward Manzhouli, Manchuria, less than a hundred miles away.

"How far is this train going?" Klara asks the man next to her.

"To Harbin. But first, we've got to cross the border into Manchuria. You look shocked."

"It's just unbelievable."

"It's a miracle," he replies, as he crosses himself.

Although on the one hand the passengers are happy, they realize they'll never see their homeland again. And so, they handle the pain differently. For Klara, she's burning her bridges behind her. She knows she'll never return, so she dismisses any sorrow she might possess. After a while, nobody will know where she came from.

Halting often along the tracks, passengers are allowed to get off and walk along the embankment. At one such stop, Klara climbs down also and, though weary, she hobbles along the track, head down, arms hanging at her side. She can't connect with anyone to engage in conversation to exchange ideas. A deep depression begins to settle in.

Back in her car, she begins to walk through the train and looks at the sleeping passengers, most spouting deep lines of worry on their tired faces. She spots a face she knows coming toward her in the aisle. He stops. Her eyes lock with his.

Neither flinch.

He doesn't say anything.

She doesn't say anything.

They stare at each other.

To each, the other looks different.

He's lost weight. A pale, thin, face. Sunken cheeks. Eyes deep in sockets. His nose is red.

She can't remember. "Who is he? I know him."

Neither smile.

"I believe we met somewhere," he says.

"You look familiar, too."

"Were you ever in Chelyabinsk?"

"Several months ago. What's your name?"

The moment he says "Dmitri Abramovich Dudin," she becomes dizzy and grabs his arm. Yes, he's Dmitri, Vladimir's colleague who was on the train and fell off when the carriage he was riding in rounded the curve just before Ekaterinburg.

"But you're dead," she wants to say, but can't get the words out.

"What happened to you?" he says, helping her into an open seat.

They keep their voices low, even while they talk as if they had not seen each other for years. Neither notices that the train has come to a standstill. She tells him that Vladimir's dead, though some say missing; and that while Mischa, her brother, who's now a Red commissar, has popped up from time to time, she doesn't know where he is.

As for his own story, he says he can't remember what happened to him after he was pushed by the conductor from the train.

"I must have been on the ground for a long time. A peasant family took me in. They nursed me. Why, I don't know. I burned whatever documents I had. My saviors forged new papers for me. I hugged and kissed them and said good-bye. God has saved me. I'm going to survive and so will you, Klara, believe me," he says. "Klara, I won't let you die. We must live. We owe that to Vladimir wherever he is."

The train is stuck. No movement at all. As the hours pass, Dmitri notices Klara's sallow face, her tired eyes, her dry lips, all symptomatic of millions of Russians caught in the cauldron of this horrific Civil War and trying to break out.

For two days, the train does not move: Waiting for food, fuel, another engine, engineers, it rests at a squalid railway station. The two walk up and down the tracks. Dmitri wraps a blanket around Klara. The blanket, which he took off a dead person in the station, is soiled, but it serves its purpose and keeps the chill to a minimum. Dmitri scrounges up some bread and meat with the money she gives him.

Several days pass. Klara keeps losing track of time, especially during the night when she can't sleep. One night, she dozes off and wakes with a chill. She has a fever and she's sweating.

"Everyone out. Out, out," commands the harsh voice. "You'll have to stay here till the next train comes along. Don't worry, it'll stop for you. I'm sure you'll all lie down on the tracks," he snickers. "*Dosvidanya.*"

The next morning when she awakens, she notices Dmitri's looking at her. "What is it?"

"I met him, your brother Mischa. He didn't bother me. He's still a Red commander, guerrilla fighter, harassing the enemy. He sent me back to you. He wants to see you, Klara. He has known your whereabouts ever since you left Irkutsk. He's here in Zabaikalsk."

"Please Dmitri, it's too much. I can't. He murdered the man I was to marry; I'm more and more convinced of that."

"Your brother's your best friend."

"Once I needed him. But that was then. Now is now."

Klara realizes she has made a mistake talking this way to Dmitri. She has to be cautious. She must try to mask her feelings.

"Stop talking like that," she says to herself. "Most people'll think there's something wrong if you constantly badmouth your brother. Don't go down that road. Dmitri might get the idea you're manipulating him. So far, he's been nice. Be careful. Mull it over. Better that way. Even people you dislike can be your angel."

"Dmitri, you convinced me. Take me to him."

The musty-smelling room in the cabin in the hills contains a large round, wooden table adorned with dirty ashtrays and unwashed whiskey shot glasses, a few plates on an old table with four chairs, and a cracked leather couch along the wall.

Tears come quickly; happy tears that roll down her cheeks.

"Can't stand you. Damn it. But I guess you're still my brother."

"As they say, the feeling's mutual," answers Mischa softly and with a slight smile on his face. Sensing that she is hungry by the way she looks at the kettle on the old-fashioned stove, Mischa provides her with hot milk, an egg, and fresh bread.

For a long time, brother and sister don't talk.

"Everyone in the family will shun me now because I can't marry. How can I? No man will have me. I can't give them children."

"God is sparring with me. He's killing everyone dear to me, but keeping me alive. I'm almost raped in Odessa, but the molester is shot. Then on the Chelyabinsk to Irkutsk train with you, shotgun pellets find my leg and stomach and I become sterile. Then I end up in a hospital after one of your gangsters bangs my head with a rifle butt. Later, I'm spared death when bandits attack a jewelry store in Chita. God, stop teasing me. Take me already."

She sobs again, as Mischa remains silent.

"Oh, if only you hadn't killed Vladimir, none of this would have happened," she says out loud, turning her bloodshot eyes down toward her barren belly and adding, "he never would have left me. Now he's dead."

But she realizes she should stop attacking Mischa. She needs him.

"Did Vladimir know you couldn't have children?" asks Mischa.

"Yes, I told him the last night we were together. He didn't seem upset. He took it well, though I know how much he wanted children. That's the way it is with his people, even though his father is a well-known Communist. Later on, he said, we could adopt if we wanted to. And the next day, you shot him."

"Please, Klara, stop it!" Mischa does not say that Vladimir may be alive; he's probably just missing. But she'll never believe it. She's had to convince herself that he's dead; otherwise, he'd have caught up with her.

"Nothing exists for you here," he counters. "Move on. Find Papa. He'll help you. Later, you and Papa will bring Momma and the girls over. Right now I heard they're fine, though Odessa has been a battleground. Those fleeing our troops have congregated in the city. So go."

"It's easy to say, 'Pick yourself up. Fight on. Don't quit. Keep at it.' I've had to act the tough young lady. Can't stand it anymore. And I don't need your speeches. And at what cost? My life? Just because I gave my word, can't I change my mind? The sacrifice might not just be worth it. So what that I promised? What if the promise is too much? Does that mean I keep going despite everything?" She wants to slap him, she's so angry. But she controls her rage. So she leans on his shoulder and cries and cries pouring out her anger in tears.

He doesn't know what to say. If only he can convince her he didn't kill Vladimir.

Something's wrong with the whole story, thinks Mischa. My men searched the area. They didn't find a body. He just vanished. Yet even in all this turmoil, somebody would have heard something; especially about a Red Cross officer who as everyone knows has a famous Bolshevik father. Unless, of course, he fled on purpose.

And as if a revelation has penetrated Mischa's fatigued brain, he comes to the conclusion that Vladimir, discovering she couldn't have children wanted nothing to do with her. Despite his protestations, he couldn't bring himself to be saddled with a barren wife and leave the Siberia he loves. Who knows? Maybe he thought we Bolsheviks would win and if we won, well; he'd better leave and get back quickly through the lines and to Red territory so he could be on the winning side. Besides, he reasons, Klara's a Jewess and even with all his idealism, he felt in the end it wouldn't work.

The two are silent. In a few minutes, she wipes her eyes and breathes heavily. He's learned not to be sentimental, or so he thinks he has.

To Mischa Rasputnis, it still isn't the catastrophe she's making it out to be. He just can't get excited about it. Maybe there's a good side to all this: She doesn't have to marry a *goy*. She can get to America and start a new life, even if trouble looms ahead when she finds Father. Apparently he's not masking his thoughts too well, either.

"Mischa, are you listening?"

"Yes, I'm sorry. I feel bad for you."

Again silence, this time for several minutes. She's ready to move on and she realizes that she never asked him about Olga, the female Cheka officer. "Mischa, whatever happened to Olga? Did you ever find her?"

He doesn't answer.

"I guess you don't want to talk about it," she says.

"She's dead. Back then, after you and I parted in Irkutsk, I moved on to Chita. But when I'd return to our base back across the Volga, I'd ask about her. Usually, they'd answer: 'she's at the front.' One day, however, they didn't reply; they wouldn't tell me what happened. Only later did I find out that as she interrogated a prisoner, her fellow officer left her for a few moments. In that short time the prisoner somehow managed to stab her with a hidden knife he had buried in his underwear; escape through a back window and get into town. But the Cheka moves fast. Her comrade, who found her dead was charged with being derelict in his duty and shot immediately. When they found the prisoner, they hung him in the village square.

"Olga was buried in a grave in the small cemetery behind the barracks. A wooden Red star marked her resting place and whenever I return to this camp,

I lay flowers on where she sleeps. Such a beautiful person," he whispers. "She didn't deserve to die like that." And with that, this so-called tough Red commissar breaks down in tears, and as he sobs, he tells Klara that he's now even more committed to the Communist cause.

"I'll kill every White I get my hands on."

The two hug each other. They are drained. A few minutes pass until Klara utters: "If I get out of this alive, I'm never going to tell anyone about my problem or Vladimir, or even that you're a half-brother."

"I won't tell either. What good would it do?"

So in this desolate part of Siberia, a pact is made between brother and sister. For now, the secret is shrouded. Virtually everyone holds a secret as a prisoner in the mind. And the jailer in her mind knew that she had to keep the secret hidden in solitary confinement. But Klara recognized that in a fit of anger, Mischa could spill it all out someday. Be that as it may, she'd do everything in her power to keep it buried deep down in the pit of her body, as if it was fastened to the bottom of a volcano.

The two don't talk for a long while. Klara straightens up, wipes away the tears, puts a smile on her face and says:

"Tell you what, brother. I learned a lot from my ballet group. Whenever they messed up on the floor, they'd go back to the *barre*, back to basics. They were such wonderful people; I miss them. Dancing was like food for all of us. I'm going back to my mission, even if it kills me," she says with a sly snicker that will remain her marker for life.

"You've still got a long way to go," answers Mischa. "Anyway, we should get some sleep. It's late. You can have the couch. My men'll take you back tomorrow. Good night."

Klara gets up and embraces this "brother of hers," as she likes to call him.

"Klara. Get out of this cursed land. This war's going to last a long time," he says as he kisses her on the forehead, sure in his heart he'll never see her again.

Next morning, Mischa's gone. He leaves her ten rubles. Again she's abandoned and again, her heart is lonely. The night after her return, she dreams again. She hears her father's voice, calm but firm, instructive, affectionate: "Klara, put your mind to the task. That's all you have to do."

Simple words, "Put your mind to the task." The words lift her; it'll be her new motto.

She must remember not to talk too much. Nobody has to know she's from Odessa. "If nobody cares where I'm from, do they care where I'm going?" she mutters.

26

The Chinese Eastern Railway, September 1918

In travel, a shortcut that speeds you quickly to your ultimate destination is a welcome sign, especially after a tumultuous journey. Ever since Klara Rasputnis boarded the train in Chita, she has taken advantage of a shorter route to find her father. She has been a passenger on a relatively new railway, the Chinese Eastern Railway that links Chita—via Harbin—with Vladivostok in the Russia Far East. The CER route drastically reduces the travel distance required along the Trans Siberian Railway and its northern route in Russia to Vladivostok. The new line crossing Manchuria remains Chinese in name only, for the Czarist government maneuvered an agreement with China in which the Russians laid the tracks along a zone in Manchuria. That zone, in effect, had become a Russian crown colony.

Despite the fact that Manchuria may be occupied by bandits and gun lords, the political climate soothes Klara and the refugees. They are out of the clutches of the Cheka. Jews now turn thoughts to their future. They hear that in 1917, the course of Jewish history has changed with the historic British Balfour Declaration: "His Majesty's Government views with favor the establishment in Palestine of a national home for the Jewish people...."

On the train from Manzhouli (Manchuria Station) to Harbin, Klara will meet up with a new wave of young Jews who are marching with their feet to fulfill the age-old dream of Zion restored. They are called "Zionists."

•

Klara and Dmitri are stuck in this forsaken outpost right at the border. No trains. They find a spot on the floor of the single boarding house in Zabaikalsk.

The next morning, both are quiet until Dmitri tells Klara, "We've got to do something quick, or we'll be here forever. Maybe we can get to the part of the border that that isn't guarded and cross over there. We can get a train from there. We've got to keep moving."

"Yes, but how?"

"Come on. Let's go out to the street. We'll check out the area to see if anyone is guarding the border and if we can cross."

They walk up and down the main street. They try and find out what's going on at the crossing.

"Nothing's here," she says.

"Wait, Klara. Patience."

"I know. I know. But 'we've got to get out of here' are your words."

"Just be patient."

"Easy for you to say."

"Okay. Have it your way."

Arriving at the border on the Russian side, the two notice there're no guards, at least not outside the sentry post.

By now large crowds have joined them and are walking slowly to the crossing known as the Manchuria Station. No one comes out of the guardhouse on the Russian side and the barrier's up. Half-ripped flags flap in the wind. Welcoming signs hang loose. A downed, muddy banner states that pedestrians should "Cross Here Only! Violators will be shot!"

"Too quiet," says Dmitri. "Something's wrong. My God! Look over there, on the ground outside the door. The guards are dead. Must have happened last night. Nobody's come to their rescue. Nobody's moved their bodies. Welcome to Manchuria, everyone."

"Like God parted the Red Sea," a man pipes in. "God's with us."

"Better yet, I like the Russian saying, 'God and the Tsar are far away,' responds Dmitri.

They cross the road, past the guardhouse with its windows full of bullet holes. Silence. The men bow their heads and then look at the sky, the fields, the trees and realize they're leaving home. Planning to do so is one thing, but when it comes to tearing themselves away from Mother Russia and the life they have lived as Russians, some have second thoughts. Quickly, they overcome the reluctance. It's life or death. Yet they're cautious. They sense an invisible message in the sky: "Free you may be, but not out of danger yet."

"A new life's beginning for us," says Dmitri, trying to make his words sound encouraging to Klara. But inwardly, his stomach churns with the start of what everyone calls homesickness, as if a nurse took the infant from the mother's breast before getting full.

Not Klara; she smiles, a smile that telegraphs, "I'll make it to a new land. And I'll forget this country."

In a few hours, Klara and Dmitri fight their way onto a Chinese train on the line that will take them through Manchuria. Having bought some food near the station for the long haul to Harbin and having paid on board for the tickets with the money Mischa left for her, they relax a bit. They know they have to travel through the countryside, a countryside that resembles a large refugee camp of Whites, Reds, Greens, partisans of all persuasions; guerrillas, desperados, foreign troops; all of them quite capable of confiscating their food, and beating or killing them.

"Look," shouts Dmitri, "the road sign; 600 miles to Harbin."

The train slowly chugs along unsafe, often cracked tracks. Passengers scan the horizon for bandits. Their melancholy thoughts return. Long ago, Dmitri had been forced to abandon his old girlfriend, Dunya; she's gone and he doesn't even know where she's living, or if she's even alive at all.

As for Klara, she realizes she never had a chance to say good-bye to Vladimir. And now he's gone. Dmitri will have to protect her. A harsh rain lashes the cars. A raw wind bores through broken windows. Chilly fall winds make them shiver. Klara closes her eyes as the train keeps going and clacking, stopping and clacking, moving and clacking without a schedule, without attention to speed or safety, ever southward.

"You know, Klara," continues Dmitri, "I used to get the shakes. I drank too much. After my fall from the train, I swore I'd never drink again and I haven't. It's the curse of Russia."

Klara doesn't answer. She's asleep.

Next morning, their train stops. Everyone scampers out; men to one side, women to the other. There's a stream nearby. They wash. The daily routine begins again. This nation of weary bodies is moving away from danger.

"Do you smell the change in the air? We're getting closer to Harbin," says Dmitri. "Milder here. We're going south."

The wind warms her body. She senses sexual warmth again. She cools her desire; too much pain regarding Vladimir. She grieves for him. She will never shed him, never.

That night, a familiar dream reoccurs. She is in a bedroom in a very fancy apartment house in Odessa. A newly installed telephone rings. A young person picks up the phone and begins talking. It's a familiar voice. He's a soldier, tall and blond. Who is it? She can't recognize him. The trooper puts down the phone and sees her. Walking over, he sits on the edge of the bed and pulls her to him. She slides into his embrace.

"How did this happen?" he asks looking down at her and planting kisses on her brow.

"Who was it?" she asks herself next morning as if she was questioning the town gossip.

"You know who," says her voice.

"I don't, I don't. Tell me. Tell me. I'm not sure."

No answer; the voice is gone.

"Oh my God!" Klara yells as the train stops the next morning and they open the door to see what's causing a delay. "Look who's here! I don't believe it. Osip. Over here. Is it really you? Come over here. Here we are," she says, reaching out to him as he boards the car. "My God, you've lost weight. Your face's thinner. Anyway, how did you find us? I know nothing ever happens by accident on this stupid line."

"I'm Armenian. Remember?" answers Osip, having pulled himself up into the train car. "Followed your tracks. Not hard to pick up. We have our spies. Anyway, you shouldn't have run away from me," he says angrily. "I got in trouble with Mischa. He didn't think you were healthy enough to go. It doesn't matter anymore, I'm also getting out of that hellhole."

Klara puts her arm around his shoulder and pulls him close to her. He's her security, too.

"But I had to give you the slip. You were getting too oppressive. Had to get going," she says.

"I saw Mischa yesterday. We talked and he sent me on my way."

Turning to the stranger, she realizes she hasn't introduced them.

But first, "Dmitri, meet Osip. Osip, meet Dmitri."

"Klara, I also brought a friend with me," says Osip as he waves to a tall, young lad still standing on the tracks. "Come on up, Shlomo."

"Now there's a nice looking boy," is her first reaction to the newcomer. She can see his muscular arms, thin body, brown hair combed back. How did he get such perfectly fitting clothes? she wonders

Osip interrupts her train of thought when he whispers, "He's a nice guy. But he talks a lot, especially about Zionism."

"Where're you from?" asks Dmitri, thinking to himself, Klara and I were a couple, now suddenly we're a group.

"I'm from Kiev," discloses the newcomer. "On the one hand, I miss it. My father moved to Kiev to better himself. He didn't want his family to be poor. Thrown out of his family's lumber business by a jealous and crooked uncle. 'A falling out of the brothers,' he would say. I think he wanted to avoid mean and sarcastic relatives. They're trouble."

Shlomo relates how he later joined the Red Guards who promised him freedom from Czarist oppression and anti-Semitic officials.

"Lies, lies," he continues, "Jews who flock to the Reds are making a big mistake. Yes, there's an alternative. Get out while the going's good. Let 'em emigrate to Palestine, the Jewish homeland. The Russian borders are still open."

They're all tired, so they sit down on the floor and though difficult, try to sleep. The hard wood stiffens their backs. Not easy, though they get used to it. They pool what little money they have; it's enough to keep them from starving.

"We're almost there. But we must be careful in this part of the world," Dmitri says as the engine's bells ring and the train lurches forward.

Exiting the station, the train snakes past Lake Dalai Nor and rolls across the steppes.

"Thank God we're out of there," says Klara though a deep foreboding begins to creep into her mind. She cries again. Her life keeps changing as the train moves further and further away from home. Putting distance between her and her former home causes pain. "But wait," Klara says to herself, "perhaps the most dangerous part of this damn terrible trip is over. Is it? How will this end?" she asks, sobbing quietly. She leans her head on Dmitri's shoulder. She's exhausted.

As the train moves on, the passengers notice a fortified station building across the field adorned with apes, dragons, and other Chinese ornaments. Klara watches Chinese carts with their two high wheels cracking the hard soil. Beyond them, camels are at pasture.

After climbing several gradients, the train picks up speed across these flat lands of the Manchus. Gazing out the window, passengers note little habitation and much grass for grazing.

With Manzhouli behind them, this young, boisterous group, now part of a caravan, is on its way. They form a friendly quartet. Dmitri, Osip, Shlomo, and Klara. Riding the rails of the Chinese Eastern Railway, they're all heading for Harbin, the largest commercial center in northern Manchuria.

The train moves across fertile but sparsely populated land in Heilongjiang and Jilin Provinces and begins to follow the Sungari River and like a fired bullet, heads straight to Harbin.

The road to Harbin, however, is fraught with the danger of a new tyrant who sticks knives into people's ears, or beats them with sticks on their genitals.

"We were lucky in Chita," continues Dmitri in a talkative mood. "We avoided Ataman Semenov, the bastard who rules that town like it was his own. Now, we have to watch out for Baron von Ungern-Sternberg who moves his troops in and out of the area."

"So what's unusual about that? Killing Jews?" interrupts Shlomo. "Happens all the time. You don't need a lesson in history. Heard about the Kishinev pogrom in 1903? They slaughtered Jews who did nothing to defend themselves. No more. We won't lie down as sheep. In Palestine, we'll fight. That's why every Jew should be a Zionist. That's the only way we'll return to our homeland."

A smile lights his face as he glances at Klara. "Think about it," he says and walks away.

Later that day, Shlomo's not discussing Zionism, Communism, or Socialism. He and Klara are planning what they would do when they get to Harbin. Jewish refugee groups and Jewish clubs and a large Jewish colony live alongside

White Russians. Though they reside in their own neighborhoods, the Whites have brought their anti-Semitism with them from Mother Russia.

Harbin stands as a fishing village and the only Russian city beyond the borders of Russia. Czarist government flyers describe the municipality as "A Russian City on Chinese Territory."

Osip tells Klara there's money to be made in Harbin. "But be careful in that town. Not everyone's rich. Some have to sell everything to get out, everything that is, except their fur coats," Osip smiles. "You've got a lot of deserters, prisoners of war, and even penniless nobles roaming the streets."

Osip doesn't tell her that some refugees are offering their bodies to soldiers hungry for sex and that white slavers are sneaking into town, pouncing on young girls and kidnapping them.

"My God," thinks Klara, "it never lets up, the same fears, the same anxiety I had going into Moscow, into Chelyabinsk, into Irkutsk, Chita, I have them now heading into Harbin, and there's still a long way to go. Will I ever make it?"

27

On the outskirts of Hailar, Manchuria, one misty September morning in 1918, four young Russians lean out of the passenger window of their halted train on the Chinese Eastern Railway. They are 500 miles from Harbin and they are smiling and laughing and slapping each other on the back. Each one of them has only one oft-spoken sentence: "Harbin, here we come."

The four are so charged up that for the first time in a long time, they jump, not walk down the few car steps. Eager to go into town, eager to walk down a town street and not worry about being picked up by the police, they hurry into the station fortified with artillery and guards. The walls are covered with designs of apes, dragons, and Chinese ornaments.

Dmitri and Osip exit together. Shlomo, who finds Klara very attractive, gently takes her hand and motions her to a different direction. She obliges.

Dmitri doesn't try and stop Klara. He can't; she has a mind of her own. Even though a bit jealous, he doesn't tag along.

He knows Klara won't last long with Shlomo. She's as stubborn as he is. He wants Palestine; she, America. Dmitri sees that that with the disappearance of Vladimir, she has once again begun her search for her father.

Meanwhile, for these young Russian travelers, the scenery has changed: They gaze at Chinese carts with their two high wheels pulled by camels along streets. They observe a blend of Russian and Mongolian log cabins, some with yurt-style roofs, standing tall in this, the "Pearl of the Grasslands," city of fifty thousand, a gateway between China, Mongolia, and Russia, a caravan road that runs from Urga, the capital of Mongolia to Manchuria.

Shlomo and Klara wander the streets, looking in the stalls along the make-shift marketplace. They laugh and with nearly the last of their money, they treat themselves to Turkish coffee and *baklava*.

Free from care and enjoying the surroundings in this market and commercial center, they start arguing whether the conductor bellowed a 20-minute stop or an hour respite. Shlomo insists, an hour; she, 20 minutes.

"Don't wonder off. We may have to run back," warns Klara. "Let's head back to the station."

Freedom, however, is too much for them. They're oblivious to everything. They forget their world, the time, even their companion of the moment. To Klara, Vladimir is walking beside her.

"I am sure it was 20 minutes," she again tells Shlomo, this time convinced. But her warning is too late; the final three beeps sound from the train blocks away.

"The train. It's going. We missed it," screams Shlomo, "and Dmitri has all our tickets!"

"All our stuff. All our clothes!" shouts Klara, her face wrinkled, her hand atop her head, her eyes wide open with anger. "Pray that Osip and Dmitri got on the train. Some pioneer you'll make. I told you 20 minutes. The train only runs once a day, I was told. We're stuck in this town until tomorrow morning."

"Where're we going to sleep? My God. The station's a filthy mess. Could be typhoid around here, too. Besides, at night, they'll cut our throats," he says.

"We need money. I'm out. Just a few rubles left."

"Same here," says Shlomo, though Klara wonders how he's broke when he's going all the way to Palestine. On what? But she's in a similar position with her journey, though she still has the pearl necklace her mother gave her and the rubies and the ring from Vladimir. She's certainly not going to cash them in now, unless ...

"We've got to get something to eat," she states emphatically.

"You know, Klara, we could always pick up some needed cash."

He sees a smirk on Klara's face. She's laughing at him. "Robbery? An option? You, the idealist," she teases. " I guess it's okay for the poor to steal from the rich. Didn't Lenin say: 'Loot the landlords! Seize their estates! Rob their jewelry stores!' Don't you know your Communism? The only problem; this is China. These people don't agree with Comrade Lenin. Still, I'm all for it."

Smiling, he realizes that Klara takes other peoples ideas and thoughts and uses them to back up her singular desire to move on, and if that means stealing, so be it.

"Well in that case, forget any kind of petit theft. No small-time job for Klara and Shlomo," he says. "Banish the thought. Not here. If they catch you even stealing a toy, they shoot you. Worse than Arabia where they cut off your hand if you take something that's not yours, but at least they let you live. So, if we're going to pull off a robbery let's make it big."

Later that evening, Shlomo and Klara sit in the doorway of an abandoned hut.

Finally, Shlomo breaks the silence:

"When I went to the outhouse by the station, I learned from a peasant that a villa outside of town belongs to a Baron Simonoff. There's a concert tonight and everyone in town is going, including the Baron and his family. I got the address. We can hit the house."

"Oh? And get caught? And how do you know someone won't be in the house?"

"I'll check it out first. I'm a professional. We've no choice."

"Where's that house? Let's go."

The troika's bells sound like ringing doorbell chimes. The horses grunt as their feet pound down on the road's hard surface. Klara and Shlomo have been standing for a few hours waiting for this very moment. Finally, the Simonoffs' carriage begins to move and picks up speed. The occupants' laughter pierces the cool Manchurian night. They are jovial; their faces are lit; they seem ready for the anticipated joy of the theater. Shlomo and Klara are silent, mere statues among tall, birch trees planted around the circular driveway. They watch the carriage fade away into the bright moonlight. Looking up Klara can see that the moon is high in the sky. "Please moon. Protect me!"

"Just relax, Klara. Relax," says Shlomo showing whose boss of the operation. He circles the house and when he comes back, he puts his hand on Klara's shoulder as he whispers instructions to the girl whom he hopes will be his wife.

"Nobody's in the house. We only want valuables we can put in our pockets: Jewelry. Cash, preferably bills. No coins. Don't grab or touch anything else. All we need is enough to get to Vladivostok," he says, somehow feeling that if anyone does walk by, he would be able to overcome them with a pistol hidden in a small bag he took with him from the train. He can stand guard while Klara does the dirty work.

"I heard you," she answers impatiently. "You've said that five times already. Bad enough I have to rob a house and become a common thief. Don't make it worse."

"I'll be waiting here," replies Shlomo, ignoring her remarks, and yet feeling guilty and wondering if he's right to let her go alone into the house and pull off the robbery while he stands watch. He hopes he's right and nobody's there, even though he did look through the windows and when he went inside, checked part of the dwelling. Not a soul.

"See the back door over there? Go through it," he says in a calmer voice. "When you get into the house, go straight through the hall, up the stairs and into the first bedroom on the right at the top of the staircase. The jewelry, whatever those bourgeois Simonoffs are not wearing tonight, will probably be in one of the drawers. Believe me, whatever you get is enough for the tickets, some meals. Don't get greedy," he adds in a serious tone, which she knew by now means he's worried about pulling it off.

"I'll be on my best," she says, reaching her hand up and moving it slowly along his black stubbled cheek. "I'm glad you're with me. I know you'll be here if I stumble," she says, wondering what she'd have done if he was not there and she missed the train.

"Now go," commands Shlomo. "Remember, just money and jewels. Don't be frightened." Immediately she's off across the flat lawn. Even in running, her ballet training shows. Despite the old shotgun injury, she still has that special lift. She gracefully leaps across the small field like a gazelle.

Quickly passing through the back door, she moves down the long hall that contains family portraits. She doesn't stop to see their names, as she is eager to climb the steps to the second floor.

"The bedroom. The bedroom. Where is it? Here! Shlomo was right," she says to herself. Right over to the bureau, she goes.

"Top drawer, nothing. Middle drawer, nothing again. Bottom drawer, yes, yes. There it is, the jewelry box." She dumps its contents on the master bed. Ripping off a nearby pillowcase from a cushion, she stuffs it with bracelets, rings, watches, and earrings. "Such jewelry. Enough here to buy ten rail tickets and passage across the Pacific," she says to herself. "How could people be so stupid as to leave all this lying around?"

The full moon shines through the window's lace curtains as if it's a beacon for her. It reminds her of the night in Odessa when she awoke and saw the moon, only that moon was red, blood red. Tonight it's white and the light signals that she'd better move on.

"Downstairs. Move Klara." Her legs follow her commands. The steps pass quickly under her feet. Turning to go back down the hall, she spies the library.

"Damn it," she mutters, "I can't pass a library without looking at the books."

A few spotlights above the four tall shelves have been left on. If she had her way, she'd take all the tomes in this bookcase. Perhaps she can lift a small volume and hide it under her sweater. Her eye quickly finds a strange title, *The Possessed,* by Fedor Dostoyevsky. She has heard about this book. The writer takes up the cause of the little man.

"Hell no, I'm not going to read him. He's a known anti-Semite. Why read anyone who insults your religion," she says under her breath, returning the book to its dusty spot. She looks down to the end of the shelf to see what book she can grab when a log cracks in the smoldering fireplace reminding her of Shlomo's words, "Only cash and jewelry."

She's about to leave the library when an antique desk near the wall catches her attention. Had not Shlomo told her to look in desk drawers for cash or bank notes? Her pent up zeal and anxiety bursts out as she pulls out one drawer after another. And finally, she reaches down and pulls out the bottom one whose lock she bashes open with a stone ashtray.

"Eureka!" she shouts: Envelopes with bills, one of them with hundreds of rubles. Another with American dollars, and another, British pounds, and another, German marks, and another, Japanese yen.

"He's so brilliant that Shlomo," she says, stuffing the envelopes into her pillow.

"Out now. Go out. Back door," she tells herself. But she halts again.

"Oh my God! There. On the dining room table, roses. Beautiful, fragrant real roses, a dozen of them in a vase, no less."

She plucks out a single rose from the forest of roses. The rich red petals are so soft and smooth. They seem to Klara to be made of velvet. As she fondles a flower, the poem by the Englishman Thomas Moore, "The Last Rose of Summer," comes to her mind. She promises herself that when she gives this love potion of a single rose to Shlomo, she'll recite it. In jest, of course.

"Shlomo can never be my permanent love; he's going to Palestine."

A note has been attached to the vase. "To Naadia, with love."

She can't hold back the tears that swell in her eyes. Vladimir couldn't send her flowers. Sorry Naadia. I had a lover, too, reflects Klara, wiping away her misty eyes and out she goes, stopping for a second to inhale the flower's eternal rapture.

Fortunately for the two, an unscheduled train comes through an hour after the break-in and stops to pick up passengers. The Siminoffs are not back from the concert, so they can't report the burglary. Boarding, Klara and Shlomo eagerly await the sounds that means music to their ears, the clatter in their carriage, the familiar hoot, and the final lurch forward. Finally, they settle back in their seats. They're instructed to keep the blinds down. No reason to tip off bandits in the hills that a train of refugees and loot is passing through.

The train whistles as it rolls through village after village.

"When will we ever get there?" someone shouts.

But then, up ahead, just past a dry landscape of dead trees, there's a river, a bright river, and with it an unexpected shout, a hoarse man joyously yelling to the top of his lungs: "We're crossing the Sungari River. Almost there. Harbin, here we come!"

On arrival in the early afternoon of October 12, 1918, Klara's 18th birthday, the two youths locate Osip and Dmitri at the railway station. Waiting for a day and a half, with nowhere to go, nothing to do, the young men took turns watching for the incoming trains, counting the minutes and hours as they stand in the crowded terminal. They have the luggage.

Since the taxis are all taken, they grab rickshaws. It's exciting for them to watch the coolies lift the poles, lunge forward and run in rhythmical manner toward the business district.

A short while later, three ragged, disheveled-looking young men and a tall, thin, attractive woman, check into Harbin's fanciest hotel, the Hotel Moderne, whose name is carved in cyrillic letters above the massive concrete structure. The youths are shown to a three-bedroom deluxe suite with a breakfast room, a sitting room, and a bathroom. The bedrooms have double beds. Klara has her own room, a wonderful birthday gift; she will pamper herself.

The four pay cash for a week, tip lavishly, and admire the Turkish-rugged hallways. Shlomo points out that nobody questions where people get money or if they spread it around without restraint, for in war, people will grab up any hard currency.

"Welcome to Harbin; in winter, the coldest place on earth," they are told by the concierge. Later in the dining room, after a few vodka toasts to Klara on her birthday, their Chinese waiter happily jokes with them and even relates that it only snows twice a year in Harbin.

"The first time it snows, we get out our winter clothes, as the snow is a herald of bitter weather. And the second time it snows," he continues, "we get out more winter clothes. It really gets cold here," he says, seeing their smiling faces and not wanting to disillusion them.

28

China waits. No hurry. One day Japan will take Harbin and then China will retake it. But for now this railway center is Russian. "Let the intruders call it their own," says China. Even if the town displays onion-shaped Russian church cupolas, even if its street and store signs are in Russian-language letters, even if sections of this Manchurian city are called, "Moscow of the East," or "Manchurian Paris," even if White Russians or Japanese live here, Harbin someday again will be Chinese.

By 1914, 69,500 residents representing 53 nationalities, including 25,000 Jews, will call Harbin home. The city is crawling with White refugees, many of whom hate Jews, even if those Jews, like them, are fleeing Bolshevism.

But it is not clear who is in charge as Russians, Cossacks, Japanese and Chinese troops sit and eye each other.

•

Dawn in Harbin.

A Russian storekeeper opening his front door, looks up to the sky and grimaces. "More rain," he says to himself and enters his own personal world of demands, haggling, and yelling. Yet he is happy; he and his family are safe. A Chinese peddler, setting up his wooden stall in front of the grocery store, displays necklaces of imitation pearls and homemade paper flowers. A fruit storeowner opens the door of his shop. A haberdasher put on his store lights. The tearooms are not open yet; it's too early.

Horse traders flock to the city selling hardy Mongolian ponies, which are harnessed in pairs to the droshkies.

Harbin prides itself on being a city of contrasts. On the one hand, cabarets, theaters, and whorehouses have made it a boomtown with smartly dressed women visiting fashionable shops. On the other hand, it has become a city of beggars and panhandlers who once were millionaires, but lost fortunes in the recent inflation that has hit the country. The ruble is worthless. But for Klara and her three comrades with strong foreign currency, money will never be a problem; the heist in Hailar will pay for it all.

Klara knows she is narrowing the distance between her and her father. But she has to be careful. Harbin streets are filled with idling soldiers. Robbery and rape are a daily occurrence. After weeks in smoky, crowded trains, she indulges herself with soapy, perfumed hot baths in the hotel and begins to peel off layers of anxiety as she dons newly purchased silk dressing gowns over her relaxed skin.

Klara and her three fellows frequent the Café Mars, a favorite of the expats. There, they watch and look out for friendly Jewish faces. She discovers that most Harbin Jews thrive in this Russian-look-alike city. Families, with names like Bonner, Kabalkin, Pautushinsky, Skidelsky, and Soskin, deal in export-import, textiles, furs, dry goods, and general merchandise.

The sign on the two story wooden building reads "Harbin Hebrew Association." Long lines of refugee families with their tired faces, their hunched-over bodies, their crying children begin to snake around the weather-beaten structure at five o'clock in the morning. When the two tall wooden French doors finally open at nine, the noise outside is subdued and the rush inside begins for these excited and emotional families into a massive hall decorated with blue and white bunting, the colors of the Zionist flag. Hung around the hall are a few pictures of Theodor Herzl, the founder of the Zionist movement, with his long black beard, his Messianic smile, his redemptive eyes. It is doubtful if anyone, except Shlomo, notices him or even knows who he is, as they rush to find an aid worker.

As the morning proceeds, the Association room becomes smoke-filled as everyone seems to light up cigarettes at the same time, much to the chagrin of the Chinese cleaning staff who laugh at the overexcited Russian, Ukrainian, Polish, Lithuanian, Latvian, Estonian, and Bessarabian Jews, all talking at once, switching from Yiddish to Russian, back to Yiddish, to Ukrainian and Polish, and back again to Yiddish.

When they are not talking, they mill around the crowded hall and wait their turn to see an advisor. Some men play chess on make shift benches. Some women breast-feed their infants. Some read torn, yellowing newspapers. Some knit. Some wait for a letter, a pass, a friend, a supervisor. Boredom loosens their tongues as they stand around in the corridors of this framed building in a city on the banks of the River Sungari, they ponder and pontificate on world events in Moscow, Berlin, and London.

"Got to get out of here before winter" says one.

"Did you know Harbin is called the ice city?"

"Where you going?"

"I'm staying put. There's money to be made here."

"You crazy? Russia's done with. Manchuria's done with. Leave now."

"Where to?"

"The only place in the world where we can live as Jews, Palestine."

"No. America. America. That's the Promised Land."

"Maybe you've heard about my cousin in Brooklyn. He's from Kiev."

"What's his name?"

"Cohen."

"Cohen?"

"Do you know how many Cohens there are in Brooklyn?"

"No. I won't trade you rubles for cigarettes."

"Stay here. Free lunch."

"I bought white rolls on the corner. Imagine that. White rolls. Not black bread."

The Russian residents of Harbin are called *Kharbintsy*. Stalked and often robbed by swindlers; exploited by thieves; approached by opium traffickers; mugged by men, women, and even children, the refugees try to survive. If they are lucky they hole up in filthy crowded apartments, three or four families in a unit. Some even set up house in cold cellars.

Klara is frightened in Harbin. But as in Russia, she has the boys to protect her. She's not intimidated by a group of men. Her room in the hotel suite is across from Shlomo's, one of the few balcony rooms overlooking the busy thoroughfare. Klara's room boasts beautiful gold wallpaper, a Persian rug, a four-poster bed that invites sleep and a mahogany *amoire*.

She and Shlomo often walk through the arch that spans the street leading from the Russian quarter to the Chinese quarter. Though she has seen filth in Russia, Klara flinches when she spots dead rats as big as small terriers filling up the gutters in the alleyways.

One day, they all head for Fu Dzya Dyan, the town and home of a million Chinese. Once it had been a small village inhabited by a few poor fishermen. Then the railway came and with it coolies, merchants, adventurers, businessmen, and promoters and of course, opium dens that they constantly observe, but don't enter.

The group of four goes through the arch and move down the narrow road, lined with irregularly roofed buildings and wooden balconies. Rainbow banners and streamers fill the streets with gorgeous colors; lanterns swing overhead. Pigtailed men in black satin robes and round black hats move by inviting shops. Women, with bound feet and Manchu girls with normal ones, saunter pass busy stores. Elderly Chinese women hobble on tiny, distorted toes.

Who said Chinese treat Russians as foreign devils? They smile and make way for the four who move quickly past several undertakers' shops. Piled almost in front of the doors are huge coffins painted red, black, and gold. Next door is a whorehouse where gaily dressed, painted, doll-like-girls sit, each in her house doorway. They look clean, yet Shlomo tells Klara they give off an oppressive smell if you get close to them.

"How do you know?"

"That's what I heard," he blushes.

Only Osip stays back at the hotel. That's because he's sick and doesn't dare go out of his room. He doesn't want to be far from a toilet.

On one such walk around town, Klara's eyes suddenly open wide: "Look. Across the street. A bookstore. A Russian bookstore. Let's go in." She has not seen such a store in months. She realizes she has not even seen a book, except for those fleeting moments back in the mansion where they stole the money. She scans the shelves, "There he is again. That mad Russian. That anti-Semite. I'll take it this time," she tells the clerk, "*The Brothers Karamazov,* by Fedor Dostoevsky. Only because I'm out of his pogrom-ridden country."

The next day as they saunter down the street, Klara gets close to Shlomo and whispers in his ear, "Let's go shopping. "

"How much you need?"

She's silent.

"Here," he says, "taking out a wad of bills and counting out two thousand rubles. "I want you to look like a queen. My queen."

"I'll take that. And that."

"Wrap that up."

"That silk blouse. How much?"

"Five hundred rubles," the clerk answers, not impressed with a teenager entering a luxury shop and buying out the store, until the young person gives him a large ruble note as a tip.

"Can I try on that dress? Thank you?"

"Do you have this sweater in my size?"

Three hours later, Klara Rasputnis returns to the hotel laden down with three bags, and a hatbox.

29

For several days, Shlomo and Klara go to the Association hall. There they wait and while they pass the time, they notice two men stand guard at the supervisor's office.

"Enough. We've been here over a week. To hell with this," Klara mutters. "Let's go."

Shlomo, already used to Klara's assertiveness, needs no prodding. They casually walk up to the guards as if they have an appointment. No questions asked; the two open the door.

"*Shalom Aleichem,*" she says to the first person inside the door, an older man, slightly bent, an unkempt beard, a large black skull cap on his head.

"*Aleichem Shalom,*" answers the man, showing his diseased gums as he displays a broad, wide-open smile. He motions to chairs in front of his desk. Klara smiles. Shlomo looks sad, impatient.

Klara has prepared her speech.

"I'm Klara Rasputnis, and I need your help."

"I'm on my way to find my father, Cantor Gershon Rasputnis. He was in Vladivostok, but I think he's probably in Canada by now. I'm going there to find him. I heard your organization helps people. Please. Help me."

"Rasputnis. Rasputnis. I know the name. Vladivostok, yes," said the man trying to hide the frown that furrows his brow. "Something's not right there. Something happened. I can't remember what," he says to himself.

"Is he alright?"

"Yes. It's nothing. You're right. He's definitely in Canada."

"Please get me a pass out of here," says Klara, trying to change the subject and not stir up any negative, buried thoughts about her father, if there are any. She's not inquisitive now.

"I also need a ticket," chimes in Shlomo. "Except, I'm going to *Eretz Yisrael,*" he says straightening up as he pronounces the words, "the Land of Israel."

"So, you're not going together," he raises his eyebrows as if puzzled. "Such a nice Jewish boy," he winks at Klara. "Anyway. None of my business. For you, Klara, better to go to Vladivostok. This place is full of bandits. You can't stay here. The American Army's in Vladivostok. They're good men. Not like the Japanese brutes."

"I don't want to go back to Russia again," she says indignantly.

As I said, Vladic is not Communist or White Russian really. Anyway, that's our gateway for Canada. For now the Allies are there and they run the show. The Jewish community will aid you. See Rabbi Simon in the next office. Give him this paper," says the official, handing Klara a paper with a special Association stamp. "I'm sure he can help."

Klara repeats her plea to Rabbi Simon. "Help me. I've been through a lot," she says purposely, choking on her words and whimpering slightly.

The Rabbi gets up and put his hand on her shoulder. "Easy child. China does that to you. Swallows you up. It's natural. Actually," he continues as he looks at the paper Klara hands him, "I have your records. I've got good news for you. On Thursday, you can leave for Vladivostok. A train is leaving at eight o'clock in the morning. In two days, you'll be there. Be on it. When you get to the station in Vladik, a Mr. Teplitsky will meet you. He'll have a sign, 'HIAS.' That stands for 'Hebrew Immigrant Aid Society.' You can pick up the tickets and some rubles for the journey, outside in an hour."

"Young man," he says turning to Shlomo, I see you're going to Palestine. You can go on Friday. You'll go with the group of young people who are leaving for Shanghai. Also eight o'clock in the morning at the train station. The group'll have a sign, *Hechalutz,* pioneers. Good luck. Here are your documents and some Chinese spending money. Four days to Shanghai. Off you go," he says, standing up and closing his eyes. He places his hands on their shoulder and recites the ancient blessing, "*May God bless you. May God keep you. May God watch over you.*"

The two smile reverently, and even take the money. They don't really need it. But who knows what will befall them in the days ahead? That night after a rowdy gathering with Dmitri and Osip, both of whom had too much to drink, she ponders her next move; she's going without a protector. She'll be alone; Dmitri and Osip have announced they're staying in Harbin to make money.

Klara sits alone in her room. Maybe I ought to go with Shlomo. He'd protect me, she thinks as she begins folding some clothes and packing them away. "However, life's not easy there," she realizes. "The Land of Palestine, swamps, malaria, summer heat, desert. Trouble with the Arabs. No. Not for me."

Indeed she's troubled. Last night she dreamt about Mischa. To her, he's always the bad guy. In her dream, she's looking for him. Yes. There he was across the street, watching her, following her, protecting her. But there were other faces around her, too. Father, Momma. They're waving good-bye.

Wakening the next morning, she walks over to the window and gazes down on the street. Her eyes scan the neighborhood as if looking for someone. "If that brother of mine follows me in my dreams, that means, he'll show up again.

Where exactly will he turn up next?" she asks herself as someone knocks loudly at the door.

Opening the door. Shlomo, bleary-eyed, comes in and sits across from her. Her robe's slightly opened, and he can see the top of her uncovered breasts.

"I've been thinking Klara. I've got an idea," he says, though his eyes fix on her beautiful, soft milky skin. As he's trying to get the words out, desire overtakes him.

"Don't start that again. Don't pressure me with the Zionism stuff," says Klara, seeing his dark eyes focusing on her body while trying not to make it obvious what he wants.

"He doesn't have to hide it; he's mine," she laughs as she can see the bulge between his legs. She moves closer to him and he to her. But he can't stop talking about his obsession.

"I'm going. I have to," says Shlomo as his lips tighten. "Come with me to Palestine. Don't go to America."

By now, he's fixated on having Klara. He rises and bends down and kisses the top of her chest. Smothering her soft skin with kisses, he gently opens her robe, and squeezes her breasts and kisses her already hardened nipples. She yields. It doesn't matter if she's vulnerable. She'll imagine it's Vladimir. Lifting her up from the chair and disrobing her, he leads her over to the bed where he quickly and clumsily unbuttons his pants and struggles out of them. Seconds later, they are on the bed and as he enters her he can only utter:

"I love you Klara. If only ..."

They make love again in the early morning. They don't talk, but Klara notices Shlomo's energetic, alive.

"If you have any, even a little love for me, you'll come with me."

"I can't."

As much as he tries, he fails to convince her.

Finally, smiling, he blurts out, "I'm starved. When is lunch served in this glorious hotel? Should be about now. Let's go. Our last meal together."

"Yes" she answers sitting up in bed.

She begins to dress.

He watches her.

Downstairs, they enter the busy dining room whose deep red chairs and tablecloths give the banquet area a gaudy, plush look. A balalaika orchestra serenades the diners.

"Table for two, please."

"*The couvert* is 200 rubles," responds the *maitre'd*. He's new and doesn't know Klara and her escort. "One hundred for each of you," he says in a surly tone as he gives them the once over as these so-called hosts and hostesses make it their duty to do.

"What's the matter? Can't we have money? We do have it, you know. Do you think we robbed a bank?" she says with a straight face, adding sarcastically, "Can we come in now?" She places a 200-ruble note into the hands of the startled *restauranteur*. "And here's something for you," says Klara handing him a 20-ruble note, which brings a bright smile to his dour face. He shows them to a well-positioned table.

As they finish their meal of *zakuski*, *pirozhky*, *kasha*, and hot *blini*, Shlomo looks directly at Klara. "You know, going to Vladivostok is just as dangerous as going to Shanghai. Partisans attack the Vladivostok trains, too. Come with me," he pleads. I'll protect you."

"You don't give up, do you?"

They are quiet.

As she gazes at Shlomo, she realizes he has also been her protector, her advocate, just like Vladimir. But she has learned to look out for herself, no sentiment when it comes to: "is it in my interest?"

"Shlomo, the money from the robbery."

"What," he grimaces, as his head jolts to one side.

"You know, the cash, the bills, and the money you got for the jewels from the robbery. I know you spent a lot on us: clothes, meals, treats. And I know you gave Osip and Dmitri funds. But that was a very big haul."

"Well," he replies, regaining his composure, "I was bringing the rest of the money to the kibbutz. I thought and still hope you'll come with me."

She doesn't reply. Instead, she stretches out her right hand and with her palms up, she moves her four standing fingers up and down to her palm, in an obvious gesture and with a firm voice, slowly utters, "Shlomo, give me the money."

He knows it's useless to argue with her.

"I'll be right back," he says and leaving the table he walks to the lobby and returns in a few moments.

"This is enough to get you to America and back, believe me."

She smiles, takes the packet from his hand and looks into the pouch, stuffs it into a small bag then gets up from the table and as she does so, kisses Shlomo on his forehead and turns to leave.

"Klara, you didn't say thank you."

She doesn't answer.

Next morning, the gray-stoned station is shrouded in fog. The chill penetrates her bones. The station is jammed with Chinese and Russian soldiers in full war kit, heavy packs, overcoats, as it is already getting cold. Klara hopes that maybe now after Harbin, she'll find permanent peace.

Shlomo, too, is on his way again from this city of sin that in reality has been kind to him. Happens sometimes—the so-called dissipated city can welcome you with open arms.

The two youths, Klara and Shlomo, eyes almost closed, lips tight, foreheads frowning, silently await the signal to board. Amid the confusion and bustle, they speak.

"Good-bye Klara."

"Good-bye Shlomo. I'll write you. Where?"

"Kibbutz Degania, Palestine."

"Kibbutz Degania, Palestine. That's all you need?"

"Yes, it's simple.

"Someday you'll change your mind. I'm sure. It's better there, Klara. Dangerous, but a better life. A good ideal to live for. Besides, we'd be together."

They hug. She smiles. He frowns.

"The Chinese have an expression," she says. "'The journey of a thousand li begins with the first step.' That's about a mile and a half. So here goes again. I guess my first step is up onto that train."

"Oh, I almost forgot. This letter came for you by a man who said he knew your brother; I didn't get his name."

"Thanks," she says, seeing the familiar writing on the envelope. It's from Mischa. She holds it tight as a piercing whistle breaks their new thoughts.

Shlomo takes her elbow and helps lift her up the first step. He hands up her suitcase. Three bells and the steam pours out from the train onto the platform. She stands at the top of the steps and blows him a kiss. As the train chugs out and moves slowly along the platform, he stands and watches. He realizes he'll never see her again. She knows it, too. He turns around and walks out of the Harbin Railroad Station. He doesn't look back.

The train runs along the coast in the misty grayness of early morning. Finally, she takes the letter out of her bag. As she reads it, a smile breaks over her dour face. Her lips are slightly parted. She feels her eyes open wide.

Dear Klara,

I hope this letter reaches you in good health. Sorry had to leave you so abruptly. But the war has heated up. Battle lines are drawn, Reds versus Whites.

We may never see each other again. I have tried to watch over you, but you are too far away now and Osip informs me he has moved off your trail. I guess from here on in you are on your own. Be careful.

Don't trust anyone.

Alas, the Whites are still after me. Unfortunately, they know about you. I wouldn't put it past them to try to get to me through you. They're capable of that. That is why it is best that I leave you. You don't know where I am and that's good!

I really tried, but I couldn't find any trace of Vladimir. I repeat, even though I know you won't believe me, my troops did not kill him that day in Chita. And like it or not, there's no evidence that he's dead.

We shall meet again, after the war, I am sure. My love to Papa. Don't worry about Momma and the girls; they're fine.

Love,

Mischa.

"That bastard. Why does he write he has no proof Vladimir's dead," Klara almost utters the words out loud as the train plows its way toward the Russian port of Vladivostok. "Trying to put doubt into my mind. With all his nice talk, it's my bastard brother who has deserted me."

"Be careful," says the conductor. Too many half-starved *mujiks* and criminals now terrorizing everyone," he warns.

She listens.

30
Vladivostok, November 1918

In October, the Czech Legion is unwilling to fight in Russia any longer. Since Czech independence was declared on October 28, the Czechs beat a hasty retreat out of Russia. They are disheartened with the Whites.

On November 11, 1918 World War I ends. The German surrender and the ensuing Armistice, coupled with the withdrawal of German troops from Russian soil, leave a power vacuum that the Western Allies have neither the means nor the will to fill. The Soviets becomes the undisputed master of great areas of Russia that are vital to the survival of their new empire which the Communists will name in 1922, The Union of Soviet Socialist Republics (USSR).

•

Three days after Klara Rasputnis departs Harbin and two days after she crosses the Chinese border back into Russia, she arrives in Vladivostok.

"I've made it," she says to herself. "I feel like a sprinter crashing past the finish line in a long marathon."

The war's far away. The train has carried her through the haunts of the Manchurian tigers, which are the most dangerous of Asiatic carnivores, except for brown bears that roam through the lush summer greens covering the countryside.

In hilly Vladivostok, Klara'll be able to smell the salt waters of the Pacific Ocean. As she approaches the end of the rail line, she's anxious to see this "Lord of the East," this ice-bound city, Russia's main naval and military base in the Far East.

"Winning. I'm winning," she says to herself. "Getting there. The end's in sight. Only that body of water between me and Papa."

Klara's train enters the outskirts of the port city on an early chilly fall morning. Even in the winter, the locals agree Vladivostok is blessed with a mild climate. The city boasts one of the world's finest harbors for naval and military operations. One defect, though: three-and-a-half months of ice stop maritime traffic.

Klara Rasputnis has one desire only, not to remain here longer than necessary; her goal is to board one of those sea-going steamers and embark across the Pacific.

In the Golden Horn Bay itself, a dense fog rolls in off the ocean, its gray waves seem to float above one, as if the visitor is sitting in a thick walled cauldron of pea soup. And yet, the minute one looks up to see the depth of the cover, the dusty mist of the day dissolves, leaving a clear blue sky. Klara can see the Chinese and Korean junks being unloaded.

About 60,000 people reside in the town. Half are Russian with a few Europeans, as well as Americans, while the other half includes Chinese, Japanese, and Koreans. Stone and brick houses, government buildings, banks, schools, churches, hotels, and theaters are planted firmly on this Gibraltar of the Russian Far East, this Pacific coast port of Siberia founded in 1860 and situated on a narrow strip of hilly land extending into Peter the Great Bay at the head of the Sea of Japan.

Greeting travelers of the world are muddy, unpaved streets, open sewers, grim military barracks, and warehouses, unpainted wooden houses, and mud-plastered straw huts belonging to Chinese and Korean settlers.

Klara smiles as the train approaches the station. She watches soldiers in her car hurry through their last drinking exercise. Forming letters with rows of small glasses on the table, they write the names of their girlfriend on the table. Each glass is filled with vodka and the drinker gulps down contents of the glasses that form the letters of his lover's name. What a bunch of drunks, she thinks.

She has learned how to overcome loneliness, loneliness that creates fear and anxiety and depression. Mostly, she succeeds. Sometimes she just goes to sleep.

She's stronger now. More disciplined. She has had help; her boyfriends have provided her security in her flight. During the days in Harbin, she became even more calculating. Planning, scheming, talking to everyone whom she liked; whom she thought wouldn't harm her; finding out who had the power to help her, to keep her moving on her quest, her long journey.

The anxiety returns, however. She knows it'll be worse in Vladivostok. She'll have no one here. Or will she? After all, she's attractive, smart, and above all, streetwise, she thinks as she pulls out a pocket mirror from her purse and stares at her features. Her face has changed. A few furrows here and there, lines of sadness; she is tense. Will she ever, just ever, get through this turmoil?

She's worried. Would someone, anyone from the Jewish organization meet her? "Stop it, Klara, nobody's going to be there. You know it."

"Last stop. Vladivostok. Everyone off."

She searches for the brick building that serves as administrative headquarters for the Jewish Welfare Center, which she was told overlooks the harbor. She has heard it is located behind the Versailles Hotel, only a short walk from the station to the city center. She carries a small suitcase, one she picked up in the Harbin market.

HIAS leaders apologize for not meeting her at the station to welcome her. They have greeted thousands of refugees who are streaming into Vladivostok. Her dormitory room is on the second floor and it contains four other beds all crowding their respective walls, with sheets and khaki blankets neatly tucked in. She is especially excited about the white sheet partially showing outside the blanket at the top of the bed and she imagines it cries out to her, "Come, rest and enjoy."

Another unpacking, another city, another part of the world. The only question remains: When will she get out of here?

A day later, the roar of the sea banging up against the huge wooden piles wakes her early. "Get out. Go see the city," she commands herself. In a way, she's happy she doesn't have to look for her father here; she knows he's in Canada. Now she can relax a bit, thinks Klara; "You won't be lonely walking the streets. Maybe you'll meet someone interesting, a new friend. It's happened before."

So off she goes. The cold, grey sky covers the barren hills. Down in the port area where she walks, Vladivostok looks like a war zone. Arms and ammunition are lying on the wharves near the sidings. Covering them are huge canvas tarpaulins. The city is accumulating mountains of war supplies purchased from America.

"You buy fish. Cheap price. Right off boat," yells a hawker. She descends into a market area crowded with vendors shouting their wares from booths and stalls or even coming out into the open street and shoving their products right into her face.

She passes painted women; streetwalkers from all over Russia who gather here. She can't blame them. They, too, are taking advantage of capitalism. With the huge influx of soldiers and sailors arriving daily in this *entrepot*, girls are in demand. Romantic words are the first ones a young Russian woman learns when it comes to foreigners in Vladivostok, especially for Americans. "I love you. Give me a kiss, honey. Take me to America."

Vladivostok has become crowded with Allied troops. The Americans disembark from their ships sporting knapsacks and boy-scout-looking hats. They march with Philippine mules that they unload as soon as their boat docks. The mules occupy the vacant space along the wharf near the U.S. warship, "*Brooklyn.*"

She decides to board a tram that stops in front of the building. One approaches so she gets on, puts a few coins in the collection box and pushes by soldiers who turn their heads to admire this thin, tall woman who still carries herself like the ballet dancer she once was.

The tram lets her off at the top of one of the main hills next to an observation post.

"Oh my God," she says out loud, unable to restrain herself as she gazes over the Golden Horn port of Vladivostok. "At last. You out there: Pacific Ocean. Take me to Father."

"It's the Sea of Japan," says a voice in Russian behind her. Before she can complete her turn about, she knows that the male voice is not Russian.

He's tall, with dark brown hair, kind, with sparkling blue, wide-open eyes; a slight smile. He's a sailor, a foreigner with another strange, small flag patch sewn on the top of the left arm of his shirt, red and white stripes and in the corner, white stars on a blue field. He wears a pressed, white uniform, polished black shoes, a white sailor hat and a small kit bag with a long strap.

Neither talk. They stare at each other. Sizing each other up, seeing if there's any attraction whatsoever, even a little—all this while the terrifying wind rips through the hills and around the fortresses and chills the pair.

"What country?" she asks pointing to his insignia.

"America! You must be from here?" he asks politely in broken Russian.

"No. Odessa. Passing through."

"Where're you going?"

"Where everyone wants to go. Your country, the golden land."

"Yes, everyone wants to come to America. You too, I guess," he says smiling, showing his clean, white teeth. They are straight, perfectly formed, no spaces. She has never seen anyone with teeth like that; they glimmer. Russians flash stained teeth, crooked teeth, broken teeth, gold teeth, no teeth. How could anyone have teeth like that? she wonders. God bless America. "Do you have entry papers?"

"Not yet," says Klara. "But I hope to get them at the Consulate here or in Japan." So far so good. Thank God she isn't talking to a Japanese soldier.

"Good luck with getting into the Consulate. Long lines. You have relatives here?" queries this sailor who realizes the young lady before him has to be one lonely girl. He's a long way from home, too, and he has felt something pulling him toward this Russian girl.

"Yes," Klara fibs.

"That's important. They can vouch for you. What about in the States?" he asks, in a tone that suggests he really seems interested.

Klara, already good at picking up a kind note, a nuance of friendliness, a feeling of sincerity, and not just mouthed platitudes, figures she can trust him. Better to tell the truth and smile nicely, she thinks, for her journey has taught her how to entice a young man.

"Sorry," she says. "I exaggerate. They're really not relatives. Friends of relatives. You know, friends of the family. They're helping me. To tell the truth, I'm at the Jewish Welfare Center behind the Versailles Hotel."

She wants him to know this information, that she's Jewish. She feels better she's telling the truth, at least closer to the truth, only because she sees something in this sailor, something that attracts her. Besides, he looks Jewish.

His face lights up and his words burst forth in Yiddish:

"You're Jewish? Funny. You don't look Jewish." he laughs. "I'm Jewish, too."

"Really," and a smile overtakes Klara as they sit down on a nearby bench.

His broken Yiddish sounds better than his Russian, easier for Klara to understand him. He tells her he's from a place called Brooklyn, just across the river from New York City. Brooklyn's a city in itself, he points out grinning, "and as luck would have it, guess what's the name of the ship I'm on, you got it, the SS Brooklyn. Anyway, a lot of Russian and Polish Jews live in my city." He explains his family runs a kosher bakery. He has a younger brother, Joshua. His parents work from morning to night, opening the store at four in the morning, and closing at nine. Half-day Friday; closed Saturday for the Sabbath. He and brother Josh help out. While he loves his parents, he enlisted in the Navy to get away from the store.

"They work like slaves," he continues. "Not for me. Don't want any part of it. If I stayed, they'd make me work there," he confides. "When I'm finished here, I'm going to college. I'll save money. Maybe the Navy'll help pay for school."

"Why's your army and navy here?" Klara asks, trying to keep the conversation going.

"Supposedly, we're to guard military stores and help the Czechs. Got to protect the Trans-Siberian railway, east and south of Khabarovsk. Do you know that city?"

"Heard of it. Never been there."

"On top of that, we're watching the Japanese. Don't trust them. They're cruel. I saw one of their soldiers kick an old man in the stomach and they use their rifle butts on women. They believe everyone's inferior to them."

At first, Klara speaks to the American in measured tones. Often, she has to rephrase her words into very simple Yiddish. She had honed her story very well. She's told it a thousand times, it seemed. She has been sent by her family in Odessa to find her father in America. She has to go the long way around, through Siberia because of the war in the West. Now, she hopes to get a boat to Japan. And from there, she'll board an ocean liner for the U.S. and be reunited with her father. Then, they'll bring over the rest of the family.

"Since you're going to the States, can I give you some English lessons?" he asks, focusing his eyes directly into hers and silently messaging, 'I want to get to know you.' "And you could teach me Russian."

"Good idea. When?" she asks eagerly.

"How about tomorrow. Tomorrow at four o'clock. I get off then. Is that good for you?"

"Fine," answers Klara, looking at her watch. "Oh, it's getting late. Must get back."

"I'll walk with you."

"You don't have to," she tries to insist politely, knowing that he will anyway. After he extends his arm, she puts her arm through his so that they walk arm-in-arm down the hill to the tram as the sky begins to darken over the hills bringing on a sudden chill to Klara who leans closer to this new friend from a far away city called Brooklyn.

"By the way, my name is Sid. Sid Goldstein. I'm American."

"My name's Klara. Klara Rasputnis. I'm Russian."

They walk down the hill. Assigned to port security, Sid is billeted on his ship. "I'll pick you up here at the Jewish Welfare Center," he says when they reach the hostel.

"Not a good idea," replies Klara, recalling the rules about men entering the dormitory.

"If you'd like, we could meet me in the lobby of Versailles Hotel. It's really okay. I'll be on the lookout for you," he replies.

"Fine," she says and turns around and walks directly into the center.

Sid Goldstein waits a few minutes and stares at the entrance of the center, the home of a new friend.

Our young couple meets every day at four o'clock. Sid Goldstein is free to roam the city. As long as Klara's with him, there's no danger for her. Walking with Sid, she wonders why recent dreams about Vladimir have become so pleasing. "What a sweet dream," she says to herself upon awakening.

Outwardly, Klara's happy. The war is far away in Europe and the Bolsheviks are a long way off in western Siberia. The city is bustling in the neighborhood around the main street, the Svetlanskaya. A few luxury apartments with little gardens out front enhance the broad avenue. Well-dressed men and women enter and leave the buildings, and always, quiet, polite bows by guards and doormen.

From her window at the Welfare Center, Klara can look out at Vladivostok, the city that sprawls in an amphitheater of hills overlooking the Golden Horn. Allied and Russian freighters stand at anchor, loading and unloading precious cargo. Toothless Mongolian merchants with long black queues of hair braided over their bare backs and their bald heads turning this way and that, shout, cry out, and flay their arms as they hustle potential clients.

"Two rubles, only two rubles for this nice, juicy watermelon."

"Come inside Yank. Have your fortune told."

"Upstairs. Have smoke. Chinese girls. Pussy different. Suck you. Come up. You see."

Side streets are lined with multi-lingual Korean tailors, and Japanese hairdressers. Hawkers announce their wares in poor French, street Russian, Chinese pidgin, and English. They sell everything imaginable: buttons, thread, pens, slippers, cold drinks, pants, dresses.

Welcome to the entrepot of the Russian Far East.

Klara never goes out alone, except for the short walk to the Versailles to meet Sid. Sometimes she'll walk with the young people from the Welfare Center. Many of the girls are orphans or have lost relatives and friends on the long journey. As they stroll, they tell their stories, sometimes even stopping to cry in the middle of the street as they recall a loved one.

Much to Klara's chagrin, Hannah is always warning them about sailors. "Soldiers are safer," she says.

Tanya, who had been in Vladivostok for several months, points out it's hard to get papers for passage. "I've been waiting and waiting. You need an affidavit from a relative."

Luba reminds them: "Don't go down Bolshaya Street. People are sleeping in sheds. Look's pretty bad."

Some accept their fate of being stuck in this unwanted city. "Don't complain. It's better here than in the countryside."

Klara notices that once a day, the Red Cross doles out watery *borsht*, a few potatoes and pieces of meat to refugees from the "Red Terror." Former shopkeepers, managers, artisans, even Cossacks in their long black coats, wearing astrakhan caps and flashing cartridge belts across their chests, line up every day for this handout. Children scrounge for rolls in the garbage. Former professors, lawyers, architects, and merchants beg. Klara often thinks how she has been living a gypsy lifestyle—always packing up and moving on. Disturbing nights. Little sleep. Paranoid thinking, so much so that she has reached the point where she trusts no one. But then again, there's Sid.

One day sitting in the hotel lobby and waiting for her American sailor, she realizes what has been happening to her. "I'm not alone. Sid's with me; just like Dmitri and Shlomo were with me."

Funny name, "Sid," she reflects. He'll do anything for her. He buys her little trinkets and a pair of earrings. They hold hands. They kiss. He tells her he loves her. They talk about America.

They have known each other for several weeks now and Sid never misses a day to be with her. But one cool fall day, a Tuesday, he doesn't show up at four o'clock.

"Where is he?" Klara mutters to herself, noticing it's after four.

"Hell. I'm not going to wait for him. Ten more minutes, that's all. I'm not standing by for anyone. Why do I have to always be waiting for soldiers? I had to wait for Vladimir till he got off duty, and look what it got me?" she protests to herself.

"What if he's hurt?" she asks in a worried tone. "I'll go look for him. But where? Maybe down by the wharves. He says he's usually around there. Nothing'll happen. I'll be careful."

Off she goes. Out the door. Up Bolshaya Street. Down Svetlanskaya Street.

Although she averts her eyes from sailors who beckon to her from crowded doorways, she's pleased they find her attractive.

"Hello pretty one. Come on over. Have some *piriozhki* with us. A shot of vodka, perhaps? It's cold out there, the vodka surely'll warm you up."

From the street, she sees a lot of Yanks enter and leave a two-story building. Something odd about the place. Looking up, she can see through the balcony railing: Doors open and close, and inside, it looks like gambling's going on. In other rooms, young girls go in and out. Men sit on benches inhaling from long stemmed pipes.

"Out of here. They'll think I'm one of them," she whispers. As she hurries up the street she notices a half dozen Chinese fellows are following her. "Better get away."

Just then on her left from a docked motorboat, a sailor waves to her. She walks over to the pier. Better a sailor than the menacing Chinese behind her.

"Don't you dare get on the boat," she reminds herself.

The Chinese pass by.

Meanwhile, Sid arriving late, hears from the hotel receptionist that Klara told her she was going to walk down to the harbor.

"What! Is she crazy?" he yells at the desk clerk. "They'll kidnap her. There's a slave trade out here. If she doesn't know better, you certainly do. You should have stopped her, it's getting dark!" he shouts back as he makes his way out the front door, brushing aside a few surprised visitors.

It takes Sid only five minutes to find Klara. She sees him first and runs to him. "Klara, Why? You know better. Want to end up in the harbor? I was so worried about you," he blurts out as she moves to him and lowers her head on his chest. He hugs her and holds her tight. Embarrassing her, he kisses her forehead and smothers her again with kisses and they walk off together.

"Can't live without you."

"Can't marry you now."

"Why?"

"A Russian officer."

"Where is he?"

"In Chita. Probably dead. I'm not sure. Never found his body," she says, bursting into a choked laugh. Then tears and more tears. She can't stop. She thinks she's over it. With Shlomo, she could go on. He was a rebound. But the lies she tells herself all seem to fall by the wayside with Sid. The thought that Vladimir could be alive surfaces at this moment. Kind, sweet Vladimir. Her body swells at the thought, the impossible thought that he's alive. No, he's dead. She firmly believes that if he was alive, he would have contacted her already.

"Vladimir's dead, Vladimir's dead," she whispers, sobbing quietly in a low voice.

Sid guides her to a nearby café. The two sit in a separate little section reserved for foreigners. A group of sailors chat at the next table, oblivious to the young couple. The service men are alone, too; they converse in male talk and gulp down vodka.

Sid says nothing. He just holds her hand tightly. Though hurt and angry, he realizes her tears stir something in him and releases an outburst of deep love for this Russian lady for whom he feels he has waited for a long time in his young life. As she sighs, his affection for her arouses him. Her defenses are down. Alone, the scene could have been different. They feel a whole world is watching them. "Come on Klara. Cross the ocean. It's time," a voice whispers in her ear.

Returning to the dorm, she finds a letter on her cot. She caresses the embossed-seal on the off-white stationary and even gives the official-stamped-envelope of HIAS a little kiss. She carefully places the document, which includes Japanese currency and a passenger ticket under her makeshift pillow. "Tomorrow morning, I sail," she repeats several times to herself as she examines the shipping tickets and instructions on boarding.

"Thank you God," she mutters. She's tired and closes her eyes and quickly falls asleep. Yet, as she drifts into unconsciousness, her head begins to ache. She can't control her troubled mind. She tosses and turns and fights with the makeshift bed. All my loves are dying, if not physically, then spiritually, she thinks, "Papa's dead. Vladimir's dead. Sid's dead." The words themselves, however, never get out; she swallows them; they die on her dry lips. "He's dead. He's dead," she wants to shout.

Deep in slumber, she watches herself opening her eyes. She dreams she lifts her sore head and gazes around the large, musty-smelling dormitory. Nobody is up. Nobody moves. Nobody's looking at her. Nobody hears her shout. She watches herself fall back onto the hard cot, no mattress, no springs. She's quiet now. Her eyes are closed. Her body relaxed. Her hands stretch to hug the rock-like bundle of torn, sweaty, clothes that serve as her pillow: She thinks she is sleeping and she is, but as she dozes, she mumbles:

"My God. What if Papa is dead? What if when I get to Canada, I can't find him?" she says, straining every muscle to sit up. "All this, and he's dead. No! My father's alive and I'm going to him," she utters confidently in her sleep.

Awakening before dawn, she packs her suitcase. After the sharp clicks of the metal latches of her bag snaps shut, she sits on the traveling bag for a few minutes and silently reflects. "So long Vladivostok. Bye darling Sid." She leaves the sleeping hostel for the short walk to the harbor.

A few hours later, she stands on the upper deck of the *SS Nippon Maru*. She's going east to the Land of the Rising Sun. No dream; it'll take 36 hours to get to Tsuruga located on the west coast of Japan. Later that morning at the Welfare Center, the director, staff, and guests wonder why Klara left so early in the morning, without notice, without a good-bye, and without official papers.

31

Boat to Japan, December 1918

With World War I ended, Great Britain, France, Japan, and the U.S. keep their promise to effectively assist the White armies. But their aid is limited, though Japan ups the ante with about 70,000 troops. Yet the Americans, in line with President Woodrow Wilson's instructions and under Major General William S. Graves, try to remain neutral in Vladivostok.

The followers of a former commander of Russia's Black Sea Fleet, Admiral Aleksandr Vasilevich Kolchak, lead a *coup d'état* in Omsk on November 18, 1918, and disband the Siberian government, known as the Directory. Kolchak establishes a military dictatorship and proclaims himself, "Supreme Ruler of Russia." His supremacy is recognized by the Archangel government in the north and by White General Anton Denikin in the south. Kolchak wins a few battles, gets across the Urals, and almost reaches the Volga in his dash to overthrow the Bolsheviks. At the same time, Denikin's army advances from the south and threatens to link up with Kolchak's army.

However, Kolchak overshoots his supply and communication lines. By late spring, 1919, he retreats He can't unite pillaging bands of peasants and Cossacks who recognize no authority other than their own. He can't control Siberia unless he holds large sections of the Trans-Siberian railway, which he fails to do and so dooms the White cause. That summer, the cities of western Siberia fall to the Red Army. By November, 1919, Kolchak's army is falling apart.

Kolchak flees eastward, but he is stopped by the Czechs, betrayed by them and the Allies, and handed over to his enemies in Irkutsk. He and his prime minister are tried and shot on February 7, 1920, their bodies dumped into a hole in the ice in the Angara River.

Meanwhile, in the south, General Denikin occupies virtually all of the Ukraine and advances on Moscow. He captures Orel on October 14, 1919 and heads for Tula. "The entire fate of the Soviet regime hinges on the defense of Tula," notes author Orlando Figes. The White Volunteer Army appears unstoppable to take Moscow. But the Whites lack sufficient troops and supplies to sustain their advance to the Russian capital, 108 miles away. Hammered by the newly formed Red cavalry, the Whites retreat to the south. "Never again did they threaten to break through into central Russia," adds Figes.

A White Army group under the command of General Yudenich fails to capture Petrograd, though the Whites reach the city's Pulkovo Heights on October 20. But Trotsky rallies the workers of the city and defends "the birthplace of the revolution." To honor his role in the defense of Petrograd, Trotsky is awarded the "Order of the Red Banner," the first such order of its kind.

Shattered by their almost-victory turned into defeat in October 1919, the Whites regroup in the south against "the rapidly strengthening Red Armies."

•

As Klara stands on deck of the *SS Nippon Maru*, a bitter wind comes off the Bay of the Golden Horn where Allied ships rest at anchor. She watches the waves leap up against the sturdy steel bulwark of her vessel. Soon she'll be far from the Siberian coast. From the moment she boards the *SS Nippon Maru*, she keeps repeating to herself that there's a long way to go. But when she recognizes the name engraved on the American cruiser moored across from her slow-moving vessel, her face flushes with the red blush of a teenager in love. Making sure she's reading the name of that ship correctly, she repeats the word *Brooklyn* over and over again. It's Sid's home. As the *SS Nippon Maru* passes the *SS Brooklyn,* the American ship's four tall stacks begin to pump out huge puffs of pale smoke as if in a good-bye salute from Sid. Klara realizes she didn't have time to tell him she was leaving. Maybe it's better that way, she thinks.

The wide, blue sea welcomes Klara Rasputnis of Odessa. The brutal Civil War vanishes behind her. She left home in the winter of 1917, it's now the winter of 1918. During the three-day voyage to Japan, she'll mull over how she can get from there to America.

Klara's letter of departure, emigration pass, and instructions informed her that after she found her cabin, she should contact a retired Russian naval officer. She was merely to ask any crew member to point out the "Admiral," obviously not the ship's captain, but the man everyone calls the "Admiral." This gentleman often travels back and forth from Russia to Japan. He'll watch out for her, the letter said.

Alone on the boat and not having a companion in Japan will be extremely difficult, she realizes. She might even be in great danger. As Klara looks out at sea and seeing the land recede, she murmurs, "Good-bye Russian homeland. I'll never see you again."

She doesn't have a chance to philosophize whether Russia had been good to her; it hadn't; or whether Russia had been good for her family; it hadn't; or to its citizens, it hadn't; or to its Jews, for sure it hadn't—and yet, it was home. Suddenly, she feels a gentle touch on her arm, which frightens her.

"You must be Klara," says a soft-spoken male voice. "Don't be afraid. I'm the Admiral."

"How do you know my name?"

"I have before me the most beautiful *devushka* on board, and I know it must be you," says the short, burly, broad-shouldered, middle-aged man dressed in a fashionable suit.

"That's what you say to every woman. You startled me," she says staring into his jovial, blue eyes that seemed to reinforce his endearing comment. His thick salt-and-pepper-hair, cut very short, gives him an air of maturity; he's old enough to be her father. On his pinky, he sports a small gold ring with a subdued diamond set in the middle.

She's not afraid of him. To keep him off guard, she gently confronts him with: "You're not going to molest me, are you?" a touch of mockery in her voice.

"No. Of course not," he answers, chuckling. "But I can tell you're going to America. It's written all over your face. Everyone smiles when they leave Russia," he says pausing for a moment. "Well, not everyone, I suppose," he adds, noticing Klara's questioning eyes.

"You don't look like an Admiral."

The Admiral tells Klara that while he's called the Admiral, his real name is Isaac Saltzman, a Jew from Minsk, White Russia, which he describes as a landlocked western city about as far from the ocean as you can get. He's the product of the Vladivostok naval base where he trained as a seaman and rose in the ranks. The Navy sent him to engineering school and gave him further technical training. He even sailed to San Francisco aboard a Russian frigate and admired American know-how.

He tells Klara that after 30 years in the service of the Czar, he has retired and has found a part time job in the maritime industry, with the Nagamatsu Shipping Line, owners of the *SS Nippon Maru*. That's why he travels a great deal to Japan. He says he has a wife and five sons.

The Admiral cuts a formidable figure: Full chest, a crew cut, bulging muscles and a fast moving gait. Since he's Jewish, he has offered to help HIAS, the Jewish immigration society, by chaperoning individuals and groups across the straits to Japan, including young ladies.

"So, tell me young lady, where you going?"

"As if you didn't know. Well, right now, I'm on a Japanese transport, under a Japanese flag and I'm headed for what I've heard is a very strange fairyland called Japan. But how do I get out of there once I get there? That's my problem."

"Just follow your nose," he says laughing, adding, "that's how you'll get to America."

"Of course, I'm going to Seattle, America. Then up to Canada. My father's there."

"How're you getting there?"

"By boat."

And they both chuckle as the Admiral pipes up: "You're right. You can't walk on water. Or can you?" They laugh again.

"Seriously, I don't know how I'll get there. It's taken me about a year to get this far. The Jewish hostel is in Yokohama. Since I'm going there, I'll ask them."

"Getting late," says the Admiral, ignoring her remark. "Right now, I'm going to my cabin. They probably stole everything I own. Don't leave any valuables in your room."

"Valuables? Don't have any. Besides, I haven't even found my cabin," she says.

"Good night. See you in the morning."

On the *SS Nippon Maru,* Klara shares a cabin with a Russian woman, Lydiya Koslov. She's older, a teacher in her forties. As is the Russian custom, they begin talking by sharing food, though Klara has only black bread. Lydiya hands Klara a chicken wing. "God," she thinks, "when did I last have chicken?"

"Chicken," she repeats out loud. "Reminds me of home in Odessa. You see, I've never been out of Russia," she tells Lydiya. "Now, I'm going to the strangest land in the world where the sky supposedly is always blue."

"What a shock you'll get when you set foot in Japan," says Lydiya, rising and closing the porthole. "God, it's windy out. Must be going through the Tsugaru Straits."

Next morning, Lydiya begins to teach Klara customs of Japan.

"Sometimes, they put on a blank face and stare at you. Don't be upset. And don't yell if you're in a communal bath and all of a sudden a whole family comes in, husband included, and you're naked and they're naked."

"You're joking."

"No. Their attitude toward nudity is different. They're not ashamed or embarrassed in the nakedness of the human body. In the west, nudity is all about sex. Here it's less complicated. They say the causes of modesty and self-consciousness lie in our minds. It's immodest to look at a naked man or woman or stare at a person's private parts. Anyway, in Japan, the nape of the neck is considered the most beautiful part of a woman's body."

"What about food?" asks Klara, wanting to talk about something else.

"Pretty much all they eat is fish and rice, with eggs, vegetables, vermi-celli. There's seaweed and pickled roots, cakes, and sweetmeats. Sake, tea, and sugar-water are the only drinks. An amazing country. God is truly shining on this land of the rising sun."

Three days later, the *Nippon Maru* arrives on the mystical coast of Japan. The clear sky stands above her, soft and gray, with a tinge of blue.

"What you'll see, Klara, will be a miracle," says the Admiral as they stand on deck watching the never ending inlets and the landlocked bays that line the shore. She takes in the panoramic sweep of mountains, the terraced tiers upon tiers, the valleys with paddy rice fields and sacred mountains from which blows a cold, December wind.

"Japan is growing rich; China's impoverished. In 25 years, it'll be Asia against the West. Mark my word, Klara, one day Japan will take on the giant, America, and then ..." He stops for a moment, his voice rising, his eyes bulging and burning with fervor. Klara stares at him as he bows and mutters "*Banzai.*

"Sorry, I get carried away."

"You certainly did," replies Klara thinking it strange, a Russian gloating over the virtues of a country that humiliated the Russian people in the 1904 war.

On land, the custom house is a beehive. Short-stature officials in blue uni-forms of European pattern and leather boots are very civil to the passengers. They open and examine the baggage, and immediately strap them up again.

Clanking out of Tsuruga, the train climbs through narrow valleys and tun-nels. The Admiral continues talking about Japan and while he does, she pre-tends she's listening, but she's really catching glimpses of the blue sea framed between two mountains. She notices long agricultural villages with old houses and beautifully thatched roofs.

People are bathing in the rippling streams. Lydiya was right. These people jump right in with no clothes. As the train moves along the riverbank, Klara sees a tall, beautiful young girl, naked, stand up and unembarrassed, wave to the train. The Admiral turns away, albeit slowly.

Just outside of Yokohama, on the western side of Tokyo Bay, the passengers forget the discomfort of the long journey when members of the train crew serve spice cakes. She's hungry and gobbles down the filling refreshment.

"Don't eat too much," cautions the Admiral. "We'll have a nice room, fire-place, and a view from the Grand Hotel. Meals'll be brought to our room; caviar, champagne."

Klara smiles. For an instant, she welcomes the idea of a view of a harbor and a sumptuous meal. Then, as if she has been clobbered by a sledgehammer descending on her head, she blinks and lets out a quiet gasp, which the Admiral, rambling on, doesn't hear.

"Something's wrong here," she repeats to herself. "The Admiral mentions a hotel. What about the Jewish hostel? During the whole trip, the Admiral never once discusses the hostel. He pays for extra drinks and snacks on board. He buys her gifts, a good luck charm, a bracelet. He gives her doses of Japanese history and customs."

"What about the hostel?" Klara asks in an unruffled way.

"Oh, we'll have plenty of time. We don't have to report there until the day after tomorrow," he says nonchalantly, avoiding her eyes.

Bastard. He's kidnapping me. Who is he? Why would HIAS entrust me to this lecher? I've got to get out of this. But how?

Her first thought actually becomes her plan of escape. *When we arrive at the hotel, I'll get away. I'll scream.*

As they begin to get off the train, she recalls the HIAS letter said, "When you get off the train, someone from the hostel will be there." For the first time in a long time, she feels really frightened.

The Admiral and Klara are met by a guide who holds up a sign with the word, "Admiral." Outside the station, they get into a *jinricksha*. Men pile their baggage into their tiny two-wheeled carriage and speed off into a bewildering labyrinth of turns and alley-like streets. Miniature gardens and groves of cherry trees flash by them. A 10-minute ride in a jinricksha brings them to the hotel. During the ride, the Admiral looks at the sites and hums some tunes.

He's visualizing the bed scene, thinks Klara, who has summoned up courage ignited by total anxiety. *I'll give him a sex scene he won't forget.*

At the hotel front desk, the Admiral is busy signing them in and not looking about.

Suddenly, Klara lets out a scream. "Oh my God, give me a handkerchief!" she pleads with the Admiral who immediately pulls one out of his suit jacket's breast pocket.

"Klara, what's wrong?"

"Oh goodness gracious, I'm sick," she shouts as she spews mucus into her handkerchief.

While he turns around to the desk again to finish signing them in, she quickly takes her middle finger and stuffs it down her throat. No one sees her fast, methodical movement.

"The bathroom. Where is it?" she demands, gagging on the words.

The clerk points across the hall, and moves toward her. "I'll take you there."

Covering her mouth with her handkerchief, she begins to retch up vomit as she follows the clerk. Halfway across the hall, she whispers to him:

"Go back. Tell him, I'll be okay. Few minutes in the bathroom," she smiles embarrassingly.

Inside, she quickly recovers. She looks out the door and there in a corner of the lobby, away from the view of the front desk is her suitcase. If she can get to that corner, without being seen, she can run out the rear door of the hotel.

The clerk behind the front desk of the counter is talking to the Admiral who is filling out forms and who has his back to Klara. When the clerk turns around for a moment to get the key from the wall box, Klara walks calmly to her bag, picks it up and leaves via the side door. Hailing a jinricksha she takes out the letter of instructions from her bag and shows the driver the address, along with some Japanese money.

"*Hai Hai*," he says in Japanese, nodding his head, and off they go.

"He was to bring you here," says Mordechai, head of the hostel. "We trusted him. Wait. I've got a picture." Pulling out a photo from the desk drawer, he hands it to Klara.

"No. Of course it's not him. But who would want to do this to me?"

"The question is who sent you the permission letter and instructions to leave Vladivostok? And why?"

"Oh, my God. But it was written on very fancy stationary with a HIAS letterhead."

"Not good enough," thinks Mordechai who's sure someone wants her. Not the white slave trade, either. They could have done that anytime, anywhere, and not gone to the expense. They want to grab her here in Japan and either get something out of her or use her as a bargaining chip, he decides, adding he would have to look into this.

"Come. I'll take you to your room."

Next day, Mordechai shows Klara the daily newspaper.

"That so-called Admiral of yours was found dead in the Grand Hotel. Someone left a Black Dragon Society dagger deep in his neck.

"God. I hate him. But what a way to die."

"The Admiral paid the price for not delivering you to the Japanese. What do they want from you, anyway?"

"How should I know?" replies Klara innocently.

Silence. Distrust enters the room. Mordechai knows she's covering up something. But then again, all the refugees from Russia hide the truth. Who's she protecting? Who wants her?

"What did you say, Klara?" asks Mordechai, goading her somewhat but realizing she'll never talk.

"Nothing. Nothing."

Klara's convinced that she'll now have to wait her turn to depart from the Land of the Rising Sun; Mordechai is suspicious of her. And she's in the first country that's truly different than Russia; even Harbin had too many Russians to be considered truly representative of China. Shrouded in oriental mystery, scenic beauty, sacred mountains, cherry blossoms, quiet inlets, landlocked bays, green hills, and a snowcapped Mount Fuji, this island nation's mystique overcomes her.

In teeming Yokohama, the hostel's located near the Bund, which is the main street for foreign offices and businesses. Klara has to be careful. Didn't Lydiya tell her that according to guidebooks, it's absurd for any woman to be in Japan without an escort, the 'height of impropriety.' Klara feels at home at the hostel. Besides sleeping rooms, the facility boasts a dining room, a tiny library, a reading room, and a small synagogue with a single Torah. Most of the hostel's guests are newcomers from Russia. Most arrive with nothing; just the clothes on their back. They're all given some spending money, but not very much since they get all their meals at the hostel.

After the vast landmass of Siberia, Yokohama begins to grow on her. The breeze lifting up the tang of the sea to her nostrils gives her encouragement.

Returning from her walk one day, Klara asks Mordechai: "Why is it taking so long for me to leave? I've been here several weeks already."

"Only the American Consulate can give you papers to board the ship," he replies; "we just have to wait. And, let me warn you, please don't go near the consulate; you'll only be turned away. And stay away from the police. The Japanese often give up Siberian refugees to the Russian government. Why, you could even be put on a ship back to Vladivostok," declares Mordechai.

Klara smiles. She has learned when someone says, "don't do it," it just might make sense to do it.

One day Klara ambles past a large concrete building. "Ah, the American flag," she utters. Sid taught her how to recognize the American flag, the "stars and stripes," he called it. Next day, Klara makes her way through narrow alleys on her way to the Consulate compound consisting of houses within houses.

Two American and two Japanese soldiers stand at attention outside the structure. Joking with them is a young Japanese civilian, known as "Joe, the guide." He has a chair and from time to time, unlike the guards, he sits and relaxes at the building entrance. He's muscular with broad shoulders for a short person. His narrow face features a thin nose and his dark black hair has grown long, covering both his ears. He obviously trims the part above his forehead, for his hair is combed down and the hairline from temple to temple, above his eyebrows, is straight.

Even though he speaks Russian, she remembers the girls warned her to be careful. He's very clever. Yes, he can get you papers all right. But he extracts a big price. "I must do this," says Klara to herself as she approaches the guards and civilian. Cautiously, she walks up to the soldiers, yet directs her question to Joe.

"What time open?" she asks him in English.

"It's open now. Where're you going in the States?"

Klara explains how she just arrived from Vladivostok and she's on her way to Canada, to be reunited with her father.

"What a coincidence! I'm going with Consul Flannigan to Vladivostok. We're going to visit American troops. The Embassy is sending us to see if everything is okay; if American troops need anything special. We report to State Department. I'm going as translator," he says excitedly. "You must have been through a lot, Klara."

"Yes," she answers, her head beginning to droop down on her chest. She's tired. Lack of sleep had wearied her. She yawns a lot. She longs to wake up and go back to sleep in clean sheets, yes, and if there was someone she loved, to arise in the middle of the night and make love to him, and then fall back to sleep until she wakes naturally. That's the best kind of sleep. That's the kind of sleep she had with Vladimir.

"Joe. Joe. You've got to help me," now putting on that ingratiating voice that has stood her in good stead. "Promise me you'll introduce me to this Flannigan so he can stamp my papers.

"Hard because he's a bully with women." His last comment is not lost on Klara. "Anyway, let's try. Let's go talk to the guard."

Joe approaches the U.S. Marine who looks at Klara. Joe waves her forward. Klara walks up to the gate.

"Can I see your papers?" demands the Marine in a stern voice. Glancing at Klara's documents, he ushers her inside and into a waiting room. "Someone will come and get you. He's in there. Have a seat. This outer door is always open," he says and puts his hand on the knob. For some reason, the door doesn't open. Seeing it's locked, he takes out his key and unlocks it. "He'll come for you shortly from that inner room."

Klara stares at the sign, "Consul Michael Flannigan."

Ten minutes. Twenty minutes. Nobody calls for her. Her eyes get drowsy. She's falling asleep again. They're waiting outside for me. The Hell with it. She gets up, opens the outer door and knocks on the inside door.

"Come back in a few minutes." Perhaps Klara does not hear correctly, or misunderstands. Or perhaps she does. Checking whether the door is locked—it isn't—she turns the handle and pushes it open.

Klara could only stare in disbelief. There in front of the desk, is Flannigan standing upright, his muscular back, the bare white cheeks of his rear-end staring Klara right in the face.

As he bends over to pull up his pants, she can see the bottom of his testicles and his hairy ass. Her first reaction, under other circumstances, would be to giggle and then laugh; for to her, it seems hilarious.

Flannigan turns, his face distorted. "Who the hell let you in from the outer door, it was locked. I locked it myself," he says as he moves slightly sideways, but his behind still faces Klara. He moves around the desk and drops into his chair so he won't be exposed anymore.

Sitting up on the desk and partially blocking Klara's view is a frowning young Japanese girl, her bare feet hanging over the table. She, too, is partially dressed; her bra's still on so all she can do is put her hands over her crotch, which she does. But Klara can see the short, black curly, pubic hairs between her legs, her smooth stomach and belly button. At her feet is her pile of clothes. She begins to whimper as she leans over to pick up her panties.

Klara's first inclination is to get out, but by now she figures out she has the consul right where she wants him. She has discovered him in a sex act, and having traversed a war zone where she has heard a few stories of couples caught fornicating in public places, she realizes that if you have something on someone, you better use it fast, no matter what. Klara Rasputnis is not averse to blackmailing the consul and his lady friend, who by now is yelling, "Get out of here!" Quickly closing the door and standing inside the room, she lifts up her hands palms up facing the girl. The command could not be clearer: "Stop. Don't move. Sit where you are."

"Get the hell out of here! Can't you see ... Who let you in? Who are you to interrupt me? I'll call the guard," threatens the man, his face still flushed.

"I don't think you do that," says Klara. She figures he's bluffing. "You no position to call," she adds, glancing at the female who again tries to pick up her clothes. But Klara again stops her by raising her hands: "Sit!" Her fist is clenched. She will punch the woman if necessary.

Taking her papers out of her pocket, Klara hands them to the shaken Consul.

"First, honorable counselor, please sign the papers."

"The papers! Okay! Quick! I'm expecting someone," he sneers, shaking all over. He sighs, signs and puts down the pen. She places the papers in her pocket and leaves.

Joe's waiting outside the gate.

"What took so long?"

"Oh nothing. Just a lot of paper work."

"But the consul. He's supposed to be so mean, so ... how could you?"

"When a man is mean and a woman wants something from him, you either sweet talk him; or you lift your skirt, or you blackmail him with something he's trying to hide."

They walk for a short while. Joe bows. Klara bows. They bow again. She gives him ten British pounds.

He takes it and smiles, a smile that says, that's twice as much as he normally gets. Her eyes tell him, 'Don't you dare.' He obeys.

The next day, SS *Tatsuta Maru* leaves on its maiden voyage, with a passenger list of 440, and ninety crew members. On the passenger list, which includes a group from the hostel, is Klara Rasputnis, a Russian national, bound for Seattle.

32

Good-bye Yokohama, December 1918

History repeats itself. Momentous events that occurred in Klara's short life in Russia will happen again. While the first Russo-Japanese war occurred in 1904; another will reoccur in 1945 when at the end of World War II, the Kremlin at the last minute joins the Allies, revenges itself on Japan, and snatches up Manchuria and various Pacific islands.

Even the route that Klara's ship will take across the Pacific in 1918 will become the path for future conflict. In a surprise air attack, Sunday morning, December 7, 1941, at a harbor they called "the Pearl," the Japanese will sink American battleship after battleship, cruiser after cruiser, destroyer after destroyer. Despite the loss, the U.S. will emerge victorious four years later.

•

On a cool, rainy winter day in 1918, Klara Rasputnis glimpses Japan for the last time.

Standing in the Yokohama port dock and followed by a long line of fellow passengers from her hostel, she waits to board the *Tatsuta Maru*. Her eyes are glued on the gangplank conveying her up to yet another new home. She can only imagine the boredom that lies ahead. Nearly a month's journey to get from Japan to Seattle, via the northern route. The *Tatsuta Maru* is late in loading. Huge cranes lift crates onto the vessel. Sampans bob in the water. Small boats drift out and return to pier. Tugboats stand by ready to push giant craft out to sea.

Nobody seems to mind a late departure, certainly not the large Russian passenger group of about one hundred from the hostel. Visibly excited, laughing, with no panic, no anxiety, they are sure they're going to board. They know their long ordeal is over. Nothing bothers them on this, the last leg of their journey. Next stop: America.

Haym Gross is in charge of the group of young men and women from the hostel organized by HIAS. Tall, round faced, with a small nose, thinning brown hair, he's the leader because he's the oldest at 31 years of age. He speaks Russian and Polish and English. He has been stranded in Japan for several years awaiting a visa, so he knows some Japanese.

"Got everything," he asks his young but often forgetful passengers who are seeking shelter from a heavy summer storm off the bay. Torrential rain pelts them. Passengers and crew alike huddle in the makeshift sheds that serve as departure exits while immigration officials check exit papers.

Now the ship's loudspeaker announces that upper deck passengers can come aboard. The wealthy passengers promenade forward. As if winners of a beauty contest, they flaunt their luxurious hand luggage, their affected smiles, their bows to friends and officials, their dainty waves and their short, polite steps upward. No pushing and shoving here.

As their turn arrives, the group from the hostel is told to line up in single file. Klara, knowing enough to run quickly to the front of the line, stands among the first few dozen who begin moving forward.

Several port officials approach and begin yelling at the inspectors who were watching each person as they sauntered up the gangplank. The inspectors stop the procession.

"What's going on?" asks the teenager in front of Klara who notices Haym Gross becoming engaged in a frantic discussion with port officials. He is moving his hands wildly. He even stamps his feet and points to his documents. He's wiping his forehead with a crumpled handkerchief.

"We can't all go," he yells back to his charges. "Another group behind us has priority. We just happened to board first."

"No. No," shout the young people, and the line begins to move forward with everyone jostling for a position up front.

"Quiet. Stop. Don't push or none of us will get on," yells Haym. "I'm trying to get most of us to board. Patience!"

The youngsters obey and the rush forward halts, as does the rain.

Klara has held her spot. One youth tries to get ahead of her. "I haven't come over six thousand miles for you, bitch, to push in front of me," she tells one girl from the hostel as she grabs the intruder's arms and like a javelin thrower hurls her back to her original spot.

"I'm only number ten or so from the front. Please God, get me on," Klara mumbles to herself.

Meanwhile, Haym continues talking to the officials. Only this time, he, too, is calmer, mainly because a few soldiers with rifles, their bayonets glistening in the sunshine, have moved into position alongside the clerks and inspectors. He has done his best and slowly the line begins to move forward again onto to that precious movable bridge

Klara watches the face of the guard counting the bodies going up as she gets closer.

"Keep going," she says silently. "Four more. Just four more. Two more. One more." Then she looks into the face of the guard, the cruelest countenance and the coldest eyes she has ever seen.

She will never know why she did what she did. Maybe it was from everything that she had learned on her long journey. Maybe it was what they call feminine charm summoned from instinct. Or maybe she was prepared to trade her body for a passage across the ocean to safety: She smiles at the soldier and winks and this cold statue of a man grins back and and gestures Klara Rasputnis forward.

She walks up slowly, each step measured. She doesn't look back. She doesn't try to see who got on and who didn't. When she gets to the top, she jumps over the last step of the *Tatsuta Maru* gangplank, and yells, "America! America!"

Reaching the main entrance hatch, Klara is sent below to two dormitories where everyone scampers for a lower. Klara takes an upper.

"The boat leaves in a half hour," someone yells.

"Better unpack quickly. Put your suitcases under the bunks," Haym shouts from the doorway. "As soon as you finish, come up to B Deck. We're allowed there. Bring your passes."

Klara hurries. Where should she put her toothbrush?

Over the loud speaker comes an announcement: "Passengers! Please take your lifejackets and proceed to designated positions. Follow drill instructions written on the door of your quarters."

"Oh, why don't they shut up," declares a voice behind her. "Such nonsense, these drills. Everyone knows there aren't enough lifeboats to go around. It's so stupid."

Klara knows that voice, a voice you don't forget. It's like a mother's voice, it lasts forever. Her hand covers her mouth, muffling a scream. Afraid to look, she mutters. "Oh my God, I don't believe it!"

The other young lady, still mumbling insults toward imaginary ship officials, turns at the same time. They stare at each other. Their mouths open. Their eyes tear. Their hearts throb. They raise their hands high and wide and hug each other.

"It's you."

"Who else?"

"Can't be."

Even in a frantic bear hug, they look at each other, smiling, laughing, crying.

No more words. No more questions. They know what each had been through since that train ride from Odessa when they first met. They remember they agreed to take the next train that came along after they had been dislodged. They recall what a mistake they had made when they argued and split up. They picture themselves standing again in that whorehouse in Irkutsk. They relive their second parting that long-ago day, each believing the other was wrong to continue their chosen path. None of this matters anymore, what occurred between them, happened.

"Take the lower," Klara commands

"Still trying to be the boss," answers Rachel, smiling. They hug again.

"When did you board?"

"About ten minutes ago. We must be in different groups."

"We'd better go to that stupid boat drill."

"You'll look good in an orange life vest."

"This time, don't you dare leave without me," says Rachel, quickly unpacking her meager cosmetics.

"And you? Don't be so stubborn, answers Klara.

Up on deck, after the drill, they look out onto the harbor and beyond to the blue Pacific. Mr. Gross had told them it meant "peace," *pacifico*, in Spanish. A Spanish explorer by the name of Balboa had given the vast ocean its name. Balboa sounds new worldish to Klara. "Balboa. Balboa," she repeats over and over again.

A bell rings in the engine room. A short blast and the motors begin to hum and quicken. The ship moves. The tugs push. The engines throb. The ship rolls a little as it heads out to sea. Most passengers line the rails and shout to someone on shore. The hostel boys and girls have no one to yell down to; or throw kisses to; or wave to no one comes to say good-bye to them. Their parents, their uncles and aunts, their boyfriends and girlfriends are elsewhere. These young refugees can only say: "Good-bye Japan. Good-bye Russia. Good-bye Old World."

As the engines hum louder, orders are barked to the crew. Inching from the pier, the liner heads out to sea as two young women stare at the dark, heavy sea they are to traverse for twenty-eight days. The two feel the salt in the air as their steamer cuts through the sparkling blue Pacific Ocean spreads itself before their eyes. Eventually, raging icy winds will toss and turn the ship now sailing due northeast. Swirls will churn up the sea and passengers will have a hard time navigating on deck. Holding on to wet, cold railings will cause their fingers to ache.

That afternoon, as the SS *Tatsuta Maru* plows its way across the Pacific, Klara and Rachel lean against the deck rail and watch the waves sink and rise, just like a suction cup. Sometimes the waves batter the hull of the ship, but fail to shake the ocean liner off its destined course.

"Klara, I remember you telling me about that young man you really liked," says Rachel, not looking at her friend but gazing out to sea.

"He's dead. Vladimir. He was with the Red Cross," Klara says.

"Oh Klara! I'm so sorry," she says, still not looking at her, but remembering something.

"It's ok, I just don't talk about it."

Rachel puts her arm around Klara and pulls her toward her.

Perhaps it's the ocean, the sea breeze, their touching, but it is at that moment that Rachel recalls what one of her whores in Irkutsk told her about a strange fellow, a nervous Red Cross officer who picked her one night. He said his name was Vladimir and when he was on top of her he cried several times, "Klara! Klara!" He said after that he was on his way to Moscow, summoned by his father. The girl said he seemed terribly frightened, like someone was following him. He kept looking at the door and mumbled something about a Bolshevik guerrilla after him. Scared, the whore hustled him out.

"Let's go back to the dorm," Rachel says, realizing with deep clarity that, for the sake of Klara's sanity, she must keep this memory secret forever.

The sea shines as the ship stands tall in the water. The Japanese enforce the class system, especially for meals and entertainment. First class in first class, second class in second, steerage in steerage. Everything's organized. At night the ballroom is full of giddy people. The orchestra plays Strauss waltzes. Passengers drink. Lovers kiss in the moonlight.

Klara's hostel group, exhausted from months of malnutrition, emotionally drained, and physically spent, lounge on deck when possible. They can only go up certain hours; they're in steerage.

To keep herself busy and pass the hours, Klara stumbles out of her bunk and for the first time in such a long time, reads a book. She has not touched a book since she bought one in Harbin. The book she now holds in her hand is *The Jewish State* by Theodor Herzl, the founder of Zionism.

One cloudy Saturday up on top deck chairs, Rachel is reading a short story about a Jewish family living in poverty in Poland.

"*Cholent*, Klara, *cholent!*" screams Rachel.

"Where? What you talking about?"

"Klara. I can taste it now. It's *shabbos* today. We should be eating *cholent*. Can't you taste it? I can smell the stew's aroma all the way from the Ukraine to us right here on deck. Simmering beans, meat, lentils, potatoes. Oh no, this isn't relaxation. Back in Odessa, we really had peace during the *shabbos* meal."

Klara, too, has been daydreaming. The night before she again dreamt that Vladimir—at least she thought it was Vladimir—held her in her arms. The two were locked in a long and profound kiss.

"*Cholent?* Cholent. You had to bring that up now. Next, you'll ask me about my family. My father? 'Where is he? Have I heard any news?'"

"Well?" replies Rachel. "Obviously you want to talk about it. Speak. Let's hear it. Get it off your busty chest," she says snickering.

Turning toward Rachel, Klara leans forward and stares at her friend. Without thinking, without checking her words, she confides in this young lady who has been with her since the beginning of this long, long journey.

"What a rat, that Mischa. Just to aggravate me, he once told me, Papa was running around with women. A ladies' man. Can you imagine my father having paramours? We never knew if Papa actually arrived in Canada, until recently when I found out he has a position as a cantor in Canada. That's what the rabbi in Harbin told me as I left his office."

"Do you think fathers are angels?" Rachel interrupts. "Your mother's back in Odessa. Right? Taking care of little ones? Right? And father is a runabout. Right? And you've almost died trying to find such an ingrate. Right?"

"Oh, keep quiet," replies Klara, not angrily, but in a tone that suggests that down deep, she knows Rachel utters the truth.

"You know," Klara goes on, "when I was running, bribing, stealing, and even sinning in love, I forgot that noble purpose of my trip. Oh yes, it was always there. The real goal, however, was to get here, to win, to overcome. Forget idealism. Back in Siberia, I didn't have time to think. Now, out here, in the middle of nowhere, where one can perhaps lose one's memory of all those terrible incidents and struggles, the problem comes back again. I am running to meet a man who deserted us, who made us suffer, my sisters and mother, and me, too. And you might as well know, Mischa is only my half-brother."

"What?" exclaims Rachel, quickly leaning forward, wanting to hear more.

"It's true. Isn't that something! Zlota's my stepmother. But my real mother's in America, according to Mischa. You know, maybe that's why my father left us in the first place, to find her."

"Klara, children never know the whole truth. We don't find out till much later, if ever. Now that you're here and landing in a few days in Seattle, you'll discover what really happened. He's still your father, however."

"What about my mother back in Odessa? Who's standing by her? What am I to do?"

"Go to him. Like I said, he's your father. Get the truth out of him if you can. Mischa could be exaggerating, trying to push his agenda on you. You never know. Sort it out. Then get rid of it. Live a new life. That's what I'd do," says Rachel.

The two turn away from each other, and gaze at the stormy sea. They close their eyes. They dream of cholent: with its simmering beans, meat, lentils, and potatoes. The days drag on.

On deck one day, Klara stares at the carpet of rolling waves, punctuated here and there by a sudden white bursting splash booming out of the blue waters, and as she gazes up at the dull white sky blotched with parallel lines of blue, she vows that she will never travel again, especially on a long sea voyage.

The days pass. Twenty-eight of them; some on stormy seas. A heavy overcast sky follows them the whole 4,257 miles to Seattle.

Haym has made sure their documents are in order. They are briefed and know what to say when they land: "Remember: No illness. No diseases. Don't cough. You're in good health. No membership in the Bolshevik Party. Yes, relatives are waiting for you."

A day later! Early morning. Raining. Dark clouds envelope the passengers standing on the top deck; first class passengers are downstairs waiting to be the first to disembark.

Nobody waits for Klara's group. Nobody greets them. No parents. No relatives. Just the usual HIAS-Welcoming Committee. Thank goodness at least for that.

"Always rains here," Klara hears a sailor say as the ship enters the port.

"Where's the Statue of Liberty?" someone asks.

"Not here, stupid. No Statue of Liberty here. Only in New York. This is Seattle."

"Look! A sign."

"Klara, you know some English. What's it say?"

"Welcome to the United States of America."

33

Seattle, January 1919

After the Germans left Odessa in 1918, the French landed in that Black Sea port that December. They were followed by Greek, Polish, Senegalese, and Algerian detachments. In April 1919, Trotsky's Bolshevik forces ousted the French who evacuated Odessa only to be occupied by Grigor'ev's partisans. Then White General Anton Denikin's forces took Odessa in August 1919. But the Red Army returned and captured the city early in 1920, the year the Communists defeated White armies.

In March 1920, General Denikin is dismissed after his panic retreat south to Novorossiisk, the main Allied port on the Black Sea. Because too few Allied ships are on hand to pick up his troops, thousands of Whites cannot escape in this botched evacuation. General Dinikin's successor, General Baron Peter Wrangel gathers the remnants of the Denikin armies and makes one more attack against the Reds. But he also will be defeated by the Soviets. His units, plus about 100,000 civilians are evacuated on Allied ships to Constantinople in mid-November 1920.

Most of the Allies were out of Russia by the end of 1920.

Through those years, the Rasputnis women waited for Gershon or Klara or Mischa to rescue them. Help would only come, as we shall see, in 1921. The Civil War had come to an end in Siberia, although the "Far Eastern Republic" survived until 1922 when it collapsed because of the full withdrawal of Japanese troops. Throughout Russia, the aristocracy and the industrial and commercial 'bourgeois' were liquidated; many of them put on barges and "drowned with all their children," wrote Vasily Grossman in his masterpiece *Life and Fate*. "...From the beginning of the Revolution, Lenin and the Bolsheviks feared the restoration of the old order. The surest way to prevent this was to rip it out by the roots and kill it," explains author Douglas Smith in *Former People*. So after millions had been killed, millions exiled to prison camps, millions forced to emigrate, the bitter struggle that tore Russia apart ended in a pyrrhic victory for the Russian people: They moved from being the property of the Czar to slaves in a Communist super-state that dominated every aspect of their lives.

•

American flags flying in the breeze.

Sid would be proud of her. She learned that the U.S. just added a star for Arizona, making it the 48th state.

One more obstacle coming up, Klara thinks.

"Ah, yes. Here they come." The immigration inspectors look like a line of charging bulls moving out of a coral into the bullring. "They do look mean," she observes.

"Line up. Line up."

"You over there. Get in line."

"Me?"

"Yes, you. If I have to tell you again, I'll ship you right back to your Jew-loving Bolshevik homeland. You're probably one of those Red kikes," he says, walking right up to Klara and putting his face just a few inches from hers.

Their noses almost touch. But Klara has traveled thousands of miles through death, destruction, and demeaning experiences. She stares right into the eyes of this crude interloper of hate. Her eyes and her hate meet his. She doesn't move.

He blinks and backs away.

"Get back into line," he mutters.

"That fuckin' Cossack," Klara shouts back to Haym Gross who stands behind her as they walk down the gangplank. "I see they're here, too, the bastards." she declares thinking of every swear word she can, though not uttering all of them.

"Even in America, they hate Jews. Some 'land of the free, home of the brave,'" she adds recalling the words from the national anthem that Sid was always trying to teach her, though to be fair, he warned her that although Jews had a good life in America, anti-Semitism existed.

"Hatred? Hatred's everywhere, Klara," replies Haym. "You just happened to pick a rotten egg from a good dozen."

Reaching the bottom of the plank and stepping onto the pier, they are forced to stop. Someone up ahead is on their knees and kissing the ground.

"What an idiot," Klara whispers. "Keeping us waiting. A great country, maybe. But kiss its soil? Who does he think he is, Yehuda Halevi?"

"Yehuda who?" questions a young girl, Shoshana, standing behind Klara and Mr. Gross.

"You don't know the great Hebrew poet, Yehuda Halevi? responds Klara, happy once again to be part of a group discussion. "Seven hundred years ago, longing for the Land of Israel, he sailed from Spain. Legend has it that as soon as he arrived in the Holy Land, he bent down to kiss the holy ground. But just as his lips touched the earth, an Arab horseman rode by; drew his sword; and slew him."

"I'm not getting down on my knees," agrees the girl. "I'm here. That's enough."

Standing together, Klara, Shoshana, Rachel, and Haym scan the large crowd standing outside the fence, many with homemade signs held up over their heads. Scrawled on them are names in Russian and English.

Just then, a shout, a long, loud, happy yell from their group. A shriek that turns their heads as a hostel member begins to wildly wave his hands and screams with excitement: "That's me Yankele Rosenblatt."

His relatives rush along the fence to the gate; they all kiss and hug.

Klara's little group stands idly by, faces somewhat drawn, speechless.

Shoshana steps into the void.

"Where actually are we?" she asks Shoshana as they stand about on the pier. "It's America, I know. But it's the other side. The backdoor, right? Most enter the United States through the front door: New York, Philadelphia or Baltimore. Why did we pick the back door?"

"This is what they call the Pacific Northwest," says Shoshana. "Seattle's a big city and its one of the closest ports on the eastern side of the Pacific. A quarter-million people. Boomtown. Gateway to Alaska and get this," she continues, "Russia once owned Alaska. Gave it away to America. Fools we were. Even though the Americans thought it was a joke to buy it. They called it a 'folly.'"

"Keep together. Keep together," Mr. Gross commands. A group of American youths from HIAS who speak Yiddish come up to them on the pier. The young people gather around to listen for their names to be called.

"Rachel Galobovsky."

"Here."

"Klara Rasputnis."

"I'm Klara."

"Please go over there to the bus," says a woman introducing herself as Hannah. "Good news, Klara. We found your father," she states in Yiddish. "And here's a letter from him."

"Oh. Thank God. Thank you. Thank you so much. Where is he?"

"He's in Winnipeg. But he's traveling to Vancouver to meet you. He'll be in Vancouver tomorrow at a Mr. Cohen's house. You'll stay here with us overnight. Early tomorrow morning you'll go by train to Vancouver, which is north of here, not far. A Mr. Cohen will meet you at the station and take you to your father."

"Thank God it's over. He's alive. Will my father be at the station?"

"That's all we know. Mr. Cohen'll probably tell you more. He'll be there. We'll give you a pass, tickets, some spending money and an affidavit to cross the border into Canada. Unfortunately, you'll have to go alone. But from what we heard, that shouldn't bother you."

Klara nods.

Dear Klara,

Thank God you are alive.

I cried with joy when they told me you were alive and on your way and that you're landing in Seattle. At services today at the synagogue, I recited the prayer, 'Gomel,' the prayer that you had completed a safe, but dangerous journey.

Until then, I never heard from Momma or anyone these past several years. Apparently, my letters never got through.

Oh, how I miss you and mother and the children. And Mischa, I hope you have had some news of him. I'm afraid to ask. I, too, had to go east through Siberia, as you know. The war stopped me from getting to Bremerhaven in Germany. It wasn't so bad in the East then, long before the Revolution and the Civil War that I'm sure you endured. I ended up in Vladivostok where I got a job as a cantor. I did well there. More about that later. Suffice to say, they liked me.

Klara stops reading, and thinks, "What did he mean, 'I did well there.'" She's suspicious. "If he did so well, why didn't he send us money?" She continues reading the letter.

No one believed that I was a cantor. I had no certification. So I had to audition. They let me pray in the synagogue. I was good.

To make a long story short, I finally got papers and came to Canada where our relatives in Ottawa helped me get a position in Winnipeg. Nice city. But very cold in winter. Flat land; reminds me of the steppes of Russia. Lots of Ukrainians here, too. Just like home. Only here, it's a free country and they keep their Jew hatred to themselves. They like me here. Now all I want to do is to see you and hug you.

I worry especially about Mischa. I met a Mr. Davidoff. He is from Kiev. From what I told him, he figures Mischa became a Communist. You don't want to use the word, 'Communist' here. There's a big Red scare on. We don't even say we're Russian. They think every Russian Jew's a Communist.

Please God, when we meet, tell me Mischa and the family are well. I hear terrible reports: death, starvation, hunger, bloodshed. Women and children harmed.

I pray every day for you and Mother, Mischa, Ann, Lillian, and Sonya.

See you soon. Love, kisses and embraces. Your father. Gershon.

Klara Rasputnis folds the letter, inserts it neatly into the torn envelope and with a fixed gaze, wonders in what direction is Canada. She figures it's due north.

Several hours away in Vancouver, Gershon Rasputnis looks out of a bay window in the direction of Seattle in the United States.

A day later: A large porch, with tall white pillars in front holding up a slanted roof. On the second and top floor, topped by a cupola, is a large bay window. There at the window, stands the silhouette of Cantor Gershon Rasputnis, middle-aged, portly, a man of God. He watches the street. He can see down to the blue shining Vancouver harbor, to the sailboats, to the port, to the railroad station. He doesn't know exactly when his daughter will arrive. He cares, but not enough to go down and greet his daughter at the station. He's not alone; Ruth Rosenthal has been with him all week.

Across the Canadian border, a passenger train hurtles along the Pacific shore, through the tall American timber forests, past sparkling lakes and rivers. Amidst the hissing, the vibrations, the clatter of the rolling stock, a bright sun shines down on the train cars, one of which carries Klara Rasputnis, daughter of Cantor Gershon Rasputnis. Covered with green, the trees shade the hot passenger cars.

Closer and closer the train wheels churn. Klara, who gazes out the window, is still reading the book by Theodor Herzl. Later, she picks up discarded magazines to look at the pictures. She eats the snacks from her HIAS food basket. She wonders what she will say to her father. She knows that when she meets him, the words will evaporate. She doesn't know what to expect. Soon she will be at the Canadian border.

"Ah, oh. They'll be another bastard inspector there. Keep quiet. Act the dummy. Just stare ahead."

At the border station, suitcases are unloaded; placed on the platform. Passengers get off and stand alongside their luggage. Klara casts a shadow over her small satchel.

An inspector stops in front of her. She hands him her documents.

"Is that yours?" asks a tall, blond young man with smiling blue eyes, blond hair.

"Yes," she says, bending over to get it.

"No. Don't bother," he counters with a smile. "Welcome to Canada. Welcome to British Columbia. Thanks. You can get back on the train, if you'd like. Here are your papers."

Seated, Klara sees snow-topped mountains and a sign. Twenty-five miles to Vancouver.

34

Vancouver, January 1919

"Vancouver!" bellows the conductor. Last station-stop. Everybody off!"

Dark, rainy clouds hide the masts of the fishing fleet nestled in the harbor. White orange-beaked seagulls flap their wings. In a few hours the chilly fog will burn off and newcomers will gaze at the surrounding snow-covered mountains surrounding this port city.

Klara can hear the first morning blasts of tugs pushing barges; of freighters moving back and forth with the tide. Soon this harbor will be alive and the girl from Odessa hopes she can become a new person.

Klara's stress melts away. She feels buoyant, realizing that people who have accomplished what she's achieved without giving up become sure of themselves. Stepping off the train she walks briskly along the cement platform toward the gate. Head up. Shoulders back. She walks as a tall soldier, a smile on her face. The station is practically empty. Looking right, left, straight ahead, she searches for a friendly face.

"Papa," she says to herself, "I did this for you. And you're not even here to meet me. I'm your daughter."

At the gate, an older, well-dressed man, short in statue, is holding up a sign. Written in Russian and English is the name "Klara." She likes seeing her name in English. She spells out the letters as she approaches the sign: K-L-A-R-A.

"How do you do. I'm Klara."

"I'm Benjamin Cohen, a friend of your father's. Here you are at last. Welcome to Canada. Welcome to Vancouver. How was your journey? says this rather stout, balding man looking at her as if she had just come off a luxury berth on the Winnipeg Clipper.

Mr. Cohen leans forward and picks up her small suitcase and nods to the right.

"Where's my father?" she asks politely.

"He's waiting at my house. It's only a short walk through Gastown. This way."

"Is he sick?"

"No! Of course not. What gave you that idea? Because he's not here? Well, he sent me instead. Wants to greet you at home."

Klara doesn't say a word. She's oblivious to her surroundings. Her stomach tightens. Small beads of perspiration sprout on her forehead. She's excited and anxious at the same time: What's it going to be like if his first wife, Gittel, is with him? she wonders as she follows dour Mr. Cohen along the cobblestone streets of the Gastown district. She doesn't notice the four-story buildings, the gin mills, cafes; the sweating, rough and tumble young men sitting on bar stools peering deep down into whiskey-filled glasses.

By now the street is full of people: Chinese, Japanese, American Indians, Poles, Ukrainians, Anglo-Saxons. Rushing about, they jostle each other as they make their way into various shops.

Klara marvels at the light brown skin of the natives who resemble Buriats, though these Canadian Indians don't have slanted eyes, she realizes. Everyone seems to be mingling nicely in this city of more than 100,000 persons.

"Why didn't my father come to the station?" she again questions Mr. Cohen, trying to hide her annoyance.

"Well, I guess you really have to ask him, I'm afraid. Maybe he felt the station's not a good place. Too public. You know, he's staying at my place. His lady-friend's there, too.

"His what?"

"His lady-friend."

"Who's that?"

"Don't you know? Didn't he write you?"

Klara is silent, turning her face away from Mr. Cohen.

"I guess you didn't know. No problem. He'll sort it out for you. Let him tell you, himself," says Mr.Cohen, in an angry voice. "Let's go. Just 'round the corner."

"Is that Gittel?" asks Klara, wondering if her father had finally reunited with her. "No. It's Ruth. Ruth Rosenthal from Winnipeg. That's the city where your father's a cantor. A fine city; a real *shtetl*. Anyway, it's not my business. Let him tell you."

On the morning of Klara's arrival, Gershon Rasputnis has lost all track of time. He remembered he asked Cohen to meet Klara at the station. He hopes the train is late as he recalls the pleasure of last night when he bedded Ruth Rosenthal. He's glad he brought her with him; too lonely to make such a long trip without companionship. Now, it's very hard to leave the half-naked woman next to him.

But reality has a way of closing in on Gershon Rasputnis, even when he basks in the warmth of the female body. Still, he has his ways and he's sure he'll find an explanation to pass off to Klara.

He knows that within minutes, Klara and Benjamin Cohen will arrive at his two-story house, a house with a large porch, featuring tall, white pillars in front holding up a flat, tiled roof.

He and his woman quickly dress.

"There he is. He's looking out of that second floor window. See him up there. Ruth's there, too," exclaims Mr. Cohen, as the pair reach the house.

"Yes, I see him," mumbles Klara. "But there's no woman up there. I only see a ghost, Mr. Cohen, a ghost."

Klara begins to laugh, short gasps of soft laughter, then sounds of louder laughter.

"I got it all wrong," mumbles Klara, forgetting that Mr. Cohen is beside her. "Was this whole insane trip for nothing? Rachel was wrong. Mischa was right. He warned me Papa cheated on us. He deserted us."

Klara looks up to her father and repeats the lady's name, "Ruth. Ruth." She can see her father standing there, smiling and signaling excitedly. She can't see the woman.

"He's waving at me," she says. "Making signs that he's coming down. But there's no woman there; there's only a ghost."

Growing light-headed, she repeats over and over again, his girlfriend's name, "Ruth."

The street begins to sway under her feet. What kind of name is that? In her almost blank mind, she decides none of this makes sense. Another woman. Klara loses her balance and begins to fall, muttering, "Gittel, Ruth."

Falling slightly backward, she slides straight down in a sitting position. She's unconscious.

Mr. Cohen can't believe his eyes.

"What happened?" yells the distraught man entrusted to escort his friend's daughter. "Damn it! How did I get into this," he whispers as he tries to lift Klara up from the grass.

From the second floor bay window of the two-story house, Cantor Gershon Rasputnis, a middle aged, grey-haired, portly man, watches his daughter fall to the ground. So he does what every father has done since Abraham, Isaac, and Jacob: He runs to rescue his child. Out the door, down the hall-steps, out the front door and the descending front steps of the porch, he goes. He doesn't look up. He doesn't move his head right or left. Breathing heavily, panting, sweating, he just runs and runs and runs and runs.

He can't keep running, however. His weight holds him down; so he's walking now. Arriving at the scene, he yells out, "Oh God. Help us."

Exhaling and inhaling continuously, he finally shouts:

"Stop. Don't move her. Cohen, what happened?"

"She fainted."

"I can see that."

"I don't know. Unless ..."

"Unless, what ...?"

"She seemed upset. She said she saw a ghost," reveals Mr. Cohen, not repeating the part of Klara's declaring her father deserted and cheated on them.

"A ghost. I knew I should have told her about Ruth. Too much of a shock, I guess."

The two keep Klara sitting by propping up her back.

"Water. A glass of water," Gershon hollers in vain.

Nobody's around to fetch it.

Opening her eyes, Klara utters: "What happened? "Where am I?" She moans as she looks at the two-story house on the cobblestone street.

She gazes into the tight-lipped, frowning face of Gershon Rasputnis and begins to cry. "Take me back to Odessa. I want my mother!" she shouts.

"She'll be here soon. I promise you," answers Gershon and he, too, begins to cry like a baby.

35

Epilogue

Klara quickly recovered as one often does at the end of a long illness. When she fainted, Ruth Rosenthal, realizing that an ambulance might be called, as well as fearing the arrival of the police who would question her, fled the house. What Gershon didn't know was that his paramour was an illegal immigrant and an anarchist. Not having much money, she literally went along for the ride from Winnipeg to Vancouver, a poor young lady on a vacation. Had she stayed, all three of them could have been picked up and possibly deported because of the "Red scare" then engulfing Canada and the U.S. Later Klara would recall that at the time, much concern in government circles surfaced regarding a Communist takeover. After all, the Reds were preaching, "World Revolution."

Klara and Gershon would go to Winnipeg in Manitoba. But their time together was brief. He contracted liver cancer that shriveled his robust body to mere bones. Klara took care of him day and night. He died seven months later. The whole city turned out for his funeral; he was, after all, a popular and successful singer in a city that prided itself on its cantors.

Bitter that her father had behaved the way he did after he deserted them in Odessa, Klara eventually realized that she couldn't mend the past. She never divulged details of her own journey. Gershon never asked. They never discussed Ruth Rosenthal or Gittel, his first wife and Klara's true mother, a woman Klara would never seek. Too much bother; too much pain. Besides, she truly loved Zlota.

But Zlota, who never learned of Gershon's death, did not make it to Canada. Just before she was to sail, she perished in a fire. Flames that burst from the space heater had caused an explosion. She perished instantly. An unidentified young man was seen fleeing the burning house.

The three young sisters, all teenagers, managed to survive, partly because Mischa did provide them with money. They were not at home at the time of the fire; they were arranging their transport to Romania and then to Bremerhaven, Germany, where they would pick up their steamship line tickets to America. Klara paid for the tickets and they arrived in Winnipeg in 1921.

Klara never danced professionally. Her left leg had lost strength from the wound she received on the Siberian train. She did, however, open a dance studio in Winnipeg. Each student became her son or daughter. She was enthralled with ballet, and in her free time helped support a local company.

As for Mischa, Klara at first attempted to trace him. Ads were placed in the Russian and Yiddish papers in the Soviet Union as well as the U.S. and Canada. No luck. Klara always confirmed what Ann, Lillian, and Sonya knew: "Mischa ran away, joined the army, and disappeared." The family did not talk about him. Only Klara would repeat his name to herself, usually followed by "that bastard." She never believed his story that he was not responsible for the death of Vladimir, in Chita. Sometimes, though she just uttered the name, "Mischa." Sixty years later, his name sounded softer, gentler to her. His baby-like face had grown dim. She never forgot his caressing smile, his romantic eyes, his lack of anger except when cornered. As much as she disliked him, he would always be her brother, not a stepbrother.

Yet, a year before she died, sister Sonya received a letter saying Mischa was alive and was somewhere in Canada. Since Klara ruled the family with an iron fist; since she spouted opinions on everything from what the daughters of her sisters should wear to punishment for an errant nephew, she was able to keep Sonya silent. She blamed Mischa for everything and didn't want him back in her life. She hoped she could keep the secret of Vladimir and the details of her journey and how her father had left the family from getting out in the open. Everyone knew that she traveled alone through Siberia, but the details, the happenings, the incidents, remained a secret. In her mind, she had been engaged to Vladimir. He was the only one that mattered. No one could take the place of what to her became his God-like soul. The experience with Vladimir never faded from her mind nor did a sense of betrayal of her father Gershon who deserted the family. Suitors knocked on her door but knowing that she couldn't bear them children, she spurned them all. Besides, from one point of view, she didn't need boyfriends anymore; she was secure financially with her studio, and safe in Canada. Nevertheless, she did go out at times and entertained male friends. In the end, they would drop her. She was just too bossy they would say.

"Men," she sneered.

Klara's nephews and nieces always wondered why this statuesque and attractive woman never took a husband. A shrug of the shoulders was the answer from the elders. She never brought up her past even when arguing with her sisters whom she supported until they married. As a nephew once quipped, "it was her way or the highway."

Since Gershon and Zlota never told the children that Klara was the child of another woman, and Mischa never had a chance to tell his sisters about Klara and her journey, neither the Rasputnis sisters, nor their offspring ever knew that this oldest sister was only a half-sister.

As for the Lubavitzes, the family that didn't wait for Klara at the train station in Odessa, only the Lubavitz son survived. He ended up in Baltimore. Hearing that Klara Rasputnis and her sisters in later years had moved to that city from Winnipeg, he established contact with her. He was not sure why the family deserted Klara, but he vaguely remembers taking an earlier train, for fear the one that they were all supposed to board in Odessa, might never leave. His father believed in catching the first train in; who knew when the next one would arrive? He also told her that his mother had been beaten and thrown off a speeding train outside of Irkutsk and at the next stop, his father was shot and his sisters were torn away from the family, never to be seen again. He himself jumped out of the slow-moving train before it reached that station's platform and avoided death.

"Their luck ran out," Klara would say.

Klara always knew there're no secrets in families. Yet, Mischa, who knew facts about his sister, facts that only he could know, lived up to his agreement; that is, almost. At least he waited until she was dead. He would prove that family secrets are only half buried; they often rise like a phoenix because of resentment, jealousy, thoughtlessness, misunderstanding, slips of the tongue. In families nothing is buried.

At Klara's funeral in Baltimore, an old, hunched-over man who resembled Klara and her late sisters stood at the cemetery gate. During the service, he talked to one of Klara's nephews who related that the stranger kept saying, "I'm Klara's journey."

He told the shocked nephew things that only a member of Klara's immediate family could know.

At the end of the service, in which the rabbi cited Klara's trek through Siberia, the nephew turned to find the stranger. But the old man had left the cemetery. Just down the road, outside the gate, however, the nephew saw him getting into a car. The young lad began to chase the vehicle as it sped off.

"Uncle Mischa. Come back. Please come back!"